Judith Lennox grew up in rural Hampshire and studied at the University of Lancaster, where she met her husband; they have three adult children. She began writing in the mid-eighties and, since then, her powerful historical novels have been highly and widely acclaimed. Her novels *The Winter House* and *A Step in the Dark* were both shortlisted for the Romantic Novelists' Award.

BEFORE THE STORM

It's 1909 in Lynmouth in Devon, and when Richard Finborough catches sight of Isabel Zeale her beauty captivates him, and he immediately wants nothing other than to be with her. Aware of shameful secrets in her past, Isabel has no intention of letting anyone into her life. Undeterred, Richard pursues her, and eventually wins Isabel's hand in marriage. The decades pass and Isabel and Richard raise a family through the turbulent times of the First World War and the 1920s. As her children reach adulthood, Isabel is convinced her secret is safe. Until an old acquaintance emerges from the shadows, turning her world upside down. To protect the happiness of those she loves, Isabel must confront what came before, and live with the consequences . . .

Books by Judith Lennox
Published by The House of Ulverscroft:

SOME OLD LOVER'S GHOST
THE DARK-EYED GIRLS
WRITTEN ON GLASS
FOOTPRINTS ON THE SAND
THE WINTER HOUSE
THE SHADOW CHILD
MIDDLEMERE
ALL MY SISTERS
A STEP IN THE DARK

JUDITH LENNOX

BEFORE THE STORM

Complete and Unabridged

CHARNWOOD
Leicester

First published in Great Britain in 2008 by
Headline Review
an imprint of
Headline Publishing Group, London

First Charnwood Edition
published 2009
by arrangement with
Headline Publishing Group
An Hachette Livre UK Company, London

British Library CIP Data

Lennox, Judith
    Before the storm.—Large print ed.—
Charnwood library series
    1. Birthmothers—Fiction 2. Adoptees—Fiction
3. Family secrets—Fiction 4. Great Britain
—Social conditions—20th century—Fiction
5. Great Britain—History—George V, 1910 – 1936
—Fiction 6. Large type books
    I. Title
823.9′14 [F]

ISBN 978–1–84782–501–8

Published by
F. A. Thorpe (Publishing)
Anstey, Leicestershire

Set by Words & Graphics Ltd.
Anstey, Leicestershire
Printed and bound in Great Britain by
T. J. International Ltd., Padstow, Cornwall

This book is printed on acid-free paper

To Ewen and Amanda, with love

Part One

The Red Queen

1909–1928

1

In the autumn of 1909, Richard Finborough was driving through Devon when his motor car began to falter. A storm had got up since he had left his friends, the Colvilles, earlier that afternoon, and he had a growing suspicion that he had taken a wrong turning, heading across Exmoor.

He pulled into the side of the road. Rain lashed his face and a strong wind tugged his coat and threatened to blow away his hat. The light was failing and the wind whipped dead leaves from the beech trees. An inspection of the de Dion's bodywork showed him that the car had a damaged rear leaf spring. Reluctantly, he abandoned his original intention of spending the night in Bristol and began to look for a place that would offer him shelter. A few miles ahead, a fingerpost pointed to the town of Lynton. The car lurched as he took the turning.

In Lynton he booked into a hotel. The next morning, he rose and breakfasted. After he had arranged for the car to be taken to a blacksmith for repair, Richard decided to go for a walk. The town of Lynton perched high on a cliff, overlooking the Bristol Channel. Lynton's sister village of Lynmouth lay below: from his vantage point, Richard could see that the continuing storm was whipping up white horses on a heavy sea. This part of north Devon was nicknamed 'Little Switzerland'. Richard could understand why — the incline of the hills and paths was dramatic; the houses seemed to cling precariously, struggling to keep hold of the cliff.

He headed down towards Lynmouth. The violent wind and the steep incline of the road meant that he had to watch his footing. Two rivers, in torrent because of the heavy rain and laden with branches torn from the trees in the narrow, wooded valleys, joined into one in the small village of Lynmouth before meeting the sea. Cottages clustered round the harbour. The tide was in and the fishing boats were moored to the quayside, the weather judged too foul, Richard supposed, for fishermen to venture out to sea. The flurries of rain were frequent and heavy: the landscape seeped water, sea and rain, like a sponge. Richard silently cursed the de Dion for marooning him in the middle of nowhere, in such weather.

His eye was caught by a flash of red at the far end of the harbour arm. Out of the storm-lashed greys and browns of water, sky and cliff he picked out the figure of a young woman. She was standing beneath a squat stone tower on the sea wall that reached protectively round one side of the harbour. Shading his eyes from the rain, Richard made out a flare of blue and white skirt beneath a red jacket and a banner of long black hair. The wind buffeted her and the sea spray rose high above her; not far from her, the waves churned angrily. She was standing too close to the edge, he thought — a freak wave and she might be swept away. The precarious position from which she had chosen to watch the storm troubled him, and he was relieved when she turned and began to walk back towards the quayside.

Curious, Richard waited in the shelter of a doorway. As the woman neared him, he saw that she was drenched. He suspected that she must have been out in the rain for some time. He raised his hat as she passed him and she turned, noticing him for the first time. Then, with a toss of her wet black hair, she looked away and headed up the road that led back to Lynton.

★ ★ ★

4

Several times over the next day he thought about her. That black hair, that proud carriage, as, with her trailing skirts and soaked red jacket, she had passed him. Her haughtiness, her queenliness — a red queen, he thought.

The storm slackened and the fishing boats set out to sea. Ragged clouds trailed along a sky of washed-out blue-grey. Debris clogged the gutters and there was a line of flotsam and jetsam thrown up high up on the rocky shore.

Out of season, there were few other guests staying in the hotel. The dining room revealed a scattering of elderly gentlemen who Richard assumed were year-round residents, as well as a young couple, perhaps on their honeymoon, who giggled and held hands at their corner table. As the waitress served him, Richard interrupted her chatter to ask her about the woman at the harbour.

She looked blank; he prompted, 'She was young . . . in her early twenties, I would guess. Black hair — and she wore a red jacket.'

A plate of plaice *au beurre blanc* was set in front of him. 'Oh, you mean Miss Zeale, I expect, sir.'

'Miss Zeale?'

'Zeale's a Bridport name, but she don't come from round here. Bristol, maybe, I don't know.'

'But she lives in the town?'

The waitress gave a nod of the head in a vaguely inland direction. 'Up at Orchard House. Miss Zeale was Mr Hawkins's housekeeper. He died three weeks past, poor old gentleman.'

The following morning, Richard obtained directions to Orchard House before walking up the steep hill that lay behind the town. To either side of him was woodland, pierced by deep rocky clefts. At length, a narrow lane, pocked with puddles and enclosed by high hedgerows and tall beech trees, led off from the main road. The air held the tang of wet earth and fallen leaves.

The house was easy to find, its name announced in curling wrought-iron letters on the front gates. The whitewashed building was set back from the road behind a garden that had been battered by the storm. An iron and glass veranda, weighed down with climbing plants, ran the length of the house. Richard thought the place had a closed-up look, the curtains drawn, the gates firmly shut.

He was about to turn away and head on up the hill when the front door opened and Miss Zeale came out. She was wearing the red jacket again, this time over a dark skirt.

Richard opened the gate. 'Miss Zeale!' he called out.

Frowning, she walked towards him. 'Yes?'

'I wonder if I might trouble you for a glass of water.'

A moment's pause, as though she was considering refusing him, and then she said, 'Wait there,' and went back inside the house. She returned a few minutes later holding a glass.

'Thank you.'

'How do you know my name?'

'The waitress at my hotel told me. I'm Richard Finborough, by the way.'

She had folded her arms across herself and turned aside, seeming not to notice his outstretched hand. As he drank the water, he flicked a glance at her profile, noting the straight, somewhat Grecian nose, the full curve of her lips, and the almost translucent pallor that contrasted so strikingly with her black hair.

He thought there was a tension in their silence; to break it, he asked, 'Have you lived here long?'

'Two and a half years.'

'It's an isolated spot.'

'Yes. I like it here.' She turned to face him. Her eyes, a very pale greenish blue with a ring of darker colour around the rim of the iris, were hostile. 'If you would excuse me, I have work to do.'

'Yes, of course.' He handed her back the glass. 'Thank you for the water, Miss Zeale.'

★ ★ ★

She intrigued him. Those eyes, of course, and her unusual and astonishing beauty, so unexpected, out here in the wilderness, like discovering an exotic flower on a compost heap.

Richard considered himself to be a fair judge of beauty. Among all the pampered princesses of his acquaintance in London, he could think of none who outclassed Miss Zeale. And her cold dismissal challenged him. Good-looking, affluent and confident, he wasn't used to being dismissed, especially by a servant.

In the afternoon, a message arrived at the hotel, telling him that the de Dion was ready. Waiting in the cottage parlour, he fell into conversation with the blacksmith's wife. Talk drifted, as he had intended it to, to Miss Zeale.

He asked, 'She doesn't come from Lynton, does she?'

The blacksmith's wife snorted. 'Not her.'

'Where, then?'

'Couldn't tell you, sir. Keeps herself to herself, that one. You'd think yourself lucky to get the time of day out of her.' A duster swept with unnecessary briskness across the mantelpiece. 'She'll be gone soon enough, I dare say.' The tone of voice hinted that, in the opinion of the blacksmith's wife, Miss Zeale could not leave Lynton soon enough.

'Because of her employer's death?' he supplied. 'Which will mean, I suppose, she must look for another place.'

Another snort. 'Oh, I shouldn't worry about the likes

of her. Her sort always falls on their feet.' A tap on the window told him that the blacksmith had arrived; Richard went outside to collect the motor car.

Waking early the next morning, he saw that the sky was a shimmering blue, the streets and houses licked gold by the sunrise. He had planned to depart for London first thing, but instead he found himself dressing and leaving the hotel, breathing in great lungfuls of cold, salt-tinged air as he headed through the town. His route took him past the church where, among the yews and gravestones, he spied a flicker of movement. He stood motionless, watching as Miss Zeale emerged from the churchyard. She was wearing black, this time, and her face was veiled. He noticed that one of the graves, not yet marked by a headstone, was scattered with roses.

'Good morning, Miss Zeale,' he said.

'Mr Finborough.'

He found himself foolishly gratified that she had remembered his name. 'I thought I might head uphill. May I walk with you?'

She said indifferently, 'As you wish.'

As they walked, his remarks on the beauty of the day and the violence of the storm met with no response. Any question she answered as briefly as possible.

They reached Orchard House. Glancing up at the lovely old building, he found himself saying, 'You'll be sorry to leave, I dare say. A place like that, you'd miss it.'

Her face was still covered by the veil. When she spoke, her voice was as cold and as hard as ice.

'I know what they say about me in the town, Mr Finborough.'

Startled, he stared at her. 'You must excuse me — '

'Whatever stories you have heard, they are not true. Whatever tittle-tattle has reached your ears, you should forget. And now, if you would be kind enough to let me past . . .'

He realised that he was standing in front of the gate. He held it open and she entered the garden.

She addressed him once more. 'Please do not try to speak to me again. All I ask is to be left alone. Please find the courtesy to let me be.'

Then she walked to the house. He watched her shut the front door firmly behind her and then he walked away.

★ ★ ★

Driving back to London, pushing the de Dion as hard as he dared, Richard's rage consumed him for much of the journey. Miss Zeale's tone of voice had been an insult, and as for her words — she had spoken to him with a scorn he would have reserved only for his laziest employee or a dishonourable business acquaintance. Reaching the city, he went straight away to his offices and took out his fury on his assistant, John Temple.

Richard Finborough had lived in London for seven years. He had left his home in County Down in Ireland at the age of eighteen, knowing that there was no future for him there. The Irish Land Wars and subsequent Land Purchase Acts had left the family estate, Raheen, impoverished and reduced in size until only the house and thirty acres of parkland remained. When Richard was sixteen, his father had died, blaming the British Government for its betrayal of Anglo-Irish families. Richard did not share his father's bitterness, and besides, he had no wish to live as a farmer or landlord. And he had witnessed young in life the destructive nature of disappointment, how it eats away at you, changes you.

So he had been relieved to leave the estate in his mother's care and travel to London. He had quickly come to love London. He loved it because it seethed with energy and activity, and because you could almost smell the money. Buying and selling was London's business; it permeated the streets and buildings. London's pulse beat hardest in the City and in the docks, where the great ships unloaded their cargoes from the Empire, filling their holds with the products of cotton mills and iron foundries before setting off again across the globe.

Richard had worked first for an import agency, in the offices of a family friend. After three years, he had branched out on his own. He had discovered that he had a natural business acumen, that he was capable of both cool-headedness and ruthlessness, and that he had a nose for which industries might thrive and which had peaked and would decline. As soon as he reached his majority, he sold his father's remaining investments. Most of the stocks and shares earned him little, but a piece of land in a prime area of the city, the last fragment of what had once been a substantial London holding, realised a large sum.

With the profit from the land deal he had paid off the most pressing of the debts on the Irish estate. There was enough money left over to buy a tea-packing factory and a small button-making workshop in the East End of London. A beginning, he thought: the beginning of the empire that he, Richard Finborough, would create. Once, the Finboroughs had been wealthy and powerful, with splendid properties and acres of land on both sides of the Irish Sea. Time, the course of history, and his father's ill-judged expenditure had taken away all that. Richard's ambition had been fired by loss, fed by his early exposure to the possibility of ruin. He would not rest until the family rose once more from the ashes, its assets secured, a modern dynasty.

Arriving back in London, he worked late and did not return to his Piccadilly mansion flat until well after nine o'clock that evening. By then, his anger with Miss Zeale had diminished, punctured by other more complex emotions. Refusing his manservant's offer to prepare him supper, he changed and left the flat. After he had dined at his club, he made his way to a reception at a house in Charles Street, knowing that Violet Sullivan would be there.

Violet was the younger daughter of a wealthy industrialist, Lambert Sullivan. Richard and Violet had enjoyed a flirtatious, sparring acquaintance for some months. Violet was pretty and self-assured; Richard had once or twice toyed with the idea of marrying her. Her small, neat, rounded figure was alluring, and an alliance with the powerful Sullivans could only be to his advantage.

Tonight, though, she failed to charm. Her coquettish taps of her fan and her girlish laughter seemed contrived and arch. Her face, with its ivory skin as smooth as a peeled almond, seemed vacant, her conversation uninformed. Miss Zeale's features, with their mysterious, otherworldly beauty, intruded in Richard's mind's eye as he and Violet conversed.

He left the reception early. The sky was clear, stars piercing the darkness. He walked aimlessly for a while, enjoying the cool of the London night after the overheated room. Then, in a private booth in a pub, he ordered a brandy and soda and found himself reliving, yet again, that morning's scene.

I know what they say about me in the town, Mr Finborough.

The previous day, the blacksmith's wife's disapproval of Miss Zeale had been undisguised. It didn't take much imagination to work out why she might be an object of censure. Miss Zeale's pride, her reserve, her desire for solitude, and her beauty, of course, would all provide fuel for resentment and gossip. He guessed that she was unconventional, and small, remote communities are often suspicious of a lack of convention.

Richard finished the first brandy and ordered another. Miss Zeale's neighbours' disapproval would have one likely focus, of course: her morals, or supposed lack of them. Men would desire her and women would envy her. His own interest in her — his questioning of the waitress and the blacksmith's wife — would have provoked shaken heads and knowing comments. Unwittingly, he may have added to Miss Zeale's difficulties. Worse, it now occurred to him that she had believed his interest in her *fired* by gossip. That she had thought he had spoken to her because he believed her easy, available.

Richard put his head in his hands. It was all he could do not to groan aloud at his clumsiness. Forget the woman, he told himself. There were hundreds of beautiful women in London and hundreds of miles between Lynton and London. He need never see her again.

His thoughts pleasantly blurred, Richard walked across the city to the house of his mistress, Sally Peach.

★ ★ ★

During the days that followed, Richard forced himself to concentrate on his work and to plan for the future. The tea-packing factory had potential, but its present premises were too small to allow for expansion, and the button-making workshop wasn't much more than a shed in which rows of women worked, squinting in the poor light. Both businesses must grow in order to survive and prosper. The labouring classes were starting to demand higher wages: once the bulk of the population earned more they would be able to buy more, and Richard intended to capitalise on that. He knew that the days when a businessman might cater only for the wealthy were over, and he had no intention of being left behind by changes he was convinced were inevitable. He wouldn't make his fortune selling exclusive teas to the rich, but he might make it by selling a cheaper yet smartly packaged tea to the less well-off.

As for the workshop, buttons made of mother-of-pearl, shell and glass were all very fine, but they were slow and expensive to manufacture. For some time now, Richard had been searching for a cheaper, more adaptable material. Earlier in the year, he had made the acquaintance of Sidney Colville, a polytechnic-trained chemist who was interested in the properties and use of casein plastics. A strange, shy, unsociable man, given to shutting himself away for weeks with his work and refusing to speak to anyone, Colville spent much of his time in the West Country, with his invalid sister, Christina. Richard found himself thinking that it was time to pay the Colvilles another visit.

He made his arrangements with the Colvilles and gave instructions to John Temple to cover for him in his absence. He wasn't self-delusional enough, however, to believe that his only motive in returning to Devon was to find out more about casein plastics. This time, he thought, he would tread carefully. Sidney Colville and Miss Zeale had something in common: both were tricky customers.

★ ★ ★

It was mid-afternoon when Richard reached Lynton and the sky was already darkening. Impatient to see Miss Zeale, he did not, as he had intended, book into the hotel first, but took the steep, narrow road that led to Orchard House.

He parked the car and, peering over the gate, caught sight of Miss Zeale in the garden. Something seemed to

13

twist his heart and he was aware of an odd mingling of emotions: pleasure and fear and — what was it? — anticipation, as if he was about to embark on some long and difficult journey. And recognition — though they had exchanged only half a dozen sentences, she seemed familiar, as if he had known her for a long time.

For several minutes, he watched her unnoticed. The wind buffeted the exposed hillside garden, tugging at her uncovered hair and billowing out her skirts. It seemed to him that she worked with a driven, almost angry energy. A slash of the scythe, and a tangle of brambles were felled. A wide sweep with the rake at the browned horse chestnut leaves that blotted the lawn, and they were gathered into pyramids. But the wind had got up and, even as Miss Zeale worked, leaves spiralled from the heaps. Her shoulders drooped, as though she was tiring.

At the sound of his footsteps on the cinder path she turned.

'Here,' he said. 'Let me help.'

Taking off his coat, he tossed it over a branch of the tree and seized the rake.

She said furiously, 'What do you think you're doing?'

'Sweeping up these leaves before they're blown away.'

'Please go, Mr Finborough.' Her voice shook with anger.

He continued raking the small piles of leaves on to the patch of waste ground beside the lawn. 'It's a big garden to manage on your own.'

A silence, then she said stiffly, 'A Lynmouth boy used to come up to do the heavy work but he hasn't been for a month or so.'

'Why not?'

She gathered the two halves of her jacket protectively round her. Her gaze settled coolly on him. 'Why do you think, Mr Finborough?'

'I've no idea.'

14

'He doesn't come — or his mother doesn't let him come — because I'm here on my own now. Because I might infect him with my wickedness.' She spat the word out.

Anger and exertion had given colour to her pale skin, intensifying her beauty.

He said, 'Might you?'

He thought she might slap his face; but then, once more, she seemed to droop a little. 'Why must people always believe the worst?' she said bitterly. 'Isn't life hard enough without seeing sin where it doesn't exist?'

'People get bored, I suppose. These little towns must be dull enough, especially in winter. Anyone at all different provides fodder for rumour.'

She looked down, frowning. 'I don't try to be different. I have only ever tried not to be noticed.'

'You shouldn't mind the gossips.'

'I don't. Not for me. But that they should ~~have~~ of criticised *him* . . . '

'Are you speaking of your employer?'

'Yes.' The frown deepened. 'Charles became very frail during the last months of his life. I dare say I gave him my arm as we walked through the town. Or maybe I helped him off with his shoes when his rheumatism was so bad he couldn't stoop to undo them, and some busybody walked past the gate as I was doing so. That people should choose to misinterpret things in such a vile way disgusts me.' She looked up at him. 'Why have you come here, Mr Finborough?'

Now, all the leaves were gathered together in a heap. 'Because I like bonfires,' he said with a smile. He took a lighter from his coat pocket and struck it. The dry leaves caught and smouldered. 'To tell the truth, I came here to apologise to you, Miss Zeale. I realised, after I returned to London, that I must ~~have~~ of put you in a difficult position. I wanted to explain to you that I had no ulterior motive in speaking to you that day.'

15

'You have driven here from London?'

'Yes.'

'And you expect me to believe that you came all that way to say this to me?'

'Not at all. I have business near Woolacombe.'

'*Oh.*' She flushed.

The fire had spread, flames darting from the crackling leaves.

'When we last met,' Richard went on, 'I was stranded a long way from home. Under those circumstances one tends to find oneself talking to whomever one catches sight of in the street. I noticed you the first day I came to Lynton. There was a gale and I always like to watch rough seas so I walked down to Lynmouth quayside. I saw you on the harbour arm. I was concerned about you.'

'Concerned?'

'You were standing in the shadow of the old tower. You were too close to the waves, I thought.'

She gave a short, dismissive laugh. 'I go to the Rhenish Tower when I need to think. It's a habit of mine. I like it there.'

'What were you thinking about?' He caught himself quickly. 'I'm sorry — how intrusive of me . . .'

There was a silence, and then she glanced back at the house and said, 'It's no secret. I was thinking of my future. I shall have to leave here soon.'

He remembered how she had seemed to perch too close to the edge of the stone parapet. 'You looked . . . precarious.'

'I was safe enough. What would you have done, Mr Finborough, if I'd fallen into the sea? Would you have dived in and rescued me?' Her tone was mocking.

He said evenly, 'Yes, I think so.'

'How very gallant, to be so concerned about someone you did not know at all.'

'Have you never been so in need of company, Miss

Zeale, that you'd talk to a stranger you saw in the street?'

Her expression became guarded again. 'Once,' she murmured. 'A long time ago. Not now.' The fire was dying down; the animation vanished from her face and she shivered. 'I must go. I have work to do. Good evening, Mr Finborough.'

★ ★ ★

Richard made sure not to return too soon to Orchard House. He spent the next few days with the Colvilles in the cottage they had rented near Woolacombe, where Sidney Colville, in an expansive mood, scrawled on scraps of paper, trying to explain the chemistry of casein plastics to him. Every now and then they went out to take some fresh air. Sidney, a keen ornithologist, pointed out sea birds to him. Richard listened politely and thought about Miss Zeale.

Back in Lynton by the end of the week, he made it his business to find out about her. Enquiries told him that Miss Zeale's Christian name was Isabel, and that she had begun to work at Orchard House over two years ago, in the summer of 1907. Charles Hawkins, her employer, had been the headmaster of a boys' preparatory school until his wife's death seven years previously. Though Mr Hawkins' eccentricities had been tolerated in the town, his housekeeper's were not. Miss Zeale's dress, her accent, which lacked the Devon burr, her refusal to respond to curiosity about her past: all had aroused resentment. Even her fondness for reading books had fuelled her neighbours' suspicions. Richard concluded that in the eyes of her neighbours, Miss Zeale had committed that most heinous crime: she had got above herself. Her darkest sin was only hinted, however. No one quite had the nerve to say to him that Isabel Zeale had exploited her position as housekeeper

17

by becoming Charles Hawkins' mistress, though the insinuations were plain.

The next time Richard saw her was in town. He had walked to the harbour after breakfast; heading back through Lynton, he caught sight of her ahead of him. She was wearing her red jacket and was carrying a shopping basket. As he watched, a group of men, falling out of the pub, jostled her on the pavement, knocking her basket out of her hand. He heard laughter and jeers as a loaf of bread tumbled into the gutter and a bag of flour split open, showering the cobbles.

Miss Zeale stooped to gather up her belongings. A cabbage had rolled to Richard's feet: picking it up, he headed quickly to her side.

'Here,' he said, putting it into her basket. 'I'll help you with the rest in a moment.'

She grasped his sleeve. 'No. Let them be.'

'They struck you deliberately. I saw it. They shouldn't be allowed to get away with it.'

She said, her voice low and urgent, 'If you speak to them they will only torment me more. Mr Finborough, you will leave here in a day or two, but I must stay. I have nowhere else to go.'

Reluctantly, he nodded. He helped her pick up her remaining packages. The bread lay in the mud and her newspaper was soaked, the pages turning to papier-mâché.

He said, 'At least let me replace some of these things.'

'No, thank you.' She was very pale. 'But if you would be so kind as to walk a little of the way home with me — just to make sure . . . '

He took her basket and they walked up the pavement together. A voice called out to them just before they reached the corner of the street. 'Like rich men, don't 'ee, my lover? Rich old men suits 'ee best!' There was a ripple of laughter. Richard saw Miss Zeale whiten and set her lips.

He gave her a few minutes to regain her composure and then, as they headed uphill, he asked, 'Who were they?'

'The Salters? They're fishermen — brothers — they live in Lynmouth.'

'They are acquaintances of yours?'

'There was a time when — ' She broke off, biting her lip. Then she murmured, 'I was very lonely when I first came to live here. I may ~~have~~ passed the time of day with Mark Salter once or twice. It was foolish of me, because he interpreted it in the worst possible way.'

'Are you often troubled like this?'

'They're braver now Mr Hawkins is no longer here to protect me.'

'Braver?' He glanced at her. 'Is that what you call it?'

She tossed back her hair. 'They don't frighten me. Mark Salter fancies he wants to marry me. They make out I've offended them because I've refused him. As if I would ever marry such a low, ignorant man!'

They had reached the narrow wooded lane that led to Orchard House. She held out her hand for the basket. 'I'll be quite all right now, Mr Finborough.'

'Nonsense. I'll see you back to the house.'

They walked along the narrow lane. The branches of the beech trees cast a lacework of shadows across the road; beyond the beeches, a thicket of hazel blocked the hill and the town from view.

There was a sharp, intense pleasure in walking with her, side by side through the flickering gloom. So one of those village louts wished to marry her, he thought; what, then, did he, Richard Finborough, want of her? He desired her, of course, yet his need for her was not only physical. He wanted something else as well: her attention, perhaps, her appreciation. He wanted to erase the indifference to his company that she didn't trouble to hide and that irked him.

19

They reached the house. Indecision showed momentarily on her face as she opened the gate, and then she blurted out, 'May I offer you a cup of tea, Mr Finborough?'

He thanked her. As they headed down the path, she told him that the house was to be inherited by the nephew of her former employer, a Mr Poole, who lived in India. 'A letter came from Mr Poole this morning,' she explained. 'He plans to sail to England as soon as he's able to make arrangements. I had hoped . . . '

'What?'

'That Mr Poole would decide to remain in India. That he might allow me to look after the house for him. Foolish, I know.'

'Isn't it possible that he'll keep you on as his housekeeper?'

She opened the front door. 'Mr Poole has a wife and children. Some busybody would make sure to tell Mrs Poole about me, I don't doubt, and then I would be dismissed.' She went into the house; Richard followed her. 'And besides, I don't think I could bear to remain here with strangers.' Her eyes, that pure, pale turquoise, met his briefly as she added, 'You see, I did love Charles. Oh, not in the way the gossips accuse me of — but I did love him.'

Entering the house, he felt, along with interest and curiosity, a flicker of triumph, knowing that he had stormed the outermost ring of a citadel. An elephant's-foot umbrella stand stood in the lobby beside the tweed coats and oilskins hanging on pegs. There were three globes on the windowsill, arranged like the planets spinning in space. In the hallway, books were stacked on tall shelves that rose from floor to ceiling. Some of the books were new, but many were old, their spines hanging from cat's cradles of threads. Through the open doors of the rooms that led off from the hall, Richard glimpsed more shelves, more books.

20

The wooden floors gleamed; the rooms smelled of beeswax and lavender. 'It's a lovely place,' he said. 'I can see why you'd be sorry to leave it.'

Her hand stroked the worn oak of a banister. 'It's been my sanctuary.'

'Tell me about your employer.'

It was the first time he had seen her smile. 'I've never met anyone like him. Charles knew . . . oh, *everything*. He was so kind to me. He taught me so much. He let me read any of his books I chose, any of them.' There was wonder in her voice. 'He reminded me of my father, though my father hadn't had the same chances in life.'

'What happened to your father?'

'He died of tuberculosis.'

'And your mother?'

'She died not long after I was born.'

She headed deeper into the house, opening a door at the end of a corridor. Richard found himself in a large kitchen. Saucepans, their copper bottoms polished to pinkish-brown brilliance, hung in descending order of size along the far wall. Crockery was stacked tidily on shelves and the sink and floor gleamed.

He put the basket on the table. 'What will you do when you leave here?'

'I shall look for another position.'

'In Devon?'

'I don't think so. Mr Hawkins made sure to leave me a good reference, but you'd be surprised how tales travel. I think I'll have to go to another part of the country. I'll hate to leave the West Country, though. I've been happy here.'

She went to the sink to fill the kettle. He took the opportunity offered by her turned back to admire her figure, noting the narrowness of her shoulders and waist and the swell of her hips.

She asked him, 'Has your business in Devon been successful, Mr Finborough?'

'Yes, I believe so.' He told her about Sidney Colville and his interest in casein plastics. 'They're the material of the future. It's extraordinary stuff — you can mould it into any shape, dye it any colour.' He grinned. 'Have you any idea what it's made of, Miss Zeale?'

'None at all, I'm afraid.'

'Cows' milk.' He laughed. 'Isn't that extraordinary? I intend to manufacture buttons out of cows' milk. But I must understand the science before I invest money in the process.'

'Mr Hawkins once cut a flower in half so that he could show me all the different parts. He said that you couldn't understand anything properly until you knew how it was made.'

'Very sound advice. Some things are harder to get a grip on than others, of course, but I find that if I persevere I always get there in the end.'

She had moved to the far side of the room, still wary of him. 'I expect you do, Mr Finborough,' she murmured. 'I expect you do.'

★ ★ ★

Richard rose early the next morning and left the hotel before breakfast. He found himself heading up through the town and along the tree-roofed lane as if dragged by some physical force. The sun was not yet fully up and mist swirled in the ferns and brambles: out of it the trees seemed to rise unrooted to the ground. His thoughts rushed and he felt edgy and unsettled, filled by a restless energy.

Reaching Orchard House, he saw that the front gate was swinging open. The tidiness of the garden had been sullied by a trail of rubbish. Potato peelings and fish-heads rotted on the cinder path, and old newspapers curled round the stems of the roses. More garbage fouled the veranda.

The front door opened and Isabel Zeale emerged, holding a broom. She started, seeing him. 'Foxes,' she said quickly. 'They make such a mess.'

He knew that she was lying. The foxes who had visited the house in the night had human faces. But her expression was defiant, and he knew it would be a mistake to challenge her.

'I'll help you clear up,' he said.

'There's no need.'

He ignored her. 'A shovel would be the best thing. Is there one in the shed?'

When all the rubbish was in the bins she invited him into the house to wash. Emerging from the cloakroom, he said, 'Breakfast, we need breakfast. I'm sure you cook a good breakfast, Miss Zeale. They always burn the bacon at the hotel.'

In the kitchen, he talked to her as she cooked. He told her of his boyhood in Ireland, fishing in rivers and playing on the beach. He told her how he had wept, leaving home at the age of eight to go to boarding school in England, and how he had counted off the days until the school holidays. As he spoke, he sensed everything with great clarity: the aroma of the frying bacon, the tanginess of the marmalade, the sound of spitting fat and the soft pat of her footsteps as she moved about the flagstoned floor. And, most of all, the sight of her — the black curl that clung to her cheekbone, the single button undone at her cuff — because she had dressed in haste that morning presumably — which revealed an inch of her wrist. He would have given a year of his life to be able to run his fingertip along that slender white wrist, to press his lips against that small V of skin, to smell her, taste her. He felt dizzy with longing for her, almost sickened by it.

She put the plate in front of him. 'Are you well, Mr Finborough?' he heard her ask, and he realised that his hands were hovering over the knife and fork, that he was quite literally losing his grip.

'Perfectly well,' he said, and he began to eat, though he had lost his appetite, and Miss Zeale's excellently cooked bacon and eggs tasted of nothing at all.

★ ★ ★

That afternoon he walked along the cliffs to the west of Lynmouth. Standing on the headland and watching the waves crash on the rocks below, he thought about Isabel Zeale. In his mind's eye he pictured her proud, erect stance, her thick, lustrous black hair and fair skin, and those pale aquamarine eyes. What was it about her that held him so, that forced him to remain here, when every rational thought, every iota of sense, told him that he should go back to London and never see her again?

He had fallen in love with her, he supposed. A raw sound escaped from his throat, something between a groan and laughter. The wind turned, wheeling a blast of rain into his face. He had managed the first twenty-five years of his life without falling in love — why should it happen now, and in such a place, with such a woman? Isabel Zeale's position in life was markedly inferior to his. She was a servant, a housekeeper. Her reputation was doubtful, to say the least, and as for her character — she was proud and aloof, sharp-tongued and viperish. Perhaps, he thought with wry amusement, this was all he deserved for the times he had pretended love for form's sake, without feeling it a bit. For the débutantes he had danced with, the knowing young misses he had flirted with, and the married women who, bored by their rich old husbands, had been happy enough to take a young and enthusiastic lover.

The rain thickened and he headed back to the town. The sea was a sulky pewter and the light was fast failing. He knew he should leave Lynton; common

24

sense told him he must leave and never return. What possible business had he here, paying attentions to a woman like Isabel Zeale? He knew that it was not enough for him to be the kind friend who carried her shopping and swept up the rubbish that ruffians had dumped on her veranda. It would never be enough. What, then, was his purpose in visiting her? Would he persist, wearing her down, until he had enforced on her some kind of emotional bond, some perception that she owed him something? To do so would be vile, an exploitation of his superior wealth, strength and class. It would make him a worse man than the Salters.

Isabel Zeale was penniless and friendless and would soon be homeless. All her independence and hauteur did not alter the fact that she was that most defenceless creature, a woman alone. Her startling beauty only increased her vulnerability. The kindest thing he could do would be to pass on to her the name of a widow or an old married couple in need of a housekeeper.

Yet he could not even do that for her. What limited involvement they had depended on his failure overtly to recognise her inferiority to him. To point out her lower status would humiliate her. He guessed that her pride was essential to her, that it held her together in some way and that she would prefer him simply to return to London.

Which was what he must do, and as soon as possible, without any further delay. He must put an end to this attachment, this obsession. Though the thought of never seeing Isabel Zeale again hurt him more deeply than he would have believed possible, he knew it was the only sensible thing to do.

As soon as he reached the hotel, the clerk handed him a telegram. It was from John Temple, informing him that a fire had broken out at the tea-packing factory and asking him to return to London immediately. Richard packed his bags quickly, paid his bill and left the hotel.

Driving out of the town, he came to the junction in the road. The route to Bridgwater and, ultimately, London, lay before him.

He braked sharply. His fingers drummed against the steering wheel and his eyes fixed on the wet, murky darkness ahead. He thought of the fire and the factory and all the necessary actions he must take. He was aware of time passing and the clock's ticking, and of a mixture of impatience and anger.

He struck the steering wheel hard with his fist and swung the car round, heading up another road. When he reached the lane that led to Orchard House, he plunged into the tree-fringed gloom. Low branches thwacked the bonnet and the gleam from the de Dion's headlamps seemed hardly to lighten the murk. Rain pelted against the windscreen and he almost drove past the house, struggling to pick it out from the night. Stepping out of the car, he found himself ankle-deep in a puddle.

The gates were closed, the porch was unlit. Still, he knew the way by now, and he strode up the path between the flowerbeds and rapped his knuckles loudly on the door. Only a narrow glint of light showed round one of the windows and he had to knock a second time before he heard footsteps from inside.

The door opened a crack. He addressed the sliver of light that sliced open the darkness. 'It's me, Richard Finborough,' he said. 'I apologise for calling on you at such an hour, Miss Zeale, but I have to leave straight away on urgent business. There's been a fire at one of my factories and I must return to London. But I couldn't go without speaking to you first.'

'It's late, Mr Finborough.'

'Please.'

A moment's pause and then she opened the door. He followed her into the parlour. A sewing basket stood beside an armchair and there was an open book on a side table.

'I'm disturbing you. I apologise again.' He did not sit, but moved restlessly around the room. 'You told me that you'll leave this house as soon as your employer's nephew arrives from India. And that he'll be here in, what — a month or so?'

'I believe so.'

'And you mean to look for another post?'

'I've already begun to. I must do — I have a little money saved, but . . . ' She fell silent, reddening slightly.

'The thing is that I find it hard to think that I'll never see you again.'

She said drily, 'I dare say you'll manage, Mr Finborough.'

'No. I don't believe so.'

'Mr Finborough — '

'Please, hear me out.' He frowned. 'I was quite content before I met you. I had my work and my London friendships, and they were enough for me. That day my car broke down I had every intention of leaving this tin-pot little town as quickly as possible and never seeing it again.'

She said coldly, 'I have never sought your company.'

'No,' he said, and gave a short laugh. 'I certainly can't accuse you of *that*. Yet I find that when I'm away from you I can't stop thinking about you. And when I'm near you I — '

'Oh, spare me, please!' she cried, and he broke off, startled.

'Miss Zeale?'

'Don't you know that I could write your lines for you?' Her voice shook — with anger, he realised, jarred. 'I've heard them before — the declaration of undying love, the inability to live without me — and all the rest of it!'

27

'I'm sorry if I bore you,' he said stiffly. 'But let me speak.'

'No. No, I won't.' She had moved away from him, her arms folded tightly round herself. 'I refuse to be insulted. There is nothing you could say that would make me alter my plans one jot.'

He frowned. 'Nothing?'

'Nothing at all.'

Some stubborn streak made him persevere. 'When we first met you made your aversion to me plain. But lately I had begun to wonder whether you disliked me less. Miss Zeale — Isabel — '

She interrupted him, 'Do you imagine that you are the first? If so, then you are mistaken. I have been plagued by men like you ever since I came to Lynton!'

Her words shocked him into silence. In her mind, she had bracketed him with those ruffians who had assaulted her in the street, brutish fishermen from the hovels of Lynmouth. He said slowly, '*Men like me* . . . Tell me, Miss Zeale, what would a man like me do next?'

She went to the door and opened it. 'Please don't insult me further. Please go.'

'I want you to say it.'

He heard her furious exhalation of breath. Her hands were knotted together, the knuckles white. 'Very well. Next you would offer me money. Tactfully or otherwise. I expect *you* could be tactful, Mr Finborough. And then, perhaps, you would rent me rooms in Barnstaple or Exeter. And then — '

'So that's what you think of me,' he said angrily. 'You thought I had come here to make you my mistress. You thought I had come here to *buy* you!'

'Hadn't you?'

He hardly trusted himself to speak. He looked away to the window, to where the wind blew the branches of a climbing rose against the glass, so that it made a sound like tapping fingernails. His anger slipped away and was replaced by disappointment and disillusion.

'The truth is,' he said, 'that I came here to tell you that I love you.'

She made a contemptuous hiss. 'You can't possibly!'

'What makes you so certain?'

She took a step towards him; he almost thought she might strike him. 'I may live in a *tin-pot* little town, Mr Finborough — I may be merely a housekeeper — but I am not *stupid*!'

'It never occurred to me that you were.' His fury returned. 'Cold, yes — reticent, of course — rude and disagreeable, certainly. But stupid — no, never.'

'I'm sorry if I've given you the wrong impression. I'm sorry if you feel I've given you any encouragement — '

'Oh, you haven't, Miss Zeale, you most certainly haven't!'

'In that case, there can be no excuse, no excuse at all for your coming here. Mr Finborough, I thought you too much of a gentleman to add yourself to the list of those who torment me!'

There was a moment's silence, in which her words seemed to echo, and then Richard picked up his hat and gloves. 'Thank you for making your feelings so plain, Miss Zeale,' he said. 'Thank you for being so — so explicit. As my company is so obviously distasteful to you, I won't trouble you any further.'

He left the house. A few minutes later, he was driving back down the lane. Be damned to her, he told himself. He was better off without her. He should be thankful for his lucky escape. Yet he did not feel relieved, only wretched, as, with a squeal of tyres, he pulled the car out of the lane and on to the road to London.

He drove fast, too fast for the narrow roads and the foul weather. The wheels of the de Dion threw up thick ribbons of water; once or twice he felt them lose traction and had to fight to regain control of the car.

Reaching a small hamlet, he parked and went into a pub, where he ordered a whisky. As he drank, he caught sight of himself in the mirror over the mantelpiece, saw his white face, his wild red hair darkened by the rain, and in his eyes a mixture of fury, resentment and hostility. No wonder the barman had hastened so to pour out his Scotch, he thought with grim amusement; no wonder the rest of the drinkers stood well away from him.

Afterwards, he went back outside to the de Dion. He did not yet start up the engine, but sat looking out of the window to where the blurred black shapes of the houses merged with the rain. He could blame her for leaping to conclusions, he thought, or blame himself for mishandling the situation. But the truth lay deeper than that, a truth he had not yet admitted to himself. He could no longer imagine a future for himself that did not include Isabel Zeale. Reminding himself of her social inferiority or the brevity of their acquaintance was futile; reminding himself that common sense dictated he fall in love with a woman of his own class, a woman who might bring money to the marriage, was equally unproductive. He was already, in some way he did not pretend to understand, tied to her.

So far in life, he had had whatever he wanted. He craved all the best things the world had to offer — power and wealth and success. Having made up his mind to restore the Finborough fortunes, he was already striding ahead, recovering much of the ground his father had lost. As for women, he could say with all honesty that he had never yet been refused.

Richard closed his eyes and dozed for a while. When he woke, the pub had closed and no lights showed in the cottage windows. He turned the car and headed back towards Lynton. The rain had stopped and the sky had cleared. Driving along the tree-covered lane to Orchard House, he glimpsed a full moon flickering between the branches overhead. Reaching the house, he parked and waited.

Some hours later, with the coming of dawn, he climbed out of the car and stretched his legs. The temperature had plummeted and a crazing of ice, like filigree silver, edged the puddles. As he walked down the cinder path he thought he saw the gleam of an oil lamp in the house. Then the door opened, and Isabel Zeale, a shawl wrapped over her nightgown, her hair loose and tumbling down her back, came out.

She walked down the path to him. As she neared him, he saw that she looked fatigued, her face pale and darkly shadowed.

'I'm sorry if I woke you,' he said. 'I've tried to be quiet.'

She whispered, 'What do you want of me, Mr Finborough?'

'I apologise for offending you last night. But I'm not sorry for telling you I love you.'

Momentarily, she closed her eyes. 'Mr Finborough, if you have any kindness in you, any respect for me at all, then please go.'

He shook his head. 'Not yet. You asked me what I wanted of you. I want you to marry me, Isabel. That's what I want.' He raised a hand, cutting off her words. 'Don't say anything now. I must leave for London. But, think about it. Please think about it. I shall return here in a week's time. You can give me your answer then.'

He walked away. He had a last sight of her just before he headed back down the lane. She was standing in the garden, a column of white, motionless, frozen.

★　★　★

In London, between relief at the news that no one had been injured in the fire at the factory and surveying the destruction of the premises, Richard amused himself by

31

sending gifts to Isabel Zeale.

Hothouse flowers the first day, a great sprawling bunch of them, transported by rail from a florist in London all the way to Lynton. In a bookshop in Charing Cross, he chose a volume of poetry by Christina Rossetti, bound in red leather, the pages edged in gold. Inside the flyleaf he wrote 'To Isabel, with love from Richard'. It pleased him to think of the many times he might write that dedication in years to come.

The next day, he sent her a camellia in a pot, the day after that a sheaf of periodicals showing the latest fashions. Then a black silk umbrella with a mother-of-pearl handle because it rained so much in Isabel Zeale's part of the world.

He thought of her, alone in her citadel, before he chose his last gift. He had the delivery boy transport the wicker basket containing a King Charles spaniel puppy by hand all the way to Lynton. His note in the basket said, 'His name's Tolly. All Finborough dogs are called Tolly, I've no idea why. R.'

No perfume, no silk stockings, no jewellery, nothing that presumed an intimacy that did not yet exist. He intended to woo her, not to frighten her away.

At the end of the week, he drove down to Devon again. Heading into the West Country peninsula, he felt exhilarated and alive. In the morning, he called at Orchard House.

'Marry me, Isabel,' he said.

'No.' The word squeezed out of her; she looked panicked.

Richard nodded, undaunted. 'Then at least come for a walk. I need to stretch my legs after driving so far. We'll take the dog.'

He chose a route that led along fields above the town. As they walked, he told her about his week — the fire, the loss of business, the urgent search for a new factory.

It was a cold, misty day, and at the highest point, where the pastureland gave way to gorse, they looked down on to clouds that blurred the valley below. Ahead of them, fragments of cloud raced along the curve of the hill. A winter's sun had begun to burn the mist away.

They headed downhill, towards the Valley of Rocks, where wind, water and frost had sculpted strange formations out of the sandstone and limestone. The rock columns and tumbled conglomerations of stone and boulder towered high above the steep grassy coombs. Beyond lay the sea.

'I can see why you like this part of the country,' he said. 'One day, I'll buy you a house down here.'

She said, her voice quick and low, 'Surely you can see that marriage is impossible. Surely I don't need to point out to you *why* it's impossible.'

'Nothing is impossible if you put your mind to it.'

'Nonsense,' she said sharply. 'You say that because you have never lacked for anything. Plenty of things are impossible.'

'I've never found it so.'

'Mr Finborough — '

'Richard, please.'

'Then, Richard, I can't possibly marry you. You're only . . . you're only *pursuing* me in this fashion because you've been thwarted. I expect you're used to getting your own way.'

He threw back his head and laughed. 'I dare say I am. But that's not why I want you to marry me.'

She whispered, '*Why?*'

'I told you. I love you.'

'I expect you've been in love before.'

'No, I don't think so. I thought I was, but I was mistaken.'

She glared at him. 'Do you feel sorry for me? Is that why you're saying these things? If so, there's no need.

I'm perfectly able to look after myself. I've done so for years.'

'Do you think I'm asking you to marry me because I pity you?' He shook his head. 'Come now, Isabel — such a notion beggars belief. There are many young women in a far more pitiful state than you. Should I offer all of them my hand in marriage?'

'Then I don't understand,' she said faintly.

Far below, at the foot of the steep red-sandstone cliffs, waves crashed. Richard stood near the edge of the precipice, testing himself, feeling the void beneath him.

'I should be in London now,' he said, 'looking for new premises for my factory, yet I'm here, because it seems to me the most important thing in the world that you should agree to marry me. I want to care for you. I want to protect you. I want to take you to London and I want to show you Raheen. I want yours to be the first face I see when I wake in the morning. I want to grow old with you. There really is nothing more to it than that.'

She turned away, her lips pressed tightly together. They walked on, down the valley, towards the coast. He made her list her objections to their marriage one by one. He knew that he could knock them down, annihilate them, and then she would have nothing left to argue with.

'We met only a few weeks ago,' she pointed out. 'I don't *know* you, Richard.'

'That's easily repaired. We can have as long an engagement as you wish, though I should have thought a short one would suit you better. And if, when you come to know me, you still find me repulsive, well then, I shall have to accept defeat.'

'I don't find you repulsive.'

He sensed how much the admission had cost her. 'Then that's a start,' he said lightly.

At the bottom of the hill, a stream gouted into a small cove. Jagged grey rocks lay piled in the cove; Richard gave her his hand as they scrambled over them. The dog ran ahead, barking at the sea. On the beach the tide had gone out, leaving in its wake gritty grey sand and gleaming coloured pebbles. In a rock-pool a maroon plum of an anemone waved its tentacles and a tiny pale green crab, feeling the vibration of their footsteps perhaps, scuttled beneath a stone.

'Our difference in rank makes it impossible for us to marry,' she said, with finality. '*That* difficulty is insuperable, you must admit.'

'Nonsense. That doesn't trouble me at all.'

'*Richard*!'

He liked the way she said his name, even when her voice was taut with exasperation. 'What is it?'

'It's quite simple — you are rich and I am poor!'

'If you marry me, you'll be rich. Not yet, Isabel, but I mean to be rich one day. And besides, I've been poor. Not so long ago, my family lost almost everything.'

'What you speak of isn't *poverty*,' she said bitterly. 'Poverty is wondering where the next meal is coming from or whether you'll have a roof over your head in a week's time. Richard, *listen* to me! My father was a clerk to the bursar of a large estate in Hampshire. When he became ill he lost his job and we had to leave our home. When he died, I went into service. I was a nursemaid to a family in Kent before I became Mr Hawkins' housekeeper. Men like you, Richard, don't marry women like me! They make us their mistresses, but they don't marry us!'

'I want to marry you. And that's all that matters.' When a wave crashed nearby, he brushed the spray from her cheek with his fingertips and saw her shiver. 'Become my wife, Isabel,' he said softly, 'and you can put all that hardship and privation behind you. You'll have the comfort and happiness you need and deserve. Marry me, and you'll never want for anything. Marry me, and you need never be lonely again.'

He thought she was wavering, tempted. 'Your family . . . ' she murmured.

'My mother will love you. I have no one else.'

'If we were to marry then you would be a laughing stock among your own people. Your friends would desert you and your employees would lose their respect for you.'

If we were to marry . . . He could feel her resistance crumbling, like a sandbank swept by waves. He felt a rush of excitement and pleasure. 'Perhaps at first there would be some talk,' he acknowledged. 'But people would lose interest and move on to the next scandal soon enough. London isn't like Lynton. All sorts of people make their way in London, people of different position and religion and race. And besides, once they knew you, they would come to love you, as I do.'

'You must have social obligations. I would let you down.'

'It's no great endeavour,' he said airily, 'giving a supper or knowing how to dress for the opera.'

'No, Richard.' A quick shake of the head. 'I've been in service long enough to know that these things *are* a great endeavour and that there are a thousand mistakes to make, and a thousand ways I would fail you!'

'Do you think I'd care if you muddled up the cutlery?'

'You would care when your friends were embarrassed for you at some grand occasion,' she said quietly. 'You would care when they pitied you. You would come to regret having married me. You would be ashamed of me.'

'Never.' He seized her hands. 'I would never regret marrying you. Never, ever.'

'Richard — ' she gave a sigh — 'I am not the kind of woman you should marry.'

'You are, Isabel, I know you are.' He felt calmer now, sure of himself, never so certain of anything in his life. 'I couldn't bear to find myself hitched to some mincing little miss who'd have hysterics whenever I said a cross word or who'd complain if I refused to dance attendance on her at every moment. That kind of woman wouldn't suit me, because I would crush her. You are strong-minded and courageous and independent, and I need that, I need it so much.'

She set her mouth, looking away from him as they headed back to Lynmouth. 'I'm not educated, like you,' she said. 'I left school when I was twelve.'

He pushed her objection aside with the sweep of a hand. 'No one expects girls to waste their time with years of schooling.'

'But what would we talk about, what would we say to each other?'

'We would talk about all the things we haven't had time to say yet. And perhaps sometimes there would be no need to speak. It would be enough to be with each other.'

'That sort of marriage . . . does it exist?'

'We could make it exist.'

She frowned. 'You are too idealistic.'

'No, I'm a practical man, Isabel. I'm not a fool, not some lovesick young idiot who's asking you to marry him on a whim. I dare say we'd have cross words sometimes, you and I. I'm not always sweet-tempered, I admit it. But if there's love — if there's a strong enough love — then I believe that nothing else need matter.'

'Oh, *Richard*! You might think yourself passionately in love with me now, but that sort of love doesn't last! How will you feel in one month, or six, or even a year? Sooner or later I would tire you — sooner or later you'd wish you'd married someone else, someone of your own kind. You'd end up hating me and wishing yourself free!'

'No.'

'You can't know that.'

'I know it as well as I know anything.'

'But I — ' She broke off.

'You don't love me — is that what you were going to say? Do you dislike me?'

'No, not at all. But attraction isn't *love*. It doesn't last, it isn't certain, it can be broken.'

'Attraction might do for a start, don't you think? And love can grow, can't it?'

'What if it doesn't?' she said bluntly. 'What then?'

'It will. I'll make it grow. It's a risk I'm prepared to take. And besides,' he said, feeling himself growing impatient, 'enough of this shillyshallying. If this were a business proposition, then I'd point out to you how much I can offer you — a home of your own, security and a position in society. Looked at practically rather than sentimentally, what have you to lose?'

'You mean, what alternative have I?' Her voice was bitter. 'Do you think I don't know? A post as a cook or a housekeeper. An attic room furnished with leftovers and a fireplace that's never lit. An employer who expects me to bob curtsies and to know my place. My pleasures the servants' dance at Christmastime or a book borrowed from the penny library. Do you think I don't dread all that, fear it, that I haven't put off my fate for far too long already?'

They had reached Lynmouth harbour. Richard said softly, 'It doesn't have to happen. Come to London with me and you'll never have to endure such humiliations again.'

There were tears in her eyes. 'You don't know me. You might think you do, but you don't. You don't know how I've lived or what I've done.'

'How old are you, Isabel?'

'Twenty — but I don't see — '

'So you're five years younger than me. I find it hard to believe you've done anything so very terrible. And if you have — if you've stabbed a wicked stepmother and buried her body in a ditch, well then, that's in the past and it's no concern of mine. If you marry me, you can start again. You'll have a new name, a new home in a new city. You can put all the hardships you've suffered behind you. So marry me, Isabel. There's no reason on earth why you should not marry me.'

She gasped, and pressed her knuckles against her mouth. Eventually, she said, 'Wait here, if you please. I must think.'

Richard followed her path, a flare of red and black, along the harbour arm until she stood beneath the shadow of the Rhenish Tower. The tide was coming in fast, and now the boats in the harbour, beached at low tide, were afloat. From the harbour, the incoming sea was funnelled up towards the river, the speed of its progress visible along the stony bed. Richard was able to make out the point where sea and river met, where they clung to each other, mingling, fighting, insepa-rable.

It was late morning and the bay was bathed in a golden light. Richard sat down on a bench, the dog at his feet. At length, he looked up and saw Isabel walking back towards him. As she approached, he stood up. He knew himself unable to disguise the mixture of hope and fear that infused his features.

She drew level with him. 'What you said to me about my past — did you truly mean that?'

'Of course. Your past is no concern of mine. Marry me, Isabel.'

'Yes.'

He only just caught the whispered word. Elation ran through him. He took her in his arms; a tremor of emotion ran over her face. 'Isabel, my Isabel. Say it again. Say that you'll marry me.'

'Yes, Richard,' she whispered. 'I will.'

★ ★ ★

They travelled up to London the following day. Richard engaged a suite of rooms for Isabel in a small, exclusive hotel in a quiet street behind the Strand. In the interval between her departure from Devon and their marriage, she had fittings with dressmakers, shoemakers, milliners, glove-makers and corsetieres.

Dining together on the night before their wedding, Isabel wore a gown of pale green filmy stuff, trimmed with lace and narrow black ribbons around the bosom. Richard thought how the fine clothes suited her, a fitting foil to her strange and severe beauty.

Tonight, she was quiet and she picked at her food. He put it down to apprehension about their wedding day and tried to distract her by talking of Paris and Ireland, which they would visit on honeymoon. After the first course, she excused herself and left the dining room. When she returned, he noticed that her pallor had increased.

'I ordered *crêpes au citron* for both of us,' he said. 'I hope you like them.'

Her hands were knotted on her lap. 'Richard, I can't marry you.' Her voice trembled. 'I'm very sorry, but I can't.'

He said soothingly, 'You're just a little nervous, my darling. You'll feel much better once tomorrow is over.'

'No.' She shook her head violently. 'It's not nervousness. This wedding — it cannot take place. I should never have let things go so far.'

'Isabel, you're being irrational.'

She bit her lip. 'In Lynton, when you asked me to marry you, I believed then that you were sincere. But when I came to London, when I saw how you lived, I thought . . . '

'You thought what?'

Her eyes, which were wild and distracted, met his. 'That I must have been mistaken. That you couldn't possibly marry me. That you meant to take me as your mistress after all.'

The head waiter came to the table, a minion pushing a trolley behind him, preventing Richard's angry response. Then there was a great deal of histrionics with spirit burners and crêpe pans. When at last they were alone again, he said, 'Good God, Isabel! How can you say such a thing?'

She flushed. 'I see now — I see that I have misjudged you.'

'And having realised that I am not a liar,' he said furiously, 'that I have not deceived you, *now* you talk of being unable to marry me?'

'I *can't.*'

'What are you saying? That you'd rather become my mistress? That you want no permanent tie — that you would prefer to pursue your career unhindered by the fetters of legality?'

Anger flashed in her eyes. 'Richard, that is unworthy of you!'

'What else can I believe?'

'This is my fault,' she said bitterly. 'I can't blame you for being angry with me. I can't blame you for thinking the worst. But I can't marry you, Richard. It would be wrong of me, I know it would . . . '

She looked tired and distraught; he reached across the table to her. 'Give me your hands,' he said and, after a few moments, she did so. 'I'm not angry with you,' he said gently. 'But you are frightening me. Don't speak like this, please, my darling.'

Her lids lowered; he heard a small sigh escape her. 'Richard, there's something I haven't told you — '

A voice hailed them, interrupting her. 'Good Lord, Finborough, is that you?' A tall, curly-haired man was threading his way between the tables. 'I say, of all places, to find you here!'

Richard cursed under his breath. Then he rose.

41

'Isabel, let me introduce you to an old friend of mine, Frederick McCrory. Freddie, this is my fiancée, Miss Zeale.'

'Well, you're a dark horse, Richard.' McCrory's gaze settled admiringly on Isabel. 'Delighted to meet you, Miss Zeale.'

'Freddie and I were at school together,' explained Richard.

The men talked, the moments passed and the waiter cleared away the uneaten pudding. Then Freddie took his leave of them. Shortly afterwards, refusing coffee and brandy, Richard and Isabel left the restaurant.

Flakes of snow floated in the darkness. Richard said, 'Do you mind if we walk a little? Is it too cold for you?'

Isabel shook her head. They walked to the Embankment. The water of the Thames seemed gelid, viscous, as though the surface had just begun to turn to ice. Beneath the shadow of a plane tree, Richard took her in his arms and kissed her. It was the first time he had kissed her properly, unrestrainedly. He had kept a distance from her during these strange, unreal weeks before their marriage, knowing the importance of preserving her reputation. Now, though, he ran his hands beneath the fur lining of her pelisse, feeling bones and flesh beneath the silk of her bodice, and he crushed her to him, as if by doing so he could make her a part of him. And the miracle happened and he felt the passion he had always sensed in her awaken, felt the frost with which she surrounded herself warm and turn to liquid, like the river, heard her murmur his name, saw her throw back her head, her eyes squeezed shut, as they clung to each other.

When, eventually, they drew apart, he said softly, 'The day you agreed to marry me, I thought I was the luckiest man alive.' His kisses changed, becoming gentle and tender; he cupped her face in his palms. 'I've taken you away from all that was familiar to you, haven't I?

42

I've taken you from your home, from the place that you love. Forgive me for that — I see that it was selfish of me.'

She murmured, 'There is nothing to forgive, Richard.'

'Don't be afraid, Isabel, my darling. I promise you I'll look after you; I promise you I'll care for you. I promise I'll make you the happiest woman in the world. Let me do this for you, please.'

There were tears in her eyes; he drew her to him, cradling her head against his shoulder. 'You would break me if you were to leave me now.' His voice was unsteady. 'I don't think I would survive it. You cannot do it. I could not bear it.'

2

She thought she began to love him that night. She saw through his forcefulness and ardour, and for the first time glimpsed the tenderness and vulnerability that lay beneath.

Was that why she lost courage, and didn't tell him about Alfie Broughton? Because she had begun to love him?

She hoped so. It was a better reason than all the others.

★ ★ ★

Twenty-four hours later they were married.

Richard Finborough was tall, broad-shouldered and strongly built. His hooded eyes were a dark greenish hazel, his features were powerfully delineated and his mouth had a sensual curve. His thick, close-cropped hair was a coppery red.

Isabel had never liked red hair. It went too often with temper, pride, arrogance. When she had first found herself attracted to him, she had felt disconcerted. She had thought him a spoiled, indulged young man, accustomed to having whatever he wanted. She had not taken his courtship seriously, had been unable to believe that someone like him could love her. She had ignored him, insulted him, closed the door in his face. Only after she failed to drive him away had she begun to think he might be sincere. Still, she had not believed that he would marry her.

The day he had first seen her, standing beneath the Rhenish Tower during the storm, she had been grief-stricken and afraid. She, who by the age of twenty

44

had already made so many new beginnings in her life, had been almost unable to face the further alteration in circumstances that Charles Hawkins' death had prompted. Where would she go, what would she do? She had felt weariness and apprehension, and a disabling kind of dread, and it had occurred to her, standing that stormy morning on the harbour arm, soaked by rain and sea-spray, that she need only take a few steps forward and then there would be no more decisions, no more new starts, no more losses to absorb and endure. Something — habit, as much as a Christian rejection of self-harm, she later thought — had made her turn away from the roiling sea and walk back to the village. That Richard Finborough had seen her that morning troubled her. She hated to expose a glimpse of her darkest self to a stranger: it made her feel that she had given a part of herself away.

That first night of their honeymoon, in their bedroom in the Crillon Hotel in Paris, Richard removed her coverings one by one. A pearl necklace trailed, cool and slippery, through his fingers. An evening gown of rose-coloured silk chiffon tumbled like a flurry of petals to the floor. Strong, competent fingers untied petticoats of taffeta and chantilly lace and bows of ribbon. Unlacing her pink coutil stays, he bent and kissed her breasts. He left her silk stockings and her long white gloves till last. His mouth brushed against the nape of her neck; his hands, touching her, ignited desire in her. Her body moved in rhythm with his, her pleasure coincided with his.

In the aftermath, along with release, she felt, again, that sense of betrayal. What if she should come to love him too much, this arrogant redheaded man who had forced his way uninvited into her life? Could you not choose who you loved, could your emotions never be in tune with your intellect, your self-control?

After a fortnight in Paris they left for Raheen,

Richard's birthplace in County Down in Ireland. Miraculously, Richard's mother was not the disapproving dragon Isabel had anticipated, but was talkative and welcoming, only occasionally revealing flashes of the stubbornness she had passed on to her son. Large, imposing and neglected, Raheen House stood half a mile from Dundrum Bay. Walking along sands slick with the outgoing waves and with the purplish-grey silhouettes of the Mourne Mountains like a mirage across the bay, Isabel experienced moments of calm and contentment.

Yet Raheen disturbed her, as if the cobwebs and decay that veiled the outermost rooms of the house enshrouded her at night, eroding her defences. She wondered whether it was the proximity of the sea that made her dream of Broadstairs, whether she could hear, while she slept, the murmur of the waves or smell the salt in the air.

In her dream, she was walking along the beach with the Clarewood children. She was wearing her nursemaid's uniform, but her feet were bare and she could feel the damp sand squeezing between her toes. The pram wheels ran smoothly on the glistening, compacted surface; shells and pebbles dotted the shore like grey and white pearls. Ahead of her, Adele and Elsie ran splashing through the sparkling water. It must have been late in the day because the Punch and Judy booths had been packed away and the bathing machines wheeled out of sight. The sun was sinking towards the horizon, painting the sea with gold, and washing the waves with shimmering brightness.

Then she turned and looked down and saw that the pram handle had somehow slipped through her fingers, and the pram, with baby Edward inside it, had disappeared, and the girls were nowhere to be seen, and she was standing alone on the wide, empty beach.

* * *

Isabel woke, her face wet with tears. Beside her, Richard slept deeply. She lay awake in the darkness, thoughts of Broadstairs, the Clarewoods, Alfie, tumbling through her mind.

She had been seventeen years old when she had met Alfie Broughton, and the object of men's interest for some time. She had been adept at the cold shoulder, the swift put-down. Alfie had changed all that. Until then, she had not known what it was to look at a man and to want him. Nor had she known that you could discover delight in the spark of an eye and the sound of a voice. At what point, she wondered, could she have prevented the disaster that had so slyly overtaken her? If they had not met, that afternoon on the beach? If she had not watched him emerge from the waves, cloaked in sea and sun? What magic, conjured up by the minstrels' songs and the warm air, had made her fall for Alfie Broughton?

* * *

Isabel Zeale had started to work for the Clarewoods at the age of fourteen, after her father had died. Her mother had died when Isabel had been six months old; she had no brothers or sisters. She had applied for the post as a nursemaid to a family living in Broadstairs because she had always loved children and because, coming from a landscape of forest and clearing, she had longed to see the sea. Glimpsing it for the first time, dark blue and silky and constantly changing, she had stood still, in a sort of rapture, clutching the bundle containing her clothes and her father's books as the summer holiday crowds bustled round her.

The job with the Clarewoods suited her and she became fond of her charge, three-year-old Adele. Elsie

47

was born not long after Isabel started to work for the Clarewoods, baby Edward two years later. Mrs Clarewood rarely interfered with the running of the nursery, and Isabel loved the seaside, especially in summer, when rules slackened, and the servants — Mrs George, the cook-general, and Liddy, the parlourmaid — cut corners, heating up leftovers and skimping the dusting.

She first met Alfie on a warm Whitsun afternoon. It was their half-day off so she and Liddy headed to the beach. Bathing machines, pulled by horses or strong men, carried the swimmers into the water. The men bathed in one part of the beach, the women in another. The sands were crowded with holidaymakers, the better-off in bathing suits, the poorer people in their ordinary clothes, lobster-faced in the heat. Isabel wore the new dress she had made for herself, a candy-striped blue and white cotton. Liddy, who was a chatterbox, talked constantly. Watching the minstrel show, Isabel felt the warmth of the sand through the soles of her boots.

In the ripple of applause at the end of a song, a young man approached them. 'Enjoying the show, girls?' he asked.

'What's it to you?' said Liddy, but smiled, because he was handsome.

'Just asking,' he said.

Alfie Broughton's eyes were the dark, black-brown of treacle toffee, and his hair, with its crisp black curls, made Isabel want to run the palm of her hand across it and feel its springiness brush against her skin. A black moustache curled jauntily above his curved red mouth.

He took a bag of fruit bonbons from his pocket and offered it to them. He was a manufacturer's agent, he explained. He sold cigarettes and confectionery to the shops and stalls of the seaside towns on the Kent coast. He was staying in a lodging house in Broadstairs; each day he travelled from town to town, taking orders for humbugs and lollipops, marshmallows and Turkish delight.

They walked to the pier, threading through the day-trippers, passing the whelk stalls and the ginger-beer men. Alfie bought three penny ices: as he scooped the last of the ice cream out of the little glass dish with his forefinger, he said to Isabel, 'Here,' and put his finger to her mouth. She licked off the ice cream and then blushed at the sweetness and the warm saltiness of his skin.

On the beach, Alfie kicked off his shoes, threw off his jacket, rolled up his trousers and waded into the sea. Glancing over his shoulder, he called out, 'Coming in, Isabel?'

Liddy tutted disapprovingly, but Isabel remembered swimming in slow, dreamy Hampshire rivers, the dark green weed clinging to her ankles. Her frock, petticoat and corsets weighed on her like armour. She unlaced her boots and peeled down her stockings. After the first ice-cold touch of the water, she picked up her skirt and petticoat and waded in deeper. The sea rippled round her ankles and, beneath her feet, the sand moved, forming hollows, making the solid ground shift. In the distance, Alfie had become a black shape against the blue of the sea. Then he dived, and a long moment passed before his head broke through the waves.

As he walked back to the shore, Isabel saw how his curls had been flattened by the water, and how his white shirt clung to the broad triangle of his chest. The sun glittered on the waves and she had to shade her eyes to shut out its brightness.

In the weeks that followed, he courted her with ice creams and lollipops, with sherbet fountains and liquorice bootlaces. Alfie's friend, Jim Cottle, took the three of them out on his fishing boat. Liddy perched beside Jim in the small cabin while Isabel and Alfie sat in the stern. They picnicked on pink and white marshmallows at Pegwell Bay. In the shadow of the cliffs, Alfie made Isabel close her eyes as he posted a chocolate drop into her mouth. She laughed as it melted on her tongue, but her laughter turned to shivers when he pressed his lips against hers and his taste mingled with the chocolate.

He told her his dreams. He was going to travel. He was going to sail to America — he wanted to see a different country, a new country. He was going to own a shop. 'I won't be at someone else's beck and call for ever,' he said.

'Your beau', Mrs George, the Clarewoods' cook, called him, and Isabel felt a thrill of pride. Alfie was the handsomest man in Broadstairs; all the girls turned to look at him as he walked along the promenade.

As the summer lengthened, the sun blazed down on the sands day after day. Out to sea, fishing boats floated on the limpid water; on the beach, the ladies' parasols clustered like white barnacles. A lazy, opulent heat settled over the prim little town. At night, embracing her in the gloomy basement area behind the Clarewoods' house, Alfie ran his fingertips down the small, knobbly bones of her spine. On the cliff-top, alive with gorse and harebells, he undid the tiny buttons of her blouse.

He had a tenacity, Alfie Broughton, that his carefree manner and easy charm did not immediately reveal. Isabel could look back on those months as a series of skirmishes, all of which Alfie had eventually won. One thing had led to another, she supposed, the holding of hands to a kiss, a kiss to an embrace. Like the dominoes the Clarewood girls liked to set up in the nursery, when one fell, everything tumbled. Piece by piece, he fought over every part of her.

Yet it would be a lie to say *he made me*. She had wanted him, all of him. Sleepless at night in the nursery she shared with Adele, Elsie and Edward, her

50

imagination had conjured up prettier girls, more obliging girls. Jealousy, dark and bitter, had been as powerful as desire.

So you could put it down to the August sun, which had seemed to bleach the colour from the sea, leaving it pearl grey and glaring. Or perhaps the touch of his hand, turning her to fire, had mesmerised her. Or had it been his voice, murmuring in her ear, *But I love you, Isabel, I love you so much. Don't you love me at all? And besides, if there's any trouble, we can get married, can't we, sweetie?*

His only deception had been those words, dropped carelessly, she later realised, as a bargaining counter. But in the end, she had let Alfie Broughton make love to her because she had wanted him to. Because she had longed for him. Because she had ached for him.

★　★　★

The menace and glory of her dream lingered into the morning. After breakfast, while Richard dealt with estate business and his mother exercised the horses, Isabel explored the house.

The two wings that sprouted out from the main building had been built by his father, Richard had told her, but they had been little used, expensive white elephants almost from the day of their construction. There was a melancholy air to these rooms, which were redolent of failed dreams and ruined ambitions.

In a glass cabinet she discovered a bone rattle and a pair of baby's shoes. Taking them out of the cabinet, she ran a fingertip along the yellowed lace as her thoughts rushed back to Broadstairs. As the summer had faded and the holidaymakers and day-trippers had left the town, Isabel had realised that she was pregnant. She had seen Mrs Clarewood endure the same symptoms during her pregnancies with Elsie and Edward — tired

51

all the time and sick as a dog every morning.

She told Alfie about the baby. It was late, and the children were asleep in bed. She and Alfie were in the basement area at the back of the house. Through the scullery window Isabel could make out the shape of a packet of washing soda and a bar of household soap.

'A baby . . . ' he repeated. He let out a breath. 'Lord, Isabel, you know how to bowl a fellow a blinder, don't you?'

'We'll get married, won't we, Alfie?' She clutched his hands.

'Yes, yes.' He eased the irritation from his voice and smiled. ''Course we will.'

Relief made her lean against him, gripping him tightly. 'At the church?'

'Whatever you like, sweetie.'

Days passed. Alfie loved her, he was going to marry her. They would live in a little house by the sea: Isabel pictured her child playing on the sand.

Yet, peering out of the nursery window at night, she could not make him out, darkly handsome among the bins and bicycles. She wrote him a note: when he did not reply she told herself that he must be away on business, stocking the shops of Kent with sticks of rock and barley sugar.

When she became uneasy, she went to his lodgings. His landlady told her that Alfie had gone away. 'Owes me a week's rent,' she added crossly. 'Didn't leave no forwarding address neither.' Her eyes ran over Isabel's belly as she spoke.

The next day, her half-day off, she scoured the town, calling at Alfie's favourite haunts. Panic rose inside her as she ran from shop to café. As she hurried along the beach, the sand dragged nightmarishly at her feet. No one knew where Alfie Broughton was; no one had seen him for more than a week.

Isabel put the baby shoes back in the cabinet. It had

taken her a long time to accept that Alfie had gone for good, that his promises of love had been a lie. Such a well-worn story: the lover's betrayal, the jilted girl. Not even *original*. Should she ~~have~~ told it, with all its terrible compromises and consequences, to Richard? Of course she should.

Yet she had not. She had had her reasons, some of them shameful, some less so. Richard Finborough had forced his way uninvited into her life. Hadn't she tried, over and over again, to repulse him? And then — *your past is no concern of mine*, he had told her, and now it must be no concern of hers either: she must forget Alfie Broughton and her child, must erase them from her mind as though they had never existed.

And besides, hadn't she suffered enough? Hadn't she earned the right to put the past behind her, to begin again? Should she remain unmarried and childless and without love for the remainder of her life, and all for one terrible mistake, made when she was only seventeen years old?

Isabel put on her coat and hat and left the house. Crossing the lawn, she headed towards the sea, invisible in the mist that shrouded Raheen. Black, dripping branches crisscrossed her path; above her she could make out the pale disc of the sun behind the clouds. The trees cleared and she walked through a field, the hem of her skirt soaked by the long grass. At the top of the rise, she looked out to the bay. There, the mist had thinned and a silvery light played on the water. Half a dozen cows, escaped from their field, jostled each other on the sands.

Alfie Broughton must be her secret, kept for ever. No one must ever know about him. In marrying Richard Finborough she had cut herself off from her past with a clean slash of the knife. 'Isabel Zeale has gone,' she murmured aloud. 'Now, I am Richard Finborough's wife.'

A voice called out her name. Turning, she saw Richard crossing the grass to her. The winter sun, she thought, this green and dreaming landscape, this man. Her heart lifted and she ran down the slope to him.

★ ★ ★

At first they lived in a rented house in Kensington. Married to Richard Finborough, she was able to feed her mind, to satisfy its aching hunger. The first year of her marriage was marked by a series of beginnings: the first time she saw a ballet, the first time she attended an orchestral concert, the first time she visited an art gallery.

Richard took her to the button workshop and to the new tea-packing factory in the City of London. One afternoon they went to the docks, to Butler's Wharf, where the lightermen unloaded the tea chests from the ships. She saw how Richard loved to be in company, how he revelled in it, how he had the great gift of being equally at ease with all classes, from the women who laboured in his factories to the grandees with whom they dined.

She learned to move among people who assumed luxury and ease as their right. She went to house parties and balls, she shared dinner tables with titled ladies and financiers and entrepreneurs. She attended the races at Ascot and watched the boats at Henley. At the theatre, sitting in a box high above the stage, framed by crimson velvet curtains and gilt putti, she felt herself displayed, on show.

She hated it. She knew that her difference marked her out. The habits and customs of the new world in which she found herself bewildered and excluded her. Though she had always prided herself on being well-spoken, she lacked the mangled vowels of the aristocracy. Seated at some great lady's dining table, she must choose from the array of silver, china and crystal that surrounded her, must not hesitate and give herself away. She must rise when her hostess rose and leave the dining room in the same order of precedence she had entered it. She imagined her fellow guests noting her errors, seeing through the fine clothes and the jewels to what she really was. She thought she heard them whispering about her. *Where on earth did Richard find that quaint little creature? Pretty, but not quite the thing, of course.*

On terraces and in drawing rooms, she held up her glass of pink Oeil de Perdrix champagne to the light and saw it turn to the colour of rubies. At house parties, the breakfast dishes, warmed over the burners, overflowed with plump, pink kidneys and golden kedgeree. At dinner, footmen wielded damask napkins as they served oysters, turbot, game, pastries, savouries, fruit and champagne. All that she ate was disguised, made duplicitous, given a French name, garnished with herbs, drowned in pools of sauce or cloaked in whipped cream. A pineapple became a boat with a gelatine sail; meringue swans were reflected on mirrored glass. She, too, presented to the outside world a self that was false, as much an artifice as those bedecked and gaudy desserts. Her mouth dried, caught at the edges of conversations about people she had never met, places she had never been. She had not the years of upbringing and habituation that the others had; her virtues — of economy and endurance and independence — had no place here.

It took her a while to realise that she felt, along with nervousness, contempt for these people she must mix with. She scorned their frivolous conversation, their ignorance of the real world and their ridiculous, wasteful habits. The idiocy of having to change her frock three or four times a day! The stupidity of having to eat a peach with a knife and fork, instead of picking it up in her hands! The wastefulness of the house parties shocked her, the unfinished plates of food, the mountains of grouse after a day's shooting.

Other discoveries shocked her more. At night, after the guests had gone to their rooms, she heard the pitter-patter of feet along the corridor and the echo of laughter as a bedroom door was opened and closed.

'They've been lovers for years,' Richard told her when she voiced her suspicions. 'Everyone knows.'

'But they're not married to each other.' Along with shock, Isabel was aware of distaste. 'Their husbands . . . their wives . . . '

'Oh, I'm sure they know exactly what's going on. No doubt it suits them.' His fingers brushed her cheek. 'Don't look so scandalised, darling. It's how the world is.'

'Not *my* world.'

'This is your world, Isabel. This has become your world.'

His voice was light, but she caught something unyielding in his eyes. She thought of how, sometimes, he drifted away from her side in the course of an evening, and how, always restless, his hand tapped against his thigh as his eyes roamed round a room. She had noticed how women flirted with him and how their glances followed him. She knew that he was easily bored, that he loved anything new. Sometimes, her fear and her jealousy almost choked her — would he leave her, as Alfie Broughton had left her? Would he regret this reckless marriage, forget her, desert her?

She said, 'I would never do *that*. Never, Richard.'

'Take a lover? I should hope not.' He sounded amused.

They gave their first dinner party in March. There were people he owed invitations, he told her, and others whose acquaintance he needed to cultivate. On the evening of the dinner the house whirled with servants polishing glasses and cutlery, and shaking coal on to the fires. Glorious aromas issued from the kitchen.

Three-quarters of an hour before the guests were due to arrive Richard went upstairs to the bedroom to change. When he opened the door, Isabel was sitting on the bed, wearing her chiffon petticoats.

'Good Lord,' he said 'aren't you ready yet? Where's the maid?'

'I sent her away.'

'Why? You need to get a move on, darling, they'll be here soon.'

She shook her head. 'Richard, I don't think I can do this.'

He glanced back at her. 'What do you mean?'

'I can't go through with it.'

He said bracingly, 'It's only a dinner party, darling.'

'All those people — '

'You've met most of them before.'

She was nauseous; her stays pressed uncomfortably into her stomach and the thought of eating a five-course dinner sickened her.

'Can't we cancel it?'

'Now? Don't be ridiculous.'

'We could say that I was unwell.'

'Why on earth should we say that?'

'Because . . . ' What was the cause of her nervousness: telling him what she suspected, her certainty growing with each passing day, or this dreadful ordeal that she must go through?

She said evasively, 'I'll drop something — or I'll say the wrong thing.'

As he unbuttoned his shirt, a cufflink leaped beneath the dressing table, and he cursed. 'I can't see why you're making such a fuss. I never thought you lacking in courage.'

'Don't you know that every day I feel as though I am walking on ice?' Her voice rose. 'Don't you know how often I have to catch myself, to stop myself curtsying to people who once would have been my betters? Or do you prefer to forget all that? Tell me, Richard, how many of your acquaintances know what I was before I met you?'

'They have no need to know.'

'How many?'

'A few. My mother, of course — the Colvilles — '

'You see,' she said bitterly, 'it's as I said: you're ashamed of me!'

He looked angry. 'That's nonsense.'

'Is it? Can you honestly say that our marriage hasn't harmed you at all? That it hasn't made people think less of you?'

A sweep of the hand. 'Do you think I'm troubled by a few invitations less from the stuffier sort of hostess? Isabel, why are you doing this? Why do you torment yourself?'

She sat down on the bed. She whispered, 'Because I'm afraid of losing you.'

'Losing me?' he cried, exasperated. 'Why should you lose me?'

'You might meet someone prettier or cleverer.' Her voice was anguished. 'Someone of your own class.'

'There's no one prettier, no one cleverer. So I ask you again, why torment yourself over something that will never happen?'

She looked away. She murmured, 'Because I love you.'

'You say that as though it was a catastrophe.'

'Perhaps it is.'

His fingertip stroked her cheek. 'My darling, how can it be anything other than miraculous that we found each other and that we love each other?'

'I thought we were too unalike for love.'

'Unalike?' He laughed. 'I suppose we are. But as I'm your husband, isn't it just as well that we love each other?'

Then he went to the wardrobe. Isabel saw him flick aside the gowns hanging inside: blue, green, mocha, the succession of colours dizzied her.

'Which one are you wearing?'

'*Richard*. I told you. *I can't.*'

He drew out a black velvet gown. 'You should wear this.'

He took her hand, pulling her to her feet. She stood stiffly, like a mannequin in a shop window, as he eased the gown over her head and fastened the hooks and eyes and twitched the rich folds of fabric into place.

He swung her round to face the mirror. 'You are my wife,' he said. '*That's* who you are. *That's* all that matters. *You are my wife.*'

Isabel stared at her reflection in the mirror. Black dress, black hair, white skin, the only colour her red lips and pale eyes, which closed as he began to kiss her neck in a trail of small caresses. His hands slid round her waist, his palms were flat against her belly before moving down to follow the curve of her haunch and thigh.

'My darling, beautiful Isabel,' he whispered — and then he was tearing at the hooks and eyes and the dress was slipping to the floor in a pool of black velvet and he had swept her up in his arms and carried her to the bed. There was the rustle of silk and the hiss of lace as he pushed aside her petticoats and entered her.

All over in a soaring, intoxicating moment, and then they were lying on the bed, wrapped together, fighting for breath. It crossed her mind that if this was love, then it was a strange thing, this savage arousal that sometimes seemed to her almost combative.

Afterwards, he dressed her, a tender unrolling of silk stockings on to her legs, his mouth brushing her shoulder as he laced her stays.

As he fastened the buttons of the black velvet gown,

she found the courage to say, 'Richard, I think I'm expecting a baby.'

His hands stilled. 'When?'

'December, I believe. A few weeks before Christmas.'

'A son, to carry on the business.' His voice was full of wonder.

'Or a daughter,' she murmured.

'A son first,' he said firmly, and kissed her.

As he clasped a pearl necklace round her throat, he said, 'I was once at a dinner where a very grand old lady dropped her false fringe into her bowl of soup. She fished it out and mopped it up with her napkin and didn't pause for a moment with her hunting yarn. You just have to have the nerve. You can get away with anything if you have the nerve.'

★　★　★

Philip was born in early December. He was a healthy baby, weighing nine pounds, with a sheen of red hair and a lusty howl. With the safe arrival of her son, it seemed to Isabel that she had put the past behind her for good. She engaged a nursemaid to help care for Philip, a pleasant Cornish girl called Millie.

Two months after the birth, they moved into a house in Hampstead. A short distance from the Heath, their new home was large and roomy and had a walled garden. At the bottom of the garden was an orchard, where the sound of traffic from the road was almost inaudible. Isabel imagined sitting there in the summer, playing with Philip.

She engaged five servants — the cook, Mrs Finch, two maids, a gardener, and Dunning, the handyman, who chauffeured the car in Richard's absence. Before they moved in, Richard had had a telephone and electric lighting installed and the old stable block converted into a garage. He left the furnishing of the house to Isabel. She had the rooms papered in soft shades of pink and cream and gold, and she visited the antique emporia and furniture stores, choosing a carved Elizabethan chest here, a modern lampstand there. In the late afternoons, she saw how the sun filtered through the coloured glass in the windows, making pools of jewelled light on the floor.

In the hot summer of 1911, the sky took on an opaque, glaring quality, as if it had been sealed behind glass. On the streets, the traffic moved slowly, seeming to press against an invisible barrier. At midday, clerks and shop girls rolled up their sleeves as they ate their packed lunches in parks where the sun had bleached the grass to straw. In the docks — in the heart of London — the city's sullen, angry mood deepened. Unrest spread from Southampton, where the dockers had downed tools after the crew of the liner *Olympic* had gone on strike. After Winston Churchill's intervention, the dispute seemed to be settled, but then, following a blazing June, discontent erupted once more. By the beginning of August, with the temperature in the eighties, much of the London docks were at a standstill. Ships lay unloaded at their moorings. Heaps of fruit — exotic peaches, bananas and pineapples — rotted on the wharfs. The great markets of London, Smithfield and Covent Garden, were as empty as a poor man's larder.

Richard's temper worsened as the Finborough tea-packing factory fell idle, its workers laid off, chests of Ceylon tea imprisoned in the holds of the becalmed ships. The button-making workshop scratched along, their stocks of materials dwindling by the hour. Five days, a week at most, he told Isabel, and he would have to lay off the women who worked there too.

But by September, the temperature had dropped and the dockers had settled their dispute, and the Lords had backed down, allowing the passage of the Finance Bill

61

through Parliament. By then, Isabel knew that she was pregnant again. A daughter this time, she hoped. A daughter to dress up in pretty clothes and take to the ballet. A daughter to replace the daughter she had lost.

★ ★ ★

In the March of 1912, Richard visited a factory in southern Germany that made products from Galilith, a casein plastic. On his return to England, he took a taxi from Victoria Station to the button workshop.

As he crossed the courtyard, his assistant, John Temple, hurried out to meet him. 'Thank God you're here, sir. Mrs Finborough is unwell, I'm afraid. She's gone into the nursing home.'

Shocked, Richard said, 'It can't be the baby, it's not due for another month or two.'

'They do sometimes turn up earlier than expected.' John Temple was father to a large brood of children. 'I'll look after things here. Don't worry about the business.' Briefly, his hand rested on Richard's shoulder.

At the nursing home, Richard was told that his wife was in labour and that he could not see her. Twelve hours later, their second son was born, five weeks early. As a doctor took him aside and told him that the lives of both his wife and his son were in danger, something seemed to freeze inside Richard. It was not possible, surely not possible, that he would lose Isabel. That would be too terrible, too *unfair*.

The doctor was murmuring about difficult births and hoping and praying, and Richard roared, 'Then what are you doing, standing here talking to me? Why aren't you with her, why aren't you making her better?'

Richard was left alone in the waiting room. A nurse brought him a cup of tea. He drank the tea and smoked, as much for something to do than for any desire for a drink or a cigarette. The worst of it was his utter impotence. Somewhere in this wretched place, Isabel was suffering, and he could not do anything to help her. They wouldn't even let him see her — though, when he threatened to lose his temper again, the nurse said kindly, 'But if you come with me you can see your son, Mr Finborough,' and he found himself stumbling up a corridor and being led into a small, white room.

What he felt most of all for the tiny, purplish scrap in the cot was resentment. And dislike. If God had just then required him to choose between his wife and his son, he would have chosen Isabel without a moment's hesitation.

A sister, crackling with starch, came into the nursery. 'The vicar is here, Mr Finborough, if you're ready.'

Richard stared at her blankly. Then he realised that they were telling him that the child must be christened. The unsaid words hung in the air: *in case he dies.*

'We hadn't decided on a name. Isabel — '

The kind nurse who had brought him the tea said, 'I've always thought Theodore was a nice name. It means gift of God.'

Not much of a gift, thought Richard sourly, his gaze returning to the scarcely finished little creature in the cot. Why choose a name for something that probably wouldn't last the night?

But he said brusquely, 'Then let's call him Theodore. Theodore Thomas Finborough.' Thomas had been Isabel's father's name.

After the brief christening ceremony, they let him sit with her at last. Isabel was asleep. The colour had drained from her face, leaving it the grey-white of bone. She looked old and exhausted; seeing her, it seemed all too possible that she might die. As Richard sat by her bedside, holding her hand, he thought of all the times he could have been a better husband to her: his occasional flirtations — insignificant, of course, but he knew that she hated him to so much as look at another woman — his insistence on her company to the social occasions he knew she loathed, and his wretched temper, that came too easily to the boil, and made him say things he later regretted.

It was only Isabel he loved, only Isabel with whom he wished to spend the rest of his life. She had intrigued him the first time he had seen her, standing on the harbour arm at Lynmouth, and she had continued to intrigue, madden and captivate him ever since. If he had not met her, he knew he would have gone on drifting from one love affair to the next, greedy for physical pleasure, his emotions uninvolved, his heart and spirit eventually wearing thin. Isabel had given him a home and a family, an anchor, a future. He knew that he was a better man for loving her. *Let me keep her*, he prayed silently, *and I'll never be selfish again.*

His prayers seemed to be answered, because throughout the next week both Isabel and the baby's health slowly improved. Richard's sense of shock, however, at the discovery that he and his family were vulnerable, remained, though he admitted it to no one. It was a month before Isabel and the baby were able to come home, longer before he began to feel any attachment to his younger son. Theo slowly lost his skinned rabbit look, though he remained small and thin and dark.

Time passed, and when Richard saw the two boys, Philip and Theo, together, he always noticed how Philip, with his fiery hair and sturdy frame, outshone his little brother. Yet he discovered a particular tenderness for Theo, as if to make up for the lack of love that had marked his birth. He imagined the day when his two sons would join him, working for the family business. He imagined his dynasty expanding, growing stronger, more powerful.

★ ★ ★

They spent their Christmases in Ireland, their summers in Cornwall. Philip and Theo's steps echoed in the dusty rooms of Raheen; holidaying in the West Country, there was the tang of salt and sea pinks along a jagged, rocky coast of fishing villages and hidden coves. For Richard and Isabel there were days of celebrations and laughter, and other days of quarrels and raised voices that spread through the house like thunderstorms. And then there were the nights when they made their peace, when their bodies expressed the love for which they could not always find the words, skin speaking to skin, bone speaking to bone.

Isabel learned to run the house with smooth, unobtrusive competence, presiding over formal dinners for Richard's friends and colleagues, and giving relaxed, intimate supper parties for the friends she had made among the artists and writers of Hampstead. On fine summer afternoons they gathered in the garden, where someone played a guitar or a poet read out his latest composition. Richard called her friends 'Isabel's Bohemians', and liked to tease her about them.

The boys, red-headed, rumbustious Philip and dark, intense Theo, scrapped in the garden and rampaged through the rooms. Philip's tantrums, when he was thwarted, seemed to make the walls swell and gasp as he screamed and drummed his heels on the floor. Theo's expression, when Philip threw a tantrum, amused Isabel. 'He looks so *incredulous*,' she said to Richard, 'as though he can't quite believe that anyone could choose to make so much noise and fuss.' Every now and then, seeing them together, Philip and Theo, Isabel felt such a rush of pride and joy that she paused, trying to hold on to it. But it was like catching thistledown and could not be retained.

The war, when it came, caught both of them unawares. For some years now, Richard had been concerned about the situation in Ireland, what with the

Unionists flexing their muscles and practically threatening civil war, and Sinn Fein causing trouble in the south. Irish politics had a way of flaring too easily into violence and rebellion, and Alice Finborough was alone in that remote, empty house with only the servants for company. Private armies — the Ulster Volunteers in the north and the Irish Volunteers in the south — were raised and trained. British soldiers mutinied, refusing to turn their weapons on their own people. Richard's mother dismissed his suggestion that she leave Raheen and stay for a while in England. Richard, reading her letter, cursed her intransigence.

Ireland distracted them, which was why, Isabel supposed, the conflict in Europe took them by surprise. The assassination in Sarajevo of Franz Ferdinand, the heir to the Austro-Hungarian empire, by a young Serbian separatist, had consequences neither of them were able to predict. Europe, with its old jealousies and emnities, was a powder keg: the assassin, Gavrilo Princip, lit the fuse. Fear, nationalism, pride and opportunism stoked the flames and the continent echoed with the scraping of swords drawn from their sheaths.

Still, Richard did not believe that there would be a war. There was no need for war, he said to Isabel, no true cause for war. Each state was bound one to the other by trade and by blood. King George V of the United Kingdom, Kaiser Wilhelm II of Germany and Tsar Nicholas II of Russia were cousins, linked by their common ancestor, Queen Victoria. In their correspondence, they addressed each other affectionately: 'Dear Georgie', 'Dear Willy', 'Dear Nicky'. Why should they choose to destroy themselves?

Yet in the warm, restless August of 1914, armies were packed into railway carriages and entrained to frontiers. And in the dog days of summer the first shots were fired.

Why did he enlist? Because, Richard supposed, his entire life had trained him for this moment: the loyalty of the Anglo-Irish to the Crown, his years of Officer Training Corps at school, and even the rabbits he had shot in the sandy dunes on the coast of County Down. On the damp walls of Raheen hung rusty swords and portraits of military men in scarlet. You didn't question it.

Isabel did, though. The evening Richard told her that he had joined up they quarrelled more bitterly than ever before. The boys hid in the nursery and the servants cowered in the kitchen.

'You could have stayed with me!' she screamed at him as she pummelled her fists against his chest. 'You didn't *have* to!'

Ah, but I did, he thought, as he took her in his arms and kissed until he felt her tense body relax. It was what he and his class were *for*.

★　★　★

Isabel always believed their daughter was conceived that night. The discovery that she was pregnant compensated in some measure for Richard's leaving, at the beginning of November, for an army training camp in the north of England.

Sara was born in 1915, at the end of May, in the bedroom of the Hampstead house. The evening sky, glimpsed through the window of the bedroom, was a changeable mixture of apricot and violet. The soft, variable light flickered on the sleeping infant's face. Isabel stroked Sara's curved, peachy cheek with her fingertip. Such a pretty baby, she thought, and was aware of a deep and sustaining joy.

3

In the late summer of 1915, Richard was posted to France. By then, the war on the Western Front had solidified into a stalemate, the two great armies confronting each other, defended by vast earthworks that ran from the Channel coast to Switzerland. Because, early on in the war, the Germans had been able to capture the hills and salients, the British and French were confined to the lower ground that was in some places only just above sea level.

Quickly promoted to the rank of captain, Richard's existence became bounded by the narrow underground confines of the trench and by the routine that went on day after day. Stand-to at dawn, followed by stand-down an hour later if there was no sign of an enemy attack. When it was light, the men's rifles were cleaned and inspected and, after breakfast, duties were given out. The maintenance of the trench was never ending: new saps and support trenches must be dug, existing earthworks must be be shored up, reinforced and repaired daily. Rations must be brought in, and the enemy lines, two hundred yards or so away, must be observed using a periscope or a mirror fixed to the point of a bayonet. Attacks were mounted from the trench to capture a ridge or a barn; at night, wiring parties were dispatched to repair the defensive barbed wire entanglements or to prise out information about enemy defences. All this had to be carried out while their lives were constantly at risk. The men, Richard noticed, had learned to sleep whenever they were not required to perform a task.

Richard's sergeant was called Nicholas Chance. Chance was tall, over six foot, broad-shouldered and strong. He had sharp blue eyes, dark brown hair and a distinctive, angular face, and he handled the sandbags they used to reinforce the trench as if they weighed no more than bags of sugar. Richard soon discovered that he could rely on Nicholas Chance. Give an order and Chance would carry it out with a cheerful efficiency that always contained a dash of nonchalance. Ask for volunteers for a night patrol and Chance would step forward. He was quick, thorough, intelligent and brave.

In September, an Allied offensive was mounted on the Western Front with the intention of taking the pressure off Russia to the east. The French attacked the German lines in Champagne while the British offensive was launched at Loos. Before the attack, there was a bombardment along a six-and-a-half-mile length of the front. Then poison gas was released across no man's land.

The onslaught began. Richard's regiment was in the reserve trenches. Soon they saw the wounded men coming back through the lines. To begin with, there were the men who had been gassed by a faulty canister or a sudden gust of wind in the wrong direction. Then came the walking wounded, limping or clutching lint to their heads, and then the men borne on stretchers. Motor ambulances drove past: sometimes the injured men called out and waved from the back. Once, Richard heard singing drifting over from another trench, familiar ragtime and music-hall songs.

You thought something was going to happen one way and then you discovered, in the passing of moments, that you had been completely wrong. If they had long ago lost the optimism of the early days of the war, they still clung to the conviction that Britain would, in the end, prevail. Loos taught them that they were, for the time being at least, mistaken. The German troops were better prepared, better defended and better armed. The British soldiers went over the top and were mown down by German machine guns.

Taking cover in a shell hole in no man's land, Richard looked round to rally his men and discovered that the great majority of them were dead. Many who were still alive were wounded. Only he and Nicholas Chance and a couple of dozen private soldiers survived the battle of Loos unscathed.

What remained with him afterwards was a deep and lasting anger and a loss of trust in the men who planned and equipped the war. Richard had always possessed an instinctive faith in the wisdom and competence of his superiors, but that belief was destroyed by what he had seen at Loos. Now he found himself questioning everything — at times, he even found himself doubting the existence of God.

At home on leave that Christmas, he kept his disillusionment to himself. He had established a code in his letters to Isabel, a series of phrases to let her know whether he was on active duty or behind the lines and which part of the theatre of war he had been sent to. But this emptiness, this rage, was harder to communicate. He told her about some things but not others. He told her about the rats and the lice but not about the cats that nested in the corpses. He told her about the exhaustion and the fear but not about the dismembered leg sticking out of the parapet that one of his men liked to hang his tin hat on. He had learned how sights, sounds and even smells could stay with you, slicing a gash through the way you had once looked at the world. He could not see the point of passing on to Isabel his knowledge of suffering and brutality. It would be like deliberately infecting her with a painful and damaging disease.

He spent most of his leave at home, avoiding the parties and dances that were taking place in this feverish, wartime London. He took the boys to the Heath to play ball, and it lightened his heart to see Sara, a pink and gold sort of baby, entranced by the glass baubles on the Christmas tree. He went into the city only to check on the factory and workshop, which he had left in John Temple's capable hands.

The war had thrown up both problems and opportunities. Chests of tea destined for the Finborough factory found their way to the sea floor with frustrating regularity, sent there by German gunboats and U-boats. Meanwhile, the button workshop flourished, manufacturing military buttons and insignia.

At the beginning of January, Richard returned to France. It was a cold, wet winter and the trenches and dugouts filled with slimy mud. The soldiers' tea was diluted with rain, and mud mingled with their food. They were cold and wet while they ate, worked and slept. They forgot what it was not to be cold and wet.

Reinforcements had been sent to replace the men who had died at Loos. Sergeant Chance chivvied and bullied them into shape. One day, rounding a traverse in the trench, Richard came across Chance pinning one of the new men to the earth wall by his throat. Seeing Richard, Chance let the soldier go. Yet it took a second or two, Richard noticed, before the powerful grip relaxed.

'Saunders is an idle bastard, sir,' Chance said afterwards, when he and Richard were alone and Richard questioned him about the incident. 'He was supposed to shore up the supports on a sap. He said he'd done it, but half the wall caved in overnight. People like him get good men killed.'

'Every regiment has men like Saunders,' said Richard. 'We're supposed to bring out the best in them.'

'The best?' Nicholas Chance looked scornful. 'There is no best to bring out, sir. A clip round the ear is all that men like him understand.'

'Perhaps,' said Richard mildly. 'But not blue murder.'

A few days later, Richard took a patrol out after dark

71

into no man's land. They were to find out whether one of the enemy's forward listening saps was manned. Their faces blackened with cork, they carried rifles and sheath knives as they wormed their way on their stomachs towards the enemy lines. If they kept low and moved quietly, it was hard for the German snipers to notice them. When, every now and then, the sky was illuminated by a trench mortar, they lay still, feigning dead. To one side of Richard, Nicholas Chance moved like a snake across the mud, invisible in the darkness.

They were a few yards from the sap and were cutting through the last of the barbed-wire entanglements when they heard voices. They all became motionless. Heads in steel helmets appeared briefly above the parapet and Richard caught a few words of German. Richard lay still and breathed shallowly. Now and then, the soldiers in the German trench exchanged a sentence. Cautiously, Richard glanced up at the barbed wire. A few more cuts and they could be through, and then they might easily overpower the enemy. Sergeant Chance seemed to have the same thought: Richard saw him raise his wire-cutters.

Without warning, there was the loud clatter of Maxim guns, quickly followed by flashes of fire from their own rifles. Soon, the raiding party were running back through no man's land and scrambling over the parapet into the British trench.

'How many men back?' Richard asked Chance.

'Ten, sir. No dead, two wounded. Not bad. They were firing over our heads — we were that close.' Chance gave a sudden burst of laughter. 'I wonder what old Fritz was rattling on about, back there.'

'They were complaining of stomach aches. Comparing symptoms.'

'You speak German, sir?'

'A little,' said Richard. 'I did some business in Germany not long before the war.'

After the injured men had been sent back to the reserve trenches and Richard had sent his report to HQ and stood down the men, he offered Nicholas Chance a glass of brandy in the dugout.

'I've travelled about a bit myself, sir,' Chance told him. 'Only in England, mind, never abroad.'

'What did you do before the war, Chance?'

'I was born in Buckland, in the Vale of White Horse. I couldn't see myself as a farm boy, though, so when I was fifteen I went to London. I took a job with a firm selling agricultural equipment and feedstuffs because it let me move around a bit.' He took a photograph out of his wallet and passed it to Richard. 'That was how I met my wife. I was travelling round East Anglia. There she is, sir, that's Etta, and that's our baby, Ruby.'

Richard looked down. Etta Chance had a round, pretty, dimpled face. A curled fringe fell to her eyes and she was smiling sweetly, if a little nervously, for the camera. She had put on her best dress, Richard guessed, festooned with frills and ribbon bows, for the studio photograph. All he could see of the baby was a grumpy little face in a sea of lace.

'She's a corker, isn't she?' Chance said proudly.

'Very fine. And the baby's — ' after a moment's thought, Richard settled on, for safety — 'bonny. Is she your first?'

Chance nodded. 'Have you any children, sir?'

Richard opened his cigarette case and showed Chance the photograph inside it. 'That's Philip, my eldest, and there's Theo, and that's my little girl, Sara. And this is my wife, Isabel.'

'They're all very handsome, sir.'

'Aren't they?'

As the sergeant made to leave the dugout, Richard said, 'You did well tonight, Chance.'

'Thank you, sir.' He grinned again. 'For a moment, out there, I thought I'd had it. Poor old Nick Chance, I thought, lost in the wild blue yonder and never going home.'

★ ★ ★

In March, the company was moved down the line towards Serre, near the River Somme. One night, Richard took out a patrol to repair the company's barbed wire entanglements. Wiring parties were never a popular job — they were exposed, out beyond the parapet, using their muffled mallets to knock the steel pickets into place, in the path of any stray bullet or shell, their vulnerable position liable to be lit up by the trajectory of a trench mortar.

The night was quiet, the moon showing only every now and then between racing clouds, and the repairs were carried out without incident. As he gave the order to return to the trench, Richard caught sight of the body of a British soldier, lit up by the fitful moonlight. He decided to drag the corpse back behind the lines, so that the man could be given a decent burial. But when he tried to lift it up, the head, which was more decayed than he had thought, came off in his hands. He stood there for a moment, paralysed, staring at this awful *thing* that he held, and then, retching, let it fall.

He must ~~have~~ OF gathered his men together and led them back to the trench because the next thing he knew, Sergeant Chance was saying, 'Would you like to try some of mine, sir?' and handing him a flask.

Richard drank and choked. 'What the hell is this?'

'I won it in a card game,' said Chance.

It disturbed Richard that he remembered nothing between dropping the head and finding himself in the dugout. He looked down at his hands. As he rinsed them, using water from a jerry can, he heard Chance ask, 'Are you all right, sir?'

'Yes, of course.' He managed a half-smile. 'Wiring

parties always make me a bit jittery.'

Chance nodded. Then he said, 'Do you sometimes think we might be stuck out here for ever, sir?'

Richard glanced at him sharply. 'What do you mean?'

'Well, we never *get* anywhere, do we, sir? We capture a farmhouse or a pimple of a hill and once we've got it, we defend it mightily. But what for? It's still only a ruined farmhouse or a hill. And then we rush about, trying to blow up their trenches and they try and blow up ours, and what does it gain us? What, really?'

'I suppose, if we weren't here, the Germans would just march into Paris.'

'Yes, sir, I suppose so.'

There was a silence. They lit cigarettes. Chance said, 'When you see the trenches the Boche have — proper rooms and passageways, much fancier than ours — I wonder if maybe we'll start doing the same. We'll build ourselves bigger and better trenches, and then maybe one day there'll be whole cities beneath the earth. We'll live — ' he gave a snort of laughter — 'like moles.'

Richard suppressed a shudder. He glanced down at his hands again, twisting them together as if to wash something away. To change the subject, he said, 'Tell me how you met your wife, Chance. It was in East Anglia, wasn't it?'

'Yes, sir. I was travelling round the Fens. Have you ever been there, sir? Good farming country, so it was rich ground for the tools and machinery I was selling.' He shook his head. 'But what a wilderness! I like hills and valleys and nice little woods. That's proper countryside. Out there it's as flat as a pancake, flatter than this even, not a hill in sight. And the ploughed fields are as black as coal and the wind goes right through you and comes out the other side. Gloomy old place, I can tell you, sir. No wonder the lot of them are as mad as coots.' He drew on his cigarette. 'Anyway, I was in a seed merchant's in some dreary little hole of a town when I looked through the window and saw this lovely girl. I hadn't seen a pretty girl in days, so I wound up my business smartish and left the shop. I offered to carry her bags for her. She was all weighed down like a mule — Maude always made Etta do all the shopping.'

'Maude?'

'Etta's bitch of a sister, sir. Maude Quinn thinks herself too grand to go shopping. Etta wouldn't let me help at first, but I talked to her for a while and she must of ~~have~~ seen I was a decent sort of chap because she let me walk her home.' He explained, 'Etta's parents died when she was little. Her sister, Maude, had married by then, to a farmer by the name of Quinn, so Etta went to live with them. Nineveh, the farm's called. It's in the middle of nowhere. Etta wouldn't let me walk her all the way because she was afraid her sister might see us.' He frowned. 'Funny how different two sisters can be. There's Etta with the face of an angel while Maude's as sour as an old boot. Maude didn't like Etta to have any fun. Religious, you see,' Chance added vaguely.

'But you courted her, presumably.'

Chance smiled. 'Ways and means, sir, ways and means. It wasn't easy for us to meet each other, and Etta was always scared Maude would find out, but we managed. When Etta agreed to marry me, I took the bull by the horns and went to Nineveh.' His blue eyes narrowed. 'It was a funny old place . . . grim as hell from the outside, with lots of straggling buildings looking as if they've been put together anyhow. Inside, though, I could see they had some nice things, lovely old furniture and bits of china. I used to work for an antique dealer so I knew they were worth a bob or two.' He gave a sudden bark of laughter. 'And then there's Maude Quinn sitting there in all her finery, looking at me as if I was something stuck to the sole of her shoe.'

'Did she agree to let you marry her sister?'

'No. She told me to get lost in no uncertain terms.'
Chance frowned. 'Funny thing was . . . I'm not saying I
was frightened by the old bitch, but she had something
about her. I could see why my little Etta ran round after
her. Maude has a kind of . . . ' He paused, searching for
a word.

'Presence?'

'Yes, sir, that's it, presence. She was used to ruling the
roost, Maude Quinn was. Anyhow, she sent me away
with a flea in my ear — was damned insulting, to tell
the truth.' His face darkened. 'After I'd gone, Maude
slapped Etta's face. I hated her for that.'

It occurred to Richard that you wouldn't want to
earn Nicholas Chance's hatred. Chance, like Maude
Quinn, had presence.

He asked, 'So what did you do?'

'We ran away together. Etta was twenty-one by
then so we didn't need anyone's permission to marry.
Etta sneaked out of the farmhouse one night and we
went to London and did the deed. She wrote to
Maude once we were married. She thought Maude
might come round. Not a hope. Maude wouldn't part
with a penny to help Etta and me set up a home,
even though she's sitting on pots of money, by all
accounts. I hope the tight-fisted miserable old bitch
chokes herself.' Chance's tone was cool and matter of
fact. 'I hope she falls into one of her bloody dykes
and drowns.'

He looked at his watch. 'I'd better go and make sure
the sentries haven't fallen asleep on duty.' Just before he
left the dugout, he said, 'They're calling it a war of
attrition, aren't they, sir? I think the other sort of war
would have suited me better. Etta says she can imagine
me in a red coat, charging into the thick of battle. I like
action. I like things to *happen*.'

★   ★   ★

The strain showed in each of them in different ways. Richard's commanding officer, Major Woods, became increasingly quiet and distant, only rarely dispensing either encouragement or criticism, and mixing with his fellow officers as little as the cramped conditions of the trenches allowed. He left the day-to-day running of the trenches to his junior officers, emerging from his solitariness only to communicate with his superiors down the line or to pass on orders received from above.

Nicholas Chance found his own way of enduring the dangerous stasis of the trenches. Night after night, Chance volunteered for patrols. It seemed to Richard that Chance had become fearless almost to the point of foolhardiness. He had never thought of himself as the nervous type, but compared to Nicholas Chance, he was careful. What, he found himself wondering, did fearlessness do to a man? It made you take risks, obviously, and it blunted perception. Increasingly, Richard thought that Chance almost courted danger, as if he was trying to prove something to himself — or perhaps it was only out there, with Death hovering just by his shoulder, that he was able to feel truly alive.

And his own symptoms? Exhaustion, lack of concentration and a series of lesions on his hands that were slow to repair because he picked at them in his sleep. It was as if, since the episode with the decayed head, he had never felt clean. Sometimes he thought he could smell it, the stench of decay that had soaked into his skin and couldn't be rubbed off.

Do you sometimes think we might be stuck out here for ever, sir? The battle of Loos had demonstrated, with horrible clarity, that machine guns and trench mortars made infantry attack virtually suicidal. The thick entanglements of barbed wire, yards deep in some parts of the line, were formidable obstacles to assault. Even if the British were to launch a successful attack tomorrow, and gain, say, a mile of land, what then? There was all the rest of the front, the great long line of it, from the Channel coast to the heart of Europe, defended by an army as vast as their own. How many more men would the war swallow up?

Richard tried hard not to let his sense of futility show to the men. March shifted into April, then May. Rumours of a big push to break the German defences once and for all filtered down the lines. The new troops who arrived to replace the losses included a young second lieutenant by the name of Buxton. Lieutenant Buxton, with his fair hair and fresh-faced looks, seemed to Richard absurdly young, little more than a schoolboy. His enthusiasm and cheerfulness, coupled with a capacity for hard work, quickly endeared him to even the most cynical of the men.

The preparations for the coming offensive included frequent raids across no man's land. Major Woods asked Richard to take out a patrol one night to inspect the disposition of the enemy trenches. The patrol set out after dark. Richard checked the men's weapons and his own revolver. Inching across no man's land on his stomach, he could smell the sharp aroma of the earth and he felt, once or twice, the crisp coolness of leaves beneath his palm where a tiny island of grass had survived in the sea of churned-up earth. The guns were quiet that night and a mist drifted low over the ground. Though the mist curtained them, protecting them, it blurred the landmarks, making it harder to follow their intended course, and it seemed to magnify the smallest sounds. The rustle of tiny paws as a rat ran for cover became shockingly loud. There was the click of wire-cutters as the raiding party made a path through the first of the barbed wire entanglements and then they were back on their stomachs again, their faces in the soil, scurrying over the earth — *like moles*, Richard thought, remembering Nicholas Chance's words.

Then he heard a footfall. Too late, he realised that

theirs was not the only patrol out that night. A sudden movement in the darkness and someone fired a shot, which was closely followed by a shriek. A flash of light enabled Richard to see that they had gone off course in the mist and that they were thirty yards or so from their objective. Then an explosion made him bury his face in the ground, clawing his fingernails into the mud. He heard the peremptory pat-pat-pat of Maxim guns and yelled out the order to retreat.

He must ~~have~~ ran a few paces when he seemed to hit an invisible wall and his left arm flailed upwards of its own volition. Then the explosion of the trench mortar picked him up and threw him down again hard to the ground. He had forgotten how to breathe: struggling for air, he found only a thick, warm dust, and it took a dreadful, choking effort to fill his lungs.

Overhead, another trench mortar illuminated the night sky. Fragments of shell soared high above him: he thought them beautiful, like ragged black birds against the unnatural light. Then he closed his eyes and drifted off into unconsciousness.

When he came round, it was still dark, but the mist had thinned a little. A half-moon illuminated the area in which he was lying. He saw that he had had the good fortune to have been thrown on to the sloping side of a shell crater, which offered him some protection. He looked down at himself. Though he didn't really *hurt*, he knew there was something badly wrong with him. He tried to inspect himself methodically, as he had once, in another life, inspected faulty products in the factory. His left arm was useless, dangling at his side like a piece of dead meat. When he lifted up his right hand he saw that there was a hole in his palm. He tried to stand up. *Then* it hurt, and his howl of agony prompted a fresh volley of gunfire from the enemy trenches.

He decided to make his way up the edge of the crater so that he could see whether anyone could help him return to the British lines. It took an age, hauling himself up the soft, crumbling slope by means of his right elbow and left leg. When he reached the rim he saw the men scattered, their attitudes abandoned, in the mud. He recognised Cummings and Forbes and Hall, good soldiers all of them, as well as Lieutenant Buxton. Buxton's fair curls were darkened with mud and blood. Buxton had served on the front for less than a week; he was not yet twenty years old. Tears gathered in Richard's eyes.

All alone, out in the wild blue yonder, he thought. When the terror subsided he was left with only a fierce determination to survive. Out here, he had lost faith in everything but his family: *they* were what he fought to preserve. He fought so that his sons could live in freedom and so that his wife and daughter should never have to see the things that he had seen.

So he couldn't just *die*. Not now. Yet he was losing blood; he could feel himself weakening. He would sleep a little, he decided, and after he woke he would feel up to the haul back to the British trenches.

Richard closed his eyes and dreamed of a house perched on a cliff. Waves crashed against the rocks on which the house was built, and Isabel, wearing her red jacket, stood at the front of the house, looking out to sea. As Richard walked across the shore he felt the crunch of pebbles beneath his feet and the pop of shiny brown beads of seaweed. In some halfway state between waking and sleeping, he wondered how many buttons he'd have to make to buy the house by the sea. He thought of all the millions of soldiers at the front and all the millions of buttons on their tunics. Buttons to pay for houses, dead men's buttons.

A voice roused him. 'Captain Finborough, do you think you can walk?'

Richard opened his eyes. It was still night-time and Sergeant Chance was crouching beside him. He felt a deep, drowning relief: Chance had slithered like a black snake over no man's land and had come to take him home.

'I don't think so,' he said. 'I'm sorry.'

'Then I'll carry you.'

So Nicholas Chance picked him up and ran across no man's land, with Richard slung like a sack over his broad shoulders. They had almost reached the British defences when the guns began to fire. And the last thing Richard heard as they plunged towards the parapet was the roar that burst from Chance's throat: a roar, he thought, of both fury and triumph.

* * *

Richard was taken first to a casualty clearing station behind the lines and then entrained to the British military hospital at Étaples. He thought the hospital was a more hellish place than the trenches. At night, injured men groaned and called out for their mothers. The man in the bed next to Richard wept, curled up in a tight little ball. 'Shell shock,' the nurse said to Richard, before she drew the curtains round the bed.

He had been shot through the hand and pieces of shell were embedded in his left shoulder and right leg. The day after he arrived at Étaples, they operated to remove the shell fragments. Coming round from the anaesthetic on the ward, he had to bite his lip to stop himself crying out with pain. Then the nurse gave him a shot of morphine and he drifted off to sleep again.

Ah, then, the nurses. Pretty girls, some of them, and gentle too, but they troubled him somehow. Their brisk efficiency had a hard edge, as though there was nothing they hadn't seen. He found himself thinking that he wouldn't ever let his little Sara live the sort of life those girls led. The routine of the ward, as rigid and as unrelenting, it seemed to Richard, as that of the army itself, went on. Richard loathed it. He loathed the sounds and the smells; most of all, he loathed his dependency.

Then, one morning, three days after he had arrived at Étaples, a freckled, red-haired nurse came to his bedside. 'You have a visitor, Captain Finborough,' she said.

Richard looked up and saw Isabel. In her arms, smelling her skin and her hair, he felt as though something had clicked back into place at last.

'Take me home,' he whispered. 'For God's sake, Isabel, take me home.'

★ ★ ★

They wouldn't let him go home, but after a fortnight he was sent from Étaples to a convalescent home in Kent, where he remained for the next two months. From the grounds of the convalescent home, he heard the massive artillery bombardment that was the precursor to the battle of the Somme. By the time he was sufficiently recovered to return home to Hampstead, the battle had swallowed up tens of thousands of lives, Major Woods and many of Richard's old regiment among them. But Nicholas Chance survived and for that Richard gave thanks.

He taught himself to walk without a limp and to write again. His hand never recovered completely, however, and whenever he was tired his writing sprawled in an angry, angular fashion over the page. After six months, when it became obvious that he was no longer able reliably to fire a rifle, he was invalided out of the army.

Nicholas Chance's heroism gave him his life, and one of his favourite jokes. For years after the war ended Richard Finborough liked to tell people that he owed his life to Chance.

★ ★ ★

The war left him with scars. Those on his body were visible: the purplish welts on his left side faded eventually to white, and he would always have the handwriting of a ham-fisted ten-year-old. He knew himself fortunate to have suffered no worse. By the time of the declaration of peace in November 1918, three empires were in ruins and the fires of revolution smouldered. A strange sort of victory, Richard thought. On the streets of London, ex-soldiers begged, some limbless, some muttering and wild-eyed, many with neither their health nor work. Richard always put a coin in their outstretched hands.

His other scars were unseen. Images from the war darkened his nights and cast shadows over the day. On the worst nights, he woke in the early hours, feeling himself utterly alone, all his ambitions worthless, haunted by the fear that *that* was reality, that Golgotha of rats and rotting corpses and violent death. That all this — his work, his home, his family — might only be an interlude. That nothing was safe, and one day he might yet lose everything he held dear.

He held off his demons by keeping himself busy, and by distracting himself with alcohol, and, every now and then, women. He renewed his acquaintance with Sally Peach, who had been his mistress before he had married Isabel: her simple, undemanding affection soothed him. You might as well take what pleasure you could, he thought. He knew now how easily life could be snatched away. You might be having a conversation or playing a game of cards, and a bullet or a fragment of shell could wipe you away as though you had never been. A blackness, a blankness, remained inside him, covered over most of the time, but every now and then rising to the surface. He learned to mask it with a lucrative business deal, a new conquest. The first time he was unfaithful to Isabel he was aware of a scouring guilt; the next time, he felt it less.

The years passed and he shored up his finances and consolidated his empire. *This* was how he would protect his family, by making the Finboroughs so wealthy and powerful nothing could touch them. Unlike many others, he was able to ride out the economic downturns of the decade because he had had the foresight to invest in areas of growth. A competitor fell into difficulties: Richard waited until the owner had no alternative but to sell and then purchased a large site on the outskirts of London for a knock-down price. Soon, the plastics factory had expanded to many times its pre-war size. By the mid-twenties, Finboroughs manufactured fountain pens, knife handles and a range of fancy goods as well as buttons and buckles. In 1927 Richard set up a new line making electrical goods.

The twenties were a good decade for the Finboroughs, a time of prosperity and security. It often seemed to Richard that everything he touched turned to gold. He flexed his power to mould the present to his will and the future to his own desires.

He kept the promise he had made the day Isabel had agreed to marry him. The house he bought in Cornwall was hers, his gift to her, the deeds made out in her name, to use as she wished, his way of telling her that, however busy he was, and whatever he did, he loved her. Porthglas Cottage perched on a promontory of the North Cornish coast, not far from St Ives. From the highest window, they could see out to where the waves dashed themselves against the rocks. Isabel took the children to the house each summer and Richard joined them whenever his work permitted. Philip, Theo and Sara turned brown and healthy, playing on the sand and bathing in the sea.

Since the end of the war, Richard had kept in touch with Nicholas Chance. They met each year at the regimental dinner that Richard gave at the Savoy, an enjoyable, unruly evening to which he invited a dozen old comrades in arms. Richard suspected that the years since the war had ended had not treated Chance kindly. As the twenties wore on, Chance drank more and, when he smiled, there was a bitter twist to the corners of his mouth. It was hard to tell how difficult things were, harder still to gauge what help to offer. Chance brushed away Richard's tactful offers of work, speaking instead of a seaside holiday, a new job he had been promised. Yet the army greatcoat Chance put on each year over his dinner suit, as he said his farewells at the end of the evening, had become increasingly threadbare, and it seemed to Richard there were too many new jobs, too many great opportunities that never came to much. He found himself wondering whether Chance's nature was one that easily adapted to the different demands of peacetime.

And then, in the Christmas of 1927, Nicholas Chance failed to turn up to the regimental dinner. His absence troubled Richard — Chance had never missed the occasion before. In the New Year, Richard wrote to him, expressing the hope that he and his family were well.

A few days later he received a letter. It was not from Nicholas, but from his daughter, Ruby. In clear copperplate handwriting, she wrote,

Dear Mr Finborough,

I hope you will forgive me for troubling you, but I am trying to find my father. He has not been home for four months and my mother is unwell and I need to speak to him. If you can think where he might be, or if you have seen him since you wrote to us, please could you ask him to come home?

Yours faithfully, Ruby Henrietta Chance.

Reading Ruby Chance's letter at the breakfast table, Richard felt both concern and disquiet. The Chances now lived in Reading. As he drove to the office, Richard recalled that there was a supplier in Reading he could usefully visit. He decided to kill two birds with one stone, calling on his supplier then visiting Mrs Chance and her daughter and doing whatever he could for them.

After he had seen his supplier, Richard set out to find the Chances' house among the rows of sedate red-brick houses on the outskirts of the town. Number 50 Easton Road was a small, detached villa with a high, pointed gable roof. The house was separated from its neighbours by narrow paths to either side of the building. A tangle of leafless shrubs filled the flowerbeds, and lace curtains were drawn across the bay windows.

The bell pull didn't seem to work so Richard rapped loudly on the front door. After a few minutes, it opened. He could see in the narrow aperture, some way below the level of his own gaze, a sharp nose and a wary blue eye.

'I take it you're Ruby,' he said, with a smile. 'I'm Richard Finborough, your father's friend.'

The door opened a few more cautious inches. 'Is my father with you?'

'I'm afraid not. But why don't I come inside and have a word with your mother? Is she at home, Ruby?'

There was something apprehensive about the quick flick of her glance down the corridor. But she said, 'Yes, Mr Finborough, please come in,' and he stepped inside.

The first thing Richard noticed was that the house was freezing. It was a cold January day and the interior seemed little warmer than the frosty streets outside. He would not have been surprised to see ice lining the coloured glass lozenge in the front door.

Ruby showed him into a drawing room. 'Mother, a friend of Dad's has come to see us,' she said. 'Mr Finborough, this is my mother.'

Seeing Etta Chance, Richard had to swallow down an

87

expression of shock. He still remembered the photograph Nick had shown him, all those years ago in the dugout, of his wife and daughter. You could just about tell, looking at Mrs Chance, that she had once been pretty, but there was little trace left of her prettiness now, little left of the girl who had caught Nicholas Chance's eye as he glanced out of a shop window. Etta Chance was faded and gaunt, the healthy pink washed from her pale, hollow cheeks. Worse, there was in her light blue eyes a dullness, a despair, that disturbed Richard.

But she seemed to make an effort to rouse herself, because she gave him her hand, saying, 'Mr Finborough, how kind of you to call. Nicholas speaks of you often. Won't you sit down?'

Something made him glance at the daughter and he saw that Ruby had fixed him with a beseeching glare. A sudden understanding and he said, 'I was in the neighbourhood, Mrs Chance. I thought I'd drop by. I hope it's not inconvenient.'

A silence, during which he took in the bareness of the room. There were no rugs, no ornaments, no piano, only a few books and a couple of photos in cheap frames, one of which, he thought, was the snapshot Chance had shown him in the trenches, with Etta in her frills, and the baby scowling. A few coals burned in the grate and there was a glass of water on the small table beside the woman.

Etta said, 'Nicholas is out, I'm afraid, Mr Finborough. He's — he's away on business.'

Then she began to cry. Tears oozed from her eyes and she did not attempt to wipe them away. Richard gazed at her, horrified, and then, feeling it somehow indecent to witness such misery, looked away.

'My dear Mrs Chance — I must apologise — I hope I haven't upset you.'

Ruby went to her mother's side and pressed a

handkerchief into the fluttering fingers. 'Shall I make us some tea, Mother?'

A nod; Ruby left the room. Richard thought quickly, then rose from his seat, murmuring, 'If you'll excuse me for a moment, Mrs Chance.'

The sound of clinking crockery and a running tap drew him to the kitchen. Ruby was placing cups and saucers on a tray. She was a thin, plain little thing, Richard thought, not a patch on his pretty Sara. Ruby Chance had inherited her father's strong features — unattractive in a girl, Richard thought — and her colouring was an undistinguished halfway between Etta's fairness and Nicholas's dark good looks. She was wearing a navy-blue gymslip over a grubby white blouse, and her legs, encased in black woollen stockings, looked as skinny and shapeless as pipe cleaners. A mousy brown plait hung down her back, tied with a bedraggled navy ribbon. Her eyes were her only remarkable feature. They were large and blue and well-shaped, and had an unusually piercing quality.

Ruby looked up as Richard came into the room. He came straight to the point. 'How long has your mother been like this?'

'Years,' she said.

Once more, he was shocked. 'Is she seeing a doctor?'

'No, Mr Finborough.'

Richard's eye was caught by the open larder door. He saw that the shelves were almost empty except for the odd tin and packet. He didn't suppose the Chances could afford a doctor. They didn't look as though they could afford to eat.

'Your father's been away for four months,' he said. 'Four months with no money coming in. How have you managed?'

'I pawned some things.'

Which accounted for the bareness of the house. 'Very sensible,' he said. 'Have you a maid?'

'Mrs Slattery used to come and mop the floors but she hasn't been for a long time.'

The room had a dingy, grimy appearance. 'So, the cooking, the housework — ' he couldn't imagine that poor, fluttering creature with a broom in her hand — 'you've been doing it all yourself, I dare say, Ruby?'

'Yes, Mr Finborough.'

He looked at her again, this time with admiration. Ruby Chance must be about six months younger than Sara — twelve years old, say — and yet, since her father had left home four months ago, she had managed this house by herself.

'You've done a good job, Ruby,' he said. 'But what about school? Are you attending school?'

She looked down. 'Not recently.'

'I see. You didn't tell your mother you were writing to me, did you?'

'No, Mr Finborough.' She put two teaspoons on the tray. Her eyes met his; that penetrating gaze was unsettling in a child. 'I couldn't think what else to do. I don't think there's anything more I can pawn. And the grocer won't deliver again until the bill is paid. And we can't pay the rent. They sent a letter . . . '

Opening a drawer, she unearthed a typed letter from beneath a pile of tea towels and handed it to him. It was a notice of impending eviction from the Chances' landlord.

'Surely there must be someone who can help you till Nick turns up,' Richard suggested. 'Surely you must have relatives.'

'There's only my mother's sister, my Aunt Maude.'

Richard had a vague memory of Chance telling him about a gloomy farmhouse in the Fens. 'Perhaps you and your mother could go and stay with her.'

'No.'

'No?' No ifs or buts, just *no*. He looked at the girl questioningly.

'My mother's afraid of Aunt Maude,' said Ruby. 'And I don't think Aunt Maude would help. Look.'

A second envelope was taken out from its hiding place beneath the tea towels and passed to him. This letter, dated almost six months ago, was addressed to Etta Chance. Richard scanned it. The final sentence stuck in his mind. 'As your financial difficulties are entirely of your own making, I can't imagine why you should think I might be prevailed upon to help.' Not exactly sisterly, thought Richard, as he handed the letter back to Ruby, knowing he could consign neither Etta, with her shot nerves, nor this odd little girl, to such a person's care.

He continued to try to get to the bottom of things. 'Your mother told me that your father had gone away on business. Who does he work for?'

'Lamptons, in Finlay Street. They sell brushes and polish.'

'Your father's a salesman?'

'Yes, Mr Finborough.'

Bloody dismal job, thought Richard, knocking on the doors of housewives who, most of the time, wouldn't want to know. Poor old Nicholas.

Aloud, he said, 'Have you asked Lamptons if he's been into work recently?'

She nodded, and he thought, of course you have. You may not be pretty, Ruby Chance, but you're as smart as paint.

'And I went to the police,' she added, 'but they didn't know anything either. I thought of putting an advertisement in the newspaper but I hadn't enough money.'

'Not a bad idea, though. Describe to me what happened. Did your father tell you that he was going away?' Richard had a sudden thought. 'Had he argued with someone, perhaps? Or had there been any other . . .' it was hard to put it tactfully, 'um, difficulties?'

'He told us he was going away for a few days. My

mother was upset. She didn't like Dad going away.' The kettle had boiled so Ruby folded a cloth round the handle and poured the hot water into the teapot. 'Dad had to go away a lot because of his job, so I didn't worry at first, though Mum did.'

'How long was he usually away for?'

'A week. Sometimes two.'

'Where did he go? Different places — or always the same place?'

'I don't know, Mr Finborough.'

'He left no address where you and your mother could reach him?'

'No.'

'And he's never been away so long before?'

A shake of her head. Then, pinioning him with her blue glare, she said suddenly, 'Dad didn't take his medal with him.'

'His DCM?' Patting her shoulder, he said comfortingly, 'I'm sure he'll turn up. You must try not to worry.'

Ruby made to pick up the tray; Richard said, 'I'll do that. Now, can you find me the address of your mother's doctor?'

'Yes, Mr Finborough.'

He liked the way she understood quickly — no dithering with Ruby Chance. She left the kitchen, returning a few moments later with a piece of paper on which was written the address of a Dr Simpson.

'Good girl. I'll take this through to your mother and then you go and sit with her while I drive to the doctor's. I won't be long.'

Leaving the house, Richard was aware of a sense of relief, as though Etta Chance's grief at her desertion had sunk into the bricks and mortar, casting a shadow over the house. After asking a passer-by for directions, he set off. Driving through the winding streets, he wondered whether Nicholas had simply done a bunk. It seemed the most likely explanation. Nick had had a dead-end job and a sick wife and money troubles. It crossed Richard's mind as he headed into a neighbourhood of more imposing villas that he could understand why Nick might have wanted to get away from that distraught, tearful creature.

Dr Simpson was a blustering fool, in Richard's opinion, but with some browbeating and the promise of a sum of cash, he agreed to find a nursing home for Etta Chance and oversee her transfer there. By the time Richard returned to the Chances' house, the doctor in tow, the sky was darkening. He would have to decide what to do about the girl, he realised. There was no question of leaving her in that cold, comfortless house, and she seemed to have no relations other than the parsimonious aunt, so she had better come home with him. Nicholas Chance had saved his life. If Nicholas was in some sort of trouble — and Richard suspected that he was — then the least he could do would be to make sure his wife and daughter were properly cared for until he returned.

Isabel wouldn't mind Nicholas Chance's daughter staying with them for a while, he knew she wouldn't. They had plenty of room, after all, and Isabel loved children and would have a place in her heart for another one. A quiet little thing like Ruby would hardly be noticed. She would be a playmate for Sara.

It was well into the evening by the time Ruby had packed cases for herself and her mother and a tearful, shivering Etta had been dispatched to the nursing home in Dr Simpson's care. Only on the drive back to London did it occur to Richard that he should have telephoned Isabel to warn her both of his late arrival and the addition of Ruby to the household. He had a vague recollection of Isabel telling him that people were coming for dinner . . .

Too late now: Richard pressed down the accelerator and the car gathered speed.

Part Two

The Foster Daughter

1928–1936

4

The first thing Ruby noticed was the noise. It struck her as soon as the maid opened the door, a wall of sound that almost made her take a step back. She picked out a piano playing something martial with loud, crashing chords, and a gramophone recording of a popular song, and running footsteps and voices calling out to each other.

And laughter. At one point during the drive from Reading to London, Mr Finborough had thought of some private joke and had laughed out loud. His hearty laughter had made Ruby think of a lion she had once seen at the circus: strong and powerful, it had raised its tawny head and let out a roar of rumbustious delight.

After the quiet of Easton Road, months of quiet, which had had to be maintained for the sake of her mother's nerves, the noise from the Finboroughs' house shocked her, and she did not move until Mr Finborough gave her a little pat on the shoulder, propelling her indoors. Inside, the maid took their coats and Ruby's small suitcase.

Mr Finborough called out, 'Isabel! I've brought something for you! Isabel!' After a few moments, when there was no response, he said, 'Wait here, Ruby,' and strode off down a corridor, opening doors. In one of the doorways he paused, saying, 'Darling, I'm back,' and then the door closed behind him.

Left alone, Ruby looked round her. She was standing in a hallway. The Finboroughs' hall was, she estimated, about twice as big as the sitting room in Easton Road. Light from the lamp in the porch poured through the full-length coloured glass windows to either side of the front door, washing the polished wooden floor with rose and gold. Objects in the room — pottery and paintings — caught the sunlight, so that her initial impression of the interior of the Finboroughs' house was of a gorgeous blur of vivid, burnished colours. Ruby blinked and moved closer to the radiator. She didn't seem to have felt properly warm for a long time; cautiously, she undid the buttons of her coat.

A tall glass vase containing sprigs of holly and other evergreens stood on the circular table in the centre of the hall. On the sideboard were photographs in silver frames as well as a collection of shells, a tennis ball, a stack of books and letters and pencils. Above the sideboard was a large painting of a woman dressed in a long blue skirt and a red jacket. Ruby screwed up her eyes to look at her properly. Her black hair was blown about by the wind. She was standing on a rock and behind her the sea crashed and churned. Ruby remembered a poem they had learned by heart at school: 'Break, break, break, On thy cold grey stones, O Sea!'

From the corridor, behind the closed door, Ruby could hear Mr Finborough's voice, now a little raised, but could not make out his words. From behind a different door, the martial music had given way to something slower, more haunting. Through yet another door, which was ajar, she could see a man lying on a sofa. There was a hat over his face; she presumed he was asleep. There were other people in the room with the sleeping man, talking to each other in a foreign language — one, catching Ruby's eye, called out to her: there was a ripple of laughter and she quickly looked away.

The gramophone music seemed to be coming from above. Ruby heard the faint thump of rhythmic steps. Once, looking up, she glimpsed a pair of feet running along the landing at the top of the stairs. She caught Mr Finborough's voice again, loud and cross now, interspersed with a woman's tones. She wondered what they were quarrelling about. She expected they were quarrelling about her.

A fair-haired boy wearing a navy-blue jersey wandered out of the room with the foreign people, eating an apple. Catching sight of Ruby, he asked, 'Have you seen Theo?'

Theo was presumably Theo Finborough. In the car, Mr Finborough had told Ruby that he had three children, Philip, Sara and Theo.

When she shook her head the boy disappeared into the room with the piano. Mr Finborough's voice rose clearly above the hubbub of the house: 'I said I was sorry, woman!'

A maid rushed through the hall carrying a pile of linen; a black and white cat strolled along the corridor and half-heartedly scratched its claws against the wainscoting, and a spaniel with drooping tan and white ears padded slowly across the hall. Somewhere in the distance a canary was singing. The Russians — Ruby imagined them to be Russians, White Russians perhaps, exiled companions of the murdered Tsar — had gone from the nearby room, leaving only the man sleeping on the sofa.

Ruby inspected the objects on the sideboard, tilting her head to read the titles on the spines of the books. *King Solomon's Mines* was on the top of the pile; she opened it. She had read it before — her eyes ran down a page. Finding a familiar book was like discovering an old friend. A moment's indecision, then she sat down on a chair by the window and began to read.

A short while afterwards the door to the room with the piano opened and the boy in the navy jersey came out, closely followed by a dark-haired boy. The first boy was saying, 'I suppose Lydgate will be head of house. Good Lord, can you imagine it?' to which the dark-haired boy — Theo, presumably — replied,

99

'Throwing his weight around as usual, no doubt.' Then the first boy said, 'My books, where are my books?' and Theo said, 'On the sideboard, I think.' Ruby said, '*Oh,*' and stood up, holding out *King Solomon's Mines*. They looked at her with airy disdain and the boy in the navy sweater said, 'Thanks' and took the book, and then they too went away. She caught their conversation, though, before they rounded the corner of the passageway.

'Who was that?'

'Haven't a clue. One of my mother's friends' infants, probably. This house is always bursting at the seams.'

Ruby's face was hot. Why hadn't she apologised for borrowing that boy's book? Why hadn't she smiled or introduced herself or said *something*? And — *infant* — the insult rankled.

Her initial relief at Mr Finborough's arrival — and her much greater relief that he had known what to do about her mother (recently, she had started to wonder whether they would both just starve to death) — ebbed, replaced by other, more troubling, thoughts. She wondered, yet again, when her father would come home. And what would he do when he found the house empty? This difficulty had occurred to her in the car, driving to London with Mr Finborough. What if they never found each other again? Mr Finborough had explained to her that he had left a letter on the table for her father, and another letter at a neighbour's house. He had also left a forwarding address at the post office and at the police station.

But what now, with both her parents gone, would happen to her? She had begun to feel lonely and rather superfluous, an unpleasantly familiar new-girl feeling, and she began to be afraid that here, in this beautiful and busy house, she would not come up to scratch. How long would the Finboroughs let her stay here? Where would she go if, in a few days or a few weeks, they did not want her any more? What if Mrs

Finborough did not want her to stay here at all? Indeed, it was hard to see why she *should* want her.

What if Mrs Finborough decided to send her to Nineveh, to stay with Aunt Maude and Hannah? The prospect filled her with horror. Ruby and her mother had visited Nineveh twice yearly for as long as Ruby could remember. Aunt Maude's magisterial summonses had always sent Etta Chance into a flutter of anxiety. The journey to Nineveh had been a further source of dread; they had invariably set off far too early and had to wait ages on the platform for the London train. Her mother's anxiety had intensified as they had travelled. Ruby's father had never gone with them. Why, Ruby had often wondered, had her mother continued to visit Aunt Maude when she was so obviously afraid of going there, and when Aunt Maude was always so relentlessly nasty to her? Ruby supposed her mother felt obliged because Aunt Maude was her only sister.

She tried to reassure herself. Her father would come home and then they could return to Easton Road. Once more, she looked down the corridor to the closed door. She wondered whether Mr Finborough, leaving her here, might have expected her to introduce herself to the rest of the household. Or perhaps, which seemed more probable, he had simply forgotten about her.

The front door opened again and a young man came into the hall. Tall, broad-shouldered and startlingly handsome, his coppery head marked him unmistakably a Finborough. He was wearing a leather coat and his hair was tousled, and his shoes and the bottoms of his trouser legs were muddy. He brought with him a draught of fresh air and an aura of energy and adventure.

As he took off his coat, he caught sight of Ruby. 'I say, are you all right?'

'Yes, thank you. Though I'm not sure where anyone is. Or where I'm supposed to be.'

'I thought you looked a bit lost.' He smiled and offered her his hand. 'I'm Philip Finborough, by the way.'

'Ruby Chance.'

'Chance? You're not related to the man who saved my father's life, are you?'

'I'm his daughter.'

The smile broadened. 'Then how lovely to meet you, Ruby. Are you hungry?'

'A bit.'

'I'm ravenous. I suppose I've missed dinner. I'll go and see if I can find us something.'

Philip Finborough's leaving was like the sun going in. Alone again, Ruby wondered whether he too would forget her. But Philip returned a few minutes later carrying a plate, and Ruby followed him into the sitting room.

'Are you coming to stay with us?' he asked.

'I think so.'

'That's splendid. Have you met Sara and Theo?'

Ruby shook her head. She didn't think you could count being discovered reading a book that belonged to someone else as meeting someone.

'They're probably at the pond,' Philip said. 'Here.' He offered her the plate. 'Have some cake.'

She chose a slice of sponge with pink icing. Philip asked, 'Did my father bring you here? Is he home? I need to talk to him about the two-stroke.'

She had no idea what a two-stroke was, but she said, 'He drove me here.' A moment's reflection, and then, because he seemed so nice, and because, for the first time in a very long time she sensed that she had met someone she could confide in, she said, 'I'm afraid he's cross about something.'

'Are my parents having a row?' He gave her an amused look. 'You mustn't worry about that. They're always arguing; it doesn't mean anything.' He held out the plate to her. 'Go on, kiddo, have the last piece.'

She shook her head. 'No, you must have it.'

'My mother would say you need building up.'

'But you're bigger than me, so you must need to eat more.'

Philip's roar of laughter sounded just like Mr Finborough's. He said, 'Tell you what, let's split it,' and divided the slice of cake in two, though Ruby noticed that he gave her the half with the most icing.

★   ★   ★

Isabel studied Richard's red, angry face. Don't you know, she thought, don't you know how your thoughtlessness hurts me? No, of course you don't. You never have and you never will.

She knew they were reaching a juncture when their quarrel could go one of two ways. It could gather in strength, fed by her fear and his temper, taking on a life of its own, until one of them stormed off, he to drink and rage, she to weep or to escape to Cornwall. Or, one of them would take a step back, they would laugh and beg each other's forgiveness and make their peace in bed that night. She couldn't yet tell which would happen.

She said, 'I *told* you the Horsleys were coming. And they are always such hard work. A telephone call, Richard, that's all I ask for. Then I would know.' She knew she shouldn't ask, knew deep down that it was always a mistake to betray her misgivings, but could never stop herself. 'Where were you?'

Richard was pouring himself another drink. 'Do I have to account to you for every second of my time? What on earth is it that you imagine I'm up to?' His voice was dangerous.

I imagine that you've forgotten me, she thought. I imagine that your eye has been caught by a prettier face, a younger face. I imagine that you have realised at last the mistake you made all those years ago in Lynton and that you have come to regret having married me. I imagine that I've lost you.

But she said, 'I thought perhaps the car had broken down — or there had been an accident.'

He crossed the room to her. In his arms, she felt safe again and something relaxed inside her. The anxieties of the evening — Richard's lateness, Philip's love of that wretched motor cycle — slotted into a more sensible place in her mind.

She heard him murmur, 'Your hair smells of the sea. Why does your hair always smell of the sea?'

She whispered, 'I *missed* you, Richard.'

'And I missed you.' The pad of his thumb traced the curve of her neck. 'I always do.'

She glanced fretfully at the clock. 'I thought Philip would be back by now.'

'He'll be fine,' said Richard. 'He's seventeen. He's perfectly capable of looking after himself.'

His blithe confidence reignited her annoyance. No, he isn't, she wanted to say. Was I capable of looking after myself at seventeen? *No.* I didn't know anything at all. That's why I imagine broken bodies in ditches and a policeman knocking on the door.

Richard put the stopper back on the decanter. 'I've been to Reading, to the Chances' house,' he said. 'I thought I'd better find out what was going on so I drove down this morning. Good thing I did — they were in a sorry state. The little girl was trying to hold things together, but the mother was pitiful. She couldn't stop crying, and I could hardly get a word out of her. The house was freezing and they hadn't any food. Nicholas's daughter made tea. I'm sure the tea leaves had been used before.'

'And Nicholas? Where has he gone?'

'I don't know. I'm afraid he mightn't ~~have~~ or been able

104

to take any more. I'm afraid he might have~~have~~ of just . . . pushed off.'

'He wouldn't desert his wife and child, surely?'

Richard looked troubled. 'Such a miserable house, Isabel, I couldn't wait to get away from it. Nicholas had money troubles. I had a glance at the papers in his desk while the girl was helping her mother pack. I didn't like to, but I thought I might find some clue. But there was nothing, only bills, a lot of unpaid bills.'

'Poor Sergeant Chance.' Isabel had encountered Nicholas Chance only once, many years ago in Oxford Street one Christmas. She remembered a tall, powerfully built man with a thatch of dark hair and dancing eyes and a smile that split his face in two.

She asked, 'What did you do?'

'I fetched the doctor. He was an idle, fussy fellow, but at least he's found a nursing home for Mrs Chance. Hopefully, that'll put her right.'

'What do they think is wrong with her?'

'Complete nervous collapse, the doctor said. And she has a weak heart, apparently.' Then he seemed to remember something and his face lightened. 'Anyway,' he said, with a smile 'I've brought you a present.'

Isabel's suspicions returned. Richard was a generous man, but his gifts to her were sometimes peace offerings, sticking plasters to cover a transgression he thought she hadn't noticed.

'A present?'

'A jewel.'

She expected him to take from his pocket a box or package. But there was on his face an expression that was familiar to her, of mischievous expectation, and she waited for one of the jokes, the puns that he was so fond of concocting.

'I've brought you a ruby,' he said, plainly pleased with himself. 'Only you can't wear this ruby on your finger. Nick's daughter's called Ruby. I told her she could stay with us till Nick turns up.'

'Of course she may.'

'Think of her as a foster daughter.' He kissed her. 'A temporary foster daughter.'

'I'll ask the maid to get a room ready for her. How long will she be staying, Richard?'

'I can't tell. We'll have to see how the mother does.'

'Where is the child?'

'I told her to wait in the hall.'

'Richard, the poor little thing . . . '

Isabel left the room. Catching sight of the leather coat Philip wore when he was riding his motor cycle slung over a chair in the hall, her remaining anxiety dissolved, and from the sitting-room doorway she saw them, a tired-looking girl in a grey coat and Philip, her eldest child.

★ ★ ★

Ruby had almost finished the cake when a voice said, not at all crossly, 'Philip, darling, you know you're not supposed to eat in here. And you must be Ruby. I'm Mrs Finborough. How lovely that you've come to stay with us, my dear. But I'm sorry it should be under such difficult circumstances for you.'

Ruby jumped to her feet. Mrs Finborough was wearing a cream-coloured frock of some soft, drapey stuff instead of the red jacket and blue skirt, but she was unmistakably the woman in the portrait. When Mrs Finborough stooped to kiss her cheek, Ruby caught a breath of her scent.

'Philip's been looking after you, I see.' Mrs Finborough stroked her son's face affectionately. 'A good day, darling?'

'Terrific, Mama. We got as far as Swanscombe and then Blackie had a puncture and ended up in a ditch. We got soaked, dragging the bike out.'

106

'You must get changed, you don't want to catch cold. And take the plate back to the kitchen. And when you've done that, please wake up poor Basil. Or he'll be there all night. Tell him Mrs Finch will find him some supper.' Mrs Finborough turned to Ruby. 'Would you like to see your room, dear?'

Ruby followed Mrs Finborough upstairs. At the end of a corridor, Mrs Finborough opened a door.

'Sara has the next room. I thought you'd like that.'

The room was painted sapphire blue and there was a pattern of white daisies on the blue curtains and bedspread. There was a white chest of drawers and a dressing table, pictures of the seaside on the walls, a blue-and-white-striped rug on the floor and a bookcase full of books.

Ruby's heart seemed to swell, about to burst, so that when Mrs Finborough asked, 'Do you like it?' she was unable to speak and nodded vigorously instead.

Mrs Finborough showed Ruby where to hang her clothes and where to find the bathroom. Then she said, 'You must try not to worry about your mother, Ruby. As soon as the doctors say she's well enough I'll take you to visit her. And you can write to her as often as you like, of course. Now, why don't you have a wash and brush your hair, and then we'll go and find Sara.'

Ruby washed her face and made an attempt to tidy her hair, and then Mrs Finborough took her downstairs again and out into the garden. It was dark now, and very cold, and the terraces, paths, flowerbeds and gnarled old trees loomed out of the blackness.

A pinpoint of light and shrieks of laughter drew them to the far end of the garden. Ruby's apprehension returned at the prospect of meeting Sara Finborough. The several schools she had attended, when her father could afford to pay the fees, led her to expect that Sara would be a particular sort of girl — pretty, undoubtedly, with lovely clothes and an assumption that life involved pony riding and going to the theatre at Christmas, a girl who had her own clique of friends to which Ruby might sometimes be allowed to hover on the periphery.

The pond at the end of the Finboroughs' garden was wide and circular and edged with paving stones. In the cold weather the water had frozen and the light of the torch revealed to Ruby the three figures on the ice. She recognised Theo Finborough and his friend; the third was a girl.

Sara Finborough's wavy hair was red-gold and cut to a bob level with her chin. Her features were regular, her movements easy and graceful. Seeing Sara for the first time, Ruby experienced a moment of deep, scouring longing for the same sort of undeniable, unquestionable beauty.

Mrs Finborough said, 'Sara, come and meet Ruby. Ruby's going to be staying with us for a while.'

Sara slithered to the edge of the pond and said hello. Mrs Finborough said, 'Time you came inside now. It's very cold.'

They were heading back to the house when Sara spoke.

'You can help me bury my rabbit tomorrow, if you like, Ruby.'

Ruby was touched by the offer. 'Yes, please. What did he die of?'

'Old age, I think. I was going to make a wreath, an ivy wreath. Dark green leaves are properly mournful, don't you think?' When Sara turned to her, Ruby noticed that her eyes were the same colour as her mother's, a pale meeting between blue and green.

They talked about pets and funerals for a while and then Sara said suddenly, 'How nice that you've come to stay. What a relief for there to be another girl. I get so sick of boys.'

★ ★ ★

Sara seemed to take to Ruby, as she took to all waifs and strays, and at least Ruby was not flea-ridden like some of Sara's stray cats, just a little unkempt, her stockings and jerseys knobbly with darns, the cuffs of her blouses frayed.

Isabel took Ruby and Sara to the Army and Navy Stores to buy Ruby new frocks and a uniform so that she could attend Sara's school until her father reappeared. They had lunch at Selfridges and afterwards called at Isabel's hairdresser in Bond Street, where Lucien cut off Ruby's stringy plait. With her hair bobbed and wearing a new frock, Ruby lost her hunted, slightly grubby look.

Isabel enjoyed having another child in the house. The cradle and pram had long since been put away in the attic and all the tiny white clothes wrapped in tissue paper and placed in a drawer in a spare room. The nursery had been turned into a bedroom for Sara; now, wallpaper covered the painted friezes of animals and toys. But if you looked hard enough you could still see, beneath the pattern of primroses, the bulkier shadows of a teddy bear, a railway engine and an elephant with its trunk upraised.

Bringing up children, Isabel sometimes thought, involved a series of losses — their departures first for prep school and then for boarding school, and the way in which they grew away from her, following their own interests and pastimes, no longer seeing her as the centre of their world. Her three children were utterly dissimilar. Philip and Sara had the passion that went with the Finborough red hair; Theo was cooler, more detached. Philip and Richard often clashed — they were too alike, Isabel often thought, to get along comfortably. Both were brave and strong and confident of their own power, and both saw the world in black and white and not the myriad shades of grey Isabel knew it was composed of.

Philip had inherited Richard's love of speed, of challenge and danger. His energy needed an outlet and, with a charming smile, he brushed away her warnings to be careful, not to drive too fast, to wrap up warm, to be back before ten. Isabel always felt particularly close to Philip, the son she had nursed at her breast and comforted after falls and temper tantrums. He was warm and affectionate and loyal, though he had a unforgiving side, a tendency to brood, to nurture a slight, that she suspected he had inherited from her.

Theo was harder to know. He had been small and wiry until this last year, when he had shot up. He was now almost as tall as Philip. His fine black hair framed features that had recently lost their childish roundness and that had sharpened and strengthened, giving him the look, Isabel sometimes thought, of an eagle on its perch, surveying its kingdom through a remote and golden eye. Theo was incisive and intelligent and he had a love of music and art as well as a solitary side to his nature. In Cornwall, he would go off all day on his own, to walk or to sail or to sketch. Isabel could not always tell what went on behind those hazel eyes. She often wondered whether their early separation, when she had been so ill after his birth, too ill to hold him or nurse him, had left its mark. She had not that instinctive understanding of her second son that she had of her first: there was something unfathomable about Theo, and she loved him as she would have loved anything that was mysterious and wonderful — not an entirely comfortable emotion and one that was mixed with a certain amount of awe, a certain amount of frustration.

There was nothing at all mixed about her feelings for Sara. Sara was the daughter she had longed for — pretty, lively, amenable, and blessed with a sweet, sunny nature. With Sara, Isabel went on shopping trips and evenings to the ballet and had long conversations about nothing in particular. Sara's Irish grandmother had taught her to ride, and Richard had taught her to swim and to sail the dinghy they kept in Cornwall. Isabel had taught Sara to sew and to cook because it seemed to her that these were skills every woman should have, whatever her station in life.

Sara was Richard's favourite, the apple of his eye, the daughter he adored and spoiled and indulged. At twelve years old, Sara had the makings of beauty in her fine features and unusual colouring. Isabel knew that Sara's mixture of beauty and generosity might make a dangerous combination. Beauty needed hard-headedness, even ruthlessness, if it was not to be a liability.

And how would Ruby Chance, she wondered, fit into this household? Would she find a niche for herself or would she feel overshadowed, never quite at ease? After the first few weeks, Isabel felt confident that Ruby would survive. There was a toughness about her; she was used to standing up for herself.

The news from the nursing home was not good — the doctors doubted whether Mrs Chance's health would ever be robust — and so far all Richard's attempts to trace Nicholas had come to nothing. There was the aunt and cousin in the Fens, of course, but when Isabel suggested to Ruby that Mrs Quinn come to tea next time she was in town, Ruby looked at her with an incredulous expression and informed her that Aunt Maude never went to London and didn't like to travel. Isabel decided to write to Mrs Quinn, telling her of Mrs Chance's illness and Ruby's whereabouts. Mrs Quinn's letter back to her apologised for the fragility of her own health, which meant that she was unable to have her niece to stay. Mrs Quinn hoped Ruby was not being too much trouble to Mrs Finborough and trusted that Ruby would visit her, as usual, in the summer.

Isabel came to grow fond of Ruby. There were things she and Ruby had in common. She saw in the girl her own wariness, a sharing of the expectation that she had never quite managed to rid herself of, that the good times might not last. She felt an affinity with Ruby, who, after all, knew what it was to be abandoned.

★   ★   ★

Ruby never took for granted that she had become a part of the Finboroughs' day-to-day life. It always seemed to her a miracle, a deliverance. She went to school with Sara and shopping with Isabel, and ran alongside whoever walked the current Tolly on the Heath. She had helped Sara bury her rabbit in a shoebox 'with full obsequies', as Sara put it, and sat next to Philip as he decoked the engine of his motor bike in the garage. She became used to the rhythm of the family, to Richard's business trips to the Continent, and Philip and Theo's longer absences at boarding school.

Ruby's defences were her quick mind, her sharp tongue. She had long ago learned to conceal her differences, having worked out that there were differences that attracted and differences that repelled. The Finboroughs' eccentricities — their odd friends, their noisiness, their frequent arguments, often over pudding (they had a habit of arguing over pudding, so that the crisp brown shells of pies remained uncut and jellies quivered, translucent and unbroken) — only enhanced their charm. There was nothing charming about Ruby's family's peculiarities. Her father's absences and her mother's tears, their unpredictable lurches into penury, and, of course, Aunt Maude, were all potential sources of humiliation. These were failings that were best hidden: they did not endear.

One Sunday each month, Isabel took Ruby to visit her mother in the nursing home in Sussex. Her mother looked different now, her clothes were tidier and her face was less thin. She asked Ruby questions and appeared to listen to Ruby's answers, but Ruby sensed the effort involved and imagined some well-meaning nurse teaching her mother the phrases and then arranging her in the chair and even pasting that tentative smile on her face.

Whenever they visited, her mother would say, 'And Nicholas — I've waited so long — surely you've heard from Nicholas?' and Isabel would intervene, explaining that her husband had not yet been able to trace his old friend but still had a great many avenues to explore, and Ruby's mother would say, '*Oh,*' and collapse a little, as though someone had stuck a pin in her. On the train home, Ruby would pretend to read her book, making sure to turn a page every now and then, while inside she seethed with anger and misery at the knowledge that she herself existed somewhere on the periphery of her mother's heart, cared about but not central to her existence, and that the one person she had believed loved her best had walked away from her without a backward glance.

Milestones passed: her own birthday, her mother's birthday, and still her father did not return. In August, Ruby went with the Finboroughs to Cornwall. A succession of Isabel's friends, a ragbag assortment of Hampstead poets and artists and raconteurs, all of whom, Sara confided to Ruby, were in love with her mother, journeyed down to Cornwall too, to laze on the beach and sketch the cliffs. Ruby saw how the Finboroughs regarded the nearby cove as their own: hikers making their way along the sands were treated to cold glares, grudging good mornings.

At Porthglas they all shed their London clothes for cotton dresses or shirts and shorts, and sandals. The house, which the family considered small, stood by itself on a promontory. The timber of the house had faded to a silvery grey and the patchwork construction of the walls — stones and wood and cob — seemed to ~~have~~ of risen up out of the earth. Inside, the rooms were washed in pale colours and the simple furniture was scrubbed clean or painted white. Shells and driftwood and pebbles, arranged in concentric whorls, ornamented the windowsills and hearths. Plants clustered round the windows, their leaves trailing to wooden or stone floors. Ruby understood that this serene, austere house was Isabel's, just as the London house, with all its bright warm colours and noise, was Richard's.

There were some things Ruby loved more about Cornwall than others. She disliked the boat that Philip, Theo and Sara sailed because it made her feel sick. She did not truly enjoy, as they did, swimming in the sea, because she, unlike the Finboroughs, felt the cold. She preferred to sit on a rock at the edge of the bay, a book to hand, listening to the slap of the waves on the base of the boulder.

At the end of August, not long after they had returned to London, a letter arrived from Aunt Maude.

Isabel looked up from the breakfast table. 'Ruby,' she said, 'this is from your aunt, Mrs Quinn. She asks you to go and visit her next Tuesday.'

Ruby, horrified, said, 'Oh, no, I'd rather not.'

'I think you must. Mrs Quinn is a close relative of yours. And haven't you a cousin?'

'Yes, Aunt Isabel,' said Ruby sulkily.

'That's nice,' said Isabel vaguely, and Ruby thought, well, you'd think so, wouldn't you?

Then Isabel dropped her second bombshell. 'Theo can go with you,' she said. She gathered up her post and ran a quick eye round the table to see whether everyone had finished.

Theo looked up and scowled. 'Ma, must I?'

'Philip will still be away and I have my Mother's Circle that day, I'm afraid, so yes, Theo, you are to go with Ruby.'

Of all the Finboroughs, Ruby trusted Theo least. The oddest things struck him as funny and he had a way of using long words, or saying nothing at all, that she suspected was designed to confound. If Theo had ruffled her hair and called her 'kiddo', as Philip did, she would have thought him patronising.

'It's all right,' said Ruby quickly. 'I can go on my own. I don't mind. I've been on a train by myself before.'

'I'm afraid that wouldn't do at all.' Isabel's tone was such that Ruby knew that any futher argument was futile. 'Mrs Quinn writes that you take a train to — ' she glanced down at the letter — 'Manea. Then you can walk the two miles to, um . . . ' Once again, Isabel glanced down.

'Nineveh,' said Ruby gloomily, and Theo sniggered.

★   ★   ★

Ruby and Theo caught the train from Liverpool Street. In the carriage, Theo, sitting opposite her, dozed. They had been travelling for over an hour when he opened his eyes and looked out of the window.

'Where are we?'

'Cambridge, almost.' Ruby said suddenly, desperately, 'I wish we didn't have to go. Couldn't we just *say* we went?'

Theo gave her a look. Ruby sighed and said, 'I suppose not.'

'Why don't you want to go? Do you hate them?'

'Aunt Maude, yes, definitely. Not Hannah.' There was nothing to dislike about Cousin Hannah; in fact, she seemed to Ruby insubstantial. You almost thought that if you touched her, your fingers might go straight through her.

It wasn't *that* which troubled her, but the thought of exposing her family, in all its peculiarity and unattractiveness, to a Finborough. When she imagined Theo telling Philip and Sara about Aunt Maude and Nineveh, something inside her curled up unpleasantly.

115

Theo shored up her worst fears by stretching and yawning and saying pleasurably, 'Nineveh. If it isn't bleak and windswept I shall be very disappointed. I dare say there'll be dogs too, slavering red-eyed hounds.'

He seemed, thought Ruby resentfully, to regard the expedition as a great joke. Ignoring him, she looked out of the window. Cambridge station passed in a bustle of passengers alighting from the train; north of Cambridge, the gentle folds of the countryside levelled out as they entered the Fens. The fields were striated with dykes and bore buff-coloured corn-stubble, or were black where the plough had already turned the soil. After a while, Ruby caught sight of the two towers of Ely Cathedral, floating like a great stone ship over the lower lying land.

They had twenty minutes to wait at Ely station before changing trains and heading away from the Isle of Ely, back into the flatlands. Willows and alders fringed the rivers and fields; beside a distant track, a row of white poplars shivered in the breeze, their silver leaves glittering like newly minted coins.

Theo, looking out of the window, said, 'So *flat*. What on earth must it be like in winter?'

'Cold,' said Ruby.

The train stopped at Manea station. Ruby led the way to the village. Passing shops, a church and rows of cottages and houses, they left Manea for a narrow lane across the fields. A dyke ran parallel to the lane, other dykes leading off from it at right angles and diminishing to the horizon in a series of lines that converged in a distant bluegrey point.

'Boring, isn't it?' said Ruby.

'I think it's interesting,' Theo said, surprising her. 'Atmospheric. It has a subterranean feel.'

'Nineveh was flooded once, Aunt Maude told me. There was a storm and the dyke broke. There's a mark

116

on the side of one of the barns that shows where the water came up to.'

A mile along the road, an unmarked track branched off through a copse. Cart wheels had gouged out two deep furrows in the track, and grass and nettles sprouted from the central ridge. Elders grew from the damp, mossy ground, and fungi with clammy purplish-brown caps pushed up through the earth.

Clearing the copse, they could see across the fields to the farm.

Ruby said, 'That's it. That's Nineveh.'

The breeze picked up, slicing through them as they crossed the field.

Theo asked, 'What's your cousin like?'

'Hannah? She's all right. She doesn't say much.'

'How old is she?'

'Ten.'

'And your uncle?'

'Uncle Josiah died ages ago, in the war. I can't remember him at all.'

Hearing the barking of dogs, Ruby steeled herself. Aunt Maude's dogs might not be red-eyed, but they were always ill-tempered. In the farmyard, there was the sweet, pungent smell of animals and manure. A goose ran towards them, its neck outstretched, hissing, and Ruby shooed it away.

Dogs streaked across the cobbles in a slick black blur; a voice called out sharply, 'Tom! Malachi!' and Ruby looked up.

Maude Quinn was a large-framed, imposing woman, as tall as a man. Her brown hair was scrunched up in tight curls on top of her head and secured with pins. She was wearing, as always, a black gown. The stiff, shiny material of Aunt Maude's gowns always made Ruby think of the hard carapaces of beetles.

She heard Theo, beside her, take an audible breath, and she saw that Aunt Maude was holding a shotgun.

Momentarily, the shotgun swivelled towards them, its barrel a round black void.

Then it was lowered. Aunt Maude said, 'I thought it was the Waspes.'

'No, Aunt Maude.' Ruby crossed the courtyard and Aunt Maude permitted her cheek to be kissed.

'Aunt Maude, this is Theo Finborough.'

To Ruby's relief, Aunt Maude seemed to take to Theo. 'So kind of your family to look after Ruby,' she said. Her voice purred.

Nineveh farmhouse was large and three-storeyed, built of yellow Cambridgeshire brick. Inside, ill-lit corridors snaked between rooms, branching off into darkness. A chair or a chest of drawers, placed in a gloomy corner, tripped up the unwary visitor. On the walls, the faded photographs and prints were so spotted with damp that the subjects in the portraits seemed to peer out through a sandstorm.

'We have so few visitors at Nineveh,' said Maude to Theo. 'Only the vicar — and Dr Piper used to call, but he died last year, and the new man is a Methodist, I'm afraid.'

They went into a parlour. Tall dressers displayed pint earthenware mugs and painted plates. Delicate procelain, gold-rimmed and painted with tiny flowers, nestled behind glass-fronted cupboards.

Hannah rose to her feet as they came into the room. Maude said sharply, 'Well, don't stand there gawping, girl. Remember your manners.' Hannah stammered out a greeting.

Etta Chance had once said, as they left Nineveh, 'Poor little Hannah, she always looks so washed out.' The phrase had stuck in Ruby's imagination. Everything about Hannah was washed out — her pale, freckled skin, her fine, straight light brown hair, even the print of her cotton dresses. Hannah was slight, a few inches shorter than Ruby, and she had a rushed, flat,

118

colourless way of speaking. Her gaze darted continuously. Ruby thought her rather dull and tiresome.

Over a lunch of ham, potatoes and beans, Aunt Maude complained of the difficult harvest, low milk prices and the unseasonable weather. Then she said, 'And how is your mother, Ruby?'

'She's getting better,' said Ruby.

'Really?' Aunt Maude's lip curled. 'Etta was always weak. She never had any gumption.' A short pause, in which Maude helped herself to another thick slice of ham, then she said, 'And your father?'

'We haven't heard from him.'

A snort. 'Nicholas Chance was always a bad lot.'

Ruby glared at Maude. 'He'll come back soon. I know he will.'

'I doubt it.' Half a dozen potatoes followed the ham, and several large spoonfuls of runner beans. 'Etta should never have married him. I knew his sort the moment I set eyes on him. He thought he'd be marrying into money but I never let him get his hands on a penny.' Maude's gaze settled on Ruby. 'Has your mother no idea where he's gone?'

'No,' said Ruby shortly.

'He must have sent a letter — a postcard — a forwarding address . . . '

'Nothing.'

'Oh dear. How troubling for Etta. Still, we all have our crosses to bear.'

Theo said, 'Do you use a tractor on the farm, Mrs Quinn? I'm very interested in tractors,' and the conversation turned to the superiority of horses over tractors for ploughing.

The maid cleared away the first course and brought in an apple pie and a jug of cream. 'The sugar,' muttered Aunt Maude. 'The silly girl has forgotten the sugar. Run and fetch it, Hannah.'

Hannah scurried off to the kitchen. The sugar was

fetched; Maude served the pie. Theo mentioned that he liked to play the piano, and Aunt Maude said, 'You must try my late mother-in-law's piano. I've been told that it's a very fine instrument.'

They went back to the parlour and Theo played, and Aunt Maude hummed along to the melody, one large ham-like hand beating time against the arm of her chair. Ruby glanced at the clock on the wall. Really, it hadn't gone too badly at all, and soon they could say that they must leave for the train.

Theo's piece ended. 'Charming, quite charming,' said Maude. 'Such a pleasure to hear good music. I have an ear for music, you know.'

Ruby explained about having to catch the train. Maude said, 'You must take a little gift back to your mother, Theo. Come with me.'

Maude heaved herself out of her chair and they all followed her down a gloomy, winding corridor. In the rooms that led off from the corridor could be glimpsed pieces of large, old-fashioned furniture laden with a strange assortment of odds and ends, cracked plates and old medicine bottles and clocks whose faces were framed by extravagant gilt curlicues.

Maude led them into a pantry. Through the window, Ruby could see the maid pegging washing on the line.

'Let me see.' Maude opened a cupboard and inspected its contents. 'Does your mother like strawberry jam, Theo?'

'Yes, Mrs Quinn.'

A sheet of brown paper, flattened and folded and bearing old labels and stamps, was unearthed. 'The string, Hannah,' said Maude Quinn sharply. 'Hurry up and fetch the string.'

Hannah ran out of the room. Returning a few moments later, clutching a glass jar, she caught her toe on the corner of the peg rug in the doorway and slipped and fell, dropping the jar on to the quarry-tiled floor.

There was a crash, and pieces of glass and lengths of string skittered across the floor.

'Careless girl!' Maude screamed. 'Stupid, careless girl!' Jerking Hannah to her feet, she slapped her face hard.

Ruby ran for the dustpan to sweep up the shards of broken glass. Hannah retreated to a corner of the room, weeping. When all the pieces of string had been gathered up, Maude selected a length and used it to tie up the parcel. After she had knotted the string, she clipped the ends and returned the two short pieces, which could not, thought Ruby, have been more than a few inches long, to a new jar.

Ruby and Theo left shortly afterwards. Theo carried the parcel as they made their way across the field to the copse. When Ruby looked back, she saw that Maude Quinn was standing in the entrance to the farm, one hand raised in farewell, her bulky shape magnified and darkened by the shadow she cast against the brick wall.

★　★　★

Hannah watched Theo and Ruby walk away across the field. Then the copse took them and they were gone.

She rubbed her knee, which was bruised from her fall. Her face stung from her mother's slap. She heard her mother come back inside the house, humming to herself as she lumbered from room to room. Hannah recognised the tune her mother was humming.

What a friend we have in Jesus
All our sins and griefs to bear!

Hannah shivered. Though it was a warm day, she felt cold inside. Looking up, she saw that her mother was standing in the doorway. In her hand, she held a rolling pin.

Her mother's face was distorted with anger. 'After everything I've done for you, to show me up in front of my guests. Well, you know what happens to careless girls, don't you?'

The rolling pin struck Hannah hard across the shoulders and she fell to the floor. Then she was dragged out of the house and across the courtyard to a small brick outbuilding that lay at the back of the farm. The door was opened and she was pushed inside. Then the key turned in the lock. The sound of the humming faded as her mother walked away.

There were no windows in the outhouse. The only light was the pinpoint that showed in the keyhole. Hannah knew that when darkness fell there would be no light at all. Hannah's eyes had not yet grown accustomed to the gloom and, with the familiar sounds of the farmhouse muffled by the brick walls, only touch told her where she was and what surrounded her. She crouched against a wall, her skirt wrapped round her knees.

What a nice day it had been until she had dropped the jar of string! Ruby and Theo had come and Mother hadn't been cross, and the music had been lovely. Then she had spoiled it. Stupid, stupid Hannah, who always did everything wrong. She pinched herself hard. It was her fault that the day had been spoiled, her fault that Mother had hit her and shut her in the outhouse.

An only child, Hannah knew well only Nineveh's servants and labourers. Her experience of school had been brief: she had felt odd, uncomfortable, stared at, *different*, all too aware that she was plain and not at all clever, and she had been relieved when her mother had told her she no longer needed to go. She had absorbed her mother's distrust of strangers from birth; when, occasionally, she had to run an errand to the shop in Manea, she felt eyes staring at her as she stood in the queue and, reading out the items on her list, her mouth dried and her tongue stumbled. Though there was a great deal within the boundaries of Nineveh itself that made her fearful, it frightened her just as much to leave the farm.

She knew intimately only the farmhouse and the land that surrounded it. The land was at constant risk of flooding and was protected by a complex system of pumps and drainage channels. Hannah knew the straight, high waterway of the Old Bedford River that bounded Nineveh's land to one side and the Hundred Foot Drain that ran parallel to it for nineteen miles, and she had seen each winter the floodwater that spread over the grassland and the wildfowl that sailed on the glassy inland sea.

At the age of ten, Hannah was familiar with the rhythm of the days and the rhythm of the seasons. Her mother rarely left the farm. Maude Quinn did not visit; the vicar, her solicitor, and the few neighbours she considered her social equals called on her. Her forays into the outside world were momentous occasions, driven by crisis — a bill unpaid, an offence taken. The dogcart would be dragged out of the barn and Maude would drive away dressed in her black gabardine coat and a cloche hat decorated with greenish-black feathers. In her mother's absence Hannah felt a mixture of apprehension and relief. The almost perceptible tension that lay over Nineveh disappeared along with the dogcart. Hannah could walk across the courtyard without fear of being slapped for dragging her feet; she could have sat, if she had had the nerve, in her mother's wicker chair at the back of the house, watching the sun sink behind the orchard. On her return, Mother might be triumphant because she had beaten down a foe, or she might be enraged because she had met with insolence or resistance.

In the darkness, a soft sticky strand drifted across Hannah's face. She gasped. A cobweb, she told herself, it's only a cobweb. There was a rotten, mushroomy smell. Fearful of every footstep, terrified of encountering some nameless horror, Hannah crept towards the light. Tomorrow I'll be good, she muttered to herself. Tomorrow I'll do everything right. She sat down on the earth floor, her knees hunched up to her chest and her hands clamped over her ears to shut out the sounds as she stared up at the spark of light.

She began to sing to herself:

> 'What a friend we have in Jesus
> All our sins and griefs to bear!
> What a privilege to carry
> Everything to God in prayer!'

Waiting for Theo to say something was like waiting for a thunderstorm to break. He was silent until they were inside the copse and then he said, 'Good grief, Ruby, you do have the most peculiar relations.'

'I suppose you think it's funny — '

'Not at all, actually. That poor kid.'

Ruby thought of Aunt Maude hitting Hannah and then putting those tiny pieces of string back in the jar. Why would anyone keep pieces of string as short as that?

Then, to her surprise, Theo said, 'Don't worry, I won't say anything to the others.'

Ruby stared at him. 'Honestly?'

'I promise.'

'Not to Philip?'

'Not a word.' Theo added, in an Aunt Maude voice, 'We all have our crosses to bear.' Ruby snorted. 'And mad aunts are yours, I fear, Ruby. Despotic . . . I might have that as my word of the day.'

'Do you have a word of the day?'

'Invariably. Don't you?'

She shook her head. 'I might start, though.'

'Would you say your Aunt Maude was despotic?'

'What does it mean?'

'Tyrannical . . . oppressive . . . '

'Aunt Maude's awfully despotic, then.'

'When I saw the gun . . . '

'You were scared, weren't you, Theo?'

'It was a nasty moment.'

With the relaxation of tension, Ruby felt a ripple of laughter run through her. 'Did you think we were going to have to run for our lives?'

'Wasps . . . why was she shooting wasps?'

'Not wasps, Theo, the *Waspes*.' She spelled it out for him. 'They own a nearby farm. Aunt Maude and the Waspes have been having a feud for years.' She giggled again. 'Tractors . . . telling her that you were interested in tractors . . . '

'Perhaps I am.'

She laughed again. She felt lighter, walking away from Nineveh, as if she had put down a heavy piece of baggage. And how surprising that Theo, of all people, should understand.

On the train, Theo took his sketchbook out of his canvas satchel and Ruby watched the flickering movement of his pencil. The flat black fields rushed by and the Isle of Ely became a distant grey mirage.

They had almost reached Cambridge when he said, 'Did you notice that when your cousin cried she didn't make any sound at all?' and Ruby realised that she hadn't, and that Theo was right, and she thought how glad she was not to be living at Nineveh with Aunt Maude, and how utterly relieved she was to be going home to the Finboroughs' house.

★ ★ ★

All Richard's efforts to trace Nicholas Chance had come to a dead end. He had spoken to Nicholas's last employer and had learned that though his old friend had been a hardworking and competent employee, he had been prone to unplanned absences. If he had not left of his own accord, he would ~~have~~ of been sacked. Richard had placed advertisements in London and Home Counties newspapers, asking Nicholas Chance to get in touch with him. Only a few cranks and fraudsters replied; he gave them short shrift.

As he went through the contents of the Chances' house, he felt like one of those passers-by who stares at a road accident. Everything he discovered — the threadbare clothing, the shaving brush with the bristles worn away — spoke of grinding poverty, genteel poverty, the worst sort in some ways, because it must be hidden. In the back of a drawer Richard discovered betting slips and IOUs. He remembered Nick playing cards in the trenches — perhaps the gambling had become a compulsion. Perhaps his financial affairs had reached that tipping point when they could not be recovered. Perhaps he had known what destitution must do to his wife and child and had been unable to bear witnessing it. As the months passed, Richard came to believe Nicholas did not wish to be found.

In November, Mrs Chance left the nursing home. Her doctors thought it unwise for her to return to the house in Reading and recommended sea air. Richard found a boarding house in Eastbourne run by a Mrs Sykes, a pleasant and kind-hearted lady.

Telling Etta Chance that he had been unable to trace her husband, Richard knew that he was plunging a knife into her heart. He was condemning her to a bleak prospect, a particularly cruel limbo, still married but without a husband. It was decided that Ruby would remain with the Finboroughs in term time so that she could continue to attend the same school as Sara. She would spend the school holidays with her mother in Eastbourne.

Richard packed Nicholas Chance's belongings into a suitcase before giving back the keys of the Reading house to the landlord. Leaving Ruby to go through the case on her own, to choose any particular keepsake, he patted her shoulder and reminded her that her father was a good man, and a hero.

As he walked away, he recalled something Nicholas had once said to him. *Poor old Nick Chance, lost in the wild blue yonder and never going home.* Where are you? he wondered. What's happened to you, where have you gone? He remembered Chance's roar of triumph and fury as he had gained the British trench, and he thought how wretched it was that, having survived the war, peacetime seemed to have beaten Nicholas Chance.

★ ★ ★

Scents clung to the tweed and wool: tobacco and shaving soap and boot polish and peppermints, scents Ruby had always associated with her father.

Among the clothes and papers she found a diary. She looked through it carefully, trying to discover clues to where her father might have gone.

It told her nothing, though, and she put it aside. Unwrapping a silk scarf, she uncovered the medal. It felt cold and heavy in the palm of her hand. She touched the crimson and blue ribbon, let her finger glide over the raised silver surface of the medal. She repeated the words she had said to herself over and over again during the past year: 'Dad wouldn't have left us without taking his medal. He was proud of his medal. If he had chosen to leave us he would have taken it with him.'

She remembered how her father had liked to take her to the park when she had been a little girl, how he had made her a wooden boat to sail on the pond and had lifted her on to his shoulders as they had walked through the crowds, so that from her high perch she had been able to see further than anyone else. He had bought them ices, balancing all three on one large palm, *one for me and one for Etta and one for our Ruby.*

She missed his strength and his vitality and the way he had always seemed to light up a room. She missed the songs he sang, the jokes he made, the stories he told. She and her mother were duller without him. She missed the man he had been before he had become unhappy. She remembered the last time she had seen him: she had swung on the gate and waved as he had walked away from her. It had been a cold, bright day and the brass buttons on his army greatcoat had glinted in the sunlight as he had turned and waved to her one last time.

Ruby took a deep breath and wiped her eyes. Then she put the photographs and the medal in her pocket and closed the lid of the suitcase.

5

In the summer of 1929 Philip left school and started to work for his father. After school, Ruby liked to sit on the landing window seat, watching for him to come home.

Philip was always busy, always going somewhere, always in transit, striding through the house still doing up his cufflinks or shrugging on his coat before heading off to parties, dances and cocktails. The front door would slam and the house would seem to sit back, as if startled by his absence. Philip's friends called, fleeting, glamorous apparitions who breezed in and out of the house before hurtling down the drive in their motor cars, leaving in their wake a drift of Arpege or Turkish tobacco.

Sometimes, before Philip left the house for the evening, he put on a gramophone record and quickstepped Ruby and Sara round the room. Sometimes, at the weekend, he took Ruby out for a ride on the pillion of his motor cycle and she wrapped her arms round his waist and pressed the side of her face against his broad leather back while her hands tingled with the cold.

A year later, Theo joined his brother and his father at Finboroughs. He had been working there for six months when he returned home one February afternoon. It was five o'clock and Ruby was sitting on the window seat, reading. Theo came upstairs, unwinding his scarf.

'Hello, Rube. Where are the others?'

'Dentist. You're early.' He looked, she thought, rather distracted. The shoulders of his mackintosh and his hair were damp. Ruby said, 'Where's Philip?'

'At the Hounslow site. He won't be back till late. Were you waiting for him?'

129

'Not really.'

Theo looped his scarf around the banister. 'Philip has loads of bad habits, you know. All the girls at work are in love with him.'

'Shut up, Theo.'

'They fight to take Mr Philip his morning tea — they are most assiduous in their attentions.'

'I said, shut up.'

Theo gave her an amused look. 'You haven't got a crush on him, have you, Ruby? Not on *Philip*?'

Ruby picked up her Agatha Christie and began to read, holding the book close to her nose, as she always did.

'You should wear glasses,' said Theo.

'Have you any idea,' she said, casting him a cold glance, 'what it's like to be a plain girl with glasses? No, I don't suppose you have.'

She thought she could see, beneath his teasing, a flicker of anxiety. She sighed and put her book down again. 'What do you want, Theo?'

'A walk, I think. How about you?'

It was almost dark and raining lightly, but she said, 'OK,' and put on her mackintosh and they left the house.

Streetlamps loomed through the drizzle; on the Heath the trees were traced black against the charcoal sky. They were walking up an avenue of beeches and oaks, and Tolly was running ahead of them, when Theo said, 'I've been trying to make up my mind about something.'

'What?'

'How to tell my father I don't want to work at Finboroughs any more.'

She shot him a quick, shocked glance. His face was set; he shrugged. 'I always knew I'd hate it. I thought I'd better give it a go, though. Well, I have, I've given it six months, and it's no use, I loathe it.'

'Oh, *Theo*.'

'Quite. Only I can't help thinking my father will have a little more to say than 'Oh, Theo'.'

The assumption that both Philip and Theo would work for the business was as deeply ingrained in the Finborough family as summer holidays in Cornwall and Christmases in Ireland.

Ruby said tentatively, 'Maybe it'll get better. Perhaps if you stayed a bit longer you might like it more.'

'No, I know I won't. And I might as well face up to it now. I've been trying to work out a way of telling Dad that won't make him furious.' Theo grinned crookedly. 'Of course, there may not be one.'

Tolly returned, stick in mouth; Ruby threw it again. 'What will you do instead?'

'I want to go abroad; I want to draw. I have to find out whether I'm good enough to be a professional artist.'

'But what about — '

'Money?' he said, and she let it go, though she had meant to say, 'What about us?'

'I have some money of my own. My salary, of course — I've been saving. And Grandmother always gives us something at Christmas. And when I run out I could find work.'

'Where will you go?'

'Paris, first.' His eyes lit up. 'Then the South of France. I want to go to Provence.'

She thought how easy he made it sound. Pocket your savings and head off to Paris. 'Perhaps Uncle Richard won't mind too much. After all, he's got Philip. What do you dislike about it?'

'Oh, everything.' Theo sighed. 'I can't get excited about the things Philip and Father get excited about. And then, there's the whole thing of being the boss's son. I'm not there because I've earned it or because I have any talent for it. I'm there because of who my

131

father is. I don't want that. I want to make my own way.'

She tucked her hand through his arm as they walked back down the hill. As they reached the road, he asked, 'How old are you now, Ruby?'

'Fifteen.'

'Shame. If you were a bit older I'd take you to a pub. I could do with some Dutch courage. I feel as if I'm going to my execution.'

Richard and Theo's argument lasted throughout the evening. Eventually Theo emerged white-faced from his father's study and went upstairs without eating his dinner or speaking to anyone. Ruby saw Isabel tapping on his door later that evening, a plate of sandwiches in her hand.

Over the ensuing days the household walked on thin ice. Richard was coldly sarcastic to Theo and brusque to the rest of them. The house vibrated with tension. Once, at night, going to the bathroom, Ruby heard from downstairs Isabel's cry of anguish: 'Can't you see what you're doing, Richard? You are driving him away!'

The following morning, Ruby woke early. It was still dark: padding downstairs in her pyjamas, she caught sight of Theo in the hall, buckling his rucksack.

He put a finger to his lips. 'I thought I'd slip out,' he whispered. 'Then there won't be any more fuss. I'll get the early train. I should be across the Channel by midday. I've left a note for Mum.'

'Wait here a minute. Don't go yet.'

Ruby ran upstairs and took a bar of chocolate out of her drawer. Hurrying silently back downstairs, she gave it to Theo. 'Have this.'

'Thanks, Ruby.' He hugged her.

When he opened the front door, Ruby saw that a mist lay over the garden. Theo walked away and the mist swallowed him up. Ruby remembered that other parting: the glint of brass buttons in winter sunlight, a smile and a hand raised in farewell. But Theo did not look back.

With Theo gone, the house seemed quieter, which was odd, thought Ruby, because he was the quietest of the Finboroughs. There was a Theo-shaped hole in the family, Sara said, and Ruby knew exactly what she meant.

★ ★ ★

Richard had been certain, right up to the morning he and Isabel had woken to find Theo gone, that he would see sense and change his mind. Yet two days after Theo left home a postcard arrived from Paris.

Theo had deserted him without a second thought and, as for Philip, though Richard recognised that his elder son had a flair for the business, he also saw his faults. Philip was hard-working and ambitious; he was also hot-headed and impulsive. He worked hard and played hard. Philip often did not come home before the early hours of the morning: at breakfast, he looked pale and heavy-eyed.

Before the war, Richard had taken the decision to restructure Finboroughs as a limited company. Richard had kept eighty per cent of the shares and Sidney Colville, his old business partner, had the remaining twenty per cent. A proportion of Finborough shares had been assigned to both Philip and to Theo at their births in anticipation of the day they would start to work for the family business.

Now, it had become necessary to raise more money. For two years, Finboroughs had been using Bakelite to manufacture wireless cabinets. The line was hugely successful and needed to expand, an expensive venture for which Richard needed to raise more capital. Large pieces of machinery must be bought; new production lines needed to be set up.

His accountant recommended selling more shares, but Richard, always wary of risking losing control of the business, balked at the idea.

As they drove home one evening, Philip suggested another way of raising the money. 'Sell the tea factory,' he said. 'You don't need it any more, and Lyons, for instance, would give you a good price for it. And it's a drag on our resources.' It was Philip's unfortunate choice of word — *drag*, as though Finborough's Quality Teas were an albatross around their necks — that rubbed Richard up the wrong way. The tea factory was Richard's baby, the very first investment he had made. He refused to consider Philip's suggestion and they quarrelled. Both lost their tempers, and by the time they reached home they were no longer on speaking terms, and Richard had only time to take off his coat and pour himself a drink before hearing the roar of Philip's motor cycle as he left the house again.

★   ★   ★

Ruby spent the school holidays in Eastbourne with her mother. Etta Chance lived in two rooms in a boarding house in Elms Avenue, near the sea front. Ruby slept on a camp bed in her mother's bedroom. The evenings were worst, endured either in Mrs Sykes's parlour, listening to the wireless, or in her mother's sitting room, while her mother knitted and Ruby read a book or played patience. The passing of time was marked by the click of needles, the turn of a card. The sweaters and cardigans that her mother knitted for her were for Ruby imbued with a mixture of frustration and guilt — frustration that during the weeks in Eastbourne her life seemed to solidify, devoid of anything new, anything that amused; guilt that she was always relieved to leave Eastbourne and return to London and the Finboroughs.

Yet her restlessness touched even her life in London. Sara's pleasures — riding and swimming and tennis — were not Ruby's. Sara's future, of house parties and balls, followed by a good marriage, would not be her own. Often, during her years with the family, Ruby had mentally compared the Finborough household to a medieval court, glorious and glittering and colourful, with Richard its redheaded, powerful king and Isabel his beautiful and imperious consort. The court progressed to its summer residence in July, it entertained those to whom it gave its patronage and cast out those who had earned its disapproval. It was clannish and self-assured, and there was a cachet in being in its purlieu, a dash of glamour that clung to its most everyday affairs.

Ruby knew that living with the Finboroughs had changed her. Some of their polish and confidence had rubbed off on her. She was at ease going to the opera or taking lunch in a restaurant. She knew which shoes to wear with which frock and how to write a thank you note and how long she should stay for an afternoon call. Richard had taught her to swim and Philip had shown her how to start up a motor cycle, and from Isabel she had absorbed a certain style, an awareness of how to dress and how to arrange a house. From Sara she had had friendship, given freely and generously and lovingly. As for Philip, that first infant passion she had felt, the day she had arrived at the Finborough house, that awareness that she had encountered a dazzling, magnificent being, had never diminished. She loved Sara, she liked Theo — with some reservations — but she adored Philip. When she and Sara imagined the men they would marry, Ruby's future husband always looked like Philip.

But Isabel's chaperonage, though kindly dispensed, was strict, and gripped more tightly as she and Sara grew older — as if, Ruby thought sourly, men of evil repute lurked on every street corner, intent on seduction. Isabel thought cinemas and dancehalls unsuitable for nicely brought-up girls, and it required such elaborate arrangements, such a cobweb of lies, to secure an afternoon in Woolworths, buying lipsticks and nail polish, which must be hidden because Isabel considered cosmetics vulgar, that sometimes it seemed hardly worth the trouble.

The dangers Isabel sought to avoid were vague and unspecified. What little Ruby and Sara knew about sex was patchy, gleaned from discussions with schoolfriends and from the books Ruby read. *Les Fleurs du mal*, plodded through painfully with the aid of her school French, was frustratingly unspecific. *The Constant Nymph*, wept over and dog-eared by frequent rereading, was far more satisfying. Yet what *exactly* had Tessa and her lover done in their room in the chilly Belgian boarding house before poor Tessa had tried to open the window and, doing so, died of a heart complaint?

'As soon as you know,' said Sara, 'I mean, *properly* know, you must tell me, Ruby. As soon as you've done it.'

'I might never know. I might die a virgin, unsullied and pure.' Ruby thought longingly of Philip.

★　★　★

Sara left school in the summer of 1933. In August, Isabel took her to her dressmaker and had her fitted for half a dozen new frocks. Lucien cut her hair and her grandmother sent over from Ireland a pearl and emerald necklace and matching earrings, Finborough heirlooms. Decked out in apricot or cream or violet satin, cut on the bias, emeralds round her neck and in her ears and her hair a flame-coloured cloud, Sara took on a life of dances and parties. When she arrived home in the early hours of the morning, Ruby crept into her room. The necklace would have been dropped carelessly on the dressing table and the satin frock exchanged for flannelette pyjamas. Ruby would ask her about the party and Sara would yawn and say, 'It was dull, darling, so dull. But let's not talk about that, let's talk about something else.'

One Saturday afternoon in early January, Sara was away at a house party and Ruby was helping pack up the Christmas decorations, when Isabel said, 'Have you decided what you want to do when you leave school, Ruby?'

Ruby paused, startled, a silver bauble in her palm. 'Not really, Aunt Isabel.'

'What about teaching? You always get such splendid school reports.'

'Perhaps. Or I suppose I could be a nurse.' She plucked the idea from thin air, having recently read a biography of Edith Cavell.

'You could consider secretarial work. I'm sure Richard would be able to find you a job with the firm.'

The doorbell rang and the maid came to tell Isabel that she had a visitor. Ruby sat in a sea of tinsel and baubles. Then, suddenly, she stuffed the lot anyhow into the box, put Tolly on his lead, grabbed her coat and hat, and called out to Isabel that she was going to the Heath.

It was a cold, frosty day and the sky was a hard, pale blue. Her breath made clouds in the air as she headed up the East Heath. Calling out to Tolly, she ran up the slope, through the grass towards the edge of the pond. Blades of grass crunched beneath her feet and she remembered coming here with Theo, and Theo telling her that he was planning to leave for France. If only it were so simple, she had thought: put some money in your pocket and catch the boat train. Just now she missed Theo and wished he was here, telling her his word for the day and annoying her with his teasing remarks. She could not quite see why Isabel's question

— 'Have you decided what you want to do when you leave school, Ruby?' — had left her with a feeling of exclusion, almost of humiliation, but it had.

She reached the bank of the pond. Opaque ice had begun to gather round the reeds; gingerly, she put a foot forward, testing it. The idea came into her head without warning, as refreshing and invigorating as the cold air she breathed and as pleasurably unnerving as the notion of putting her weight on thin ice. She stood motionless, wondering why she hadn't thought of it before.

In a week's time, she would be eighteen. Eighteen was grown up, surely. She could decide what — or who — she wanted to be. Possessed of a dim, unformed yearning to reinvent herself, she had been unable to see what to turn herself into. She had no pattern on which to model herself. Her own relatives were absent, fragile or frankly embarrassing. Though she loved the Finboroughs, she was not a Finborough.

The Chances were an uninspiring lot; the Finboroughs overwhelmed. She must leave both behind. You just left, she realised. You didn't wait because there was nothing to wait *for*. You did what Theo had done — you put some money in your pocket and you walked away. Because she had no money, she must find a job. Not nursing — she was no Florence Nightingale or Edith Cavell — nor teaching, because she was sick of classrooms. And she would not work for Finboroughs, as Isabel had suggested. Richard and Isabel each had different ways of imposing their authority, but both were powerful, influential people. Her gratitude to the Finboroughs was without limit, but she had begun to see that gratitude could become dependency, and that dependency might one day lead to subserviency.

★　★　★

138

Sara hated the parties. It must run in the family, she supposed, because her mother hated them too. The first few times Sara attended grown-up parties and dances she noticed how stiff her mother was, so awkward and unlike herself as she conversed with the other mothers, and how tired and strained she looked when the chauffeur, Dunning, drove them home in the early hours of the morning. It was sometimes hard to see the point of it, both of them spending their evenings doing something they loathed.

Much of Sara's disillusion lay in the evenings' failure to transport, to transform. In smart London town-houses or in crumbling country mansions, swept of dust and cobwebs for the occasion, with the lighter squares of paint on the walls showing where a portrait or landscape had been sold to pay for a daughter's coming-out, Sara descended from icy bedrooms to hunt balls, where girls she had known for years shuffled round in the arms of their brothers and cousins, and their brothers' and cousins' friends. Her strongest feeling was one of disappointment as she circled drab ballrooms in the arms of jug-eared, pimply boys who trod on her toes and told her that the band was frightfully good. She was tall, and many of her partners were shorter than she, and while some were so shy they could hardly speak, others were conceited bores. Standing in the queue for a supper of limp sandwiches and flabby vol-au-vents, she found herself wanting to scream, or for an earthquake to swallow her up along with the supper-table and the dance band.

The proposals she received were ridiculous, farcical, impossible. In the library of a house in Shropshire, a titled gentleman forty years her senior dropped creakingly to one knee to ask for her hand in marriage while Sara bit her lip, torn between embarrassment and laughter. A boy who had been at school with Theo tried to kiss her after a tennis match. *I say, old thing, don't*

139

you think it would be jolly good fun to get married? As if, she thought, they were planning a picnic or a day at the seaside. Sweet, smitten boys asked her for her hand: sympathising with their evident anguish, she entertained a fleeting picture of herself, living in a chintzy, comfortable house in the Home Counties, arranging suppers for her husband's colleagues and doing charity work.

Other suitors offered her castles in Scotland or villas in the South of France, which might have been fun, Sara thought, had she not had to share them with a husband of unspeakable dullness. Not one of them, she confided to Ruby, had an ounce of — she struggled for the right word — dash? flair? — whatever it was that would capture her heart. Had any of her lovers been worthy of consideration, then surely she would not have made fun of them to Ruby; surely she would not have mimicked their stuttering phrases, their tics and their twitches.

Ruby had moved out of the Finboroughs' house earlier that year. She was working as a clerk at the Ministry of Labour and living in a lodging house on the Fulham Road. She had taken to wearing black jerseys or little blouses in bright colours and sweeping back her short brown hair from her face in smooth wings over her ears. She used lipstick and powder, and she smoked and went to films by herself and travelled on her own round London. Ruby's room in the lodging house had a gas ring on which she heated up baked beans and made coffee. Hessian curtains covered the windows and towers of secondhand books sprouted from the floor; a heap of brightly coloured cushions turned the bed into a sofa. The other rooms in Ruby's house were occupied by louche men who stood in the doorways of their rooms, smoking, their eyes following Sara as she made her way up the three flights of stairs.

Sometimes they called out to her, asking her to the pictures or for supper.

'That's very kind of you but I'm afraid I can't,' she always said politely.

Often, when Sara arrived, Ruby's room was crowded. Ruby's friends were as patchwork, thought Sara, as the cushions on the bed. Sara wondered whether Ruby chose them for their variety, their hotchpotch nature. Chemistry students rubbed shoulders with accounts clerks; an Italian ice-cream seller took his place on the floor between a flautist and a girl who worked as a mannequin in a department store. Some of the men wore suits, others dressed in corduroy trousers and flannel shirts open at the collar. A few of Ruby's women friends looked conventional in neat little skirts and jackets, inexpensive versions of the tweeds Sara dressed in when she stayed in the countryside, but others wore drill slacks or droopy floral frocks, from the skirts of which peeped out bare legs and grubby sandalled feet. Sara sat on the bed beside Ruby as they drank black coffee and smoked cigarettes, and talked about politics and novels and poetry.

Novels and poetry were all right — the Finboroughs knew plenty of poets and novelists — but Sara knew nothing at all of politics. Some of the conversations, in which Ruby was as fully involved as any of the others, reduced Sara to the status of an onlooker. She seemed to end up making the coffee while they rattled on about communism or Mussolini — not that she minded making coffee, but she began to notice that they expected nothing of her, that they perceived her in a different — perhaps a lesser — light to themselves. Which jolted her, because she was unused to being considered second-rate.

★ ★ ★

141

Ruby's room: a man with wild black curly hair saying, 'The trouble with any sort of absolutism is that it is, by definition, unthinking. It doesn't matter whether it's religious or political, absolutism removes freedom of speech.'

An older man, who was smoking a pipe, said, 'Is freedom of speech always desirable, do you think?'

'Of course it is,' a dark-haired girl said indignantly. 'You're just being provocative, Brian.'

'People need direction. Perhaps we should think more carefully about who to give freedom of choice to.'

'Ha! The élite only, I suppose, in your view.'

'There must be limits.'

'Once you start setting limits then the whole principle's in ruins.'

'A limit on spouting hatred, I meant.'

Brian upended his pipe, tapping the ash inaccurately into a coffee cup. 'Where would the Soviet Union be if Stalin wasn't in charge?'

Ruby said, 'Do you think that utopias can only exist when they are imposed?'

'Perhaps.'

'But what if not everyone wants the same as we want? For instance, Brian, you believe that everyone should live more or less equally, don't you, that we should have the same size of house with much the same furniture and lino and things inside it?'

'I believe that would rid us of a lot of problems — poverty, for a start.'

'But plenty of people would hate it. I shouldn't think we could even agree what sort of chair we preferred. Diana would want armchairs and Oliver might prefer basketweave and Susanne would choose something modernist and uncomfortable.'

A new voice said, 'What about you? What do you think?' and Sara, looking up, saw that she was being addressed by a fair-haired man standing by the window.

He was in shadow, squeezed into a corner of the room. His head was cocked because the ceiling of the room sloped and because he was tall. Sara's gaze settled for a moment on his face, on its slopes and angles, and found them compelling.

She said, 'Oh, I prefer deck chairs because they make me think of the seaside.'

Someone laughed. Brian murmured sniffily, 'I thought we were discussing absolutism.'

But the fair-haired man said, 'Deck chairs are an excellent choice. An example of great design, surely, both simple and useful.' Sara noticed that his voice was accented.

When, an hour later, she left the house, the discussion was still in full swing. A soft but persistent rain slid from the leaves and petals of the roses and gathered in glossy black beads on the metal railings. Pausing to put up her umbrella, Sara heard footsteps behind her. Glancing back, she saw the fair-haired man.

'Where are you going?' he asked. 'May I walk with you?'

'My brother's coming to meet me.' Sara looked up the street but could not yet see Philip's motor cycle.

'Aha, a brother. Have you many brothers?'

His hair was a darkish blond, the colour of ripe corn, and his eyes were grey and full of amusement. He was several inches taller than she and she guessed that he was a few years older.

'Two brothers,' she said 'but Theo's abroad.'

'And Ruby, the so-amusing Ruby, she is your sister?'

Sara shook her head. 'Ruby and I aren't really related at all. We're just friends. Though I do sometimes think of her as my sister. She lived with us for simply ages.'

'I must apologise, I haven't introduced myself. My name is Anton Wolff.'

'I'm Sara Finborough.'

He bowed and took her hand, raising it to his lips.

The gesture was neither flowery nor selfconscious, as it might have been from an Englishman.

'I'm very pleased to meet you, Fräulein Finborough.'

'Where are you from, Mr Wolff?'

'Vienna,' he said. 'I come from Vienna.'

'How long have you been in England?'

'For three months. I came here to study. I am a student of architecture, you see. I want to learn how to make great buildings — not grand buildings, but ones that people like to live in.' He looked down at her. 'And you, Fräulein Finborough? What do you do?'

'I ride and I play tennis and sometimes I go to terrible parties.' She thought it sounded a bit thin.

'Don't you like parties?'

'Not really. Do you?'

'It depends who else is there. With the right person a party can be magical. Don't you find it so?'

Hearing the roar of an engine as Philip's motor cycle drew into the kerb, Sara said, 'I expect so. It's been very nice to talk to you, Mr Wolff. Goodbye.'

★   ★   ★

Sara, sitting on Ruby's bed as they painted their fingernails green: 'Theo's home. We didn't recognise him at first. He looked like a pirate. Mum made him get a haircut and shave before Dad came home. He said he saw Picasso and Max Jacob dining together in *Le Boeuf sur le Toit*. He speaks French about a million times better than he did before and he smokes disgustingly smelly cigarettes.'

Theo took Ruby out for supper. He was tanned and rather thin, which exaggerated his lean, wolfish look. In an Italian café in Greek Street, Ruby quizzed him.

'What's Paris like?'

'Terrific. You should go there.'

'I will, one day. Did you starve in a garret?'

'Not a garret. On a beach in Brittany — I was homeless for a fortnight. Damned uncomfortable, sleeping on sand.'

'Have you a girlfriend?'

'Yes.'

'What's her name?'

'Celine.'

'What's she like?'

'Dark . . . tiny . . . She dances at the Paris Opera. She's never left Paris, doesn't want to go anywhere else.'

'She doesn't sound right for you, Theo. Have you been to bed with her?'

Theo twirled spaghetti round his fork. 'None of your business, Ruby Chance.'

She leaned across the table to him. 'I only want to know what it's like. No one will tell me — well, only men who want to go to bed with me, and I don't trust them.'

'You'll find out soon enough.'

'So mean. Are you a famous artist yet, Theo?'

'I'm afraid not.'

'But you're going to be?'

'No, I don't think so.' Though he spoke lightly she noticed a certain steeliness about him. 'I discovered that I can sketch well but that's about it.'

'Will you come home, then?'

He shook his head. 'I'm going sailing in the Mediterranean this autumn.'

'On your own?'

'Perhaps. I'll see who turns up.'

Theo refilled their wine glasses. 'How's the job?'

'Fine. I file things and I answer the telephone and I type letters, and every now and then I search through some hefty book to find out the answer to a tricky question of procedure. Actually, I like it. It appeals to my orderly nature, I suppose.'

'And how's your mother?'

145

'She's very well.'

'And dear old Aunt Maude?'

Ruby made a face. 'The same as ever, I suspect. I haven't seen her for a while.'

'What about Hannah?'

'Oh — droopy. That's how I always think of Hannah — *droopy.*'

A raising of his straight black brows. 'You should be kind to her.'

'Why, Theo?' She glared at him furiously. 'Because she's my cousin? Because blood's thicker than water? Not in *my* family. We walk out on each other, remember. We wander off without leaving a forwarding address.'

He threw her a cool look. 'You should be kind to Hannah because she needs you to be kind to her.'

'Hannah'll be all right. She'll probably marry some farmer with straw in his hair.'

She heard her own voice, cynical and mocking, and felt discomforted. Irritably, she drank some wine. Then she said, 'I'm trying to find my father. I want to know what happened to him. People don't just disappear, do they? He must have gone *somewhere.* I spoke to Uncle Richard about Dad. I made him tell me the truth.' Ruby recalled their conversation: Richard Finborough's attempts to avoid hurting her had been worn down eventually by her own determination to be in possession of every piece of information.

'What did he say?'

'Uncle Richard told me that my father had money troubles. I knew that — my mother had tried to borrow money from Aunt Maude. Dad was behind with the rent and there were a lot of unpaid bills. Uncle Richard thinks — he didn't say so, but I could tell — he thinks Dad was in such a mess he just ran away.'

'Have you told your mother what you're doing?'

'No, not yet.'

'Ruby . . . ' Theo frowned. Then he said, with untypical hesitancy, 'What if you find out something you might not like? What if you find out something you might have preferred not to know?'

'But it's always better to know, isn't it? A lot of things could have happened to Dad since I last saw him, I know that. He might have had an accident or fallen ill. He might even be dead.' Ruby had wondered whether, overwhelmed by his troubles, her father might even have killed himself. Though she did not think so. In all her memories, he always seemed so vital, so alive.

★ ★ ★

A cold, dark Saturday afternoon in November. As Sara waited on the pavement outside Ruby's house, tiny flakes of snow began to float down from a sky of mustard and grey. She put up the collar of the fur coat she had borrowed from her mother and heard from behind her the front door open. Looking back, she saw Anton Wolff.

'Are you waiting for the faithful brother?'

'Yes.' Sara glanced at her little gold watch. 'He's very late, though. Perhaps I should go back inside and wait with Ruby.'

'Ruby and her friends are going to the cinema.'

'Oh.'

'Maybe you should take a taxi home, Fräulein Finborough. But we could have coffee first, if you would like that. You look cold.'

Sara glanced up and down the road once more but there was still no sign of Philip. She accepted Anton Wolff's invitation not because she was chilled — the fur coat kept her warm — but because the thought of going for coffee with him excited her.

'The only good coffee in London is in Soho,' he said,

as he hailed a taxi. 'The only good coffee in England, I think.'

She teased him. 'Don't you like the coffee I make?'

'You make terrible coffee. But I like it very much, of course.'

In the taxi, she was aware of him, sitting beside her, aware also that, in being alone in a car with a man, she was flouting the most basic of her mother's rules. She said, 'I can't think what can ~~have~~ happened to Philip. Perhaps he forgot.'

'I wouldn't have thought anyone could forget you, Fräulein Finborough. But then I have no brothers. I have no idea how brothers think.'

Flakes of snow slid down the windscreen as they sped through the streets. *I wouldn't ~~have~~ thought anyone could forget you, Fräulein Finborough*. He had said it matter-of-factly, not flirtatiously. Outside, the people and buildings, glimpsed through the windows, had taken on a magical, fairy-tale air, like the painted backdrop of a theatre. Snow danced in the darkness, whirling in the aura of the streetlamps. Sara felt free and she felt grown up, and neither, she realised, were things she commonly experienced.

The taxi drew up in a narrow street. They went into a small café, where Anton spoke in German to the waiter. He smiled at Sara. 'Now I'm here with you in your furs, I can almost imagine myself in the Café Landtmann in Vienna. All the grand ladies go there for coffee and cake. If we were there, I would buy you *Marmorguglhupf*, as well as good Austrian coffee.'

'Goodness,' she said. 'It sounds lovely, darling, but what on earth is it?'

'Marbled cake. It is delicious.'

'You must miss Vienna dreadfully, Mr Wolff. It sounds so beautiful and romantic.'

The coffee arrived, rich and aromatic. He said, 'It is beautiful and romantic, you are correct. But recently,

I'm afraid, the air has seemed poisoned.' A shadow had fallen across his face.

'Why?' she asked. 'What's happened?'

'You don't read the newspapers, Fräulein Finborough?'

'Not very much, I'm afraid.'

'There was a civil war in Vienna in February. And in July, the Chancellor of Austria, Herr Dollfuss, was assassinated.'

'How awful. Is that why you came here?'

'Partly. Vienna became a dangerous place for me to be. But I came here also because, as I told you, I'm studying architecture.'

Anton told her of the places he had visited in Britain, of his journeys to Glasgow to study the work of Charles Rennie Mackintosh, whom he admired, and of his visits to Saltaire and Letchworth Garden City, to see the ideal communities that had been created there.

Sara asked him whether he had family living in Vienna, and Anton explained that though his mother had died some years ago, his father still lived in the city. 'I have tried to persuade my father to come to England,' he said, 'but he refuses.' For a moment, he looked sad. 'My father is an old man — he was nearly fifty when I was born. It's harder to uproot yourself when you are old. And perhaps, when you've seen the things my father's seen, when you've lived through wars and revolutions and famines, then the present doesn't seem too bad.'

'I really should read the newspapers, shouldn't I? But there never seems to be time.'

'Why should you want to know about terrible things?'

'Because then I'd be able to talk properly to Ruby's friends.'

'Ruby's friends talk a great deal of nonsense,' he said dismissively. 'They theorise, they do not know. Live in your own world, Fräulein Finborough, with your kind family and your lovely home and your faithful brothers.'

'Not so faithful,' she said, with a smile, 'when one goes away for years and the other forgets all about me.'

Yet, when she arrived home, having taken a taxi from Soho to Hampstead, Philip was sitting in the kitchen with his leg stuck out in front of him and her mother was cleaning the deep grazes in his leg. His motor cycle had skidded on a patch of ice, throwing Philip on to the road, and, seeing her, they both looked relieved and her mother said how sensible of her to take a taxi, and neither questioned that it had taken her an hour and a half to travel from Fulham Road to Hampstead.

In her parents' bedroom Sara took off the borrowed coat and hung it on its padded hanger. She stroked the soft dark fur with the back of her hand, and, instead of thinking, as she usually did, of all the poor animals who had been murdered to make her mother's lovely coat, she thought of Anton — Anton in the taxi, with the light from the street flickering on his handsome face, Anton in the café, looking sad as he spoke of his father, and Anton as they had parted, pressing his lips against the back of her hand.

★   ★   ★

Sara discovered that though Anton had told her he was a student, he was not registered at any university. Sometimes he sat in on London University lectures — it was easy enough, he said; he blended in with the others, and no one ever challenged him. Sometimes he worked for a friend, Peter Curthoys, who was an architect and had an office in Golden Square. He had met Peter two years earlier, in Paris, and Peter, knowing Anton's situation, put work his way whenever he was able.

He described to Sara the Karl-Marx-Hof, a vast apartment block built by the Social Democrats in Vienna. The building not only provided decent living

150

accommodation for tens of thousands of workers, but also housed kindergartens, welfare clinics, libraries, laundries and playgrounds. He told her how, during the civil war, Nazi militias had turned their fire on the Karl-Marx-Hof, hoping to destroy the equality of opportunity it symbolised at the same time as destroying the building itself.

He never tried to kiss her or to hold her hand, and they never had another opportunity to drink coffee in Soho. Away from him, her certainty that he liked her, felt something for her, vanished. Anton was pleasant and polite to everyone — perhaps, she thought, she had been mistaken in believing he singled her out.

In January, Ruby gave a party to celebrate her nineteenth birthday. Isabel agreed that Sara could help Ruby prepare for the party and then stay for the first part of the evening. An artist friend had lent Ruby his first-floor room, which was larger than her own. The only furniture in the studio was a trestle table, an easel and an old and rather dirty mattress. They covered the mattress with a colourful throw that Sara had borrowed for the occasion, and dragged Ruby's own mattress down two flights of stairs for more seating. Lengths of blue and purple crêpe paper were pinned to the walls to cover the paint stains, and they arranged the food on the trestle table — sausages and cheese and chocolate, and a jelly in which pieces of mandarin orange were suspended, Sara thought, like strange sea creatures. Someone offered to lend them a piano, and four men, redfaced with effort, hauled it up the flight of stairs.

Sara had bought Ruby three pairs of silk stockings, and a lipstick in a gloriously deep red. Isabel and Richard had given her a pair of tan leather gloves and a brooch, and her mother had knitted her a cardigan. It occurred to Sara, not for the first time, how awful it must be for Ruby not to have so much as a card from her father on her birthday.

The guests began to arrive at eight. The gramophone was playing Cole Porter; whenever a record ended, a short, bald man sat at the piano and played Liszt loudly and passionately. A space cleared in the centre of the room and couples danced. A sausage dog darted between the legs of the dancers, yapping.

A voice said, 'I wasn't sure whether you'd be here. I thought you disliked parties.'

Sara's heart skipped a beat. 'Hello, Anton,' she said.

They talked and danced, and then Sara put on her coat and they left the house together. They walked towards Putney Bridge. In the centre of the span the banks of the Thames receded away; below ran the dark river, the artery that led through London's heart. A barge disappeared beneath the bridge and the lamplight was reflected in the water.

When he touched her face with his fingertips, something seemed to melt inside her. As he drew her to him, kissing her, Sara closed her eyes. The noise of the traffic and the light of the lamps receded and all her existence was concentrated here, in his embrace.

When, eventually, they drew apart, she had a sudden, terrible thought, and she said, trying to make a joke of it, 'I suppose you're always kissing girls on Putney Bridge.'

'Always. Or London Bridge or Battersea Bridge, I don't care.' He kissed her again. His kiss was deep and lingering. Eventually, he said, 'I have wanted to do that ever since I first saw you.'

'Then why did you wait so long?'

'I wasn't sure whether you felt the same. You are like a dream, Sara — a very pleasant dream, but a dream none the less. You are here one day and not another — whenever I pause to look at you, you vanish. And you always seem so happy, no matter what is going on in the world.'

'Don't you think I'm a serious person?'

'No, not at all,' he said with a smile.

Sara heard the chime of a church bell. She glanced at her watch, disbelieving. 'It's ten o'clock,' she said, horrified. 'My father will be here.'

They headed back to Ruby's house. Sara saw the sleek outline of her father's Rolls-Royce, parked in the street. She began to run, dashing into the hallway of the house, glancing in the mirror to check her face, afraid that Anton's kiss might somehow have visibly altered her.

She heard footsteps coming down the stairs: catching sight of her father, she said quickly, 'Daddy, you're here already. I just slipped out for a breath of air. I was too hot.'

They went outside. Not far away, she could see Anton leaning against a lamp post, his coat collar turned up, his face pale against the dark night.

Her father said, 'Rum lot, Ruby's friends. Communists and foreigners, by the look of them, and I don't suppose any of them have two pennies to rub together.'

★　★　★

Richard Finborough had given Ruby the suitcase containing her father's belongings. Ruby had written to the people listed in the back of Nicholas Chance's diary, asking whether they had seen or heard of him. No one had, and there was nothing to suggest that anyone had been in contact with him later than the winter of 1927.

She spoke to her mother, trying to worm information from her without betraying the fact that she was looking for her father, and was able to piece together some of the Chance family's movements in the years between the end of the Great War and her father's disappearance. The Chances had moved house frequently, their odyssey driven by her father's search for

153

work. Nicholas Chance had left school at fourteen with no particular skills, but he had been an intelligent, forceful man who had made the most of the limited opportunities offered to him.

Ruby put off going to Nineveh for as long as possible. Though Isabel had always insisted she keep in touch with her Quinn relatives, since Ruby had left the Finboroughs she would ~~have~~ of preferred to cut off all contact with them, having some time ago arrived at the conclusion that she owed them nothing. She loathed Nineveh's remoteness, its irrationality, its air of being frozen in the past. When Maude Quinn spoke of her sister it was with contempt rather than affection; that she was welcoming and passably polite to Ruby herself was, Ruby suspected, only because of her own connection to the wealthy and illustrious Finboroughs — Aunt Maude had always been an inveterate snob. Maude had refused to help when the Chances' situation had been desperate, had done nothing at all to aid a sister who lacked her own limitless strength, and who had been, when she had approached Maude for financial assistance, close to breakdown. Had Maude answered Etta's appeal instead of rejecting it out of hand, how different things might have been! Freed from the worst of his worries, Nicholas Chance might of ~~have~~ chosen another path.

But as the months passed, Ruby sensed her lines of enquiry petering out, leaving her with little option but to speak to Aunt Maude in the forlorn hope that she might be able to shed some light on her father's disappearance. It irritated her that Theo's words pricked at her conscience: *You should be kind to Hannah because she needs you to be kind to her.*

On a cold March morning, Ruby took the train to Ely and Manea and then walked from the railway station to Nineveh. The clouds were a darker grey than the taupe branches of the willows, and the path through the copse to the farm was patched with deep puddles. The dykes brimmed with meltwater from recent snows, the landscape was heavy and swollen with water, like a sponge.

Hannah met Ruby at the gate and Ruby gave her cousin the present she had brought with her, an early birthday gift. Hannah's eyes lit up as she unwrapped the red leather purse. When her mother called out to her, Hannah stuffed the purse quickly into the pocket of her dress. She did not, Ruby noticed, show her mother the present.

After lunch, Ruby helped Hannah clear the table while Aunt Maude sat in the parlour, eating Turkish delight. Maude Quinn had put on weight since Ruby's last visit more than eighteen months before. Folds of flesh made it hard to tell where her chin ended and her neck began; her ankles, encased in thick brown lisle stockings, were as solid and shapeless as stovepipes.

Ruby said, 'I wanted to talk to you about my father, Aunt Maude,' and the humming stopped and Maude's eyes swivelled in Ruby's direction. 'I'm trying to trace him. I wondered whether you could remember when you last saw him.'

'I only met Nicholas Chance the once.' The finger-tapping had resumed, the pulse like a fast-beating heart.

'When was that?'

'That day he had the cheek to ask my permission to marry Etta.'

'Can you remember what you talked about?'

Maude's narrowed eyes were small dark holes. 'We didn't make polite conversation. I soon sent him packing.'

'Did he mention where he was living at the time? Or what he was doing? Or who he was working for?'

'As I said, we didn't make polite conversation.'

155

Tucking a sweet into the corner of her mouth, Maude said, 'Of course, he must ~~have~~ come here the one other time.' OF

'When was that?'

'When they ran away together. Etta wouldn't ~~have~~ had the nerve to do it by herself. She'd ~~have~~ needed *him* to hold her hand.' Maude's lip curled. OF

An angry response teetered on the tip of Ruby's tongue, but she managed to bite it back. Quarrelling with Aunt Maude would be like beating her head against the stout brick walls of Nineveh farmhouse. Impossible to imagine another human being ever altering Maude's opinion one jot.

Not long afterwards, Ruby made her farewells. Hannah had slipped away at some point during their conversation, so Ruby went to look for her. Easy for Theo, she thought resentfully, to remind her to be kind to Hannah. It wasn't Theo who had to put up with Aunt Maude.

Hannah wasn't in her bedroom or in the kitchen. Putting on her coat and hat, Ruby went outside. In the fields, the first blue-green spikes of new leaves were showing through the wet black soil. It had begun to rain again and water glazed the furrows. The farmhouse was surrounded by outhouses and sheds — some brick-built, with rusting tin roofs, others wooden and earth-floored or raised on columns. Inside a barn, objects both extraordinary and mundane could be made out in the dim light: half a dozen tin pails, rusted through at the bottom; a heap of periodicals, bound together by cobwebs; a stuffed curlew with a long, curved beak like a scimitar, and an old carriage, the dust dimming its black paint and gold leaf.

Ruby heard a sound. She went inside the barn. In the darkness, she saw Hannah's startled eyes, then saw her make a quick movement.

'What's that?' she asked, adding quickly, 'If it's your

secret then I won't pry. I only came to stay goodbye. I have to leave for the train.'

Hannah was biting her lip. Her gaze darted to the door. Then she whispered, 'I don't mind *you* knowing, Cousin Ruby.' From beneath a pile of dusty sacking, she unearthed an Oxo tin. As she lifted the tin down, the overlong sleeves of her jersey fell back and Ruby saw the dark bruises on her wrist.

'What happened to your arm, Hannah? Did you hurt yourself?'

Hannah frowned and tugged her sleeve down. 'I caught my hand in the mangle,' she muttered. 'I was careless. It doesn't matter.'

She opened the tin. Peering inside, Ruby saw a flint arrowhead, a brass button and the blown speckled blue egg of a robin. Hannah put the red purse in the tin, covered it with the lid and placed it back beneath the heap of sacking.

On the train back to London that evening, Ruby thought of Aunt Maude's fingers, white with sugar, delving into the box of sweets. And she thought of Hannah's tin, with its pathetic treasures. The dark bruises had stood out like a purple bracelet round her wrist. *I caught my hand in the mangle.* Ruby tried to picture the sort of accident that would cause bruises like that, but all she saw was Maude Quinn's fat white hand encircling Hannah's narrow wrist.

She wondered whether Maude gave Hannah worse than unkind words and the occasional slap. Had Maude bullied her sister too? Of course she had. Perhaps tall, strong Maude had demanded the weaker Etta fetch and carry for her; perhaps she had slapped and hurt her when Etta had dropped something or had come back late from the shops. Perhaps Maude Quinn had used her domineering personality and superior physical strength to make her younger sister the woman she was, fragile, frightened and insecure.

How miraculous Etta must have thought her meeting with handsome, generous Nicholas Chance! No wonder she had fallen in love with him. No wonder she had seen in him her salvation, her opportunity to escape. But perhaps the very intensity of her love had become a prison for him, rather than a pleasure. All too clearly, Ruby remembered the quarrels, silences and tears that had preceded her father's departure.

'What if you find out something you might not like?' Theo had asked her. 'What if you find out something you'd have preferred not to know?'

There was a possibility that neither of them had wanted to voice. What if, she thought, her father had not been running away? What if he had been running *to* something — or to *someone*?

6

Anton gave Sara a bunch of witch hazel and catkins: the flowers of the witch hazel were like tiny sunbursts. Sara told her mother she had picked them herself from the overgrown garden behind Ruby's house. They perfumed her bedroom with the scent of frosty nights and winter.

He sang to her one afternoon as she waited outside Ruby's house for Philip. His rich baritone — singing Strauss, she thought — laced across the street. Passers-by, looking up to the open window at the top of the house, saw him and smiled.

In the hallway at the bottom of Ruby's house, they kissed. Uncollected letters for former tenants lay yellowed and dusty on the hall stand and the floor was blotted with muddy footprints. Someone was playing the saxophone in a nearby room. The sound of the blues mingled with Anton's nearness and the touch of his skin. His hands rested on her waist and her cheek brushed against the roughness of his jaw. Outside, in the darkness, he wrapped her in his coat, enclosing her in its shabby black folds. She rested her head against the hollow of his shoulder and closed her eyes, breathing in the nearness of him.

★ ★ ★

A fitful, dangerous spring. Returning to Ruby's house, they saw the Wolseley parked in the street, and Isabel standing on the pavement, glancing vaguely up and down. Had she let go of Anton's arm before her mother caught sight of her? As she hurried forward, Sara thought she had but she could not be sure.

'Mummy, you're early.'

159

'I thought I'd visit Mrs Saville, at the nursing home.' Mrs Saville was a friend of Isabel's. 'I wondered if you might like to come too, darling. Ruby, dear . . . how are you . . . you must come to lunch next Sunday; we haven't seen you for so long.' Isabel kissed Ruby's cheek, but her gaze, not vague at all now, rested on Anton.

'Of course I'll come with you, Mummy.' Sara managed hasty introductions.

'I believe my husband knows a family by the name of Wolff.' Isabel shook Anton's hand. 'They live in Finchley. Perhaps you're related to them?'

'I don't think so, Mrs Finborough. My family comes from Vienna.'

A short, polite smile. Then, 'Mr Wolff, Ruby, you must excuse us. I'm afraid that Sara and I have to go.'

When they were sitting in the back of the car, her mother said, 'Has Ruby known Mr Wolff long?'

'About six months, I think.'

'What is his occupation?'

'He wants to be an architect. He's still studying.'

'He doesn't have a job? Where does he live? Are he and Ruby close friends?' Then, in a low voice so that Dunning, who was driving the Wolseley, should not hear, her mother said, 'I am not Ruby's mother. If Ruby chooses to become involved with such a man, then there's little I can do about it, except perhaps to offer advice. But you are my responsibility, Sara, and I would prefer you not to wander around London in the company of an unmarried man, whether he's Ruby's friend or not.'

'Yes, Mummy.' Turning to the window, Sara thought of Anton's fingers threaded through hers, Anton's smile as he placed a kiss on the palm of her hand.

★ ★ ★

Three weeks passed: Anton did not come to Ruby's house. 'I haven't seen him for ages,' said Ruby. 'He hasn't been in any of the usual places.'

Sara had a sudden terrible thought. 'You don't think he could have gone back to Vienna, do you?'

'I shouldn't think so. I'd have thought he'd be afraid of ending up in prison again.'

'Prison?' Shocked, Sara stared at Ruby.

'Yes, didn't you know? It was after the civil war. Anton and his father were both put in prison.'

'But why? What had they done?'

'Nothing, of course. They're socialists, so not too popular with the present regime, naturally. I'll have a look for him, if you like.'

A few days later Sara received a letter from Ruby. She had seen Anton, Ruby said. She wrote, 'He was a bit strange, not like he usually is. He wouldn't say much, only that he had been busy. I asked him to come round on Sunday but he said he wasn't free. I'm sorry, Sara.'

Sara felt a great emptiness, mixed with resentment — not of Anton, but of the restrictions that prevented her from searching him out and speaking to him. Ruby could roam the pubs and nightclubs of London, looking for him, but she, Sara Finborough, could not. No wonder he seemed to have had second thoughts about their friendship. What would a man who had travelled across Europe, who had lived through a civil war and had been wrongfully imprisoned, see in a girl who had hardly, until recently, known that such horrors existed? He had told her that he did not think she was a serious person. Had he, alone in a foreign land, been a little bit amused by her, a little bit distracted by her, nothing more? Had he got what he wanted, kisses and sweet words, and, having done so, become bored and moved on? What did she really know of him? Ruby knew Anton better than she did. Ruby had known that Anton had been in prison; she had not. Ruby had told her that she had looked round Anton's usual places. Where were Anton's 'usual places'? Sara had no idea.

Her mother, noticing her unhappiness, suggested she take a holiday. She might stay for a few weeks with her grandmother in Ireland. Sara, who loved Raheen above all other places, said that she would think about it, but instead wrote to Ruby, asking her for Anton's address. Ruby told her that Anton lived in Scarborough Street in Whitechapel, which was not a part of London Sara knew at all.

Going to see Anton required elaborate planning. Sara offered to spend an afternoon with a friend, helping choose fabrics for a wedding dress. She told her friend's mother that her father would meet her afterwards and told her own mother that Mrs Forrest would see her home.

The afternoon arrived and Sara went to the dressmaker's. After a tiresome hour of inspecting near identical scraps of white satin and chiffon, Sara waited until the bride-to-be was encased in a *toile* and bristling with pins, and then she said, 'I must dash, I'm afraid, Mrs Forrest. My father will be waiting for me.'

Outside on the street it was cold and misty. Sara hailed a taxi and gave the driver the Scarborough Street address. In the taxi, her doubts and fears receded and the inner conviction, that she and Anton had been meant to meet, returned. As the vehicle neared the river, the mist intensified. Reaching the East End, their progress was slowed by throngs of workmen coming out of the factories and docks. Sara stared out of the window at the rows of small soot-blackened terraced houses that lined the streets. Washing, patched and greyed, hung across the narrow alleyways, limp in the misty air. Children played in the alleyways, their shrieks and laughter and chants drowning the voices of the women who talked in doorways as they balanced babies on their hips. There was the smell of horse manure and of fish and chips and, in the distance, looming through the fog, the cranes and hawsers of the docks, towering over the roofs of the warehouses.

Scarborough Street was a narrow road of small houses, all squashed up close to each other like books on a shelf. The taxi drew to a halt. 'Here you are, miss,' said the cabbie. 'Would you like me to wait?'

'No, thank you.'

Sara paid the fare and the taxi disappeared round the street corner. A small girl, of six or seven perhaps, wearing a dirty pleated skirt too big for her and a woollen jersey with holes in it, stood nearby, staring at her. A short way up the road there was a coalman's horse and cart. The horse's ribs showed through its dull coat. Sara stroked its nose and received a subdued whinny in response.

She knocked on the door of the house. There was no answer so she knocked again. After a while, she heard footsteps, and a thin, dark man opened the door.

'Good afternoon,' she said. 'Could I speak to Mr Wolff?'

The man disappeared into the darkness. After a few moments he returned and told her that Anton had gone out.

Sara's heart sank. 'Do you know where he's gone?'

'No, no. Sorry, lady.'

The door closed. Sara was aware that she was a long way from home. Perhaps she should have told the taxi to wait. She suspected, glancing up and down the road, that not many taxis ventured into this district of London. The little girl had run away, and the coalman had come out of an alleyway, his back burdened with empty sacks, and was climbing on to the cart. When the horse failed to respond to his jerk of the reins, he took a stick from the seat beside him and struck the horse hard. Sara stared, horrified, then ran to the cart.

'You mustn't do that! Can't you see he's tired?'

163

The coalman, taken by surprise, paused and said, 'You mind your own business, duchess,' and thrashed the horse once more.

'Stop it! You're hurting him!'

The coalman swore; the horse began to walk, his steps despairing, Sara sensed. From behind her, she heard a voice call out her name. Turning, she saw Anton.

'That horrible man — he was beating that poor horse . . .'

Anton took her arm, steering her away from the horse and cart. 'Sara, why are you here?'

'I came to see you.'

'You should not have come. You must go. Did you come here by taxi? Where is the taxi?'

'I sent it away.'

'Then I'll find you another one.'

She began to cry — the awful man beating his horse, and Anton's anger, his distance.

Anton groaned. 'Oh God, Sara, don't cry, please don't cry.' He muttered something in German under his breath. Then he said, 'You'd better come in. Here, come with me.'

Strange smells — cabbage, spices, and unaired clothes — assailed her as they climbed the stairs. On the second landing, he opened the door to a room. They went inside.

He said, 'I did not want you to see this place.'

'I don't mind.'

'*I* do.' He sounded angry.

The few pieces of furniture were crammed cheek by jowl. Paint peeled from a wall blackened by damp. The small cupboard and the suitcase she glimpsed beneath the bed must contain all Anton's belongings. She wondered how you could do anything, how anything could ever be pleasurable in such a room.

'I'll make coffee,' Anton said. He put a metal jug on

the gas burner. 'This place has its charms,' he said lightly. 'Look, through the window you can see the docks. At night, the lights on the cranes and the ships look magical.'

She whispered, 'Why don't you come to Ruby's any more?'

A sigh. 'I thought it best we do not see each other again.'

'Darling, how can it be for the best?'

He made the coffee, placing a cup in her hands. Then, sitting down on the bed, he said, 'Listen to me, Sara. Twenty years ago, before the Great War, the Wolffs were a reputable family in Vienna. *Reputable* . . . ' He looked at her questioningly. 'Is that the right word? I mean, not a great or noble or even a wealthy family, but a good, well-liked family, a family of doctors and architects and professors. A family who had many friends and a pleasant home.'

'Respected,' she murmured.

'Yes. The Wolffs were a respected family. We had an apartment in Favoriten, a good district of Vienna. Then the war came and everything changed. My two uncles were killed in the fighting and my mother died in the famine that came after the war had ended. Many families lost everything at that time. But my father — my father is an idealist. He saw in the war and its aftermath the opportunity to make a better world. He continued to work as an architect, but instead of making grand palaces he designed homes for ordinary people to live in. I have told you about the Karl-Marx-Hof — there were many other such places built in those years, and my father designed some of them. Vienna was troubled, but though our circumstances were not the same as they had been before the war, we managed. My father spent what money he had on my education. After I left school, I was able to attend university.'

'What happened?'

'My father had lost money in the Crash of '29. When the Kredit-Anstalt Bank collapsed in 1931, what little he had left was also gone. We had to leave our home and move into a smaller place. I left university. I worked — I earned what money I could. And then the civil war broke out.'

'Was that when you went to prison?'

'Ruby told you? Yes. The charges were false, of course — many people were wrongly imprisoned.'

'It must have been dreadful.'

He shrugged. 'I dislike small spaces. I don't know why — I always have.' Glancing round, he gave a rueful smile. 'This room is so small. I long to push back the walls. Perhaps that's why I want to make buildings that have great big windows and wide rooms and no dark corners. And yes, to be confined was unpleasant. My father and I were both released after a few weeks. They had no evidence against us.'

'And then you came here?'

'Yes. As I told you, I tried to persuade my father to come to England with me but he refused.'

'And then you met me.'

His gaze settled on her. 'Since I met you, I have not felt homesick.'

'Yet you don't want to see me any more. I don't understand.'

'I have tried to explain.'

'That your family has been through difficult times — I'm sorry for you, Anton, and it must be very hard, but it doesn't explain anything!'

He rose and went to the window. His back to her, he said flatly, 'I asked Ruby about your family. She told me about your father, the wealthy industrialist. And your mother, who I met, the great beauty. And your brother, who works for the family firm. And then there's you and me. Times are hard, in London as well as Vienna. There is not much work to be had, particularly for a foreigner.

166

I hope things will change — I hope they will get better. But for now, I cannot afford to buy myself a coat, I cannot afford new shoes. So, you and I, we hide in corners. We talk in hallways. I conceal myself when your brother comes to meet you. I do not introduce myself to this brother of yours — and why not? We both know, don't we? Because he would send me away with a fly in my ear.'

'Flea,' she murmured.

'Flea, I beg your pardon, flea.' He raked a hand through his hair. 'I thought I could make it possible. I thought, if I teach German lessons in the evenings and if I rent the cheapest room I can find then I can save money, and then . . . ' He made a despairing sound. 'But then I realised how foolish I was. And how wrong it is for me to see you. This is wrong, Sara. What we have been doing is wrong.'

'How can it be wrong for me to love you?' she cried, and then, realising what she had said, she looked away, suddenly embarrassed.

She heard him say softly, 'Oh, Sara.'

'Well, I do,' she said defiantly.

'Then I am the happiest man alive.' He took her hands in his. 'Because I love you too.'

She was aware of the beginnings of joy. 'Truly?'

'Truly. But it is impossible — we cannot be together, Sara, you must see that. I saw the way your mother looked at me. I saw how she was — beautiful, like her daughter, and wealthy, and so — so *English*. I saw that she and I are from different worlds.'

'That doesn't matter!'

'Doesn't it? Sara, because of me you lie to your mother. I don't wish to come between you and your parents. I would not wish to cause such pain.'

'Then I'll introduce you to my parents. I should have done so ages ago.'

'And then what?' His eyes were bleak.

'You could come to tea — or something . . .'

'No. Your parents would not invite me to tea.' Sara began to speak, but Anton held up a hand, silencing her. 'Your parents would not invite me to their home — no, they wouldn't, once they knew how I felt about you. I should never have begun this. I should never have spoken to you, I should never have touched you. Sara, if your father knew about us then he would forbid you to see me. He would not want you to be involved with a man like me. I know that. I think you do too.'

Sara thought of the boys who sat at the Finboroughs' dinner table, who played tennis on the Finboroughs' court, and whose names headed Isabel's list when she gave parties and dances. The purpose of her mother's entertaining was to find her a husband from those sons of businessmen, financiers and landowners. She suspected that Anton was probably right and that if they found out about him her parents would forbid her to see him.

Yet, along with her fears, she also felt, deep down, a certainty that all the futility and boredom of her coming-out had been merely an interlude, something that had had to be got through before meeting Anton.

'Then we'll wait,' she said calmly. 'We'll be careful. We'll wait till I'm twenty-one and then I'll tell my parents about you. They want me to be happy. I'll make them see that I can only be happy with you, darling. I know I'll be able to make them understand. It'll be all right, I know it will.' She looked up at him. 'A year — that's not long to wait, is it, Anton?'

★ ★ ★

It was amazing how the day-to-day business of living swallowed up Ruby's wages. Feed herself, clothe herself and rent a roof over her head, and most of the week's money was gone. Though she was good at her work

168

— she knew she was — and hoped to earn promotion, it had not escaped her notice that the vast majority of her superiors were men. She thought of the government offices in which she worked as a pyramid, filled at the base with busy girls like herself along with some unmarried older women; as the pyramid rose it darkened with besuited men until, at its pinnacle, could be found a large, carpeted office housing a resplendent and forbidding grandee, a moustachioed, monocled gentleman who was seemingly too important even to see Ruby on the rare occasions he passed her in the corridor.

One evening, a sculptor called Kit, who lived in one of the downstairs rooms in Ruby's lodging house and every now and then rather half-heartedly tried to persuade her to sleep with him, was sitting in her room, drinking coffee and talking about himself. Ruby had pulled out her father's suitcase from under her bed and was sorting through the clothes and papers — army discharge papers, wage slips, a menu from a regimental dinner.

Kit said, 'What are you doing?'

'I might have missed something. It's all right, I'm listening, go on.'

'If I'm thrown out of my rooms, I don't know what I'll do.'

'Why should you be thrown out?'

'I told you, I haven't enough money to pay the rent. You couldn't lend me a bob or two, could you, Ruby?'

'No,' she said firmly. She put the papers aside and picked up the letters, which were tied in a bundle with a piece of string. 'You could get a job, Kit.'

'Good Lord, no. Actually, I had an idea. I thought I could rent out my studio in the day. Find some other artist who could use the space. I prefer to work at night anyway.'

'Where would you go?'

'I'd stay at Daisy Mae's. We never get up till midday. What do you think?'

'Good idea.'

Peering at the envelopes, Kit asked nosily, 'Who are they from?'

'Just friends. Dad didn't seem to have any relatives.' She had visited Buckland, where her father had been born. She had traced a blacksmith who had remembered her father; he had confirmed what she already knew: that her father's parents were both dead. No members of the Chance family remained in the area.

Kit said self-pityingly, 'I haven't a single person who cares about me either.'

'Nonsense, Kit, you know you've dozens of relations, you just don't talk to any of them.'

Ruby ignored the diary, having already studied it in detail, and moved on to the old jackets, shirts and waistcoats. She was aware, as she picked up the first item, of a feeling of reluctance. Clothes were so personal, they contained so many memories. As her hand dipped into a pocket or she studied a label on a collar, she knew that she was invading her father's privacy.

There were not many clothes but those that there were were of good quality. Nicholas Chance had always been smart, spruce; like his daughter, he had cared about clothes. If he'd meant to stay away, she thought, he would have taken his silk waistcoat.

'You should sell that lot,' said Kit. 'That's why you're repressed, Ruby, because you hang on too much to the past.'

From a small, hidden pocket in the waistcoat she drew out a scrap of cardboard. 'I'm not repressed,' she said absently. She saw that she was holding in her hand a railway ticket to Salisbury.

Kit said triumphantly, 'Then come to bed with me,'

as, leafing through the diary, Ruby confirmed what she had been certain of already, that none of the addresses listed were in Salisbury.

Kit was fondling her knee; she pushed his hand away, saying crisply, 'Time you went, it's late.' Then she folded up the clothes and put them back into the suitcase.

Over the next few days she found herself thinking about the railway ticket. Why would her father have bought a train ticket to Salisbury? His work as a salesman had taken him only to Reading and its immediate area. *What if you find out something you might have preferred not to know?* What Theo had really meant had been, what if she discovered that her father had left her mother for someone else? What if he had loved another woman?

A fortnight later, Ruby took a day off work and travelled to Salisbury. Arriving at the station and walking into the city, she found herself looking at the passers-by, just as she always did, searching through the crowds for *his* face.

It was market day and she bought an apple from a stall and ate it as she headed for the public library. If her father had had a mistress — if he had deserted her mother for another woman — then his mistress might have taken his name for appearance's sake, so they would be living under the name of Chance. Chance was an uncommon name; studying the telephone directory in the library, Ruby discovered there were only two Chances listed in the book, a Harry Chance, Esq., and a Mrs C. Chance. There was no Nicholas Chance — she felt a dull disappointment, an emotion that had become only too familiar to her during her search for her father.

After consulting a map and discovering that Harry Chance lived in a village to the north of the city, she decided to walk to the nearer address first. Mrs Chance lived in Moberly Road. As Ruby headed up Castle Street, a broad thoroughfare that led uphill, away from the city centre, any lingering traces of faith in her quest dissolved. Mrs C. Chance would, like as not, be a respectable seventy-year-old widow. She might be out shopping or have gone away. And even if she were at home, what on earth would she say to her?

Moberly Road was lined with sedate red-brick villas. As she reached Mrs Chance's house, Ruby saw a woman working in the garden, kneeling on the lawn, prising out bulbs from the border with a hand fork before placing them on a sheet of newspaper. The woman wore a brown skirt and a sapphire-blue blouse, and her dark hair was tied up with a red and white silk scarf. She was in her mid-thirties, perhaps.

Catching sight of Ruby, she said, 'It's a wretched job, taking out the daffodil bulbs, but I can't bear all those straggly dead leaves. Can I help you?'

'Are you Mrs Chance?'

'Yes.' The woman stood up.

'I'm trying to find a Mr Nicholas Chance.'

Her father's name had an extraordinary effect on Mrs Chance. She became very pale and still. Then she frowned heavily. 'Well, so am I, my dear.' She gave a harsh laugh. 'And have been for rather a long time. I would say, let me know if you find him, but I think I'm past caring.'

There was a phrase Ruby had read in books, which described the heroine's hair standing on end, and which she had always found improbable and assumed to be a shorthand to describe fear or shock rather than an actual physical event. But now she was aware of an odd sensation, as if she had been dipped in ice, a cold ache across the surface of her skin.

She whispered, 'You know him?'

'Of course I know — knew — Nicky.' A downward twist to the corners of her mouth. 'Or I thought I did.'

Nicky, thought Ruby. No one had ever called her father Nicky.

'Who are you?' Mrs Chance, too, looked shocked. 'Why have you come here?'

'My father's a friend of Mr Chance,' said Ruby, inventing wildly. 'He knew him in the war. He wanted to get in touch. I thought . . . '

Her imagination failed her and she fell silent. Mrs Chance said nothing but fetched a packet of cigarettes and a lighter from the porch. Lighting a cigarette, she said, 'You're telling me that your father knows Nicky? And that after all these years, he's decided to look him up?'

'Yes.'

'Why now?'

'Um — he's not well . . . '

'I'm sorry to hear that, Miss . . . ?'

A moment's pause. 'Finborough.'

Mrs Chance's frowning dark brown eyes rested on Ruby's face. 'How old are you, Miss Finborough?'

'Nineteen.'

'Where are you from?'

'London.'

'How did you find me?'

'I looked in the phone book.'

'I meant, how did you know I lived in Salisbury?'

'I found a train ticket.' Muddled, feeling sick, Ruby fell silent.

Unexpectedly, Mrs Chance gave a short laugh. 'Well, you're certainly a turn up for the books.' Then her voice altered and she said flatly, 'You're lying to me. You're his daughter, aren't you?'

Ruby couldn't speak. Something had changed in Mrs Chance's expression, hurt mingling with the anger and defiance. 'You have his eyes, you see,' Mrs Chance muttered. 'For years I've half-expected . . . I always knew there was *something* wrong . . . even then . . . '

The unfinished phrases fizzled out.

The front door of the house opened and a little girl called out, 'Mummy, where are the scissors?'

Mrs Chance said mechanically, 'In my sewing box, Anne. Make sure you put them back.' Then, dropping her cigarette end on the gravel drive and grinding it with the toe of her shoe, she said abruptly to Ruby, 'You'd better come in. I think we both need a drink.'

As they went inside the house, Mrs Chance pulled off the head-scarf and shook out her wavy dark hair. They sat in the front room, where Mrs Chance poured out two sherries. The little girl flitted in and out.

Mrs Chance explained, 'Anne's in quarantine for measles. It'll be a relief when she's back at school.'

Then she went to a drawer and took out a photograph. 'Is that him? Is that your father?'

Ruby looked down at the image. Her heart squeezed. Nicholas Chance's tall, handsome frame was a fitting foil to the young, striking woman who stood beside him, a baby in her arms.

'Yes.'

'That was taken a couple of months after Archie was born. I have — *we* have — a son, Archie, as well as Anne. Archie's at boarding school.' A swift glance at Ruby. 'Archie's thirteen and you tell me you're nineteen. Nicky and I met six months before I fell for Archie. So Nicky must have known your mother before he knew me.'

'My parents were married in 1913.'

'Married . . . ' Mrs Chance sat down. 'Nicky was *married* . . . ' Her eyes, a little wild, met Ruby's. 'Your mother — when did she pass away?'

Ruby stared at her. 'My mother's still alive.'

'Then they were divorced, surely?'

Ruby shook her head. 'No.'

'Oh, dear God.' Mrs Chance closed her eyes.

Anne skipped in, saying, 'I'm hungry, Mummy,' and

Mrs Chance took a deep breath and, steadying herself, turned to her daughter.

'Have a biscuit, darling.'

'Can I have two?'

'Yes, yes, as many as you like.'

When they were alone again, Mrs Chance took a large gulp of sherry.

Ruby said, 'Didn't Dad tell you about my mother?'

'No. No, of course not.' Mrs Chance's haunted gaze came to her again. 'I would hardly have married him if I'd known he was married already, would I?'

It was Ruby's turn to freeze, to clutch the sherry glass as though it might keep her upright. 'Dad *married* you . . . ?'

'Yes.' A crack of unamused laughter. 'That's the thing. Looks like he made a habit of it, doesn't it? The bastard, the rotten, lying bastard.' Claire Chance fumbled for her cigarettes once more, this time offering them to Ruby. 'Have another drink, honey.' More sherry was sloshed into the glasses.

Ruby whispered, 'But he's not here?'

'No. Haven't seen hide nor hair of him for years.'

'How many years, Mrs Chance?'

'Claire. Call me Claire. Good God — if we weren't *married* — I suppose I'm not really Claire Chance, am I? I'm still Claire Wyndham. All these years, I haven't even known my own name. Or — oh God — my children's.' The words were dazed, acid, bitter. 'But *you're* a Chance, aren't you? Not whatever other name it was you came up with.'

'My name's Ruby Chance.'

Claire Chance nodded and drew on the cigarette. 'Such a shock.' The hand that held the cigarette was trembling. 'Shouldn't be, though.' She said once more, 'I always thought that *something* was wrong. Even when we were together. He would never tell me much about his past. When you're in love with someone you want to

175

know everything about them, don't you? But Nicky was always *vague*. Well, now I know why, don't I?' She stared at Ruby with sudden suspicion. 'Does your mother know you're here? Did she send you?'

'No, I didn't tell her I was looking for Dad. She hasn't been well.'

'Have you been searching for him long, Ruby?'

'Years,' she said. Her voice sounded hollow.

'And you had no idea about us? You didn't realise that Nicky — No, of course not, how could you?' Claire Chance pressed her fist against her mouth. 'This is as much of a shock for you as it is for me, I suppose. You poor little thing.'

There was a silence, which Ruby broke by asking, 'You said you'd always thought something was wrong. What did you mean?'

A dismissive gesture. 'I won't pretend this isn't all terribly difficult but I suppose I had an inkling ages ago, before Nicky left me. All those weekends away, all those times he told me he had to travel round the country on business, and he was only a glorified salesman, you know. And he never had two pennies to rub together. I don't mind admitting that I thought he was quite nicely set up when I met him — he had that air, a gentlemanly way of doing things, and he was always generous. But after we married, we were constantly scrimping and saving.' She added sourly, 'I've scrimped and saved ever since he went away so perhaps it's just as well I got used to it back then. Bringing up two children on your own is bloody difficult. My parents help with the house and the school fees, thank heavens, though God knows I pay a price for that in condescending looks and I told-you-so's.'

She sat back in the chair, smoking. Claire Chance had the sort of face, Ruby thought, that could look plain, almost ugly, when she was cross or discontented, but in repose looked vivid and beautiful.

Claire went on, 'But when I found myself expecting Archie I couldn't be too choosy, could I? Not that I was reluctant to marry Nicky. Actually, I adored him. That's the awful thing, I truly adored him.' She looked deeply upset. 'He's the only man I've ever really loved. And he loved me, I know he did.' She glared at Ruby, then looked away. 'Maybe that's why I never pressed him too far. Maybe I didn't want to know. I was a coward, I suppose. I didn't want my dream to fall to pieces.'

'When did my father leave you?'

'Anne was two.' Claire frowned. 'That would make it '27. Yes, that's right, the autumn of 1927. I remember it was autumn because I had to rake up all the bloody leaves myself.' The dark gaze returned to Ruby. 'And you?'

'We saw him last at much the same time.'

A short exhalation of breath. 'Looks like he couldn't take it any more, doesn't it? Two wives, two families . . . Must have been bloody exhausting for the poor old soul, if you think about it.' Claire looked furious. 'Unless he had a third family hidden away somewhere and he scarpered to them. I wouldn't put it past him.'

'Where did you meet him?'

'In London, in the bar of a hotel in Charing Cross. I was waiting for a friend. My friend didn't turn up — Nicky offered to buy me a drink and we got talking and . . .'

Her voice went on, creating a picture of snatched meetings in station bars and evenings dancing in smoky nightclubs, a courtship that still, after distance and desertion, made Claire Chance's eyes light up at the memory. Her words painted an image of a dashing, carefree man, whom Ruby had glimpsed only rarely.

Eventually, Claire said, 'Would you like some lunch? There's enough to spare and you could meet Anne properly. After all, I suppose you're half-sisters.'

'No, thank you, I have to get back.'

A few more stilted exchanges of conversation, and then they parted, murmuring conventional phrases that failed to cover the appalling sense of betrayal that both of them, Ruby guessed, felt. In the train, heading back to London, she realised that she had eaten nothing that day but the apple she had bought earlier in the market, so she went to the buffet car. A steward brought her tea and a piece of fruit cake, and she cut up the slice of cake with great precision into eight little squares and tore each square apart with her fingers into a heap of crumbs and currants. *It's always better to know, isn't it?* she had said to Theo. But she had been wrong, so utterly wrong.

She found herself thinking about the nature of betrayal. Could anything hurt more than discovering that you had been duped, your trust taken for granted and misused? Yet she, too, carried out a betrayal. What would Isabel Finborough, who had taken her in when she had been destitute and who had treated her with nothing other than kindness and affection, what would she say if she were to find out that Sara was in love with an Austrian student called Anton Wolff, and that she, Ruby, passed letters between them and kept secret their meetings?

One question ran through her head, taunting her, as the train rattled on towards London, its backdrop the green blur of the countryside beyond the carriage window. Which of his two families had Nicholas Chance loved most?

★ ★ ★

Isabel's house in Cornwall was a mile from the nearest hamlet, reached by a narrow lane whose verges each summer frothed with cream-coloured umbels of Queen Anne's Lace. From Porthglas Cottage the land fell, first in a grassy incline and then through rocks and boulders

178

to the sands. The first thing Isabel always did when she came to Porthglas, after she had left her luggage at the house, was to walk out of the garden, down the cliff path to the rocks and the beach contained between the jutting cliffs. She needed to greet the sea, to whisper her hello to it.

When he had first bought Porthglas Cottage for her, Richard had wanted her to engage a housekeeper, someone who would live in the house and take care of it while the Finboroughs were absent. Isabel had refused. She would have hated never to be on her own. Richard might have been able to forget the presence of a servant, but she, who had been in service herself, could not. This was the first house, the only house, that she had ever thought of as truly belonging to her.

A woman from the village, Mrs Spry, came in three times a week to clean. It was Mr Spry who wrote to her about the problem with the roof. A gale had dislodged some slates, and rainwater was coming through into the single-storeyed part of the house. Mrs Spry had placed buckets to catch the drips and Mrs Spry had done his best to replace the slates, but would Mrs Finborough like anything further done? Richard was away on business so Isabel had seized at the excuse and caught the train to St Ives. On the train, she watched out of the window as the houses and factories of London and Reading gave way to water meadows and villages of golden stone. Reaching Devon, the train ran for several miles by the sea. It was not the same as Isabel's sea, grey and jagged rather than blue and pearly, but nevertheless, her heart lifted.

Reaching St Ives, she hired a taxi to take her on the final part of her journey. At the house, she quickly inspected the damage. Fortunately, there were stone flags in that part of the house. There was still one tin pail in the centre of the room; drops of rain from the morning's shower fell into it with an intermittent ping.

Isabel decided to ask the Sprys if they knew of a suitable tradesman to carry out the repairs.

She changed her shoes for gumboots and walked down to the cove. The sky was clearing, and as the sun came through, the sea gleamed, pale blue and opalescent. Waves frilled with a lace of foam licked the toes of her boots. Always, when she came to Porthglas, she felt both relief and release.

Porthglas was her refuge. It had enabled her to survive living in a city that, at heart, she disliked. It had, she suspected, helped her cope with a marriage that had often been turbulent and had sometimes been difficult. She had come to Porthglas exhausted after the children had had measles, or angry after a quarrel with Richard, and it had always healed. She enjoyed the house's isolation — even in the summer, she might be the only person on the beach and she could walk for miles along the cliff path without seeing another soul. There was no telephone and they had no neighbours. You communicated by letter or not at all. If she felt the need for company then she walked to the village and talked to the woman who owned the shop, or the vicar's wife, who was a pleasant, quietly spoken person. Or she invited her friends from Hampstead, the artists and writers and musicians whom she had always found so much more to her taste than Richard's society and business acquaintances, and they sprawled round the house, sketching the sea from an upstairs window, or confecting delicious but messy dishes in the kitchen.

Why did she feel the need to escape? Perhaps, she thought, it was because she had spent a lifetime looking after other people. She didn't begrudge a moment of it, but sometimes, now, she felt the need to stand back and take a breath.

The weather was pleasant, long days of sunshine and light breezes. The roof was repaired and Isabel worked on the garden, digging trenches and planting long, low hedges of lavender and rosemary to protect the more tender plants from the wind. On Mrs Spry's mornings, they took down and washed all the curtains, hanging them out on the line where they ballooned and billowed in a satisfactory manner before being dry enough to be taken into the house and ironed and rehung. In the afternoons, Isabel took a drawing pad and her watercolours and sat on the cliff or the beach and sketched. She liked the changeable view — however many times she drew it, it never looked the same twice.

She had been at Porthglas Cottage for a week when a letter arrived from Daphne Mountjoy. Sara was staying with the Mountjoys while Isabel was in Cornwall — Ione Mountjoy, Daphne's daughter, was an old schoolfriend of Sara's. Mrs Mountjoy wrote,

> I'm sorry to have to tell you something rather troubling. Sara said she had a headache so she did not come with us to the Everetts' picnic. But Dorothy Bryant has told me that when she was walking with her grandchildren in Green Park she saw Sara. Dorothy insists that Sara was with a man. I spoke to Sara, of course, and she told me that though she went for a walk in the afternoon she didn't meet anyone. I wouldn't worry you but Dorothy was most insistent and I would hate to think that Sara was in any sort of trouble.

Reading the letter, Isabel was at first sure that Dorothy Bryant must be mistaken. Why should Sara be in Green Park with a man? Unless it had been Philip, perhaps, or Theo, returned unexpectedly from the continent. But in that case surely Sara would have told Mrs Mountjoy she had been with one of her brothers.

Isabel recalled Broadstairs beach and a man walking out of the sea towards her — her desire, her foolishness, her ignorance. That afternoon, she packed her suitcase and telephoned from the village shop for a taxi early the next morning. The following day, she caught the train back to London. Arriving in Hampstead in the late afternoon, she telephoned Daphne Mountjoy and was told that Sara was visiting Ruby.

It was Dunning's day off so Isabel took a taxi. Crossing London, the heat that had been so pleasant in Cornwall was oppressive and she had the beginnings of a headache. She wondered if the weather was going to break — thunderclouds, grey and massive, were building on the horizon. She wondered when Richard would come home; he was always poor at keeping in touch when he was away on the Continent. Philip would know, perhaps, or she could telephone Richard's secretary, though there was something demeaning about having to approach another woman to discover her husband's whereabouts.

Then the taxi turned into the Fulham Road and she saw them: Sara and the fair-haired man, the man she had assumed to be Ruby's boyfriend. This time, Ruby was nowhere in sight, and that man's arm was around her daughter's waist, and Sara was looking up at him and smiling.

★ ★ ★

Sara said, 'Mummy . . . ' And then, feeling frightened as well as shocked, 'Mummy, I'm sorry.'

'Frau Finborough — ' Anton began.

'No, I do not wish to speak to you.' Isabel cut through his words. 'You are to have nothing more to do with my daughter. You are to leave her alone. You are never to try to see her again. Do you understand?'

Sara found herself bundled into the taxi. Her mother gave the Hampstead address to the driver in the same clipped, angry tones. Sara caught a fleeting glimpse of Anton's face as they sped away.

182

Isabel lowered her voice so that the cab driver could not hear. 'Mrs Mountjoy wrote to tell me that Mrs Bryant had seen you with a man in Green Park. Were you, Sara? Were you with that man?'

Sara whispered, 'Yes, Mummy.'

After the first crack of thunder, rain fell in thick grey rails. Girls' crisp summer dresses wilted in the downpour and men held on to the brims of their hats as they ran. Isabel and Sara looked away from each other and did not speak for the remainder of the journey.

At home, after the maid had left the room, Sara said, 'I'm sorry about all the fibs, Mummy, I'm so sorry.'

'This man — '

'Anton. He's called Anton Wolff.'

'How long have you known him?'

'Since the end of last summer.'

'*Last summer.*' Her mother's hand, which had reached out to the teapot, froze. 'Who introduced you to him?' A frown as Isabel answered her own question. '*Ruby*, I suppose.'

'I met him at Ruby's house, that's all.'

'Who else knows about him? Does Ione?'

'No, Mummy, of course not.'

'Susan Everett? The Mitchells?' Isabel named several more of Sara's friends.

'No, none of them.'

'Thank God.' Isabel closed her eyes. 'I'll tell Daphne that Dorothy was mistaken. And then, I hope, no harm will come of it. Sara, how could you do this? How could you?'

The hurt in her mother's eyes was worse than anything. Sara said, 'I'm sorry, I know it was wrong of me but I was afraid you wouldn't let me see him. Mummy, I *love* Anton!'

'Don't be ridiculous, Sara.'

Sara flinched. 'It's true. I'm not being ridiculous. I

love him. I'm sorry I lied to you, Mummy, but I had to see him.'

'A girl's reputation is so important to her.' Isabel's voice trembled and she looked distraught. 'If you lose your reputation, you rarely get the chance to regain it. People don't give you a second chance — they *remember*.' Her gaze flicked, checking the closed door. 'Tell me that this affair hasn't gone too far, Sara. Tell me nothing wrong has happened.'

Sara flushed. 'Of course not, Mummy.'

The questions, clipped and targeted, fired like bullets. 'Where did you meet him? At Ruby's house?'

'Yes, Mummy.'

'Where does he live?'

'In Whitechapel, in Scarborough Street.'

'Sara, have you been to his house?'

Sara looked down at her hands. She could feel everything unravelling: her mother was interpreting all that she said in the worst possible way.

Isabel said sharply, 'Tell me, Sara.'

Meeting her mother's eye, Sara said defiantly, 'Only once.'

'Dear God . . . ' Isabel's hand went to her mouth. 'Was anyone else there?'

'No, Mummy.'

'But you were alone with this man. Did he make you go to bed with him?'

'*No*, Mummy!' cried Sara angrily. 'I only went there because he stopped coming to Ruby's — *he* was trying to break it off but I wouldn't let him — and he wouldn't *make* me do anything! That's an awful thing to say!'

'Are you telling me the truth, Sara?' Her mother, white-faced, was looking at her keenly.

'Of course I am!'

'There's no *of course* about it, is there? You seem to have lied to me pretty comprehensively for some considerable time!'

Sara gasped. In the silence, she heard the rumble of the thunder and the sounds of the house — the tick of the clock, and a distant clattering from the kitchen — the familiar sounds grated on her over-stretched nerves.

Her mother said, her voice low, 'I'm sorry, darling, I shouldn't have said that. Forgive me.'

'I only went to Anton's house once, and I've never been there again. He didn't want me to go there and we didn't do anything wrong.' Yet she knew that, in her mother's eyes, that was untrue, and that she and Anton had gone far beyond what her mother would consider to be an acceptable limit.

She pleaded, 'You'd like him if you knew him, Mummy.'

'I very much doubt that.' Her mother's lips pressed tightly together.

'You would, I know you would!' Sara felt as though she was pushing against a solid barrier, a barrier that she must scale because her happiness depended on it. 'He's the most wonderful person — he had such an awful time in Vienna — he had to leave his home and come here — his family lost all their money — Anton and his father were even sent to prison!'

'*Prison*,' said Isabel, with a look of distaste. 'Hardly a recommendation. Darling, it doesn't sound to me as though you know the first thing about him. You've never met his family and you've never seen his home. You've only his word for everything he's told you.'

'Anton wouldn't lie to me.'

'There's no way you can know that.'

'Why should he lie? I trust him. I *know* him.'

'You *think* you know him, Sara,' said Isabel briskly. 'Men can be very clever and convincing, I'm afraid. They can make a girl see only what they want her to see. And sometimes they lie to get what they want. I know you think I'm being harsh, and I'm sure this man

— Anton — is very persuasive, and I don't doubt he seems very charming. But tell me, if he were an honourable man, would he have carried out this clandestine courtship?'

'Mummy — please — don't . . . ' Sara was weeping now.

'Darling, try not to get so upset. You'll meet someone else, someone who's right for you, I promise you you will.'

'I won't — I know I won't . . . '

Her mother was pouring out the tea. Sara's gaze fixed on the familiar rituals: the tea-strainer held over the cups to catch the leaves, the swirl of milk, the stirring of sugar.

Her mother put a cup of tea on the table beside her. She stroked Sara's hair. 'Listen to me, please, darling. Daddy and I only want the best for you. All we've ever wanted is for you to be happy.'

She cried despairingly, 'Anton will make me happy!'

'Will he?' Her mother looked sad. 'I doubt it, Sara.'

★　★　★

Since the Great War, parties of both the extreme right and the extreme left had struggled for power — and now and then seized it — in France, Germany, Italy and Spain. Germany's renewed militarism, coupled with a fascist government, just now gave cause for gave concern. Although those in Britain who clamoured for peace at any price, reminding their countrymen of the horrors of the Great War — horrors that still visited Richard in his dreams — were insistent that everyone see reason, it seemed to Richard that these days *reason* was in short supply. People were driven by a desire for security, and security had to be backed by power. A rush for power at the expense of reason gave free rein to all the demagogues, sadists and tyrants who wouldn't balk at using violence to satisfy their own ends.

Richard had thought for a long time now that there would be another war. There was too much unfinished business from the last one, too much resentment, hatred and obsession bubbling away. The realisation depressed him. These days, he was always relieved to return home after a business trip to Europe.

This homecoming was troubled, though. Isabel looked tense and Sara's eyes were red-rimmed. He hugged her, asking what was wrong, but she just said, 'Daddy, I'm so glad you're home.'

As Isabel went to check on the dinner, Philip, dressed to go out, sauntered past them and said, 'She's fallen in love with some perfectly unsuitable man, that's all,' and Sara cried, 'Shut up, Philip, you beast,' and ran upstairs.

Doors slammed. From outside, there was the low growl of the motor-cycle engine as Philip drove away. Isabel drew Richard into the drawing room and told him that Sara had, with Ruby's connivance, been secretly meeting a penniless foreign student called Anton Wolff, and that Wolff had turned up at the house the previous day, begging to be allowed to speak to her or to Sara, and Isabel had had to threaten to telephone the police to make him go away.

Then she said, 'It's my fault. I should ~~have~~ of kept a better eye on her. I blame myself.'

Richard asked questions. How could this have happened? How could Sara ~~have~~ of fallen under the influence of such a man? How old was Wolff? Where did he live? What nationality was he? What was his background and what was he doing in London?

After hearing Isabel's answers, Richard roared for Sara, who confirmed all Isabel had told him but seemed, to his fury, unrepentant.

Towards midnight, he was standing at the open window of their bedroom, smoking a cigar, and Isabel was seated at her dressing table, when she said suddenly: 'We are right, aren't we, Richard? We must keep this man away from Sara, mustn't we?'

'Of course we must. How can you ask?'

Isabel took out her earrings. 'It's just that if you had had to ask anyone's permission to marry me then you would ~~have~~ of been told that I was utterly unsuitable.'

Richard flicked ash over the balcony. He felt nothing but contempt for this man who had tried to take advantage of his daughter's innocence, this man who threatened his daughter.

'A man may marry a penniless woman,' he said tersely 'but only a scoundrel chases a girl wealthier than himself. The fellow's a fortune-hunter.'

'She seems so set on the wretched man. It's making her so unhappy.'

'Send her to Ireland,' said Richard crisply. 'That's what you should do, Isabel. Get her out of harm's way. She'll soon forget about him.'

★　★　★

Ruby was washing out her stockings when there was a knock at the door. Opening it, she saw Richard Finborough.

He came into the room. Then, in a few well-chosen phrases, he told her what he thought of her. That in helping Sara see Anton Wolff, she had betrayed the family who had taken her in when she was homeless and abandoned. That she had deceived those who had fed her and clothed her and schooled her. That she seemed to believe she owed nothing to him, Richard Finborough, who continued to pay her mother's rent and medical bills.

Ruby thought she might actually be sick. When he had finished, Richard said coldly, 'You are no longer welcome at our house. You are not to contact Sara. You are not to write to her. Do you understand?'

She thought of refusing, knew it would be pointless, and promised. The door closed behind Richard Finborough; she heard his footsteps on the stairs. The heap of stockings still bobbed in the washing-up bowl, a many-limbed octopus, and Ruby, who was shaking, sat down on the bed and cried.

★ ★ ★

After work the next day, Richard drove to Scarborough Street. A slatternly woman opened the door to him and directed him up several flights of stairs to the room that Anton Wolff rented. The heat of summer seemed to have concentrated inside the narrow, airless building. Flies battered themselves against dusty windowpanes, seeking escape. What Richard felt most of all, looking around him, was a sense of outrage that this man should have enticed his daughter to such a place.

Anton Wolff answered his knock. Richard introduced himself. Wolff invited him to come in and sit down.

'I prefer to stand,' said Richard.

As he glanced round the cramped, shabby room his revulsion increased. Just then, he hated everything about Anton Wolff, from his threadbare clothing to his accent, which brought back to Richard so many bad memories — the war, and the blaring wireless broadcasts of Hitler's speeches that he had heard in cafés during his recent business trip to Germany.

Wolff said, 'How is Miss Finborough?'

'My daughter's health is no concern of yours. I came here to ask you something.' Richard took out his wallet. 'How much do you want?'

Anton Wolff's pale face flushed. 'I don't want your money, Mr Finborough.'

'I'm prepared to go up to two hundred. On condition that you leave the country immediately.'

Wolff flinched, but said steadily, 'I told you, I don't

want your money. I love Sara. I want to marry her.'

'Do you, Mr Wolff? That won't be possible, of course.'

'Not now, perhaps, but later, when I'm in a position to marry. I want the same as you — I want what is good for Sara.'

'You are not good for Sara.' Richard put his wallet back in his pocket. 'Very well. You say you don't want money, but, tell me, do you wish to stay in this country?'

A flock of pigeons landed on the roof outside the open window. Wolff's eyes were wary. 'Yes, I would like to stay here.'

'You like England?'

'Very much. This country has given me a place of refuge.'

'You come from Austria? And you are a communist?'

'No, I'm a socialist.'

'I've never seen a great deal of difference, but then I'm not a politician. But both will be unacceptable if Austria were to fall to a Nazi government.'

'I trust and hope that will never happen.'

'Hope is not the same as belief, Mr Wolff. Have you family living in Austria?'

A startled frown. 'Yes. My father lives in Vienna.'

'Do you help him? Do you send him money, perhaps?'

Anton's fists clenched. 'Money — always money! I do not want your money, you must believe that! Not for my father, not for myself — not at all!'

'Suppose I take your word for that. I simply ask, do you help support your father?'

Anton gave an angry sigh. 'Yes, I do. I can do little enough, but, yes.'

'And how would your father manage if you were forced to leave this country? If your source of income were to be cut off?'

A pause, then Anton Wolff said, 'He would suffer. But I don't see — '

'If you insist on continuing to trouble my daughter I will make sure you are deported.' Wolff began to speak but Richard silenced him. 'I can do it, have no doubt about that. I know who to speak to, I know the arguments to make. You will be deported as an undesirable alien and you will find it impossible ever to return to England. How will you look after your father then?'

'I understand that you hate me, Mr Finborough,' said Anton Wolff steadily. 'Perhaps, in your place, I would hate also.'

'Do you swear to leave my daughter alone?'

Wolff's head lowered. 'If that's what you wish. I will promise not to speak to Sara until she is old enough to make up her own mind who she'll marry.'

'No, that won't do.' Richard opened the door. 'You say you want what's good for Sara. Very well, come with me. I want to show you something.'

Anton Wolff took his jacket and followed Richard downstairs. Outside, Richard opened the passenger door of the Rolls and Anton climbed inside. Richard drove south, towards the docks. Many-storeyed warehouses loomed to the side of them; the hooting of ships, the clatter of hobnailed boots and the shouts of the foremen, giving their orders to the dockers, filled the air.

Richard parked within sight of St Katharine's Dock. They climbed out of the vehicle and walked to the edge of the wharf. The oily grey-brown water of the Thames lapped at the rotting timbers; to one side of them, the great span of Tower Bridge had been raised to allow through a tall ship.

Richard pointed to the far side of the river, to Butler's Wharf. 'See, over there, that's where the tea-chests from Ceylon and India are unloaded. And there — ' he turned upstream towards the city — 'is my factory, where we pack the tea. I bought my first business when

I was in my twenties. I own another factory in Hounslow, which is ten times the size of the first one. My son thinks I should sell the tea-packing business, but I disagree with him. One gets attached to these things.'

'I will not be poor for ever, Mr Finborough.' Anton Wolff's voice was urgent. 'I will prosper, I will work hard.'

Richard's gaze swung away from the river to settle contemptuously on the younger man's face. 'Tell me, how long have you lived in this country?'

'Fifteen, almost sixteen months.'

'And during that time, have you prospered?' Richard's voice was laced with sarcasm. 'Are you living in a fine house, Mr Wolff — are you even in employment?'

Wolff's gaze dropped, but he said defiantly, 'I assist my friend, Peter Curthoys, and I teach German lessons in the evenings.'

'I meant proper employment, *professional* employment.'

'No.' The word was an admission of defeat. 'Not with any regularity. I have tried, but no.'

'Everything I've worked for has been for my family. I will not let anything — or anyone — hurt my family.'

'I do not wish to hurt your family, Mr Finborough,' said Wolff quietly. 'I do not wish to hurt Sara. That's the last thing I want.'

'Then you must put an end to this intrigue, do you understand?'

'I believe that Sara loves me — '

Richard interrupted, 'Sara is twenty years old. She is little more than a child. We — my wife and I — have protected her from the harsh realities of the world. If Sara has been kind to you, Mr Wolff, then that's because she has a kind nature.'

'Not kindness,' said Anton Wolff. Richard read the pain — and the beginnings of doubt, perhaps — in his voice. 'I believe she feels something deeper than that.'

'No. You're mistaken. I've seen Sara weep over a lame horse and a sick puppy. I've seen her empty her purse for a flower-seller in the street. She has a soft heart. She's very young and has romantic ideas. She felt sorry for you, Wolff, that's all, nothing more.'

In the silence, Richard heard the cry of a gull and the hoot of a steamer, heading upriver. He sensed that his words had struck a chord; capitalising on his success, he went on, 'Would you divide her from her family? If you know Sara as well as you claim to do, then you must know that she loves her family. I believe that if you were to persuade her to go against our wishes then you would break her heart.'

Wolff said desperately, 'Our marriage does not have to divide Sara from her family.'

'But it would, you see, it would. If Sara were to marry you then I would have nothing more to do with her.'

'You would do that?'

'Yes,' said Richard coldly. 'So understand this. If you were to marry Sara you would be penniless. Sara takes for granted a degree of comfort — luxury, even. She has never known anything else. Tell me, how do you imagine that you and she would live? *Where* would you live? In that slum you currently inhabit? Or would you take her to Austria?'

'Not now, but perhaps, in the future . . .'

'Ah yes, the future. That's the thing. I don't see a settled future for Europe. We've had two decades of bloody war and revolution and I don't see a glimmer of things getting better. Do you, Mr Wolff?'

'No.' The syllable was curt, angry.

'In fact, I'm afraid that things will become very much worse. So why would you wish to expose my daughter, who you claim to love, to *that*?'

'If there is a war, I doubt if England will be able to stand aside.'

'Our present political masters may not agree with you

but, yes, you may be right. But wealth and status can always buy a certain amount of protection. I can offer those to Sara — you cannot.'

A silence, then Anton Wolff said desperately, 'Love — I can offer her love.'

'I think we're both old enough to know that you can't live on love.' Richard's tone was contemptuous.

Digging his hands in his jacket pockets, Anton Wolff walked away, to the edge of the wharf, and stared down to the river. Richard went back to the car and waited.

It must have been fully ten minutes before Wolff returned to him. 'I will do as you ask, Mr Finborough,' he said. 'I promise you I will not try to see Sara again.' His expression was grim.

'Thank you.' Richard felt a rush of triumph. He held open the passenger door of the car.

Anton Wolff shook his head. 'I'd prefer to walk.'

'As you wish.' Richard started up the engine. Then he frowned. 'Oh,' he said. 'There's one thing more I'd like you to do. I'd like you to write to Sara, telling her that you don't wish to see her any more. Telling her, I think, that your intentions were never serious, and that you are in no position to court any woman, and that, though you wish her well, you consider the relationship to be at an end. There will be no need for you to mention this conversation, naturally.'

Anton Wolff paled. 'I can't do that, Mr Finborough.'

'You can. You must. You need to end this now, and cleanly. You mustn't leave Sara waiting and hoping. That would be intolerable for her. You do see that, don't you?' When there was no immediate reply, Richard said, 'There is not the slightest chance of you ever marrying my daughter. Why ruin Sara's prospects and your own for nothing?'

Richard waited. Eventually he heard Wolff say, 'Very well, Mr Finborough. I will do as you ask.'

7

Sara understood why Alice Finborough rarely left Ireland: her grandmother suited both the house and the wild landscape that surrounded it so completely that she would ~~have~~ been out of place anywhere else. Sara herself had always loved the large, sprawling house and the parkland that surrounded it, just as she loved the lawlessness of the Irish, their disdain for rules and regulations, and their easy and artful conversation. In Ireland, Sara felt free. The proprieties were not observed as strictly as they were in London; social gatherings were less formal and she was allowed to ride and walk in the countryside on her own.

Half a dozen horses were housed in Raheen's stables; years ago, when Sara had been little, her grandmother had taught her to ride. She had taught Philip and Theo to ride as well, but their attention had drifted to motor cycles and sailing boats. Only Sara's passion for horses had remained undimmed. Throughout that late summer and autumn, when she seemed to feel so oddly disjointed from everything that was familiar, she rode for miles along Raheen's paths and bridleways and over the wide, sandy sweep of Dundrum Bay.

It had been the arrival of Anton's letter that had finally made her leave London for Ireland. The shock and hurt she had felt, reading the letter, had not lessened but instead had become a part of her. Though she had burned it, she could not erase its contents from her heart. ' . . . I will always value our friendship . . . if our paths fail to cross in the future, I wish you every happiness in your future life.' She had searched the polite, frozen phrases for any evidence of love and had found none. Over the weeks that had followed, her

initial conviction that some sort of mistake must have
been made, had slowly ebbed away. The only mistake
had been her own, in misreading their situation. If he
had loved her, then he would have waited for her. *She*
would have waited for *him*. She would have waited for
years; she would have crossed oceans.

Any small difficulties she had encountered in the past
— an unpleasant classmate at school, perhaps, or a visit
to the dentist — she had overcome by refusing to think
about it. *Let's not talk about that, let's talk about
something else.* But this loss, this pain, was too deep,
too overwhelming, to be pushed to the back of her
mind. Hunting on frosty autumn mornings or lunching
with neighbours whose land bordered on Raheen's, the
same questions drummed inside her head. Why doesn't
he love me any more? Did he never love me? Whenever
she woke at night, the shock of remembering what had
happened felt new and raw. Any brief moment of
distraction only meant that she had to endure the pain
of recollection all over again.

She made herself look back at their meetings and
their conversations. When she studied them dispassionately, they seemed so fleeting — so *trivial*, you might
almost say. Half an hour in a café, a walk in a park. A
kiss, as a barge slid below Putney Bridge. Adding the
hours up, she worked out that she and Anton had spent
barely a day alone together. Could you truly know
someone in so short a time? She had not known him,
she began to think as the months went on, she had not
really known him at all. At best, she had translated
courtesy and liking into love. At worst, she had made a
fool of herself, had thrown herself at a man who had
been attracted to her and had flirted with her, but
whose feelings had not matched her own.

Or perhaps her father had been right and Anton had
been interested not in her, but her money. *No.* No, she
could not believe that.

These thoughts came to her at night, when she seemed to shrink inside herself, to feel more alone than she had ever felt before. The youngest of three children, she was not used to being alone. She was used to company, to being liked, to being loved. She was unable to see what to do, where to go; she felt directionless, all at sea.

Too much had changed too quickly. She no longer saw her parents in the same light. She had always been close to her mother, yet her mother had failed to understand how important Anton was to her. Her father's protectiveness had become a barrier, dividing her from the one person she longed for. She dreaded returning to the existence she had had before she had met Anton. The conventions of her class and the restrictions imposed on her sex, which she had for a long time accepted almost unquestioningly, now seemed unreasonable and outmoded. Loving Anton had changed her, and now something inside her raged against the dependence and childishness imposed on her.

She put on a brave face. Once her initial shock had subsided, she fended off her grandmother's questions and concern by seeming superficially to return to her usual self. She rode, she helped in the house, she went to suppers and dinners with Alice Finborough's eccentric friends. She made sure no one would guess that inside she was crumbling. Her weeks in Ireland extended to months, and by the coming of winter Sara was still at Raheen.

★ ★ ★

For more than twenty years Freddie McCrory, Richard's old schoolfriend, had been his stockbroker. In the decades of their acquaintance Freddie's appearance had altered. He had lost an arm at the Somme, and wore one sleeve of his expensively tailored suit pinned back. His sandy hair had retreated until it clung in a narrow grey band to the back of his head, his features had become fleshier and his girth had expanded. But there was still every now and then that light in his eye, that flash of enthusiasm that Richard recalled from years ago.

He saw it again one lunchtime, as they sat in Richard's club in St James's. 'Heard an interesting rumour the other day.' Freddie had lowered his voice. 'Provosts are in difficulties.'

'The machine works? They should be a solid enough concern.'

'They haven't ridden out the slump too well — too many debts, and old man Provost has clung on to the reins for far too long.' Freddie swirled the Scotch in his glass. 'Think about it, Finborough. There'll be plenty of demand for machine parts if there's another war.'

'How's the share price?'

'Going down for some time now. I should imagine the shareholders are getting a bit niggly. I'll nose around, if you like, see what's on offer.'

After they left the hotel, Freddie suggested they share a taxi back to their respective offices, but Richard declined, claiming a business appointment. Parting from Freddie, Richard headed towards Piccadilly. He was glad to be outdoors after the smoky atmosphere of the bar, and as he walked he was aware of a sense of excitement. He had been thinking for some time of expanding his empire and had been looking for a new opportunity, a new challenge. Machine parts would be a profitable area to get into — as Freddie had pointed out, if there was another war there would be huge demand for engine casings and piston rods. Or even, mused Richard, if sufficient people *believed* there would be another war ... And Provosts was vulnerable. Though Cecil Provost would cling on to the family firm for dear life, if doubts could be spread about its viability then the shareholders might be tempted to sell.

It began to rain as he walked along Jermyn Street; Richard put up his umbrella. It had been raining the last time he had been in Piccadilly, only a few days before. Then, the rain had thickened to a downpour and Richard had taken shelter in a shop doorway as, all round him, people had run for cover while a torrent rushed through the gutters.

The doorway in which he had taken sanctuary had led into a milliner's shop. The name of the shop, Elaine's, had been inscribed in black and silver on the glass door. To one side of Richard had been the solid brown marbled walls of an office block; to the other, through the shop window, he had seen hats, perched on stands of varying heights, so that they appeared through the rain-smeared glass to bob in a transparent sea. A woman's face had swum into view, behind the hats. Pale grey eyes had met Richard's, held his gaze for a second or two, then she had moved away. Shaking out his umbrella, Richard had opened the door and had gone into the shop.

She — Richard had presumed she was Elaine — had remarked on the dreadfulness of the weather. He had asked her forgiveness for making use of her doorway and she had smiled and offered him shelter until the rain stopped. She was in her late twenties, thirty perhaps. Her face was beautiful and arresting, and her platinum-blonde hair swept in a smooth sculptured wave to her shoulders. She was wearing a black dress with cream-coloured collar; simple pearl earrings and a wedding ring were her only jewellery. They had exchanged a few words; Richard had left shortly afterwards.

But over the ensuing days, he had found himself thinking about her. Thus his return to the shop.

Hearing the bell jangle as he opened the door, she

looked up and smiled.

'Caught in the rain again?'

'I thought I might buy a hat for my wife.'

'Certainly, sir. Had you anything particular in mind?'

'I'm afraid not. Perhaps you could advise me.'

'I'd be delighted to. Is your wife dark or fair?'

'Dark.'

'Tall or petite?'

'Tall — about your height, I'd say.'

'Then she could carry off a picture hat. Like this.' She took a wide-brimmed pink hat from one of the stands. 'Shall I put it on?'

'Please,' murmured Richard.

Turning to look in a mirror, she arranged the hat. The wide brim cast a shadow, darkening her unusual eyes.

'Charming, quite charming,' said Richard. 'But I don't think Isabel wears pink.'

'Navy blue, then. You can't go wrong with navy blue.'

She tried on a second hat. The same performance — her back turned to look in the mirror, the adjustment and primping, then the revelation: the smile and a downward glance as she presented herself for judgement. He wondered whether she was flirting with him.

Half a dozen hats were tried on; eventually he settled on the navy-blue hat. Richard counted out guineas while his purchase was wrapped and boxed and a receipt written out in his name.

'If your wife isn't happy with the colour or the fit, Mr Finborough,' she said, as she handed him the hatbox, 'then you must bring it back and I'll exchange it.'

Glancing out of the window, Richard saw sunshine gleaming on the rainwashed street. 'Thank you for your help, Mrs . . . ?'

'Davenport,' she told him. 'Mrs Davenport.'

★ ★ ★

Looking back, Ruby did not think there had been a single moment of revelation that she was in love with Philip Finborough, only a steady but jarring process of discovery that her childhood adoration had mutated to something that hurt as well as delighted. No one else made her feel as Philip did. His look, his touch, electrified her. He had no mannerism or turn of phrase that she did not find attractive or endearing. His presence transformed everything, from a wet autumn evening to the core of her own nature. She was a nicer person with Philip. She wanted to please him, to entertain him, to amuse him. She wanted him to pick her out of the crowd.

Yet it was hard to see why he would ever do so. Though she knew by now that you did not have to be beautiful to attract the attention of men, and that a neat figure, an air of confidence and the ability to amuse made up for a great deal, experience had taught her that there were hierarchies to everything. Philip had the background that allowed him to belong to exclusive social circles. He would always have the choice of girls who were prettier, wealthier and from better families than she. He was handsome and charming, athletic, quick and intelligent, at ease in any situation. And he had something else besides, something she had only become aware of as she had grown older: a suppressed energy, a magnetism that compelled the gaze, so that when she was with him she had to concentrate fiercely to adopt an air of insouciance, of indifference, so as not to give herself away.

One evening, Philip offered to take her out to dinner after work. They went to Wheeler's in Old Compton Street, where they ate oysters.

'At least *you* don't hate me,' said Ruby mournfully.

'Hate you?' Philip looked amused. 'Why should I hate you?'

'Because of Sara and Anton.' Ruby squeezed lemon juice on an oyster.

'Oh, *that*.' Philip grinned. 'Don't worry, I'm sure you'll soon be received back into the fold.' He poured Ruby another glass of champagne. 'Don't look so worried. No doubt sooner or later Sara will fall in love with some rich Irishman and all will be forgiven.'

Ruby remembered how Sara had seemed brighter, more alive, when she was with Anton. 'What if she doesn't meet someone in Ireland? What if she never loves anyone else?'

A flicker of distaste crossed Philip's face. 'He didn't sound our sort at all.'

'Philip, I think she really loved him.'

'Then why didn't she marry him?'

'She couldn't. You know that.'

He looked disbelieving. 'She could have if she'd really wanted to. Dad may have been furious with her but he didn't keep her under lock and key. Sara could have just walked out of the door. She didn't have to trot off to Raheen like a good girl. They could have married at Gretna Green or somewhere, and then my parents would have had little choice but to accept it. In the end, she didn't want him enough.'

There were a lot of things Ruby might have pointed out: that had Anton and Sara run away together, they would have had nothing to live on, and that daughters were brought up to be obedient in a way that sons, perhaps, were not. And besides, of all the Finboroughs, Sara was the one who tried hardest to please.

Instead, she said, 'I wonder when she'll come home.'

'She's having the most enormous sulk, isn't she?' Once more, Philip looked amused.

After Philip had seen her home, Ruby ironed a blouse and made her sandwiches for lunch the next day, and then took out pen and paper. Richard Finborough's fury had brought home to her the extent of her continuing dependence on the Finboroughs. Though she was careful with money, her civil service salary could not support her mother as well as herself, and Richard Finborough continued to pay Etta Chance's rent and bills. Ruby had begun to see how much she disliked the situation. There she was, exiled by the Finboroughs, but still dependent on them. It was humiliating.

It had been, she assured herself, a huge relief to discover that one of the Finboroughs was not cross with her. Except that being with Philip was never a relief — instead, it was exciting, agitating, nerveracking and exhilarating. She had told no one, of course, how she felt about Philip, just as she had told no one of the discoveries she had made during her visit to Salisbury. Her family had secrets — dark, dreadful ones. She would have hated Philip to know about Claire Chance. He had a proud, fastidious streak, and it made her flinch to think that the curl of his lip she had noticed when he had spoken of Anton Wolff might cross his face if he were to hear of her father's spurious second marriage.

Yet the burden of her knowledge weighed heavily on her. The discovery of Claire Chance and her children had made her see her father in a different and far more sordid light: not a hero but a bigamist, neither admirable nor trustworthy, but cheap, deceiving and shoddy. She had not her father's nature, she thought, nor his shifting allegiances. It was possible, for instance, that she could not remember when she had begun to love Philip because she had always, in her way, loved him. She had loved him since the first time she had seen him, in the hall of the Finboroughs' house, with the coloured light streaming through the windows.

She made an effort, pushed both Philip and her father out of her mind, put on her glasses and picked up her pen. The answer to her indebtedness, at least, was clear: she must earn more money. Over the past few months she had written half a dozen short stories. A few days ago she had received a letter from the fiction editor of *Woman's Weekly*, accepting one for publication. She had propped the letter on her bookcase: every now and then, she looked at it and smiled.

★　★　★

At five o'clock, Richard telephoned Freddie McCrory to discuss the progress of his acquisition of Provosts, the machine parts manufacturer. Freddie told him that he had already been able to purchase a considerable number of shares. He had bought anonymously, not yet wanting to betray his interest, and he had also, he told Richard, made discreet overtures to Bernard Provost, the younger son, overtures that had not been rejected out of hand. There were rumours that Bernard had little interest in the family firm, along with substantial debts. If he could be persuaded to part with his shares then Provosts would fall to Richard.

Both Richard's factories thrived, he had all the wealth and material goods a man could want, and yet for some time now he had felt restless and dissatisfied. There was no challenge any more, nothing to pit himself against. He had turned fifty the previous year, and at the back of his mind was the niggling fear that the best years were over, that his affairs would continue to tick over and the most he could look forward to was to hold on to what he had got.

Two things had lifted his mood, two things had restored to him his old hunger. The first was the prospect of acquiring Provosts, the second was Elaine Davenport.

At interstices in his day — driving the car or the gap between one meeting and the next — Richard found himself thinking about Mrs Davenport. He had had to return to the millinery shop. There had been a problem with the hat he had bought Isabel — it was too big, so it must be exchanged. Mrs Davenport had been serving a customer when he had arrived, so Richard had waited. He had found his gaze continually drawn in Elaine Davenport's direction. It had been hard to look at anything other than her narrow waist, which he could have spanned with his two hands, her spun-silver hair and the fineness of her skin, so translucent a bluish thread of veins was visible at her wrists. He had found himself envious of her customer, a short, stout woman — envious of Mrs Davenport's touch as she arranged the hat, her smile as they looked in the mirror.

His decision to buy Provosts was controllable and rational, his cravings for Mrs Davenport were not. Though, over the years, he had had brief flirtations with women — had, once or twice, slept with them — he could not recall feeling as he did now, could not remember this elation, this hunger. He was unsure of her feelings for him, though. She was much younger than he — and was she divorced, widowed or happily married? Was there a dull, irksome husband? Had she children? It seemed to him that, during their brief conversations, she had responded to him. There had been an undercurrent to their pleasantries. He remembered watching her trying on hat after hat, remembered her turning to him with the air of a magician casting a spell.

Richard said goodbye to his secretary and left the building. Driving out of Hounslow, he fell to planning how, once the takeover was complete, he would revive Provosts, get it up to scratch. Provosts and Finboroughs would enhance each other, and would grow together. Finboroughs' efficient distribution system would resolve some of Provosts' long-standing problems, and Provosts' expertise in machine engineering would open up new markets for him.

Reaching London, Richard headed down Holland Park Avenue instead of turning north, towards Hampstead. He parked in a side street off Park Lane and checked his watch: it was six o'clock. Typists and shopgirls were hurrying home by bus and tube; on a street corner a news-vendor called out the headlines. Anticipation coiled in the pit of his stomach as Richard walked towards Piccadilly. He knew that in going to see Mrs Davenport this time he was crossing a bridge. He thought of Isabel, had a sudden clear vision of her in her garden at Porthglas, and came to a halt on the pavement, the stream of passers-by parting as they passed him.

He loved Isabel, his wife of more than twenty-five years. He had loved her since the first day he had seen her and had loved her every day since. So what was he doing, visiting another woman? Why risk his marriage, why risk what he held most dear?

Then, looking up, he saw through the window of the shop a movement and a twist of silver-fair hair. Risking his marriage, he thought — what nonsense. How ridiculous, to exaggerate so. A smile, a few words to an attractive woman — where was the harm in that?

The 'Closed' sign was up on the glass door; peering inside, he saw Mrs Davenport's assistant, a buxom, mousy-haired girl, closing the till. Richard tapped on the door. The girl opened it and he asked for Mrs Davenport.

A curtain to a back room moved and Elaine emerged. She said, 'I'll serve this gentleman, Muriel. You can go home now. Good evening, Mr Finborough.'

Muriel put on her hat and coat and left the shop.

Mrs Davenport smiled. 'Have you come to buy another hat, Mr Finborough?' There was a hint of mockery in her smile.

Richard said, 'Not this time. I was passing and I wondered whether I might buy you a drink.'

She shook her head. 'I'm afraid that Wednesday's my day for doing the books. I used to take the accounts home with me but I find it easier to concentrate on them here. There isn't the temptation to do the housework or to listen to the wireless.'

Her refusal challenged him. 'Can't your accountant help you?' he asked. 'A dull task for a woman, accounts.'

'I have no accountant. I dispensed with his services some time ago. To tell the truth, Mr Finborough, I enjoy figures. I always have done.'

'Really? A great many people regard them as a chore.'

'Too many businesses fail because the accounts are neglected. I don't intend to fail.'

'So I can't tempt you?'

'I'm afraid not.'

'Tomorrow, then?' Suddenly, it had become imperative to him that she accept his invitation.

He saw her frown. 'I'm not sure . . . '

'Please. I would enjoy it. Just a drink.'

'Mr Finborough — '

'Look upon it as a reward for your diligence tonight. Please say that you will.'

He heard her murmur, 'Very well. After I've closed up the shop.'

★   ★   ★

Elaine Davenport watched Mr Finborough walk down the street. She noticed that he had a spring in his step. His invitation had not come as a complete surprise, but she knew she should ~~have~~ of refused him. Why had she allowed herself to be persuaded into agreeing to go for a drink with him? Especially when he had patronised her by his assumption that she was incapable of keeping the shop's books. A great many men assumed that blonde hair and a pretty face could not possibly be accompanied by a brain.

207

She sighed. She had accepted Mr Finborough's invitation because, since her husband's death, two and a half years ago, she been short of intelligent, stimulating company. Elaine Davenport had grown up in a terraced house in Hendon, in north-west London. Her father had worked in a gentlemen's outfitters while her mother had kept house and brought up Elaine and her younger sister, Gilda. The family's hold on respectability had been maintained by her parents' hard work — her father's long hours in the shop, her mother's labour in the home. The windows had always sparkled, the curtains had always been clean and white, and the lawn and hedges in the tiny front garden had been neatly trimmed. Respectability was essential to Elaine's mother. For her, events, people, clothing and furnishings were divided into two categories: nice and not nice. To be *not nice* was to be shunned and damned.

When Elaine had turned fourteen, she had started work at a milliner's in Hendon. Intelligent and personable, she had progressed quickly, moving on to a junior position in a large central London department store when she was eighteen. By the time of her marriage to Hadley Davenport she had been the most senior sales assistant in the millinery department, responsible for a number of important customers, her opinion listened to when orders for the next season's hats were being made up.

Hadley Davenport had been ten years older than Elaine, good-natured, kind and infuriatingly forgetful. They had met at a college of education, where Elaine had been attending a French evening class. French was the language of fashion and she had thought to speak some might advance her career. Hadley had been teaching history for the WEA. She had noticed him in the canteen because he had odd socks on, one blue and one fawn. They had talked, standing in the queue. The strange thing was that it had been she who had been forgetful that day. She had left her umbrella on a bench and he had returned it to her the following week.

They had married six months later. Elaine had not expected to miss her job on her marriage, but she had. The flat that she and Hadley had rented had been small and she had been able to whip through the cleaning and laundry in an hour or two. There was no garden, only a few potted geraniums on the tiny balcony and, because Hadley's teaching post at a preparatory school left them with little money to spare, she could not fill the empty hours shopping. Hadley had seemed shocked at her suggestion that she find a part-time job, so she had let it drop. Instead, she had joined an amateur dramatic club and had made use of her skills sewing costumes. She had also taught herself to cook the sort of fancy dishes her mother had never made so that she could entertain Hadley's colleagues for supper.

If some aspects of her marriage had proved a disappointment, others were a revelation. Hadley's absent-minded demeanour, and his appearance — tall, thin, with vague, bespectacled grey eyes and fair hair that was always untidy — had given little clue to his passionate nature. In bed, in making love, Elaine had found the satisfaction and fulfilment that she failed to find as a housewife. They had suited each other, and, during their marriage, had given each other immense pleasure.

Hadley's death had deprived her of that pleasure. When the policeman had called at the flat and had broken the news to her that her husband had been killed in a traffic accident, she had known, with horrible clarity, what must have happened. Hadley's death had been a consequence of the same forgetfulness that had so often exasperated her at home, leaving her running round after him, searching for his lost pen, spectacles or marking book. He had forgotten to look to left and right and had stepped on to the road in front of a bus. Identifying his body in the mortuary, she had stroked his bruised face with her fingertips and wept.

Hadley's parents hadn't approved of their clever son marrying a shopgirl, and, since the funeral, they had not communicated with Elaine. There had been no children, which Elaine regretted. When an acquaintance had tried to comfort her by suggesting that she was fortunate, at least, that she had not been left with a child as well as herself to support, she had been unable to suppress her angry response.

She had had little chance to mourn Hadley, because his death had been the first of a series of disasters. The shop for which her father had worked for more than forty years had closed down, a casualty of the Depression, leaving him unemployed at the age of fifty-seven. Her mother's health had then collapsed at a time when there was no money to pay doctor's bills. Gilda's wages, as a typist for a firm of shipping agents, barely paid the rental of the family home and the food bills.

As soon as the life insurance policy had paid out, Elaine had decided to return to the business she knew best and had used the money to buy the lease on the Piccadilly shop. The premises were not ideal — both the shop and the storeroom behind it were very small, and the shop itself was peculiarly lozenge-shaped — but she had been confident in her ability to overcome the disadvantages. She worked long hours and, after a difficult start, business began to pick up. She had a number of regular customers, a mixture of women who worked in local businesses and wealthy women who lunched or shopped in the area, and she attracted passing trade through eyecatching window displays. By means of careful economy, she was able to help support her parents at the same time as keeping up the rent on her own flat.

She had paid a price for her independence, though. It was ironic, she often thought, that though, when she had been married, she had had too much time on her hands, she now seemed to have hardly any time at all. She worked six days a week and sometimes into the evenings as well. She had little opportunity to see friends — and anyway, the friends of her marriage, Hadley's colleagues and their wives, seemed to have fallen away. She had little in common with them now. She did not miss them.

Often, though, she felt lonely. In marrying Hadley, she had moved away from her family, yet she had not replaced them with anyone else. She saw her parents fortnightly, Gilda more often. Gilda had been engaged to be married for the last three years to a garage mechanic in Hendon. Gilda would be content with Jimmy, two children and a house near her parents. Elaine knew that she had always wanted more.

What did she miss most about her marriage? She missed the fun they had had, the laughter they had shared. Though she loved her work, it was often hard, and she sometimes felt weighed down by responsibility. She also missed the sex. She missed the warmth, the physical closeness, the ecstasy. This was not a lack she could talk of to anyone. A husband could be expected to miss a physical relationship; for a respectable widow to do so would be thought tawdry, *not nice*.

She could have married again, of course. She liked men; she missed their company. Yet the offers she had received had not tempted her — she had recalled in her mind's eye that small flat and the prison it had sometimes become, and had turned them down. Instead, she had taken lovers. Both affairs had ended messily, with recriminations and accusations. Again, *not nice*.

Her thoughts drifted back to Richard Finborough. Mentally, she ran through his good points. He was pleasant, intelligent and appreciative of her, the sort of man she might like as a friend. There was a strength and solidity about him that appealed to her. Though she prized her independence, she sometimes ached for the company of someone as strong-minded as herself, someone with whom to share her problems.

But he's married, Elaine reminded herself as she locked the takings and books in the safe in the office. And he's greedy and too sure of himself: I can see it in his eyes.

★　★　★

Rain was sweeping in from the Mourne Mountains as Sara rode across the beach. A rainbow shimmered over the bay like a multi-coloured banner of silk arching in the sky. The sea was a long way out, beyond the sands and the mudflats, and was much the same shade of grey as the sky. A trail of shells and pebbles and weathered rocks, striated with greys and browns, scattered the sand.

Sara had found herself wondering how much she herself had been to blame for Anton's leaving her. Perhaps she should have fought more — perhaps she should have put aside the humiliation she had felt on receiving his letter and gone to see him, instead of retreating, wounded, to the isolation of Raheen. Had her lack of action been motivated partly by her memory of that drab little room, that lodging house smelling of cabbage and damp? Her visit to the East End had shocked her, showing her a London she had not previously realised existed. Had a part of her recoiled from what she had glimpsed? A little, perhaps.

Sara urged Philo into a gallop. A crow rose with a loud caw from behind a rock, startling the horse. Philo reared violently. The reins slipped through Sara's hands and though she fought to retain her balance she was

212

thrown from the saddle.

She must ~~have~~ been unconscious for only a second. The blackness cleared: someone was shaking her shoulder. A voice said, 'I say, are you all right?' and Sara opened her eyes.

A man was crouching beside her. He had short, blackish brown hair and eyes as dark as blackcurrants.

She murmured, 'Who are you?'

'My name's Gil Vernon. Are you all right?'

'I'm fine.' Yet when she sat up she felt sick and dizzy and her arm hurt badly.

'You had a nasty fall,' he said. 'I think you hit your head on a rock.'

Sara blinked. 'Where's Philo?'

'Philo? Oh, your horse. He's fine, just there, cropping the grass.'

He took a flask from his small canvas rucksack and poured her a drink in a tin cup. 'It's all right,' he said, 'I haven't touched it. I'd only just started when I saw the horse throw you.'

Sara took the cup in her left hand and sipped the tea. It was very hot and very sweet but it made her feel a little less peculiar.

'Started what?' she asked.

'I'm trying to map the incidence of *Ensis ensis* along this coast.' He explained, 'The razor-shell. There are various types, of course, but *Ensis ensis* is the most common.' He picked out a shell from the sand and ran a finger carefully along its straight, smooth edge.

Then he peered at her, as if surprised to have discovered her among the razor-shells and whelks. 'Do you feel better now?'

'Very much, thank you.' She gave him back the cup. 'But I think I've broken my wrist.'

'Oh dear. How awful. Are you sure?'

'I broke it before, when I was twelve, and it feels just the same. It's all right, it'll mend, it's just a frightful nuisance not being able to do up your shoelaces, that sort of thing.'

'Where do you live? Shall I go and fetch help?'

'I'm staying at Raheen House. It's only a short distance away.'

'Raheen . . . then you're a Finborough.'

'Yes.' She smiled at him. 'My name's Sara Finborough. Perhaps you know my grandmother, Alice Finborough?'

'We have met, yes, some time ago . . . ' He offered her his hand and Sara struggled to her feet. He frowned. 'The horse — what should we do about the horse?'

'Could you lead him, do you think, Mr Vernon?'

He crossed the sands to where Philo, docile for once, stood cropping marram grass and seaweed and other unsuitable things. They walked slowly back to Raheen, Sara holding her right wrist protectively against herself, Gil Vernon leading the horse. To distract herself from the pain of her broken wrist, she asked him about razor-shells and he told her about their various types, appearance and habits. It cheered her up to think of those odd creatures, burrowing headlong into the sand. His voice was pleasant and soothing, and the walk from the beach to Raheen's driveway passed quicker than she might have expected.

They were making their way between the thick copse of trees that surrounded the house when he said, 'Philo . . . that's an unusual name for a horse.'

'I expect it's an Irish version of Philip.'

'No, no. Though it might be apposite if it was — *hippos*, which may be a derivation of Philip, means horse. But Philo isn't an Irish name, it's a Greek one.'

'What does it mean?' she asked.

'Love,' he said. 'It means love.'

* * *

214

The doctor came and set Sara's wrist and examined the bump on her head and told her she must rest for a few days. Rather to her surprise, she did, and slept a great deal as well, better than she had slept for months. She wondered whether hitting her head on the rock had knocked some of the thoughts of Anton out of it at last.

Two days after her accident, Gil Vernon called. Sara was in the sitting room, on the sofa in front of the fire, when her grandmother ushered him in.

'I came to see how you were,' he said. 'I brought you these. My mother said to tell you sorry it's only berries — it's the wrong time of year for flowers.'

'Thank you, darling.' Sara took from him the great bunch of holly and mistletoe and ivy. 'So wintry and romantic. So Christmassy.'

'Your mother has a magnificent garden, doesn't she, Mr Vernon?' said Alice Finborough. 'It's a long time since I've seen Vernon Court's garden but I do recall that it was splendid.'

He stayed half an hour and they spoke of this and that, and then he took his leave.

'Are you going to look for more razor-shells, Mr Vernon?' Sara asked, and he smiled and said, yes, in fact he was.

He called most days after that. The day before Sara's parents and Philip were due to arrive at Raheen for their Christmas holiday, Gil rose at the end of his visit, gave a little cough and said, 'My mother wondered whether you would care to come to dinner, Miss Finborough. And your family, naturally.'

Gil made his farewells. Leaving the room, he frowned. 'My mother said to warn you to bring coats and jerseys, that sort of thing. Vernon Court can be rather cold at this time of year.'

★ ★ ★

Vernon Court was the most romantic house Sara had ever seen. Though she loved Raheen, no one could have¹ called it, with its square, blockish main building and grandiose wings, 'romantic'. Raheen was an expression of power; Vernon Court had been its maker's dream. It perched, frail, bewitched and enchanting, twenty miles from the western shore of Strangford Lough.

The Finboroughs arrived at Vernon Court in the middle of a December afternoon, when the sun cast a pinkish-gold light over the ivy and old roses that sprawled across the front of the house. Lichen-encrusted steps led up to a pillared entrance; as the car drew to a halt Gil came out on to the steps.

Gil showed them into a square, high-ceilinged, terracotta-coloured sitting room. The room was furnished with faded sofas, old gilt mirrors and marble-topped sideboards. Several large dogs had arranged themselves in front of the fireplace. Caroline Vernon, Gil's mother, was sitting on one of the sofas. Caroline was square and dark; she wore her coral-coloured satin evening dress awkwardly, peering down every now and then to adjust a slipping shawl or shoulder strap. She had black, straight eyebrows, and a forthright, appraising gaze, which settled on Sara as they were introduced. A maid served sherry in tiny glasses with twisted barley-sugar stems while introductions were made and the conversation ranged from the storms that had slowed the Finboroughs' voyage across the Irish Sea to Caroline Vernon's affection for London, where she had been born.

Gil showed Sara and Philip round the house. Sara was glad she had brought her stole: away from the immediate vicinity of the fireplace, the temperature plunged steeply. Begun in the eighteen hundreds, Vernon Court had been extended in both the mid-nineteenth and early twentieth centuries. The dining room, which was in the Georgian part of the house, contained a vast mahogany dining table and ranks of silver candlesticks. The tall, many-paned windows looked out on to the gravel forecourt and drive. Sara noticed that paint was peeling from the window frames and spiders' webs greyed the glass. The kitchens and pantries, which Gil indicated only by a vague wave of a hand, lay beyond the dining room.

A wide, sweeping staircase took them from a black-and-white-tiled hallway to the upper storey of the house. A great many hunting prints and old photographs and maps were arranged on the walls. Peering out of a window, Sara looked down towards the garden and exclaimed, 'Oh, a fishpond! And a sundial! And such a gorgeous little summerhouse!'

They went down a second flight of stairs. Philip disappeared in search of another drink, leaving Gil and Sara to explore alone. The high glass ceiling of the conservatory soared above them, magnifying the light of the fitful December sun. The plants had grown in great luxuriance, filling the space and pushing their way up towards the light. Vines and figs had broken through the glass panels of the roof, and now snaked out into the cold air, reaching for freedom. Withered grapes still hung on the vines and the figs had ripened from green to black.

There was a strange little room next to the glasshouse. Open at its front to the elements, only a low wall divided the interior from the outside. The walls were whitewashed and the floor was paved in terracotta. The evidence of former pastimes — cricket bats and butterfly nets — lay scattered about. Here, the spiders' webs were larger and more confident than those Sara had noticed in the rest of the house. She and Gil exchanged their shoes for gumboots and he found a torch. The twilight had deepened, and fragments of Caroline Vernon's garden — an alley edged with the sculptured columns of yew trees, a eucalyptus grove of

217

twisting pink and silver branches, a walled garden in which paths crisscrossed and meandered — were half revealed in the darkness. Wet, leafless fronds soaked the hem of Sara's green velvet evening gown.

Returning to the house, Sara pulled off her gumboots and fumbled left-handedly with the tiny pearl buttons on her evening shoes. 'Could you?' she said to Gil, and he kneeled down on the floor in front of her. Hesitantly, he took hold of her foot and slid the buttons through the small holes. She found his carefulness touching: he held her as cautiously as he had held the fragile shell he had found on the beach.

★　★　★

Richard, Isabel and Philip left Ireland for London shortly after New Year. Sara remained at Raheen. At the end of his first week back at work, Richard took Elaine Davenport to Thierry's, a small restaurant in Soho. Richard was confident that he was unlikely to meet anyone he knew there, and the food was simple but excellently cooked, the service unobtrusive.

They had met for a drink on several previous occasions. Elaine had told him that she was a widow, that she lived alone in a flat in St John's Wood and that she had owned the shop for two years. On the surface, their relationship was that of friendship. Richard knew that his feelings went far deeper, however. Elaine Davenport compelled him, mesmerised him. Away from her, he longed to be with her, wanted more of her. He wanted to embrace her, to kiss her, to run the tip of his tongue along that pale wrist to the white hollow of her elbow.

He had wondered whether to buy a Christmas gift for her. He was aware of the dangers of pushing too far, too fast, and, in the end, had decided against it and had merely expressed to her his best wishes for the season.

But a few days earlier, passing an antiques shop in Hampstead, he had seen just the thing and had snapped it up.

They had finished their first course when he slid the package across the table to her. 'It's a little belated,' he said. 'Happy Christmas.'

'Richard, you shouldn't have.' Elaine frowned.

'It's only a trifle. When I saw it, I thought of you. Go on, open it.'

Reluctantly, she unwrapped the tissue paper to reveal an antique porcelain umbrella handle in the shape of a woman wearing an elaborate hat.

'Do you like it?'

'Very much. But — '

'The hat, you see. And I remembered the first day I met you — the rain.'

'It's very sweet of you.' She was frowning. 'But I mean it, you shouldn't buy me gifts.'

'Surely one can buy a friend a Christmas present?'

'Just this once, perhaps. But no more.'

'Why not?'

Her gaze held his. 'Richard, you know perfectly well why not. For one thing, your money should be for your family, not for me.'

'I'm not a poor man, Elaine. I can afford to buy the occasional trinket without my wife and children starving.'

'But I'm not wealthy. I'm perfectly comfortable, far more so than many, but I'm not wealthy and I shouldn't think I ever will be.'

'All the more reason for me to treat you occasionally, then.'

'No, Richard,' she said firmly. 'If we're to be friends, then we must be equals.'

If we're to be friends: it was the first small indication that she expected their relationship to continue. His heart raced. But he said smoothly, 'Naturally we're equals. How could we be anything else?'

'If you were to fall into the habit of buying me gifts, like some *fin-de-siècle* mistress, then I think I might begin to feel my equality crumbling.'

Her voice was low and dry, her words took him aback.

'Richard, you need to understand certain things. I don't want gifts and I most certainly don't want your money. And I don't want to be a threat to your happiness.'

He met the pale grey of her gaze. 'You mean, to my wife and family.'

'Yes.' Again, she frowned. 'I enjoy the company of men. But I don't want — I don't want anything more than companionship, friendship.'

'You must still miss your husband.'

'In some ways, yes. I miss the sharing of little events, all those things that must seem unimportant to people outside a marriage. I miss — ' she cast a glance round the restaurant — '*this*. To dine out has always been one of my pleasures. A woman dining alone often finds it a miserable experience. We are seated in dark corners and the waiters ignore us.'

'You must have friends.'

'Not so many, now.' She gave a little smile. 'You'd be surprised how widowhood puts people off — it's almost as though it were catching. And to be honest, I don't have a great deal of time for friends. I see my sister, of course, but Gilda and I don't go out to restaurants.' She paused. '*This* is what I long for — a little glamour, a little pleasure.'

'The thrill of the new,' he murmured.

'You feel the same? I thought you might. I hate to feel stale, shut in.'

The waiter appeared; Elaine declined pudding, so Richard ordered coffees and brandy. When they were alone again, he said quietly, 'I have no wish to

220

jeopardise my marriage.'

The question hung in the air between them: *then why are you here?* She did not voice it. Instead, she said, 'I'm answerable to no one but myself at present and I find that suits me very well. If I'm honest, it's sometimes a relief to know that I'm at no man's beck and call. A great many men seem to feel independence in a woman unsettling — unfeminine, even.'

'There's not the slightest possibility of my ever finding you unfeminine. You are charming and beautiful and entrancing.' The words escaped from him, taking him by surprise. Richard added lightly, 'I've no wish to make unreasonable demands of you, Elaine. A few drinks, the occasional meal — that may give us both a great deal of pleasure.'

'Then we understand each other.' Briefly, her hand touched his.

8

Philip had moved out of the family home the previous year to live in a flat in Chelsea. It had been a relief, in some ways, because his relationship with Richard had always been combustible, and of course, at the age of twenty-five, it was understandable that he wanted his own establishment. Yet Isabel, who had always been close to her eldest child, missed him dreadfully. She missed Philip's sense of humour and the way the house had seemed to wake up as soon as he stepped into it. She missed the feeling of life and energy that always went with him; she missed the lively, noisy friends he had brought to the house.

When, towards the end of the previous summer, Sara had gone to stay with her grandmother in Ireland after that wretched business with the Austrian, Isabel had assumed that she would come home after a few weeks. Yet Sara showed no signs of leaving Ireland, and had refused to accompany the family back to England in the New Year. Her long separation from her daughter upset and saddened Isabel. She suspected that Sara blamed her in some way for her separation from Anton Wolff, but really, what else could she have done? He had been unsuitable in every way. The discovery that Sara had lied to her, and that Ruby had conspired in the intrigue, and that she herself had been utterly ignorant of the fact that her daughter was in love with a man, had shaken and unnerved her. She had recalled Alfie Broughton and the devastation that his betrayal and its consequences had brought to her life. She did not want Sara to suffer as she had suffered. She could not allow that to happen.

Her own instinct had coincided exactly with

Richard's: to put an end to the relationship as quickly and finally as possible. Though on the surface the rift between her and Sara had healed, and they exchanged frequent letters, Isabel knew that there was still a distance between them.

Theo had paid them one of his unannounced visits in late autumn. Always, when he returned to England, Isabel had a moment of delighted expectation — perhaps, this time, he had decided to come home permanently — but he had crushed her hopes almost immediately, telling her that he intended to travel round northern Europe. Isabel hid her disappointment, understanding that her flare of hope had been unrealistic anyway: Theo, the most independent and solitary of her three children, would never return to the family fold. During his visit, he had seemed reserved and quiet, and, when she had asked him whether he was happy, he had brushed aside her question. She had found herself remembering her children's infancy with nostalgia, how easy it had been to distract and console them with the promise of an outing to the park or the making of a paper crown.

With all the children gone and Richard very busy at work, the Hampstead house seemed large and empty. Isabel spent some of January at Porthglas. She loved Cornwall in the winter, loved walking along the beach while the gales whipped the waves into a frenzy. In the house where she felt happiest, she found herself wondering whether Sara's feelings for Anton Wolff had gone deeper than she and Richard had believed. Perhaps that was why Sara remained in Ireland, because she could not bear to come home. Loss could take you in different ways — you might cling on to a place that had happy memories, as she herself had clung on to Orchard House after Charles Hawkins had died, or you might flee from a town and its associations because it reminded you of a painful experience, as she had fled, all those years ago, from Broadstairs.

The evening she returned from Cornwall, Richard took her out to dinner at Quaglino's. Towards the end of the meal, he took from his pocket a small package and handed it to her.

'I missed you,' he said. 'I ended up talking to myself one or two evenings.' Opening the box, Isabel found inside it a pair of pearl and agate earrings.

It was the gift that made her start to watch him carefully. Over the years, Isabel had learned that Richard's gifts could be distractions, sops to his conscience, clumsy attempts to distract or make amends. Watching him, she noticed how often he came home late from the office. With a sinking heart she noted his variable demeanour — his preoccupation, his moodiness, his sporadic elation. Her feeling that her good fortune was fragile, unlikely to last, had, in spite of a quarter of a century of marriage, never completely left her. Her insecurity was too deeply ingrained, and besides, sometimes her suspicions had been justified. Richard had always been aware of his own power, and there was a part of him that needed to exercise that power, whether in the bedroom or the boardroom. In the twenties, his flirtations had developed into a couple of short-lived affairs. The discovery of his unfaithfulness had humiliated, enraged and wounded her. Both times she had decamped to Cornwall, refusing to return to London until she was certain both of his penitence and his love for her. It wasn't important, it meant nothing, he had yelled at her, as if *that* made it excusable. Why was he unable to see how a kiss, a glance, even a *thought* tormented her? Why could he not see how deeply she despised the easy morals of his class and their assumption of entitlement to both pleasure and power?

One evening, Richard did not come home until nine o'clock. When she asked him where he had been, instead of flying off the handle as she half-expected him to, he told her that an important business venture was about to come to fruition. For the past few months he had been planning the takeover of another company. He was sorry if he had seemed preoccupied, but it was a big step, a major venture. He looked flushed and excited as he spoke, and Isabel felt a mixture of relief at his explanation and shame at her suspicion.

Yet her relief did not last. There was some change in him she could not quite put her finger on, that could not quite be explained away by absorption in his work. Often, talking to him, she sensed that his thoughts were elsewhere; in bed, she thought there was a desperation to his lovemaking, as if he was trying to purge himself of something.

★ ★ ★

The plaster was removed from Sara's wrist at the end of January. She flexed her arm: her skin looked pale, peeled, new.

Gil drove her to Ardglass, where they walked round the harbour, and Sara looked at the boats and Gil wrote down in his notebook the different species of seabirds. Then, to celebrate her recovery, they had a beer in a whitewashed pub that looked out over the green and Gil told her about the study he was making of a new strain of sweet pea that Caroline Vernon had bred. 'The petals are white with a pale blue frill,' he explained. 'The seeds often fail to come true and have to be discarded. You have to have several generations of the correct type to be sure of getting the flower you want. I'm trying to see whether the same rules apply to other sweet peas as well to the Vernon type. Or whether it depends on the strain.'

'Multicoloured sweet peas are rather nice,' Sara said. 'So lovely and cheerful.'

He looked at her in the serious and slightly bewildered fashion that she had come to find endearing, and said, 'No doubt. But in the right context.'

When they went back to Raheen, Sara caught sight of herself in a mirror in the hall. She looked flushed, bright-eyed and windswept. Happy, she thought.

Over dinner that night, her grandmother said, 'You're fond of Gil, aren't you, Sara?'

'Yes.' She fed a scrap of ham to the dog, which was nuzzling her knees under the table. 'He's a good friend.'

'Both his father and brother died in the war, has he told you? It was a tragedy — Marcus was such a fine boy. He was quite some years older than Gil — poor Caroline lost a baby or two between the boys. Don't let Bran take all your dinner, Sara, you need to eat properly and he's fat enough already. I've always admired Caroline Vernon. She's suffered more than any one person should be expected to. I often think that was why she made that wonderful garden, because she had to find something to take her mind off losing David and Marcus.'

'And she's got Gil, Granny,' reminded Sara.

'No doubt he's a great comfort to her. More potatoes, darling? I'm afraid Vernon Court is in a sad state. It's a charming place, but as full of holes as a colander. Two lots of death duties, you see, and very little money coming in.' Alice looked up; her eyes, a cornflower blue, had lost their customary vagueness and become sharp. 'Gil must be in his early thirties by now. He has never shown any sign of marrying anyone. I tell you this only because I love you dearly, Sara, and I'd hate to see you disappointed. Your mother mentioned to me when you first came to stay that there had been someone in London.'

'Oh, *that*,' said Sara airily. 'It was nothing. And Gil and I are just friends. It's nice to have company.'

'Naturally it is and I'm delighted for you.'

They ate for a while in silence and then Sara said, 'Though men are sometimes quite old when they marry, aren't they?'

'Yes, that's true. Your grandfather was almost forty when we married.'

'Well, then,' said Sara as, beneath the table, she stroked Bran's silky ears.

★ ★ ★

Freddie had amassed, on Richard's behalf, sufficient Provost shares to make his bid for the takeover of the company public. Richard knew that Cecil Provost would be hostile to the bid — Cecil had built up the company from scratch — but he was confident the acquisition would succeed.

It had been the agreement of Bernard, the younger Provost son, to sell his shares that had tipped the balance. Strange how so often families went to the bad like that, Richard mused: one generation amassed wealth and the next spent it all. Cecil and the elder son, Stephen, would hang on for as long as possible, but, as the two Provosts no longer owned a majority share, that would not be enough to save the company. The remaining shareholders would be tempted by the prospect of a payout after a Finborough takeover.

Richard planned to give greater responsibility to Philip once the acquisition was complete. For the last year, Philip had spent much of his time in the City, at the tea-packing plant. Richard knew that Philip resented the exile that had been imposed on him and would have preferred to be in the thick of things in Hounslow, but Richard believed that the experience was good for him. Often, Philip reminded Richard of himself at the same age, desperate for challenge and excitement and power. Once Richard was in possession of Provosts, Philip's energy and enthusiasm would be invaluable.

Richard's gaze slid to the bouquet of flowers in a vase on top of a filing cabinet. The flowers were for Elaine Davenport. Earlier that day he had telephoned her at the shop. She had sounded upset and, when pressed, she told him that the shop had been broken into the previous night. Money had been taken. 'I'll come over after work,' he had offered, 'see what I can do to help.' He had heard her relief in her thanks, and had found himself wondering whether, even for Elaine Davenport, independence sometimes palled. After he had put the phone down, Richard had called a florist's and had them deliver a bouquet of flowers to his office. He glanced at the carnations and freesias every now and then; their scents pervaded the room.

He pursued Elaine Davenport with the same diligence and fervour with which he pursued Provosts. Sometimes he felt himself to be on the verge of the same sort of conquest. He could recall her every smile and touch of the hand and every chaste kiss good night. Yet he wanted more — he ached for more — and he thought he sensed a tension between them, sensed that they were both waiting, watching each other's every move.

At half-past six he left the office and drove to Piccadilly. At the shop, the blinds were down and the 'Closed' sign was up. Richard rapped on the door; after a few moments, he heard the clack of heels and the key turn in the lock.

Elaine opened the door. He gave her the bouquet.

'Richard, how kind of you,' she said. 'They're beautiful.' She let him into the shop.

'Have you lost much?' he asked.

'A day and a half's takings, the petty cash . . .' A lock of hair had fallen loose from her usually perfect coiffure, she tucked it behind her ear. 'I'm trying to work it out

228

exactly. The police need to know.'

He heard her lock the door behind him. The small back room was even more cramped than the shop — more of a corridor than a room — and the stacks of hatboxes inside it further shrank the space. She said, 'I'll put these in water' and went off with the flowers. He heard, from not far away, the sound of a running tap.

She came back into the storeroom. He asked, 'How did the thief get in?'

'Through the washroom window. There's an alleyway behind the shop. I've had a lock put on the window.'

'Are there bolts on the doors?'

'Not yet. The cost . . . '

'How much was taken, Elaine?'

'I'm not sure — I think about forty or fifty pounds.'

'A good pair of bolts will cost you less than two pounds. And that safe is too flimsy. Any competent safe-breaker would have that open in a matter of minutes. I'll give you the address of our locksmith, if you like.'

'Thank you, Richard.'

'Were you insured?'

'Not against theft,' she admitted. 'I've tried to keep down overheads as much as possible and I hoped . . . ' The sentence faded, unfinished.

'Don't you bank the takings each day?'

She sighed. 'Muriel was unwell yesterday so there was no one else in the shop and I couldn't get to the bank. I keep open at lunchtime because that's when the girls who work round here have the chance to shop. I just snatch a sandwich when we're quiet. I don't like closing up unexpectedly — it puts customers off, makes them think we're unreliable. So there was all of Tuesday's takings as well as Monday afternoon's.'

He said bluntly, 'Have the police spoken to Muriel?'

'Not yet.' She looked troubled. 'But they will do.'

'Good.' He glanced at the small desk in the corner of the room. It was littered with slips of paper. Following his gaze, Elaine said, 'Whoever did it went through that as well — looking for valuables, I suppose, though there were only pins and pots of gum. I've collected up everything and I've begun to start putting the papers in order.' She gave a wry smile. 'Still, at least they didn't find my bottle of gin.'

'Ah, gin — that sounds like an excellent idea.'

'Some days, Richard, I need it, believe me. And this is one of them.'

She left the room, returning after a few minutes with two glasses. 'It's lovely and cold,' she explained as she handed him a glass. 'I keep it in the cleaning cupboard in the washroom — it's freezing in there.'

Their glasses clinked. Enclosed in the small room with her, he could feel her physical presence, smell her perfume and see the grain of her translucent skin. His need to touch her, to feel the heat of her flesh, almost overwhelmed him.

She said suddenly, 'Oh, I do hope that Muriel had nothing to do with it! But she's a silly girl, and I wouldn't put it past her.'

He took the glass out of her hand and put it on the desk. Then he kissed her. Her fine, fair hair brushed against his face; he breathed in her perfume. 'Elaine,' he whispered. She closed her eyes and threw her head back; he kissed the white column of her throat. All thought, all calculation fled, and all that was left was longing. Through the thin silk of her blouse he could feel her warmth and solidity; kissing her was intoxicating. Around them, the scraps of paper floated from the desk to the floor like snow.

But then she pulled away from him. 'We mustn't, Richard,' she said. 'You know that we mustn't. Friends . . . ' she gave a short, nervous smile, ' . . . we must be friends, that's all, remember?'

In the morning, Isabel rang the servants' agency about the housemaid, who was off sick again, made appointments at her hairdresser and dressmaker, and took the dog, who was off his food, to the vet.

It was when she was going round the house, tidying up, that she found it. The cold winds of January had been replaced by mild, springlike weather so Richard had not taken his coat that day, but had left it on the peg in the hall. Isabel took the coat off the peg to hang it up in the wardrobe, first going through his pockets, which were fat with gloves and a scarf. Crushed beneath the pair of gloves was a piece of paper. Isabel smoothed it out. It was a bill, made out in Richard's name, from a florist's. For quite a sizeable bouquet, judging by the cost. The bouquet had been delivered to Richard's office yesterday.

Isabel sat down on the bed. There must be a perfectly reasonable explanation, she said to herself. Richard had sent flowers to an old friend or colleague who had been unwell, perhaps. Or one of the typists at Finboroughs had retired.

Yet her gaze drifted to the dressing table, to the box containing the pearl and agate earrings that Richard had given her on her return from Cornwall, and suddenly she rose to her feet, wrenched open the window and hurled the box as hard as she could into the garden below.

★ ★ ★

Philip dropped Steffie off in Enfield, where she lived with her family, and then headed back into London. The motor cycle he was riding, a 600cc Ariel, was a recent purchase, and he thought he would drop in on his parents on the way home and borrow some tools from his father so that he could make some adjustments. He liked working on his bikes, liked making those final tweaks that coaxed the best performance.

He coasted up the drive and parked the bike outside the garage. Letting himself into the house, he was about to call out a hello when he heard the sound of raised voices. Crossing the hallway, he paused outside the drawing room. He heard his father's voice, low and angry, but could not make out the words.

Then there was a crash as something struck the door, and he heard his mother shout: 'Those flowers, who were they for?'

Philip paused outside the door. His father said, 'If you must know, they were for Miss Dobson. She's suffered a bereavement.'

'Liar!' His mother's voice rose in a shriek. 'I phoned Miss Dobson! She told me she was fine!'

'You telephoned my secretary?'

'Yes, Richard! Because I need to know! And you won't tell me the truth! Who is she? Tell me her name! I want to know her name!'

Philip's fingers had frozen to the door handle. His father yelled at his mother that she was behaving like a fishwife. His mother's hissed, venomous response was inaudible. Quietly, feeling cold inside, Philip walked back out of the house.

He tinkered with the bike, but his heart wasn't in it, and after a while he put down the spanner and sat down in an old armchair with collapsed springs, and tried to reason with himself. He must have made a mistake. He had misheard, misinterpreted. His parents had always quarrelled. His mother could not possibly have meant that.

He went back indoors. The place seemed deserted; he wondered whether his parents had gone to bed. Then, hearing small noises from the kitchen, he discovered his mother, standing at the stove. Seeing him, she looked up. He saw that her eyes were red-rimmed and swollen.

'Philip,' she said, with a gasp, 'I didn't know you were coming tonight.'

'I had a few things to do on the bike.'

'I was making some cocoa. Would you like some?'

'No, thanks.' Looking at her made him angry. 'What's wrong, Mum?'

'Nothing, darling.'

'You've been crying. And I heard you and Dad yelling at each other.'

'It's nothing,' she said sharply. 'Nothing at all. It'll blow over.'

He had to ask, though everything about her demeanour warned him not to. He simply couldn't not ask. He said, 'Is Dad seeing another woman?' and he saw her become motionless, her back to him.

'Of course not. What a dreadful thing to say.' Her voice was cold.

Philip wanted to believe her. But he said roughly, 'Is he? Tell me, Mum.'

A long silence, and then she whispered, 'No. He says not.'

The milk pan was boiling over. Philip lifted it from the stove, gave his mother a kiss, left the house and drove, very fast, back to his flat.

★ ★ ★

Richard's denial of any wrongdoing had been vehement and outraged. In the aftermath of their quarrel, Isabel felt sick and shaken, her headache persisting so that she found it hard to think clearly. She longed for Cornwall, but was afraid to leave London. She needed to see him, to keep an eye on him; she needed to be sure.

A few days later, it was the cook's night off. Richard

233

was not yet home so Isabel made herself an omelette for supper. She was washing up the pan when she heard the front door open, then slam.

Philip came into the kitchen. His hair was dishevelled and his eyes were blazing. He said, 'He was lying to you, Mum.'

Isabel's heart skipped a beat. 'What do you mean?'

'Dad was at the tea factory this afternoon. When he left I followed him on the bike. He went to a shop in Piccadilly, a hat shop. The blinds were down and the 'Closed' sign was up.'

Her heart had begun to pound, but she said, 'Philip, I don't understand. What are you saying? I'm sure your father must have had legitimate business there.'

'No. They left the shop together, you see.'

She whispered, '*They* . . . ?'

'Dad and a woman. I couldn't see her all that well, it was dark and she had a veil on her hat. They went to a restaurant in Dover Street.'

Isabel bowed her head, closing her eyes. She heard Philip say, 'Mum? Are you all right, Mum?', heard the fear in his voice.

Then his tone altered. 'You don't need to worry about it,' he said. 'It'll be all right, I promise you. I'll sort it out.'

He gave her a crooked smile and then he walked out of the room. After a moment or two, she heard the front door slam, and then the roar of the motor cycle.

★　★　★

Kit had sold a sculpture and bought everyone a drink. They spilled out of a corner of the Fitzroy Tavern, a mixture of Ruby's artist friends and work colleagues. A brown-eyed boy, new to Ruby, joined the circle.

'Is this a private party or can anyone join in?'

'Oh, we're not fussy.' She budged up the bench so

that he could sit down next to her. 'Hello. I'm Ruby Chance.'

'Joe Thursby.'

'I haven't seen you here before.'

'I've only just come to London.' He had a northern accent.

'How are you finding it?'

He grinned. 'Big. Bit of a shock when you've spent most of your life in a village of two hundred people. Have you always lived in London?'

'Mostly.'

He was very handsome, his features even, his hair and eyes a matching chestnut brown. Ruby said, 'Shall I tell you who everyone is?'

'Please.'

'The man with the green jacket standing at the windowsill is called Kit. He's a sculptor. He lives in the same house as me. The woman beside him is Daisy Mae, his girlfriend. Then there's Rob, who's a painter, and Inez, who's a model, and the man smoking a pipe is Edward Carrington. Edward and I work in the same office.'

'You're not an artist, then?'

Ruby shook her head. Three short stories published, she thought — she could have told him she was a writer. But she preferred to keep her limited success private: it seemed too fragile to be exposed to public view.

'Or a model?'

She snorted. 'Hardly.'

'I would have thought you'd make a good model. You've got such a lovely thin, bony face. I like thin, bony faces so much better than round pudding faces.' As he spoke, he smiled at her.

'You're very outspoken.'

'We Yorkshiremen believe in speaking our minds. But I mean it as a compliment.'

'I'll take it as one, then. No one wants to look like a pudding. What do you do, Joe?'

'Nothing, yet. I've been walking round all day, trying to find work. I don't think they'd take me in an office, I don't look smart enough, so I've been asking in the pubs and factories.'

'Where are you living?'

'On a friend's floor at the moment. As soon as I've earned some cash, I'll find a room of my own.'

A girl's voice interrupted, saying loudly, 'You're something to do with the Finboroughs, aren't you?' and Ruby looked up.

'I know them, yes.'

The speaker was young and blonde and elegant. Her fur coat and pearls looked out of place in the raffish Fitzroy. Slumming, thought Ruby.

The girl gave a little smile. 'I thought you might like to know that Philip Finborough is trying to get himself thrown out of the cocktail bar of the Savoy. He's frightfully drunk and in a very bad temper.'

She melted away into the crowd. Ruby said, 'I'm sorry, I have to go,' and gathered up her coat and bag. She held out her hand. 'It's been lovely to meet you, Joe. I'm sure we'll run into each other again some day.'

She caught the Northern Line at Goodge Street. Enfolded in the dusty darkness of the tube, she thought about Joe Thursby and how handsome he was, and the glint of fun in his brown eyes. She had liked him, and he had been interested in her, she was certain that he had — why, then, had she left him without a backward glance as soon as Philip Finborough's name had been mentioned? Of course, she knew why. Had that girl told her that Philip Finborough was in a hotel bar in Paris, and that he needed her, then she would have put on her coat, gone to Victoria Station and caught the boat train.

Alighting at Charing Cross, Ruby headed quickly down the Strand. As she turned into Savoy Court, she saw him. Philip was leaning against a wall, smoking. She said his name and his half-lidded eyes flickered open.

'Ruby. I'd buy you a drink but the bastards threw me out.' His voice was slurred.

'I don't want a drink. Perhaps something to eat, though. Have you eaten, Philip?'

He looked puzzled. 'Don't know. Don't think so. Where shall we go? Wheeler's . . . Bertorelli's . . . ?'

She didn't like to think of Philip wrestling with oysters or spaghetti in his present state. She said, 'Perhaps we should just go back to your flat.'

He shook his head. 'Don't want to go back to my flat. I'm sick of it. Anyway, Steffie might be there.'

'Steffie?'

He said vaguely, 'I think I might ~~have~~ given her a key.'

Ruby thought quickly. 'Come back to my place and I'll make you a sandwich or something.'

'A sandwich . . . yes. Good old Ruby.' Philip lurched into the road and hailed a passing taxi.

In the taxi, he kept slumping into a corner, his eyes closing. She didn't think she was strong enough to move him if he fell asleep properly so she talked to him to keep him awake.

'How is everyone?'

'Who?' He opened one eye. 'The family, d'you mean, Ruby? Why don't you come and see for yourself? Why don't you come to visit my beloved family?'

'You know why. I'm *persona non grata* at present. Because of Sara and Anton.'

Philip's expression changed, becoming angry. 'How my father could have the bloody nerve to tell Sara — when you think what *he's* doing!'

Ruby had no idea what he was talking about. She said so, and then, in reply, Philip said, 'He's having an affair with a woman half his age. It's disgusting.'

He had spoken rather loudly and Ruby saw the cab driver's shoulders twitch. She gave Philip a nudge and hushed him, and he lapsed into silence once more. But his words had shocked her, they made no sense, and she whispered, 'Who's having an affair?'

'My father, of course.' He looked away, out of the window.

They spoke little for the remainder of the journey. Richard Finborough was having an affair. Ruby was not sure whether she believed Philip. He was very drunk, and people said foolish things when they were drunk. Yet she found herself thinking of her own father. If, a few years ago, someone had told her that her father had a second wife and family living in Salisbury, then would she have believed them? Of course not.

The taxi drew up in Fulham Road. With great precision, Philip peeled a ten-shilling note from the bundle in his wallet and gave it to the driver. Ruby steered him up the front steps, into the house, and then they slowly progressed up the three flights of stairs.

In her room, she made him a Marmite sandwich and a cup of very strong black coffee. When he had drank a few mouthfuls of the coffee, she said, 'When you said that your father was having an affair — '

'He is. With a tart in Piccadilly. She works in a *hat shop*.' His voice was contemptuous.

'How do you know?'

'I followed him. I saw him. I asked at the shop next door. They told me she's called Davenport.'

'I don't see how you can know he's having an affair — '

'Oh, Ruby, of course he is!' Philip looked enraged. 'I've been thinking about it. It probably isn't the first time. That's probably why they're always quarrelling.'

She sat down on the bed beside him. She said feebly, 'Philip, you can't know that.'

'I do. I heard them yelling at each other about it.'

'Then perhaps it was a mistake — '

'If it had been a *mistake*, then he'd have hardly gone

238

back to see her after Mum found out, would he?'

'Isabel knows?'

'Yes.'

There was a logic in what he had said; she squeezed his hand.

'He's such a bloody hypocrite! And why the hell does Mum put up with him? Why doesn't she just tell him to get lost?'

She was unable to think of a reply. 'Poor you,' she said.

'You're a good kid, Ruby.' When he looked at her like that something seemed to melt inside her.

He patted his pockets, frowning. 'Have you any cigarettes?'

'No. I'll see if I can cadge a couple off my next-door neighbour.'

Ruby left the room and scrounged two cigarettes off the Jewish translator who lived in one of the other third-floor rooms, and then went back to her own room. Philip had stretched himself out on her bed and had fallen asleep, one hand flung out on the pillow beside him. Careful not to wake him, Ruby undid his shoelaces, took off his shoes and tucked the blankets over him.

She cleared up the plates and cups and read for a while, but found it hard to concentrate. Her childhood image of the Finboroughs, of a glamorous, united family headed by the perfect couple that was Richard and Isabel, had received a knock. And besides, her gaze kept drifting to Philip, lying on the bed: asleep, he looked younger, vulnerable, his hair rumpled and his features relaxed. She put off the light, took off her shoes and stockings and lay on the bed beside him, pulling her coat over herself because it was cold. Light from the streetlamp outside seeped into the room: reaching up a hand, she let the tip of her forefinger lightly touch his brow, then trace down the arch of his nose and come to rest in the hollow at the corner of his mouth. It she had been the heroine of one of her stories, she thought, then he would have woken and taken her in his arms and kissed her passionately and told her that he loved her. But he did not wake.

When she judged it to be dawn, she rose and went to the bathroom. Splashing cold water on her face, she looked in the mirror. It seemed to her that something had changed in her, that the night had changed her.

When she went back into the room, Philip had woken and was retying his tie.

'How are you?' she asked.

'I have the most bloody awful headache, but I'm probably better than I deserve to be.' He ran his fingers through hair that stuck up in short, coppery tufts. 'Ruby, you are an absolute sport. Thank you for putting up with me. I don't deserve you.' He kissed her, then left the room. She heard him run downstairs; she put up her fingers to touch the place where his lips had touched her cheek.

★ ★ ★

Returning to her flat after work, Elaine took off her coat, hat and gloves, and lit the gas fire. The doorbell rang; she went downstairs to open it.

A young man was standing on the doorstep. 'Miss Davenport?' he said.

'Mrs Davenport.'

'Ah.' He gave an unpleasant, knowing sort of smile. Then he said, 'May I come in?'

'I don't think so. Who are you?'

'My name's Philip Finborough.'

She stared at him. The resemblance was, she now saw, unmistakable. She said reluctantly, 'I suppose you'd better come inside.'

The walk upstairs gave her a moment or two in which

240

to control her shock. As she opened the door to her flat, she said, 'You're Richard's son, aren't you?'

'You don't deny knowing my father, then?'

'Why should I?'

'Because he's married to my mother,' Philip said angrily. 'And because you're having an affair with him.'

If he had not been so offensive she might have OF explained that there had been no affair, and that she and Richard were just friends. Instead, she went to the cabinet and opened the gin bottle.

'Drink?'

'No, thanks.'

'I think I will. I would invite you to sit down, but I suspect that in your present frame of mind you'd prefer to remain standing.'

He gave her a black look and threw himself into a chair by the gas fire. Elaine sat down opposite him before saying, 'Why have you come here?'

'Why do you think? To make you leave him alone.'

'How did you find me?'

'I followed you. On the Tube.'

'How resourceful of you.' She disliked the idea of this furious man trailing her all the way back to her flat, but she ironed the sarcasm out of her voice, and said, 'Look here, Philip, I don't know how you found out about Richard and me, but really, it's none of your business.'

'None of my business? How can you say that?'

'Because it's true. What your father does is his concern.'

'Oh, come on.' He sounded contemptuous. 'I've no doubt you made sure he'd come running.'

She put her glass on the side table. 'Does it suit you to see it like that? To cast me as some sort of *femme fatale*?'

His lip curled. 'It's not a question of suiting me. That's how it was.'

'Your father seems to me capable of making up his own mind.'

He leaned forward in the chair, his fists clenched. 'You're to promise me to break off this — this *thing* with my father.'

'No.'

'You have to!' he yelled.

She said coldly, 'I think you should go now, Philip.'

'Not before you've promised.'

She went to the door and opened it. 'Please leave. If you don't go then I shall call the police.'

A long, taut moment, and then he rose to his feet. 'It's revolting,' he said, as he drew level with her. 'He's old enough to be your father.'

It had been a horrible day. The police had earlier informed her that Muriel's boyfriend had been involved in the robbery of the shop; Muriel herself had been arrested as a possible accessory. And now, this arrogant, demanding young man ... Elaine's self-control snapped. She found herself shouting, 'Get out, I said, get out!' And her Persian cat, Cleo, wandering at that moment into the flat, looked up at her with startled eyes as Philip Finborough ran down the stairs.

★ ★ ★

'Oysters,' said Gil, 'aren't necessarily born male or female. They tend one way or the other as they mature. *Ostrea edulis*, the British oyster, changes sex a number of times during its life and always spawns at a full moon.'

It seemed to Sara that Gil knew everything. He knew that woodlice were crustaceans, like crabs and lobsters, and that a spider's cobweb could be used to stem the flow of blood from a wound. He knew that most snail shells had a clockwise coil, but a very few spiralled the other way — they are freaks, he said, aberrations of nature, but fascinating too, don't you think? He knew that hedgehogs were not native to Ireland, but had been introduced around two hundred years ago, and that the common people believed that a hedgehog could predict the direction of the wind: 'Complete nonsense, of course,' said Gil, but Sara rather liked the idea of a hedgehog pointing his black, twitching nose into the air to detect a change in the weather.

One day, they drove to Killough, where small grey houses looked out over a flat grey beach. A smear of barnacled stones was strewn across the sand, and another smear of raincloud darkened the sky. Sara wrote down the birds Gil had spotted in his notebook while he looked through the binoculars. 'So much easier with two people,' he said approvingly, and Sara felt a glow of pleasure. She enjoyed noting the names and numbers in her small, neat handwriting, and embellishing the hitherto blank margins with drawings.

Gil showed her the rooms where he worked at Vernon Court. They were on the ground floor, some way away from the rest of the house. Flowers were pressed to brown paperiness inside heavy books, butterflies pinioned in glass display cases. Sheaves of paper stood by the typewriter and scientific journals were stacked neatly on the shelves. Peering through Gil's microscope, Sara saw tiny creatures flicker in a drop of water, strange beings from another world.

Even in winter, Vernon Court's garden was luxuriant. Fronds of ivy wound round old stone urns. Hollies, their frilled leaves glossily green or variegated with cream, were a backdrop for beds of fern and dogwood. On the surface of a pool, a few leaves floated, like golden coins; below them orange and pearl-white carp flickered through the dark water. A summerhouse nestled in one corner of the walled garden, and a turret, smothered in Virginia creeper, looked down to where snowdrops pushed their green and white bells through the soil.

One morning, her grandmother asked Sara how long she intended to stay at Raheen. Alice Finborough added, 'You can stay here for ever, as far as I'm concerned. It is a delight and a joy to have you, darling girl. But I know that your mother and father miss you, and I wondered when you planned to go home.' When Sara did not reply, Alice said gently, 'What is it that you're waiting for, my dear?'

What is it that you're waiting for? Walking round Vernon Court's garden, Sara asked herself the same question. She was afraid that she knew the answer. This winter had been sharp with reminders of the previous one. However hard she tried to forget, each passing week and month contained anniversaries: of the evening she and Anton had had coffee together the first time, of their first kiss on Putney Bridge, of the bunch of witch hazel he had given her, with its cold, peppery scent.

She was waiting for Anton. She was waiting for Anton to write to her and tell her that it had all been a mistake. She was waiting for him to let her know that he still wanted her, still loved her. She was waiting for the moment when she would look out of her bedroom window at Raheen and see him, tall and handsome in the old black greatcoat that he liked to wear, striding up the drive.

★ ★ ★

Caroline Vernon always took the dogs for a walk before breakfast. It seemed to start off the day the right way, as well as giving her an appetite. She took the same route, round the perimeter of Vernon Court's garden, whatever the weather.

This morning it was raining heavily. In the porch, Caroline prised off gumboots clogged with mud, shook out her mackintosh and hung it on the peg. The dogs likewise shook their damp coats and panted, their pink tongues hanging out. Caroline led them to a room at the back of the house and fed them before going to the dining room.

Gil was seated at the table, reading the newspaper; Caroline kissed him good morning and then helped herself to bacon and eggs.

'The rain looks to be set in for the day,' she remarked. 'Is the tea still hot, Gil?'

He patted the teapot. 'Lukewarm, I'd say. Shall I call Mrs Regan?'

'No, no,' said Caroline. 'I'll go myself. It'll be quicker.'

She took the teapot and headed off to the kitchen. Returning five minutes later with a fresh pot of tea, she asked, 'What are your plans for today, Gil?'

'I'm going to work on my paper. And the car has a slow puncture, so I need to change the tyre.'

'The stove's smoking again,' said Caroline, as she spread butter on her toast. 'You must find Jimmy Coulter and ask him to sweep the chimney.'

'I'll dig him out of the pub.'

'Will you be visiting Miss Finborough?'

Gil turned a page of the newspaper. 'I don't know. I hadn't thought.'

'When did you see her last?'

He frowned. 'I'm not sure. Monday . . . then there was the puncture.'

'I think you should go to Raheen today, Gil.'

'If the rain stops, I could call in on my way to the coast, perhaps.'

Caroline was silent, looking at her son. She had never, as some had supposed, resented that it had been Marcus who had died, rather than Gil. She had loved both her sons equally: her admiration of Marcus's athleticism and spirit had not exceeded the tenderness

245

she felt for her second son. Gil was far cleverer than Marcus, who, at school, had been the cheerful, charming dunce.

Yet the depth of her love did not prevent her seeing Gil clearly, and she was not unaware of his faults. At thirty-one years old, Gil could be stubborn and was often fussy, habits that he had acquired in childhood. Glancing across the table, Caroline saw that, as usual, the bacon, egg and mushrooms on his plate lay carefully separate, not touching. A small boy, he had wept when a river of gravy had lapped on to a potato. Gil liked his immediate surroundings to be just so. His fussiness was the reason why, Caroline thought, in spite of his interest in the natural world, he disliked gardening, which was not a clean and tidy occupation. Indeed, Caroline often thought that Gil's study was fired more by a need for order, and to categorise, than by a passion for life.

Yet he seemed oblivious, much of the time, to the dereliction of the house in which he lived. His lack of engagement with the difficulties that threatened Vernon Court frustrated Caroline. He did not seem to have grasped the urgency of their predicament, the need to find a solution as soon as possible.

Caroline's love for her second son was just now mixed with exasperation. She said, in steely tones, 'If you are thinking of marrying Miss Finborough, then you mustn't delay too long.'

Gil looked up, startled. She had his attention now. 'Me, marry Sara?'

'Well, why not?' Caroline scraped the last of the marmalade out of the jar. 'You are unlikely to meet a girl more suitable.'

He frowned, turning the idea over in his mind. 'The Finboroughs are an old family,' he said thoughtfully. 'They're of good Anglo-Irish stock.'

'It's unfortunate that Richard Finborough went

into trade, of course. Though, nevertheless, there are benefits to that. Vernon Court needs money. We can't go on like this much longer. The roof will fall down if it's not repaired soon.' She watched as he cut his toast into neat triangles. 'You like Sara, don't you, Gil?'

'Yes. She's a nice girl.'

It was, Caroline thought, the highest compliment he had ever paid to any woman. She felt a flicker of relief.

'You like her too, don't you, Mother?'

'She seems a sweet, biddable creature, though a little . . . ' Caroline broke off, unable to find the right word to describe Sara Finborough. Emotional? Excitable? Temperamental? And just a touch . . . *frivolous?* Yet Gil must choose his bride from a restricted circle, and one could not afford to be too fussy.

'Alice Finborough has always lived exactly as she pleased,' she said. 'And the mother — Isabel — isn't exactly out of the top drawer, I fear. But these things can be overlooked. Sara is young and healthy, and she would be a good wife for you, Gil, I'm sure of it. I wouldn't suggest the match if I didn't think she was suitable. She will bring money to the marriage, which is essential, and she will give Vernon Court an heir.' She paused for a moment, reflecting on what a pleasure it would be to have an infant in the house once more. Feminine in neither her dress nor her manner, Caroline's strong, commanding nature softened in the company of small children.

'You need to marry so that you can have a son, Gil,' she said firmly. 'The Vernon line must be carried on.'

A gust of rain crashed against the window. Caroline noticed a dribble of water ooze through one of the holes in the frame.

She said briskly, 'Apparently there was some sort of unhappy love affair in London. That was why Sara Finborough came to Ireland. You mustn't wait too long,

Gil. You must ask her to marry you as soon as possible, before she forgets about this fellow and goes back to England.'

* * *

'What was she like?' asked Ruby. She and Philip were in a pub in the Fulham Road.

'Blonde, platinum blonde.' Philip put a beer glass in front of her.

'Dyed?'

'No, I don't think so.'

He fell silent, preoccupied, his long fingers fiddling with his cigarette case. '*Philip*,' said Ruby impatiently. 'What was she wearing?'

'Something black, I think.'

'Was she pretty?'

'Of course not,' he said coldly. 'She was *obvious*. Cheap.'

Ruby pictured Mrs Davenport looking wicked in low-cut black satin and a string of pearls. 'And her flat?' she said. 'Tell me about her flat.' A tart's boudoir — what would that look like? Pink ostrich feathers and leopardskin, perhaps.

'It was . . . ' he gave a shake of his head, ' . . . I can't remember. Just ordinary, I think.'

Ruby sighed. 'No red velvet chaise longue?'

'I don't think so.' He was turning the enamelled cigarette case over and over in his hands. His eyes were narrowed — with loathing, Ruby assumed, of the poisonous Mrs Davenport.

'What did she say to you? Did she look terribly guilty?'

'Guilty?' For the first time, he looked at her properly. 'No, I don't think she gave a damn.'

Ruby was impressed. 'I suppose someone like that would be as hard as nails.'

248

'I suppose so.' But his attention had slipped away from her again. 'She won't get away with it,' he said softly. 'I won't let her get away with it.'

★ ★ ★

Mrs Davenport hadn't been how Philip had expected her to be. She had seemed intelligent and well spoken, he had thought, for a tart and a gold-digger.

At the end of the afternoon, he waited for her outside the millinery shop. As she came out of the front door she caught sight of him. '*You*,' she said. He noticed her expression of distaste as she turned to lock the door. 'Why are you here?'

'You know why I'm here.'

'If you're going to demand ridiculous promises of me then you may as well not bother, because I won't make them.' She stalked off, leaving him standing outside the shop.

A moment's blind fury, and then he ran after her. 'What? Are you still here?' she said, as he drew level with her. She turned north, up Old Bond Street, her high heels clacking on the pavement. Philip fell into step beside her.

She said suddenly, 'And, for your information, Richard is hardly old enough to be my father. Not unless he was in the habit of fathering children while just out of the sixth form.'

Which made her, he calculated quickly, thirtyish. 'That doesn't excuse what you're doing.'

'I'm not trying to excuse it. I don't believe I need to excuse it.'

Her composure infuriated him. 'He's *married*, for God's sake!'

'Yes, I know. Richard's made no secret of it.'

'So you condone adultery?'

'Adultery?' She gave a little laugh. 'Oh, Philip, you

sound so pompous. No, I don't condone adultery, since you ask. But nor do I condemn it out of hand. Everything depends on the circumstances.'

She stood at the crossing, waiting for a gap in the traffic. He said harshly, 'That's nonsense.' He watched her as he spoke. He wanted to jolt her out of her complacency. 'That's just a sop to your conscience. You tell yourself that to make yourself feel better. Some things are just wrong.'

'Are they?' She looked at him coolly. 'Tell me, have you ever stolen anything?'

'Of course not!'

'But if you were starving — or if someone you loved was starving — and you had no food, then mightn't you steal then?'

They were briefly separated, passing a news-vendor's stand and the queue of people for *Evening Standards*. When they were together again, he said, 'I'd find a way. I wouldn't let myself be reduced to stealing.'

Her laughter had a note of scorn in it, this time. 'You say that because you've never lacked for anything.'

'That's not true!'

'Oh, Philip, of course it is.' Briefly, her eyes settled on him. He noticed that they were grey, the pure, pale grey of ice covering a pond in winter. 'You are Richard Finborough's son. What have you ever had to fight for?'

'You think I was born with a silver spoon in my mouth?'

'Well, weren't you?'

This wasn't how he had intended the conversation to go. He shouldn't have felt obliged to defend himself; it was she who should have been apologising, preferably weeping, admitting she was in the wrong and pleading for forgiveness. But her jibe had provoked him, and he said furiously, 'You know nothing about me! You don't know what you're talking about!'

'Have you ever been out of work?'

'No, but — '

'Millions of men are these days. Millions have to live on next to nothing — good, hard-working people.'

'I'm aware — '

'Where do you work?'

'You know that. Finboroughs.'

'Ah, *Finboroughs*.' A small smile. 'And how did you get your first job, Philip? Did you go for an interview . . . did you speak to the foreman?'

'Of course not. But I had to start on the factory floor, same as everyone else. I had to prove myself.'

'How tiresome for you.'

'If you think it's easy being the boss's son when you're working alongside the men on the factory floor, then you're mistaken!'

A sideways glance. 'I suppose there might be some resentment,' she acknowledged. 'But your father's employees would hardly risk making their feelings overt. Tell me, where do you live?'

Her question startled him, but he said, 'I have a flat in Chelsea.'

'And you are . . . how old?'

'Twenty-five,' he said stiffly.

'Do you have servants?'

'A woman comes in to cook and clean, that's all.'

'And at work you have a secretary, no doubt.' She smiled. 'It must be nice to have all those dreary little tasks taken away from you . . . one woman to mop your floor, another to type your letters.'

'Are you implying that I'm spoiled?'

'Of course you're spoiled. How could you be anything other than spoiled?'

Yet the fire seemed to have gone out of her, and he saw, as they passed beneath a streetlamp, that her face looked tired and set. He felt a thrill of triumph; he sensed that he was beating her, crushing her down.

Oxford Street was busy with people hurrying home

251

from work, and they were able to say little. Turning up Regent Street, she gave him a disdainful glance. 'Still there? How tenacious you are.'

'I'm not going until you've promised to leave my father alone.'

She drew to a sudden halt by iron railings that looked down over a basement. 'Shall I tell you about my life?' she said quietly. 'I expect it's been rather different from yours. I left school when I was fourteen to work in a shop. A couple of years ago, I decided to lease my own place. I work nine hours a day, six days a week. I've had to make a success of it because I support my parents as well as myself. No one cleans *my* floors or types *my* letters. I do everything for myself.'

'None of that excuses what you're doing.'

'I told you, I make no excuse for what I do. I never have done.' Glancing at her watch, she made a quick, nervous gesture. 'You're wasting your time, hounding me like this. Not long after you left my flat last night I had a telephone call from my sister. She told me that my mother was unwell. They've taken her to the Middlesex Hospital. That's where I'm going now. So, Philip, if you really wish to find yourself on a ward full of sick women, then keep following me. If not, I suggest you go home.'

She walked away. Philip stood on the pavement, watching her until she was absorbed into the darkness and the crowds. Then he retraced his footsteps to where he had parked the motor cycle.

Steffie called that night and they went out for a drink. The oddest thing: there he was with pretty, jolly Steffie, who did her best to take his mind off the events of the last week, and yet every now and then Mrs Davenport's pale grey eyes came into his vision. Mixed with his rage was a resentment of her treatment of him, along with a galled awareness that he had acted clumsily, and that he had allowed her to get the better of him. She had spoken to him as though he was a naïve boy. No woman had ever spoken to him like that before. His girlfriends had always been appreciative and admiring; some had wept buckets when, eventually, he had broken it off with them.

Claiming an early start the next day, he saw Steffie home at ten o'clock and went back to his flat. After he had poured himself a drink, Philip sat down on the sofa. His rage ebbed away at last, leaving him flat and exhausted and almost overwhelmed by disillusion. Though he tried not to think about his father, he could not help himself. He remembered his father letting him sit on his lap and steer the Rolls down the drive when he was a kid, and teaching him to sail in Cornwall, and taking him to Lords for the first time. Throughout his childhood, his mother had always been there, but his father had been far less predictable — his presence had been a treat, had made an occasion special. Philip's admiration of his father had been profound and enduring, in spite of their differences. Now, he found himself wondering whether it had all been a sham and a lie, whether he had only seen what his father had wanted him to see. Whether, even, he had been packed off to work in the City rather than at Hounslow so that his father could carry on as he chose unobserved . . . whether, perhaps, Theo had gone away because Theo had found out something horrible as well . . .

Philip swallowed the remainder of the whisky in one gulp and then poured himself another glass.

★ ★ ★

Kathleen Wallace, Elaine's mother, was suffering from bronchitis. Elaine's father sat at his wife's bedside during afternoon visiting hours, and Elaine and Gilda took their turn in the evening. On her daughters' arrival, Kathleen whispered a greeting from her steam

253

tent, coughed and shortly afterwards fell asleep with her mouth open, which for some reason she could not fathom, made Elaine, looking at her mother, want to cry.

Elaine had always disliked hospitals — the legacy, she supposed, of a tonsillectomy she had undergone when she was five. Her uselessness irked her: there was little she could do except hold her mother's hand or smooth a sheet. As they left the hospital after their first visit, Gilda told Elaine that she and Jimmy had decided to bring forward their wedding. They'd have a quiet ceremony, said Gilda, no frills or bells, and after they married they would live with Mother and Father. Mother, Gilda added, needed a rest, she was doing too much.

The following evening, their conversation, sitting beside the bed while their mother dozed, was sporadic. Elaine suspected that Gilda felt as she did — that it would be somehow unsuitable to enjoy their usual amusing everyday chitchat in the austere and forbidding setting of the bronchial ward. The silence, interrupted by the clanking of a tea-trolley or the moans of a patient in another bed, gave Elaine far too much time to reflect.

The night Philip Finborough had come to her flat, her initial reaction had been one of outrage. How dare he spy on her — how dare he intrude on the sanctuary of her flat? And then he had had the nerve to turn up at the shop the following evening. Anxious about her mother and tired after a long day, she had been intentionally cruel to him and had set out to puncture his conceit and arrogance. Philip Finborough was a spoiled, indulged brat. Her refusal to stop seeing Richard had probably been the first time he had failed to get exactly what he wanted.

But why hadn't she told Philip Finborough the truth, that she was not having an affair with his father, that their relationship was merely one of friendship — an unsuitable and secretive friendship, no doubt, but friendship nevertheless? Partly because she disliked being brow-beaten, she supposed, and Philip's demands had brought out her stubborn streak.

Yet here, in the echoing unease of the hospital ward, she forced herself to confront an uncomfortable truth — that in Richard's eyes their relationship had been more than friendship. She recalled their kiss in the storeroom. Richard Finborough might have — *probably had* — considered their meetings to be the prelude to an affair. She had always known that he admired her — would she have enjoyed his company as much if he had not? Which was worse, she wondered, to be the tart Philip Finborough believed her to be, or to be a tease?

When, that morning, Richard had telephoned, she had put him off, using the legitimate excuse of her mother's illness. Later, Richard had sent flowers, a large bouquet of pink roses; Elaine had taken them home to her flat, but they had not given her the same pleasure as his first bouquet, and in the end she had given them to her mother. Arranged in an institutionally plain glass vase on the metal locker, they looked overblown and out of place. She should have put them in the bin, she thought irritably.

After leaving the hospital, Elaine and Gilda walked to Goodge Street, where Gilda would take the Northern Line to Hendon and Elaine would change at Oxford Circus for St John's Wood. Before they parted, Elaine kissed Gilda and told her that she must choose a hat for her wedding from the shop. 'Whatever you like,' she said, with a smile. 'Something beautiful.'

It was almost nine o'clock by the time she reached home. As she turned the corner, she saw the bulky shape of a motor cycle parked at the kerb outside her house. Recognising Philip Finborough, Elaine gave an exasperated sigh and strode smartly to his side.

'Oh, for heaven's sake,' she said impatiently 'not you again.'

'Have you done it?' Philip's tone was aggressive and imperious. 'Have you told my father you won't see him any more?'

'I'm not going to speak to you any more about this, Philip. Please go.'

As she went to the door and fitted her key to the lock, Elaine heard, to her relief, the growl of the motor cycle engine as Philip started up the machine. Then, a second later, there was the squeal of rubber on tarmac. Turning quickly, she saw the motor cycle skid out of control, throwing off its rider and skirling on its side across to the wrong side of the road before crashing into a tree.

She dropped her bag and her keys and ran to him. Philip lay in the gutter, motionless. She tried to call out but could not catch her breath. Reaching him, she kneeled at his side, shaking him, saying his name.

Philip's eyelids fluttered, then opened, and Elaine sat back on her heels, weak with relief. There was blood on his forehead and he looked dazed. 'Are you hurt?' she demanded. 'Have you broken anything?'

He sat up. 'Don't think so.' He shuffled on to the kerb and sat with his eyes closed and his head bowed.

Hearing the noise of the crash, people had emerged from the nearby houses. Two men righted the motor bike and parked it on the pavement. Elaine said, 'You'd better come back to my flat.'

'The bike — '

'Never mind the wretched bike! You could ok have killed yourself!' Her voice rose, unnaturally high-pitched.

He stood up unsteadily. She put an arm round him to help him along the pavement and up the steps to the front door. Her hands scrabbled, searching in the darkness for her keys and bag. Inside the house, she helped him up the stairs to her flat. In the bathroom, Philip perched on the edge of the tub while she found cotton wool and Dettol.

He winced as she dabbed at the deep graze on his forehead. 'Keep still,' she said sharply. 'I have to clean this properly. There's dirt in it.'

When she had cleaned the cut in his forehead, she bandaged it with a square of lint. 'Are you hurt anywhere else?' she asked.

'My hands.'

He must have put out his hands to save himself: the tip of each finger had been raggedly skinned off. She cleaned the grit from the wounds and dabbed them with disinfectant. He had large, square, strong hands, like Richard's. She saw, as she bandaged them, that he was very pale, and that he was making an immense effort not to shake with reaction.

'There,' she said, in the brisk tone she had adopted to disguise both her shock and the awkwardness of the situation. 'That's quite neat, isn't it? You're lucky I'm a milliner and good at close work. You've torn a good pair of trousers to shreds, but I'm sure someone will be able to patch them for you. And you'll be as handsome as ever in a short while, I don't doubt. Now, come and sit on the sofa and I'll make you a cup of tea.'

He shook his head. 'I don't need tea. I'd better go.'

'You'll do as you're told!' The words blazed out of her; she saw his eyes widen.

She took a deep breath, struggling to control herself. 'You're to sit down and rest until I'm sure that you're well enough to leave, Philip. Dear God, I thought you were dead, back there!'

'Would you have cared?'

She wanted to slap him. 'My husband died in a road accident,' she said harshly. She remembered the policeman knocking at the door and how she had caressed Hadley's bruised face in the mortuary. 'He died because of a stupid piece of carelessness, a moment's rashness. Do you think I would want to

257

inflict *that* on your parents? Do you really think that, however much you annoy me, I would want *that* to happen to you? For heaven's sake, Philip, grow up!'

She heard him mutter something that might have been an apology and then he went into the living room and sat down on the sofa. Seeing him fumbling with a packet of cigarettes, she took the packet off him and lit two, one for each of them. She rarely smoked but she needed to smoke now.

In the kitchen, as she waited for the kettle to boil, the reaction set in. She felt sick and weary, mostly of herself. She seemed to keep seeing the motor cycle skidding away and Philip thrown on to the road. There were tears very close to the surface and it took an effort to hold them back.

She carried the tray into the living room. He was sitting still, his bandaged hands resting on his lap. 'There,' she said, putting a cup of sugary tea on the table beside him. 'Drink that.' Looking at him more closely, she was shocked to recognise an expression of utter misery in his eyes.

'Are you sure you don't need a doctor?'

'No, I'm fine. Thanks.'

While he drank the tea they sat in silence. When he had finished, she said, 'I'll call you a taxi, then.' At the door, she looked back at him. 'Chelsea, wasn't it?'

He gave her the address. Elaine called a taxi from the phone box at the corner of the street. When she went back to the living room Philip was trying to thread an injured hand into the sleeve of his leather jacket.

'Here,' she said. 'Let me.' She held up the jacket and helped him guide his hand into it.

'*Christ*,' he said angrily. 'I feel like a baby.'

'Let this be a lesson to you to drive more carefully.' A silence, then she added, her voice low, 'Your father and I were never lovers. We were just friends, and that's the truth. If I haven't put it so plainly before then it's because I believe — I still believe — that it's none of your business. I didn't mean to hurt anyone. I know what you think of me — I can see why you might feel like that — but I truly did not mean to hurt anyone.'

She had turned away from him so that he could not see that she was crying. She heard him say, 'I should go,' and then the door opened and closed behind him.

★ ★ ★

Two days later, to Philip's astonishment, Elaine telephoned him.

He was at work in his office, trying to do something useful. She said, 'I've tracked you down at last. I wanted to find out whether you were all right.'

'I'm OK,' he said, 'though I feel as if I'm wearing boxing gloves all the time. I hadn't realised how useful fingers were.' In the short pause that followed, he took the opportunity to say, 'I'm sorry about the other night. I behaved like a complete idiot. I don't usually make such an ass of myself.'

'I'm pleased to hear it.' Another, longer, pause. 'Philip, there's something I need to say to you.' She broke off; he heard her give a hiss of exasperation. Then she whispered, 'I've a customer, I'll have to go. I'll phone again later.'

'No,' he said. 'I have to leave for the wharf now. I'll be there most of the day.' He thought quickly. 'I'll meet you at the Lyons at Piccadilly Circus at five.' He put the phone down before she could refuse.

★ ★ ★

He wasn't sure that she would come. He made certain to get there first and had the Nippy show him to a corner table. A few minutes later, Mrs Davenport came into the teashop. She was wearing a pearl-grey skirt and

259

jacket, edged in black, and a grey hat with a black silk flower pinned to the brim.

He stood up as she approached the table. Her gaze appraised him. 'You look a little better than the last time I saw you.'

'I was lucky, only a few scratches. The bike's worse off than me. It's still in the garage, I'm afraid — the front wheel's buckled.' The waitress approached to take their order. 'What will you have, Mrs Davenport?'

'Just tea, thank you.'

'I'm starving. You don't mind if I eat, do you?'

She shook her head. Philip ordered poached eggs on toast and tea. When they were alone again, she said, as she took off her gloves, 'I won't be seeing your father again. I've made that clear to him.'

He felt a surge of triumph. 'Good,' he said, adding as a grudging afterthought, 'Thank you.'

'You won't be too angry with him, will you? It was never anything serious.' She flushed. 'That makes me sound . . . careless. What I mean is — I needed a friend. I was lonely and Richard was kind. I'm not trying to make excuses or to ask for sympathy, but that's why it happened. I was just lonely.'

He was pleased to see that her self-possession had faltered a little. He said, 'When you told me about your husband being killed in a road accident — I hadn't realised you were a widow.'

'I suppose you thought I'd adopted a married name in a vain fling at respectability.' She threw him a cool look. 'Does it make it any better being a widow? I shouldn't have thought so.'

The tea arrived. He held up his bandaged hands and said, 'You'd better pour.' Then he said, 'What was he like? When did he die?'

'You believe in coming straight to the point, don't you, Philip?' She held the strainer over the cup. 'Hadley was sweet and clever, and hopelessly absent-minded. He died three years ago next April. As I told you, his accident was an utter, stupid waste of a life. If you'd wanted to find a way to shake me up the other night, you couldn't have chosen a better one.'

He liked her small, neat careful movements as she poured the tea; he remembered the care she had taken, bandaging his hands. He grinned. 'You don't think I'd have smashed my bike up just to make a point, do you?'

'I don't know, Philip. I suspect you have a ruthless streak.' Elaine put a cup of tea beside him. Then she shook her head and said, in an exasperated voice, 'Why do I find myself wanting to justify myself to you? It's quite ridiculous.'

'Perhaps you have a guilty conscience.'

'Haven't you ever been lonely?' Her voice had an edge; she put down the teapot. 'I mean really, truly, achingly lonely, knowing that no one you know understands how you are feeling?'

The question took him by surprise, but he searched his memory. 'When I started at my prep school, I suppose, when I first left home, it was pretty awful. But there were other new boys and I got used to it.'

'I don't suppose you've ever been short of money, either. I don't suppose you've ever wondered how on earth you were going to pay the next bill.'

'I'm in hock for the bike,' he said ruefully. 'And now there's going to be a huge garage bill on top of that.' His food arrived, he stabbed an egg yolk. 'But if you mean, have I ever been poor, then no, I haven't.'

'After Hadley died, after I bought the lease on the shop, there were months when I lived on tinned sardines and toast. Months when I knew I shouldn't buy a magazine or go to the cinema, months of knowing I mustn't buy a pair of stockings or a new scarf to cheer myself up. Everything around me was dreary and inside me there was a desert. That's what it felt like. And unless you've been through it — unless you've lost

261

someone you loved — you have no idea, no idea at all.' Her clear grey eyes were fierce. 'As I said, I'm not making excuses, I don't believe I have to. I wanted some fun, some pleasure, that's all. I hadn't seemed to have had any fun for a very long time. But I seem to have caused a lot of pain. I didn't mean to, but I did, and I'm sorry. We both made a stupid mistake and I'm sorry you've been hurt.'

Philip spooned sugar into his tea. 'But Dad was married, you knew that. It can't have been a surprise, what happened.'

She sighed. 'The trouble is, single men have a way of falling in love with a woman. And then they get hurt when she doesn't want to see them any more. And then married men, well . . .'

He leaned across the table to her. 'Do they always fall in love with you?'

'Quite often, yes.'

He attacked his toast. 'You should find some complete rotter who's only after you for your looks.'

'Perhaps I will.' Her hand reached for her bag. 'Well, that's all I wanted to say.'

'Don't rush off.'

She frowned. 'Why not?'

He grinned again. 'I need someone to cut up my crusts.'

She snatched the knife and fork from him and cut up the toast. 'There,' she said. 'Will that do?' She rose and turned to go. Then, looking back, she said, 'I feel sorry for your girlfriends. Do you make them wait on you hand and foot?'

She walked away from him. As she left the restaurant, Philip wolfed down the last of the crusts and threw a few shillings on to the table to cover the bill.

Outside, he searched around until he caught sight of her, heading towards the Tube station. His gaze moved from the loop of fair hair, just visible beneath the

brim of her hat, to her narrow waist, and he realised
with a jarring shock, that what he felt, seeing her,
was not only pleasure at having won, at having got
the better of her, but an intense and powerful
attraction.

9

Her questions were little gnawing bites at him.

What was her name? *Elaine Davenport.* She tasted the name gingerly, as though it burned her mouth. How old is she? Where did you meet her? What does she look like? Is she fair or is she dark? How long have you been seeing her?

When he protested, asking why she continued to hurt herself now that it was over, she said harshly, 'These things are never over. Never.'

Her questions troubled him, because they picked at the secret contained inside them.

'Did you sleep with her, Richard?'

'No. *No.*'

'But you kissed her.'

He remembered the storeroom, the papers fluttering to the floor, the warmth of her skin through her silk blouse, the taste of gin on her mouth.

'I didn't mean this to happen,' he said hopelessly.

'You mean,' she said, with a glance that seemed to see into his soul, 'you didn't mean me to find out.'

★ ★ ★

It had been the day he had known that Provosts was his. He had felt that he was the master of all he surveyed, capable of anything.

He had met Elaine in their usual place. 'Did you know that your son came to see me?' she had said to him.

And he had repeated, shocked: 'My son? Philip?'

'He came to my flat and then to the shop. He knows about us and so does your wife. He was very angry, as

264

he had every right to be. He made me feel cheap, actually. So that's it, I'm afraid. I thought I should tell you in person, Richard. It always seems shabby to finish with someone by writing a letter.'

'*Finish it?*' He had seemed incapable of any speech other than stunned repetition.

'Yes, of course. We mustn't see each other again.'

He had pleaded with her. There was no need for that, he had said. They must keep their distance for a while, that was all, but they could keep in touch, surely.

Her look had contained a measure of contempt. 'No, Richard, that won't do. You know it won't. I won't cause any more damage than I have done already. No meetings, no letters, no phone calls. When you've had time to think about it you'll see that I'm right.'

'But, Elaine,' he heard himself say. 'I love you.'

'No you don't, Richard,' she had said coolly. 'You desire me, and that's not the same at all.'

Then she had put her untouched drink down on the table and had walked out of the bar. He had thought of following after her but, in the end, had not. He had endured such a clashing mixture of emotions, such a fast descent from euphoria to despair, that he had felt physically ill, and had put a hand to his ribs to check the beating of his heart. For a moment, even his body seemed about to become unpredictable, unreliable.

He had left the bar and driven home. None of the rooms felt right without Isabel there. That Philip knew about Elaine Davenport dismayed him. Hard enough to speak to Isabel — impossible to discuss this with a son. It was not Philip's business, he thought angrily. Philip had no right to involve himself.

In his study, Richard began to go through Provosts' ledger-books. Yet his mind kept drifting: he remembered Elaine, in the shop, glancing into the mirror as she arranged the hat and then turning to him, her lovely face lit up by her smile. He couldn't think why it hurt so much, to put an end to something that had just been *fun*.

★ ★ ★

The first time Richard had come to Porthglas, Isabel had sent him away without speaking to him. He had hammered on the door for a while, then she heard the car engine ignite, then die into the distance. Letters arrived: she put them in the fire without reading them. She would stay at Porthglas, she would make a new life for herself, a dignified, untroubled sort of life, in which she gardened and painted and took a little part-time job, perhaps, in St Ives. How dare he inflict on her such humiliation — and with a *shopkeeper*! Yet why should she be surprised that, this time, he had chosen not some society hostess to betray her with, but a woman from the lower classes? Years ago, in Lynton, he had chosen *her*, hadn't he?

At night, she slept — or failed to sleep — in the bedroom they had always shared. In the house, reminders of summers past lay scattered around — a toy boat with a red triangular sail, a fishing-net, a doll lacking an arm.

The next time, he was angry, defensive. 'A few kisses hardly constitutes a crime,' he told her.

It was raining heavily. She had taken pity on him, had let him into the sun-room at the front of the house to stand among the wicker chairs and plantpots, his raincoat dripping on to the flagstones.

'Kisses lead to other things,' she said sharply. 'You know that, Richard. Don't talk as if you were an innocent.'

He made a disparaging sound. 'I wondered how long it would take you to start that.'

'Start what?'

'Raking up my past offences. Listing every time I've so much as glanced at another woman.'

'You *slept* with them!'

'Once or twice, years ago. It meant nothing. I can hardly even remember their names.'

'I remember their names!'

'Why? They were unimportant.' He let out a furious lungful of air. 'I wish you would learn not to be so bourgeois about these things, Isabel.'

'*Bourgeois*!' The word hurt her deeply; she found herself shouting, 'What about you? You are callous, careless — you think you can have everything you want, and you don't care about the hurt you cause!'

'Why do you *brood* so? Why do you let yourself dwell on things?'

She hissed, 'Have you any idea how it felt to have my son tell me of my husband's unfaithfulness?'

His expression altered. For the first time he looked ashamed. 'Philip won't speak to me,' he muttered. 'He hasn't spoken to me since. You shouldn't have let him involve himself. It was wrong of you, Isabel.'

'Wrong? *You* dare to say that to *me*?' Yet she found herself remembering the look in Philip's eyes, his words to her as he left the house. *It'll be all right, I promise you. I'll sort it out.* I should have gone after him, she thought. I shouldn't have let him have any part in this.

She said harshly, 'You'll never change, will you?'

'I admit that some of the fault was on my side — '

'It's the deceit I hate, Richard, the deceit!'

He took a step towards her. 'Come home with me, Isabel. You've been sulking here long enough.'

Sulking, she thought. As if this were some trivial spat and she a moody child.

'No,' she said coldly, moving away from him. 'I'd rather stay at Porthglas. I don't wish to be with you just now, Richard.'

His face hardened. 'As you wish.'

He walked out of the door. She saw him head up the path, the rain lashing at him. A flash of car headlamps and he was gone. She sat down, pulling at the rings on her fingers. *It's the deceit I hate*, she had said — she, who had lived a lie since the day they had married. They were made for each other, she thought acidly, imperfect, traitorous, the pair of them.

A part of her regretted not having gone with him. She thought of their home and their routine and the warmth of his body beside her in bed at night. She went upstairs to the bedroom and stood at the window, looking out to the sea. 'Richard,' she whispered. Her anger died, replaced by a terrible hurt and a rush of hatred for the woman who had divided her from her husband. She did not even know what Elaine Davenport looked like. She might pass her in the street, she thought, and not recognise her.

★   ★   ★

A boat bound for Bristol had been run on to the rocks in a gale and lay aslant in the bay, stricken, barrels and boxes bleeding from the hole in its hull. Objects bobbed on the sea or were scattered along the shore — a canvas shoe, a Paisley shawl, wrapped around a length of bladderwrack, and a glass jar, half-buried in the sand, containing a tawny-coloured powder. People from the nearby villages scoured the sands, picking up flotsam and jetsam.

Isabel remembered a summer they had spent at Porthglas with the children. There had been a violent storm that had thrown a fresh scattering of shells on to the shore, pink and grey and frilled with cream, their hollows clogged with wet, compacted sand. She remembered the hiss of waves and the clatter of shells as Sara had dropped them into her tin pail. And the warmth of Sara's hand in hers, and how she had kept checking that the boys, who were playing on the boat, were safe.

She looked back and saw Richard, standing near the tumbled rocks and boulders that marked the cleft in the cliff. He must have driven down from London overnight. She would have liked to walk away from him, so that she would not rub the hurt raw again, but she was cold and wet and she knew that he wouldn't just turn round and drive back to London, leaving her in peace. She headed across the sand to him.

'A wet morning for a walk,' he said.

'I like the rain. I like storms.'

'I know,' he said. 'I remember.'

He put up his umbrella and held it over her as they scrambled back over the rocks, up the chasm. Once, she missed her footing, and he put out a hand to save her, and she flinched. Touch, that had for so many years been a part of their everyday language, had become treacherous.

In the house, they hung up their wet coats. Isabel towelled her hair as she waited for the kettle to boil. She arranged on a tray bread and butter and marmalade, and took it through to the sitting room.

'Help yourself,' she said. 'You must be hungry.'

'Thank you.' He was standing at the fire, drying himself. He looked tired and drawn. He said, 'Come home, Isabel.' When she did not reply, he said softly, '*Please*. I need you. I miss you.'

'No, Richard.' She went to look out of the window. The ship that had foundered in the bay had begun to break up. The stern shivered, battered by waves.

'Isabel, please. You can't stay here for ever.'

'I can if I choose to. It's *my* house.'

'I know, I know.' In his voice there was a mixture of desperation and impatience. 'I don't know what more I can do. I don't know what more I can say.'

'Tell me what *she* gave you that you did not have from me.'

'Nothing! It wasn't like that.'

'*Why*, then, Richard?'

'I don't know . . . I didn't think . . . '

'Nonsense,' she said coldly. 'Of course you did. You always think. I know what you thought, Richard. You thought you could get away with it. You thought you could have her and still keep me. You thought I was a fool.'

'No.'

'Don't lie to me! I know I'm right!'

'I'd never think you a fool, Isabel. It isn't in me to think that. It's I who've been the fool.'

'How many more times will I have to endure this humiliation?'

'Never, I promise.'

'How can I believe anything you say?'

'I made a mistake, that's all!' His fists were clenched. 'It was just a friendship! I swear to you it was never a love affair!'

In his words and demeanour she read an evasion. Inside her, something plummeted, as if she had stepped into a lift that had fallen too fast.

'Tell me the truth, Richard. It was more than that, wasn't it?'

His fist thumped his palm. 'Oh, for God's sake, I didn't even go to bed with her!'

'No, but you felt something for her, didn't you?'

She saw his eyes change, though he looked away quickly. Her heart constricted.

When he spoke again, his anger had gone. 'Whatever I felt, it's over now. Elaine refuses to see me, so you need have no fear . . . '

'*She* finished it?'

A short pause before he answered. 'Yes. You asked for

the truth, Isabel, and that's the truth.'

She sat down, her knuckles pressed against her mouth. 'If I had not found out . . . if Philip had not told me . . .'

'It would have finished soon enough. Something like that — it would never have lasted.'

She cried angrily, 'It should never have begun!'

'No. Of course not.' He ran a hand over his face. 'I didn't think — or I thought it was harmless, I suppose.'

'*Harmless!* What a feeble thing our marriage is if I can't even trust you to be honest with me!'

He groaned. 'What else can I say except that I'm sorry, and that it won't happen again?'

She shook her head. 'No, not good enough. No, Richard.'

Looking out of the window, she saw a wave crash over the hull of the holed ship, tearing the superstructure apart. The hull was splitting in two, the masts and planking snapped like matchsticks.

Richard said, his voice low, 'Isabel, I beg of you, come home. We need you.'

'We?'

'Sara and I.'

She spun round to him. 'Has Sara come home?'

'Not yet, but soon, in a couple of days.'

'Richard, why on earth didn't you tell me? Is she all right?'

'She's very well, I believe.' He frowned. 'She wants to marry that chap.'

'Marry? Sara? Who does she want to marry?' A sudden, alarming thought. 'Not that Austrian — not Anton Wolff?'

'No, no, of course not. She wants to marry Gil Vernon.'

'Gil Vernon?'

'You remember, Isabel, we dined with the Vernons at Christmas.'

Isabel stared at him. It took an effort to wrench her mind back. Christmas, though only six weeks ago, now seemed to her a time of almost fairy-tale happiness. She remembered the beautiful, mouldering house, sur-rounded by its dark green demesne. She remembered that she had found Caroline Vernon forbidding and that it had galled her to discover that, after so long, she still preserved a vestige of her old deference to the English upper classes.

'I had a letter from him,' said Richard. 'From Vernon, asking for Sara's hand in marriage.'

'And Sara *wants* to marry him?'

'It appears so. She wrote saying so.'

'Gil Vernon . . . '

'They're a good family, an old family. The Vernons have been in Ireland longer than the Finboroughs.'

She frowned. 'Sara would live in *Ireland*.'

'It's not so very far,' he said gently. 'I know you'd have preferred her closer to you, but there are ferries and trains, and I'll drive you over there as often as you like.'

In her memory, she tried to picture Gil Vernon. 'He was dark, wasn't he, Richard?'

'All the Vernons are dark. There's some story that one of them married a descendant of some Spanish grandee washed up in Ireland by the Armada — rubbish, I don't doubt.'

She felt dazed. 'I had no idea there was anything between them.'

'No. Nor had I. It's a surprise, isn't it?'

'Their letters,' she said.

He patted his pockets, frowning. 'I don't think I've brought them.'

'*Richard*.' She had almost forgotten what it felt like to be ordinarily annoyed with him, to feel her customary irritation at the slight distance he always seemed to keep from the family, his lack of attention, his vagueness about what she knew were the most important things in the world. But so much better, she found herself thinking, to feel exasperated with him, rather than destroyed by him.

'How can I tell whether he's the right man for Sara if I can't read his letter, Richard? Or hers?'

'She seems determined to have him. And there's no reasonable objection we could make, Isabel, not this time. Gil Vernon isn't some vagabond, like that foreign fellow. The Vernons are our sort of people. And Sara's twenty-one in May, so even if I refused to give my consent — and I can see no reason why I should — they would be able to marry in a few months' time.' He paused, then said coaxingly, 'Come back to London with me, Isabel. Sara's coming home in a day or two — you can ask her all about it. And her chap — Gil — intends to come to London in a couple of weeks.' His voice softened. 'Come home, Isabel. Come home with me.'

'I can't,' she whispered.

'You can. Just step in the car and I'll drive you back to London.' He had come to stand beside her. He took her hand. This time she did not flinch. 'Forgive me,' he said.

She said bluntly, 'I don't know if I can. I've never been much good at forgiving. I've never known quite how to do it. If I forgave you, would it mean that I shouldn't mind any more?'

A quick exhalation of breath. 'No, of course not. But please understand — '

'No,' she said fiercely. 'Understanding doesn't help at all. There's no understanding, no explanation that doesn't make me feel foolish and unwanted and *old*.'

'*Isabel*. What I feel about you has never altered. You may find that hard to believe, but I know that it's true. I love you as much as I did the day I first saw you. I will always love you. Nothing I've done, nothing that's happened will change that. Come home, Isabel. Come home for Sara, if not for me.'

Though she still felt lost and fragile, liable to be torn apart, like the ship on the rocks, she sighed and said, 'Yes. Very well, I think I must.' Then, seeing his relief written on his face, she added, her voice hard: 'But this is the last time, Richard. If you ever humiliate me again, then that will be the end. I shall leave you, I promise you that.'

★ ★ ★

The first time Philip went to see Elaine Davenport, a week or so after their meeting in the Lyons tearoom, it had been to find out whether he had been mistaken in believing that he was attracted to her. Or that's what he had told himself.

'Checking up on me, are you, Philip?' she had asked, and he had shrugged and said something noncommittal.

He tried to keep away from her. He worked long into the evenings, distracted himself with friends and girlfriends, motor-biked for miles, and, more than once, got very drunk. Nothing erased her from his mind. He couldn't understand why he wanted to see someone he disliked so much. He couldn't understand how loathing could be so close to desire.

He went to see her again, calling at the shop after work. Her arched, pencil-thin eyebrows rose, seeing him.

'Hello, Philip.'

'Hello.' There was a silence, he ventured some ridiculous remark about the weather.

It was six o'clock. She turned the shop sign to 'Closed' and said, 'What do you want, Philip?'

'Nothing.' He had begun to feel angry with himself for coming here, for making such a fool of himself.

'I see.' She was wrapping a hat in layers of tissue paper. Then she said, 'If you've nothing better to do you may as well help me count the change.'

The next time, she didn't ask him why he had come. He noticed that, and puzzled over the significance of it. He remembered that she had told him she was lonely. Perhaps, in her current situation, any sort of friend would do.

Away from her, he remembered the smooth paleness of her skin and the soft roundness of arm and calf. He remembered the way she moved, the way she tilted her head to one side when she smiled and the gentle inflexion of her voice. He remembered her long, tapered fingers tying the bandages on his hand and her proximity to him — her warmth and the scent of her skin — as she had cleaned the wound on his head. He remembered how she had fought him, stood up to him, how reluctant she had been to let him get the better of her.

He realised that he couldn't go on like this. He went back to the shop. Though the 'Closed' sign was up, he could see Elaine Davenport through the window. There was another woman with her. He decided to come back another day, changed his mind and opened the door.

She looked up at him, startled. The other woman, who was trying on a hat, turned to look at him as well.

Elaine recovered herself quickly. 'Good evening, Mr Finborough.'

'I wondered if I could have a word with you, Mrs Davenport.'

'I'm rather busy just now. If it's important, perhaps you could come back another time.'

Her choice of words, 'if it's important', annoyed him, and hardened his determination to get an answer out of her tonight.

'I can wait,' he said. 'I'll come back in fifteen minutes.'

It was her turn to look annoyed. She said, 'If you like,' and went back to adjusting the hat.

Philip drank a Scotch in a pub up the road before returning to the hat shop. Opening the door, he asked Elaine, 'Has your customer gone?'

'She wasn't a customer. That was my sister, Gilda. And yes, she's gone.'

He had realised that he had no idea of her tastes. She might hate ballet, detest plays. He said, 'I've got a couple of tickets for *Glamorous Night*. I wondered whether you'd like to come.'

She paused, locking the drawer of the till. She gave a brittle little laugh. 'I hardly think so, Philip.'

'Or we could go to something else, if you don't care for musicals. A film, if you prefer.'

She turned to look at him. 'You came here to ask me out?'

'Yes.'

'For a *date*?'

'Yes.'

She laughed again. 'Why, Philip?'

He seemed to have no option but to be honest. 'Because I wanted to see you.'

'You're making fun of me.'

'Oh, for heaven's sake . . . ' He felt himself becoming annoyed again. 'This isn't exactly easy for me, you know.'

'Did you expect me to make it easy?'

'Not necessarily. But not to laugh at me.'

'Let me get this absolutely straight. You came here to ask me to the theatre. Or the cinema, or something. Not as a friend, presumably — you and I can hardly expect to be friends.'

He said levelly, 'No, not as a friend.'

She had picked up a length of ribbon and was winding it round her fingers. She shook her head. 'This is quite extraordinary.'

'I don't know why you say that. After all, we've seen each other several times since — ' he had been going to say, 'since my father'; he changed it to — 'since my accident. It can hardly have come as a complete surprise.'

'I was tolerating you, Philip, nothing more.' Her voice was cold. 'I thought I owed you at least *politeness*. You appear to have misinterpreted that.'

He said softly, 'I don't believe you.'

The ribbon slipped and uncoiled; angrily, she stuffed it into a cardboard box. 'You seem to be suggesting that you and I could become something more than friends. When you know perfectly well that your father and I — ' She broke off. Her eyes narrowed, looking at him. 'I suppose this is your way of punishing your father.'

He was taken off guard. He said furiously, 'No.'

'No? Oh, come on, Philip, why else are you here?'

'Because I admire you.'

'No, Philip, I don't think you do,' she said coolly. 'I think you despise me.'

His temper snapped. 'Do you think I wanted this? Do you think I haven't tried to stop thinking about you? Do you think it isn't degrading for me to come here and plead with you?'

'*Degrading?*' Her pale complexion had flushed. 'How dare you?'

'I didn't choose to be attracted to you!' he yelled, and then he closed his eyes momentarily, and said, 'Oh Christ. I should never have come. Don't worry, I won't trouble you again.' He left the shop, slamming the door behind him.

★　★　★

Ruby met Sara in Fortnum's. Sara, who had come straight from her mother's dressmaker, ordered tea and cakes.

Ruby asked her what her wedding dress was to be like.

Sara said vaguely, 'Long . . . white . . . '

Ruby gave a little scream. 'Sara. Properly white, or oyster or cream? Silk or satin or tulle or what?'

'Perhaps it's satin, darling. I can't remember.'

Sara told her how she and Gil had met. 'It was on the beach,' she said. 'My horse threw me and I broke my wrist and hurt my head. And when I came round, Gil was there.'

'Did he sweep you up in his arms and carry you home?'

'No, he gave me some tea and told me about razor-shells. And then we walked back to Raheen.'

The wedding was to be in three months' time. Ruby was to be Sara's bridesmaid. Ruby had wondered whether Sara had insisted on the wedding being so soon because she didn't want to have the opportunity for second thoughts — because, in the flamboyant manner of the Finboroughs, she preferred to throw herself against the hurdle of marriage, her eyes shut tight.

'Mummy wanted me to wait,' said Sara, 'but I said no. Gil wants to go to Scotland on our honeymoon and he says the midges will be up if we go any later than June.'

Struck by the awfulness of timing one's wedding to the rhythms of insect life, Ruby began, 'But, Sara — '

Sara interrupted, 'I won't wait. Not this time. It's bad enough being at home again just for a few months. I couldn't bear it any longer.' Her face was set.

'You could go back to Ireland, to your grandmother's.'

'And then what?' said Sara scornfully. 'Ride a little . . . walk a little . . . visit my grandmother's friends. I have to make my life move on. It seems to have been stuck — frozen solid — for ages.' She sounded calm but Ruby noticed that she was fiddling with her sapphire engagement ring, turning it round and round on her finger. 'For months and months I've felt as though I've been stuck behind a glass wall. Nothing feels real. I have to make myself do *something*.'

The tearoom was busy with mothers and daughters, husbands and wives, and small groups of chattering friends. Ruby asked curiously, 'Do you love him?'

'Of course I do, darling. I'd hardly marry him if I didn't love him.'

'I mean, do you love him like you loved Anton?'

'I made a mistake with Anton. He didn't love me. If he had loved me, he'd ~~have~~ waited for me. But he didn't. If he ever loved me at all, he didn't love me *enough*.'

'Even if that's true, it doesn't mean you have to marry Gil Vernon.'

'I adore Gil,' said Sara firmly. 'He's so clever and he knows so many things. I know he isn't as handsome and dashing as Anton was, but that's the point. Anton and I were too different. Gil's Anglo-Irish, and I've always loved Ireland best of all, you know that, and his family knows lots of the same people our family knows.'

She told Ruby about Gil's proposal, in the walled garden at Vernon Court. 'There's plenty of good reasons why I should marry Gil,' Sara added. 'He's my sort, Anton wasn't, he wasn't a Finborough sort of man. He was interested in politics and you know I don't know anything at all about politics. Anton had travelled a lot and the only places I've ever been are Cornwall and Ireland, and, to be honest, I've never really wanted to go anywhere else. Anton was always wanting to change the world, and I've always been happy with everything as it is. I probably wasn't clever enough for him, and that's the truth. I don't suppose I'm clever enough for Gil, either, but he likes telling me about things and I like to listen. He's had papers published in scientific journals, and he's written a book about frogs — or perhaps it was

279

toads.' She eyed Ruby. 'I plan to be his helpmeet.'

Ruby smirked. 'I'm never quite sure what helpmeets do.'

'Neither am I.' Sara took another cake. 'But I shall find out, and I shall be a very good one.'

'But what about sex?'

'Oh, I'm sure it'll be heavenly, darling. And one doesn't have to do it all the time, does one?' Sara gave Ruby an interested glance. 'Have you . . . ?'

'No, not yet.'

Sara cut her cake in half. 'Caroline has three lovely dogs and she's promised to let me walk them. And the house is an absolute dream, Ruby, you can't imagine. I'm going to love living there. It's not grand, like Raheen, but there are lots of twisting staircases in funny places and odd little rooms and you're not quite sure what they're for. Sleeping Beauty's castle — that's what I thought the first time I saw Vernon Court. I'm sure I'll be happy there. I'm sure I'll be most blissfully happy.' There was a note of determination in her voice.

A few days later Ruby received a note from Isabel inviting her to dinner to celebrate Sara's engagement to Gil Vernon. There was no mention of her exile, no reference to the events that had led to her being closed out of the Finboroughs' lives. Ruby's heart lifted. She was a part of the privileged, exclusive court once more; she was being allowed back inside the enchanted circle.

Arriving at the Finboroughs' house on Saturday evening, she felt the familiar, and much missed, pleasure of belonging. There was the chatter from the drawing room, the sound of the maids' footsteps, hurrying along corridors and stairs, the clink of china and cutlery as they laid the table, and the flickering glow of candlelight — Isabel always insisted on candlelight at formal dinners. Introduced over pre-dinner sherry to Gil and Caroline Vernon, Ruby was amused to find herself quickly dismissed as unimportant by Caroline, and subjected to a discourse on the untypical weather patterns of the season by Gil, and then, no longer engaged in conversation with anyone in particular, she stepped back and watched, enjoying the sense of being enveloped by the glitter and vibrancy that, as a child, had been such a revelation to her. Watching, she saw that Sara's months in Ireland had changed her in a way that Ruby could not immediately define, and that Isabel looked beautiful and brittle, and that Richard's expansive bonhomie was, perhaps, just a little forced.

But her gaze would always slide to one person, as if drawn there by a magnetic impulse, so that she had to make a conscious effort not to look at Philip, not to let herself drink in every curve and line of his features, or try to interpret the meaning of his stance and expression. To be in the same room as Philip meant that her every movement and word must be calculated, that she must always act, that nothing was natural or instinctive.

She went to stand at his side. She murmured, 'What do you think of him, Philip?'

'Sara's beloved? Bit of a stuffed shirt.'

'Gil told me about the Gulf Stream.'

'Lucky you. Why on earth is Sara marrying him?'

'She says she loves him.'

Philip snorted. Ruby pointed out, 'People don't necessarily fall in love with the people one expects them to fall in love with.'

'He's a bore,' said Philip crisply. 'I suppose she's marrying him for the house, the estate.'

'You know Sara wouldn't do that.' Ruby watched Sara, bright and vivid, beside her stolid fiancé. 'I think . . .'

'What?'

'I think she thinks he's romantic. They met in a very

281

romantic way, you see, when her horse threw her. I think she thinks of him as her hero. I think she sees him as her rescuer.'

Glancing at Philip, she realised that he wasn't really listening to her, so, to conceal the downward plunge of her spirits, she said lightly, 'Such a lot of people.'

'Oh, you know my parents never do things by halves. Can't give a dinner party without half London here to see what a happy, united family we are.'

Taken aback by his cynicism, she glanced at him, wondering whether he was already a little drunk. She was still searching for a safe topic of conversation when the gong called them to dinner.

★　★　★

Philip's outburst at the shop had shaken Elaine. *I admire you*, he had said, and then, *I didn't choose to be attracted to you*. If she could have passed off his first remark as a clumsy attempt to draw her attention away from his father, the outrage he had voiced only a moment or two later had contained a disconcerting ring of truth.

She was plagued by Finborough men, she thought irritably, as she pinned a dart in the bodice of Gilda's wedding dress. Pulling back a corner of the curtain, she looked out of the window and saw Philip's motor cycle, a bulky black shape at the side of the road. Why did he come here, what did he want? Was he spying on her, or was this his idea of courtship?

With a sigh, she put down fabric and pins and went downstairs. She crossed the road to him.

'Philip, this has to stop.'

'I know.' He gave a rather wan smile.

'You've been here every night this week. What do you want?'

'To talk to you.'

282

'Well, you can't. I thought I made that quite plain. Don't come here any more. I shall telephone the police if you come here again.'

She went back into the house. She had begun to pin the fabric again when the doorbell rang, a long peal while Philip kept his finger pressed on the bell.

She ran back down the stairs. As she opened the door, she said, 'Stop that, you must stop that. You'll disturb everyone in the house.'

'Then let me speak to you.'

She could have almost wept with frustration. But seeing little alternative, she said with a sigh, 'Very well. But five minutes, that's all.'

He followed her up the stairs. Letting him into her flat, she remembered the last time he had been here, on the night of his accident. She remembered helping him put on his jacket, the swell of hard muscle beneath his skin, the dusting of freckles on his forearm.

She heard him say, 'I don't suppose I could have a drink, could I?'

'I'm afraid I can't run to an extensive wine list,' she said sarcastically. 'I can do gin and bitters or gin martini, that's all.'

'A gin martini, then, please.'

She put the bottles of gin and martini, a lemon and two glasses on a tray and carried it into the sitting room. She sat in the armchair, not on the sofa beside him. There was something dangerous about him, she thought.

As she mixed the martinis, she said again, 'This has to stop, Philip.'

'I know. But I can't.'

'Of course you can. You haven't tried hard enough.'

'It's not because of Dad. I know you think that but it isn't.' She started to speak, but he interrupted her, saying, 'I've fallen in love with you.'

'No,' she said sharply. 'No, you can't possibly have.'

283

'Why can't I?'

'I should ~~have~~ thought that was obvious.'

'I wondered whether you felt the same.'

She gave a little laugh. 'Oh, Philip.'

He leaned forward, frowning. 'Why shouldn't I ~~have~~ fallen in love with you? You're a very attractive woman.'

'Only a few weeks ago you made it perfectly plain that you despised me.'

'Yes, I hated you at first, I admit it, but I don't now.'

'Listen to me, Philip,' she said firmly. 'I'm not the sort of woman you think I am. I've been married, and I've had lovers, yes, but I'm not — I'm not a tramp. So if you're here because you think I'll oblige you by jumping into bed with you, then you're very much mistaken!'

'That isn't what I thought at all.' His gaze was serious and composed. 'I think you are one of the most refined women I have ever met.'

'Refined,' she muttered. 'Good God.'

'Dignified, then. Poised. I don't know . . . '

'*Philip.*' She put down her glass. 'If you want me, then it's because you know you can't have me. That's all.'

He grinned. 'This isn't some *Freudian* thing, you know.' His eyes glittered.

'You're very young.' She heard herself adopt a brisk, world-weary tone. 'No doubt you fall in love with a great many girls.'

'No, I've never been in love with any of my girlfriends. They're often cross with me because I'm not.'

'How tiresome for you.'

'Do you hate me?'

'Hate's too strong a word.' She made herself meet his gaze. She found herself thinking what a good-looking boy he was, all long limbs and tousled hair and bedroom eyes and winning smile. She had to give herself a mental shake.

'You were a damned nuisance,' she said crisply. 'You still are.'

'Sorry.' He didn't sound penitent. Instead, he grinned again. 'This must be very inconvenient for you.'

'This passion of yours is a little more than merely *inconvenient*, isn't it?'

'How would you describe it?'

'Ridiculous. Impossible. Distasteful.'

'Because of my father?' He looked thoughtful. 'I suppose some people might think so. But I don't give a damn about him — in fact, I hardly think about him any more.'

She did not believe him, but she let it pass, and said, 'And your mother? Do you feel the same about her?'

His face darkened. 'I don't know how she puts up with him,' he muttered. 'I don't understand how she can just forgive and forget.'

'So, Philip, if I told you I was madly in love with you and we went hand in hand off into the sunset, as you seem to believe we might, what do you imagine that would do to your family?'

'Are you? Are you madly in love with me?'

'Oh, *Philip* — '

'Mix me another martini.' He rose from his chair. 'You make very good martinis, Elaine.'

She was aware of him, standing too close to her, looking down at her as she poured gin and squeezed lemon. She found his proximity disturbing.

But she gave a light laugh and said, 'There are so many reasons why you and I couldn't possibly have anything to do with each other that it's hard to know where to begin. I'm a lot older than you — '

'Five years, that's all,' he said. 'You're thirty. I worked it out.'

'How clever of you. And then, we come from very different backgrounds.'

'I know. I'm the spoiled brat who was born with a

silver spoon in his mouth and you've spent a lifetime at the coalface.'

In spite of herself, she smiled. 'Something like that,' she conceded.

'I want you, you see.'

Her hand trembled as she gave him the glass and a little of the liquid spilled. Agitated, she rose and busied herself, gathering up the ends of thread and scraps of material that had fallen from her sewing to the floor. She said, 'Perhaps, in this instance, you can't have everything you want.'

'Perhaps. And I understand how this must seem to you — the enormity of it, in one way, though it's really, if you think about it, very simple.' He drank some of the martini. 'There's one thing you haven't said, though.'

'What's that?'

'That you dislike me.'

She found that she couldn't meet his eyes. She rose and went into the kitchen, opening the bin, and dropping the remnants into it. Then she went back to the doorway.

She said coldly, 'I do dislike you. You're trying to force your way into my life when I've made it plain that I've no desire to know you. The best interpretation of your behaviour is that you are an indulged, conceited young man who's been far too used to getting his own way. The worst is that you are perverse and arrogant.' She saw him flinch.

In the kitchen, she ran the tap and rinsed her hands, then pressed them, cool and wet, against her face. She heard the front door open and shut. Her eyes were closed, her head bent. Her breathing was ragged. Then she heard footsteps behind her. 'Not *perverse*,' he said softly. 'All the other things, perhaps, but not that.'

She felt his arms go round her waist and she gasped. His lips brushed the back of her neck. She heard him whisper, 'Your heart's beating very fast. Like a bird's.'

The palm of his hand moved slowly from her belly to her breast: now, she groaned. She was pliant in his arms as he turned her to face him. Then he kissed her.

* ★ ★

Ruby had been seeing Joe Thursby for the past few months. They went to the cinema or to poetry recitals in rooms above pubs, where the resonance of the verse was punctuated by shouts and the occasional fist fight from the bar below.

Once, kissing her outside her lodging house after he had seen her home, Joe drew back and looked at her carefully. 'I always wonder what you're thinking of when I kiss you,' he said. 'I never think your mind's completely on it.'

'Oh, I'm just using you, Joe,' she said lightly. 'For material, for my stories. It's because you're so handsome. The heroic type.' She touched his face and then let herself into the house.

Before she went to bed with Joe, Ruby visited a doctor and got herself fitted with a Dutch cap. She enjoyed inventing a fiancé and a wedding and a honeymoon in Wales, it helped distract her a little from the undignified business of following the doctor's instructions as she inserted the contraceptive inside herself. A few days later, she lost her virginity in Joe's room in Euston Road. After they had made love, she rolled over on to her stomach to look at Joe, who was smoking a cigarette. She enjoyed looking at Joe; he was such a handsome man.

'Heart's Desire', her latest story, had been captioned in the magazine, 'by a *Woman's Weekly* favourite, Ruby Chance'. Sometimes she imagined her father picking up a magazine, in a doctor's waiting room, perhaps, leafing through it and seeing her name. The money she earned from her short stories enabled her to pay her mother's living expenses as well as her own, freeing her from her dependency on the Finboroughs.

She had told few people other than Joe and her mother about her writing. There was still that fear that, if she spoke about it, it would somehow evaporate, still the fear that if she stuck her head over the parapet, she would be shot down. And besides, the writers she knew — unpublished, most of them — among the Bohemians or would-be Bohemians of Chelsea and Fitzrovia preferred the experimental and the outrageous, and might be patronising or contemptuous of what she did, and might not understand her reasons for doing it. Not that *money* was her only reason, though it was an important one. In her position, she could not afford to be disdainful of money.

The only other person who knew about her short stories was Edward Carrington, from work. Edward lived with his widowed mother in a mansion flat in Belgravia. He was five years older than Ruby and worked on a different floor of the building. Edward was tall and thin, and his doleful brown eyes were set in a long, expressive face. He was one of those people who were on the periphery of several different circles of friends, including Ruby's own, but was not at the centre of any.

It was half-past one, and Ruby was eating her sandwiches in the little room set aside for packed lunches, when Edward stuck his head round the door.

'Hello, Ruby, how are you? I'm looking for Miss Chadwick.'

'She's off sick. She sprained her ankle playing hockey.'

'Goodness,' said Edward. Mary Chadwick was a very large woman.

'Quite,' said Ruby, as she slid the piece of paper on which she had been writing beneath her lunch-box. 'I assume she plays in goal.'

He came into the room. 'What's that?'

'Nothing,' she said sharply.

At her rebuff, he looked wounded, and made to go. Ruby sighed and said, 'It's just something I'm writing. It's nothing important.'

'A story?'

'Yes. It's an office romance.'

He gave a pleased bark of laughter. 'I'll let you get on, then.'

★ ★ ★

The first time he kissed Elaine they ended up in bed together. Philip felt a sense of awe at the smooth pearliness of her limbs and the fine fall of her platinum-blonde hair. Since then, they had seen each other almost every day. If work or family or friends kept them apart then they talked on the telephone, sometimes for hours. He wrote to her each day. Before he had met her, the briefest thank you note had sent him into an agony of mental blankness and pen-chewing: now, he marvelled at the way his pen speeded over the paper.

The miracle was that she felt as he did. He could tell: he had learned to recognise the symptoms. The longing to be with one person, the certainty that whatever you said would be understood. The need to touch, for your skin to brush against their skin, for your body to mingle with their body. It puzzled him how it had happened, how he had hated her and had then found himself drawn to her. Little details, only noticeable to a lover, compelled him. That her second toe was longer than her first, that the whites of her eyes had a bluish tinge, that she could touch her inner wrist with her thumb: these things fascinated him. Her tastes, when they chimed with his own, seemed to confirm their absolute rightness for each other; when, occasionally, their choices disagreed, the difference amused him.

She told him about her childhood, which had been one of day trips to Southend and picnics in the park, so different to his own, and seemed to him idyllic, enchanting in its simplicity. Only a generation or two back and her family had been Suffolk farmworkers — he liked to imagine them, tall and slender and silvery-haired, standing in a field with scythes in their hands.

They kept their affair secret, a mutual decision, largely unspoken. They went to provincial cinemas and dined in restaurants in the suburbs. Sometimes Philip borrowed a friend's car and they drove out of London. He couldn't picture Elaine on the pillion of the motor cycle, somehow, couldn't imagine her ruffled and wind-swept. He wanted to take care of her, to protect her. Yet it was surprising how often, in a city as large as London, you ran into people you knew — a business acquaintance of Philip's, encountered in a roadhouse on Kingsway, a friend of Elaine's family in the same carriage on the Tube. And though to begin with the need for secrecy only added to the excitement, after a while he found himself disliking it.

One cool, blowy Sunday in early June, they drove to Felixstowe Ferry on the Suffolk coast, where they lunched at the pub on the village green. The dining room was surprisingly busy for such an out-of-the-way place. After lunch, they walked to the mouth of the River Deben. It seemed to Philip that there were an extraordinary number of people about — fishermen in oilskins and yachtsmen in Aran jerseys, and children enjoying themselves, running around and throwing balls and generally getting under everyone's feet. He felt edgy and he kept putting his hand in his pocket and checking the box he had brought with him was still there.

A solitary artist sketched the sailing boats and fishing boats that bobbed up and down on the grey-green sea.

A mongrel darted into a puddle and spun droplets of water from its brindled coat. It wasn't quite the spot Philip had hoped for, but he said, 'Shall we sit down? There's a bench.'

'It's a bit chilly to sit. And look, see that sign up there — ' Elaine pointed to a shack with the words 'Fresh fish' chalked on its wooden walls — 'I could buy some fish for supper.'

They walked to the shack. After she had made her purchases, they headed inland, following a path through reedbeds and marshlands. As they walked, Elaine spoke of the events of her week — a demanding customer in her shop, the plans for her sister's wedding. Houseboats were moored on the greyish water of the estuary, a grubby child looked up from the deck of one as they passed.

She said suddenly, 'We can go home if you've had enough.'

He looked up at her, startled. 'Do you want to go home?'

'I don't mind. But you're very quiet, Philip. I'm afraid you're not enjoying yourself.'

He went to stand at the bank, looking down to the water, the reeds and the mud. The land seemed to melt into the sea.

He said suddenly, 'I'm a bit sick of all this, you see.'

'Us?' He caught the shock in her eyes.

'No, of course not.' He put his arms around her. 'I'm not going to change my mind about you, Elaine. You're stuck with me, I'm afraid. No, I meant all this hiding in corners. Rushing off to places in the middle of nowhere, just so we can have some time together. I think we should tell people — about us, I mean.'

'Philip — '

'I'm proud of you. I want other people to know how lucky I am. It would make it seem more real. Sometimes I'm afraid I'll wake up and find it was all a dream.'

She touched her lips to his. 'Then it's a very nice dream.'

'Dreams don't last. I want this — us — to last.'

She moved close to him, resting her head against his shoulder. He stroked her hair.

'I want to ask you something, Elaine.'

'Ask away, then.'

A family of mother, father and four small girls were heading along the narrow path towards them. Philip and Elaine stood aside to let them pass. As Philip said, 'I wanted to ask you whether you would marry me,' the smallest child slipped in the mud, landing on her bottom, then creased up her face and began to howl.

Elaine picked the little girl out of the mud and made soothing noises. Philip wasn't sure whether the howls had drowned his proposal, so he began again, 'I wanted to ask you — '

'Yes, I heard you, darling.'

The child was handed to her father, who lifted her on to his shoulders and set off down the track. When the family were out of earshot, Philip said, 'Well, will you?'

And Elaine, whose face had become very grave, said, 'Perhaps we'd better find somewhere to sit down.'

They headed inland, further into the marshes, where Philip found a section of broken fence for Elaine to perch on. He wanted to prompt her, to rush her, because the waiting was unbearable, but he sensed that they were on the brink of something momentous, something life-changing, and that to push, to hurry, as he was accustomed to doing, would be wrong.

She said, 'I would like to marry you, Philip,' and he heard the air escape from his lungs — without realising it, he had been holding his breath.

But she was frowning. 'But I don't know if I ought to.'

'Because of all that — because of my father?'

'Partly, yes. It won't make it easy, will it? I haven't

even told Gilda about you. She's so excited about her wedding and Mother's been so ill. My family will be surprised, to say the least. I don't know what my parents will think about me marrying again, though I'm sure they'd love you once they knew you. But all that pales into insignificance compared to what you would have to do. Philip, I'm not sure you understand what you might lose if you were to marry me. I dread the storm that we'd spark.'

'I've been thinking about that.' He stroked a windblown lock of hair back from her face with his fingertip. 'It'd probably mean I had to leave Finboroughs.'

'You'd mind that, wouldn't you?'

'Yes,' he said honestly. 'But there's plenty of other things I could do.'

'I don't want you to give up everything you love for my sake. I'm afraid that a marriage founded on an unequal sacrifice might not work.'

'*Sacrifice?*' He laughed. 'Marrying you wouldn't be a *sacrifice*. It would be what I most want in the world.'

'But, Philip,' she said gently, 'your parents.'

'It might not be as bad as you think. Maybe my father won't fly off the handle. Maybe he will, but then he'll forget it after a while. And to be honest, I don't know if I want to work for him any more, anyway. It's been bloody difficult, these last few months. We hardly speak. I can hardly bear to be in the same room as him, sometimes.'

'I don't want to make it worse.'

Philip shrugged. 'Dad and I rubbed each other up the wrong way long before I met you.'

'And your mother?'

'Oh, she'll come round, I know she will,' Philip said confidently. He grinned. 'Perhaps it wouldn't be so bad for me to have to manage on my own for a while. A bit less of the silver spoon.'

'And then there's me. I was married before, remember.'

How ridiculous, he thought, to feel jealous of a dead man. He had to force himself to ask, 'Do you still love Hadley?'

'In a way, I always will. But he's gone now and I have to move on. But that wasn't what I meant. I don't know that I want to be *married* again — not to you, not to anyone. Hadley was lovely, but I was bored, you see, a lot of the time. Hadley went out to work and I stayed at home and fiddled around with the dusting and the washing-up. God, I was bored!' Elaine shook her head. 'I found ways of filling in my time, of course, but how awful, to waste your life looking for ways to pass the hours.' She paused; Philip heard the hush of the reeds, stirred up by the rising wind as the clouds approached.

She said, 'The day I bought the lease to the shop, the day I collected the key and went inside and looked round and began to plan what to do with it, I felt so excited. Happy, almost. Guilty too, because it was only a few months since Hadley had died.'

'I wouldn't want to confine you to the kitchen in your pinny,' he said, amused. 'Why should I want to do that?'

'Men do, Philip.'

He caught her hand in his, kissing her fingers. 'You'd better keep the shop — we'll need the money if my father casts me off without a penny.'

'You wouldn't mind?'

'No.' He thought hard, and then said honestly, 'I would mind if you were always working and I never saw you. I would mind that.'

'Oh, I dare say we'd manage the odd supper together,' she said, ruffling his hair. She sighed. 'I suppose I should be pointing out all the other difficulties — our different backgrounds, our ages. The short time we've known each other. All that. But somehow it doesn't seem to matter as much as I once thought it did. Although . . . '

'Although?'

'There's another thing.' Extricating herself from his embrace, she turned to face him. 'I've never had a child. I never even started one while I was married to Hadley. I'm thirty, Philip. It gets more difficult for women to have children as they get older.'

'Do you want children?'

'Yes, very much. And you?'

'I want *your* children. Think of us, mixed together. They'd look quite extraordinary. What shall we call them?'

'Philip, I may not be able to have children,' she said bluntly. 'That's what I'm trying to tell you.'

'If they come, then that'll be terrific. And if they don't, then we'll manage. We'll adopt one — or half a dozen, if you like.' He put his arm round her. 'Poor darling, you're shivering.' He reached his hand into his pocket and drew out the box. 'Let me put this on your finger and then we can head back to civilisation.'

She opened the small red leather box and said in a choked voice, 'Oh, Philip.'

'It's a yellow diamond. Quite rare, I'm told. I thought it would suit you. Do you like it?'

'Very much,' she whispered

He put the ring on her finger. 'Don't cry,' he murmured. 'Don't cry, my lovely Elaine,' and she shook her head, speechless.

It was raining by the time they walked back to the pub. As he started up the car, she said, 'Your parents . . . you will be careful, won't you, darling? You will be kind?'

'Don't worry,' he said. 'I'll be tact personified.'

★ ★ ★

A 'No More War' party at a studio in Chelsea. Cartoons of Hitler, Mussolini and Stanley Baldwin in red distemper over the walls, punch tasting of boot polish, and partygoers dancing, crushed cheek to cheek, tearing off jackets, cardigans, shawls, waistcoats as the room became hotter.

'Theo!' shrieked Ruby, catching sight of him, pressing through the crowds.

He kissed her, then introduced her to the girl he was with. Aleksandra was tall and slim and elegant in tawny velvet. As the night lengthened, the music became softer, more sensuous, and couples wandered off to more secluded parts of the house. Voices, Theo's and Aaron's, who lived in the room next to Ruby's own, filtered across to her as she went out into the back yard.

It was cooler outside and there was a dusting of stars in the sky. 'Of course,' Aaron was saying, 'it is illegal in Germany for Jews to marry Aryans. It is prohibited to hold hands, to kiss, to *touch*. Life for Jews is more and more impossible. There are many shops and cafés we cannot use, many buses and trains we're not allowed to ride on. The authorities mean to make us all run away and live elsewhere, I think.'

Ruby stood in the scullery doorway, watching Theo. How nice that he had come home. How nice to see him again, to stand for a moment, reminding herself of the way his hands moved as he talked, of the curl of his upper lip as he smiled.

She crossed the yard to them. 'Darling Theo, why didn't you tell me you were coming home?'

'I like surprising people.' He put his arm round her. 'How are you, Ruby?'

'Hot,' she said, fanning herself. 'Aleksandra's beautiful. Where did you meet?'

'On a film set in Billancourt. I've been writing for a cinema magazine. Sasha was acting in this terrible film. She was the only decent thing in it. I feel very monochrome, beside her. She's a mixture of Russian, French, Jewish and a dash of Castilian Spanish, and she's lived in just about every European capital there is.'

'Everyone seems to be moving. No one seems to stay in the same place.'

Aaron smiled. 'I will live in the little room next to you for ever, Ruby, I promise.'

Theo said, 'Did you think of going to Palestine?'

Aaron shrugged. 'It's what many people hope for, to return to the Promised Land. I chose London instead. I escaped with my typewriter and my coffee cups. I like London. I'm able to work, I'm able to speak without looking over my shoulder to see who's listening. I can show my face in public without fear of violence or imprisonment.'

'Have you family in Germany?'

'My mother and father. I tried to persuade them to come with me but they wouldn't. They've lived their whole lives in the same little town and they can't bear to leave. They think things will get better.'

'Do you?' asked Theo bluntly.

'No, I don't. I did once, but not now. I have no hope now.' Aaron glanced back at the party. 'Of course it's right to be against war. Anyone in their right mind would hate war. But what if the people who govern us are not in their right mind? What if they are mad — or evil?'

Joe came out of the house. 'Getting a bit hot in there. Kit's accused Brian of being in love with Daisy Mae and Brian told Kit he was too thick to understand what a platonic relationship was.'

Theo said, 'Oh, Philip was asking after you, Ruby.'

'You've seen him?'

'Briefly.'

'How was he?'

'Fine, I think. He didn't say much. He was dashing off somewhere.' Theo flicked ash.

'Will he be there on Sunday?'

'Don't know. He didn't say.'

Ruby and Joe left shortly afterwards. As they walked down the Kings Road, Joe said, 'That bloke . . . the one whose family you used to live with . . . '

'Theo?'

'I meant his brother.'

Ruby kept her expression bland. 'Philip? Yes?'

'You went to see him that evening we first met. In the Fitzroy. Do you remember?'

Of course she remembered. Philip sleeping in her bed, her fingertip tracing his sleeping profile.

They passed closed-up shops; every now and then a car or van headed down the road. Joe said, 'You're in love with him, aren't you?'

She gave a little laugh. 'Joe, I haven't seen Philip for *weeks*.'

'It was the way your face lit up. Just *talking* about him.' There was both anger and hurt in his voice. Ruby could not think of a reply, and they walked the rest of the way in silence. When they reached her room there was a coolness in Joe's parting from her. He did not ask to stay the night.

★ ★ ★

Sunday lunch at the Finboroughs' house. That familiar, pleasurable feeling of being enfolded in light and colour and elegance. In the hall, Ruby's attention was caught by the perfume of the roses in the Venetian glass vase, the arrangement of postcards sent by Finborough friends from their European holidays, and the pair of leather gloves — Isabel's or Sara's perhaps — discarded on a wicker chair. Such beautiful gloves, of soft white doeskin, which she stroked with a fingertip.

A dining room full of old friends — the Colvilles, the McCrorys, the Temples — but no Philip. Her happiness diminished. Chatter and laughter as they ate the roast beef and Yorkshire pudding while, outside the french windows, bees buried their heads in the blue spikes of the delphiniums.

The maid brought in a summer pudding. Then the chime of the doorbell sliced through the conversation. Footsteps in the corridor: Philip opened the door.

'Darling,' said Isabel.

Philip's eyes widened as his gaze ran round the table. 'I'm sorry, I didn't realise you had company.'

'It's lovely to see you, darling,' said Isabel. 'I left a telephone message with your maid. Didn't she pass it on to you?'

Philip looked harassed. 'Perhaps I forgot — '

'Sit down, have some pudding.'

'I think I should come back later.'

Richard growled, 'Your mother said sit down.'

Philip's expression became very set. Isabel said quietly, 'Philip, please,' and he sat down, then said a quick hello to the guests seated round the table, though Ruby noticed that he ignored his father.

Dark red juice bled through the dome of the pudding as Isabel cut it with a spoon. A restrained murmur of conversation as Isabel served and the maid passed round the bowls. When she reached Philip, he shook his head.

'No, thanks. I'm not hungry.'

'Then what are you doing,' said Richard irritably, 'turning up like this, halfway through a meal?'

'I told you, Father, I forgot about Sunday lunch.'

'Everything's all right, isn't it, Philip?' asked Isabel anxiously.

'Yes, perfectly.'

'You are feeling well?'

'Isabel, don't fuss,' said Richard.

'I'm fine, Mum, honest. Actually, I came here to tell you something, but it doesn't matter, it can wait.'

'Don't hold yourself back on our account,' said Richard sarcastically. 'I'm sure all our guests would be delighted to hear your news, whatever it is.'

'*Richard*,' said Isabel.

Philip had become very still. Then, in a sudden movement, he pushed back his chair, stood up and made to leave the room.

'Damned uncivil,' Richard muttered, and, at the door, Philip froze.

When he turned to face his father, Ruby saw the fury in his eyes. '*Me*, uncivil?' he repeated. 'Perhaps I will tell you my news, after all. Yes, why not? I'm going to get married. That's why I came here. That's what I was going to say to you.'

No, Ruby thought. No, you can't.

'Married?' Isabel's hands went to her mouth. 'Philip, this is very sudden. Who is she? That girl — Stephanie — '

Philip shook his head. 'Not Steffie. I'm going to marry Elaine Davenport.'

Written on the guests' faces was a mixture of bewilderment, curiosity and embarrassment. It must be a joke, thought Ruby. A black, tasteless joke.

She stood up. 'Philip,' she said, 'please don't. You don't mean it.'

'Sit down, Ruby.' A sharp edge to Richard's voice. But she remained where she was.

Philip's eyes had never left his father's face. 'Aren't you pleased, Father? Aren't you pleased at my good news?'

Isabel was white, dazed, speechless. As Richard stood up, his chair crashed to the floor. 'How dare you?' he said softly.

Philip seemed to go rigid. But he said gently, insolently, 'Aren't you going to congratulate me, Father?'

Richard hissed, 'Get out out of my house!'

'See, I'm settling down at last, just like you always wanted — '

'Be quiet, Philip!' cried Isabel harshly. 'That's enough! Stop this, *now*!'

'Elaine and I love each other. We have done for months. We're going to get married. We — '

In a single, swift movement, Isabel slapped Philip hard across the face. He gasped and took a step back. Whirling round to Richard, her eyes wild, Isabel screamed, 'This is your fault! You are to blame for this!' and then she ran out of the room.

There was a scarlet streak across Philip's face where Isabel had struck him. But, still looking at his father, he said, his voice level, 'Elaine and I are getting married, so you may as well get used to it. There's nothing you can do about it.'

'You can't!' The words flew out of Ruby's mouth. 'You can't possibly! You hate her! You don't love her, you can't love her, I — '

Then her hand was seized and she was dragged out of the room. She heard herself sob, 'You can't, Philip! You can't!'

And Theo hauled her out of the front door, across the gravel forecourt and into the garden, where she found herself shaking, gasping and crying in an uncontrolled, gulping way that frightened her. The words poured out of her, muddled and blurred.

'He can't marry her! He can't! He hates her! He said she was cheap — he said she was a tart! I can't let him! I have to go back!'

'No.' Theo gave her a little shake. 'No, Ruby, you mustn't. Don't you see?' She stared at him. 'I thought you'd grown out of it,' he said slowly. He was frowning. His grip slackened. 'Out of Philip, I mean.'

She gave him a fierce look, then turned away. She sat down on a stone at the edge of the rockery and rubbed her hands over her wet face. 'I expect I'll always love him.' Her voice shook. 'I wish I didn't.'

'Here.' Theo gave her a lighted cigarette.

'I have to tell him,' she whispered. 'You shouldn't have stopped me.' But she didn't believe it herself any more.

He said, 'Elaine Davenport . . . she's the woman my father was seeing?'

'Yes.'

'Sara told me.' He kicked at the gravel, sending some skirling across the drive. 'What a bloody mess.'

She looked up at him. 'Theo,' she said pleadingly, 'he can't.'

'Oh, he can, you know. And anyway, he says he loves her.'

'But, Theo, he doesn't! She's a tart! She works in a shop!'

His eyes went cold. 'I didn't think you were a snob, Ruby.'

Sara came out of the front door. 'Give me a cigarette, Theo darling, I must have a cigarette.' She inhaled, closing her eyes. 'God, what a frightful scene. Philip's gone. Daddy's stormed off somewhere. Mummy's locked herself in the bedroom. Our poor old guests are trying to make polite conversation. Thank goodness Gil wasn't here. He'd have thought he was marrying into a madhouse.' She squeezed Ruby's shoulder. 'Poor Ruby — what a ruination of a lovely lunch.'

Theo said, 'I should see Ruby home. Are you coming, Sara?'

Sara shook her head. 'I'd better stay, try and pick up the pieces. Someone ought to get rid of our dinner guests. You two go.'

Ruby's head ached and she felt light-headed with crying. In the Tube train, the carriage twisted and turned, lurching through tunnels, past stations. She would have liked to have stayed on the train for ever, letting it decide where to take her, so that she would not have to pick herself up, find direction again. Her disbelief had given way to humiliation, humiliation that she had exposed herself in such a way to Theo, and a much sharper humiliation that she had attached such importance to the small signs of affection that Philip had given her, and that he had probably forgotten instantly. Humiliation most of all that she had believed herself to be his confidante, special to him, when she had hardly known him at all.

They spoke little on the journey and, climbing the stairs to her room in the lodging house, fragments of music and conversation drifted from the open doorways of the other inmates. She heard, liquid in the afternoon light, a run of notes from a clarinet. On the bed in her room were the dresses she had tried on earlier that morning; she sat down among the rayon and the silk.

'I've been such an idiot, haven't I?'

'Nonsense,' said Theo.

'Not nonsense,' she said bleakly. 'Apart from everything else, Philip's always thought of me as just a little girl.'

'What do you mean by 'everything else'?'

'Oh,' she said 'you know.'

'I don't, Ruby.'

'No glamour. Not like all of you.'

'Glamorous? Us?' He said, with a bitterness that shocked her, 'The trouble with my family is that we're so bloody self-absorbed. So self-dramatising. We can never resist an argument or a temper tantrum or the chance to make a scene. And my God, what a scene that was, one of our best.'

She looked up at him. He was standing at the window, looking out to the roofs. The afternoon sunlight silhouetted the severe lines of his profile.

She said, 'But you're not like that, Theo.'

'I detest scenes. The taking of sides.'

'Was that why you went away?'

'Maybe.' He turned to look at her, gave her a smile. 'You're not much of a one for scenes yourself, Rube.'

She picked at a blob on the front of her dress: a tearstain, she thought. 'I'm always trying to be *normal*. Because of . . . you know.'

'Nineveh,' he said.

'That — and Mum and Dad . . . ' She rose, opening a cupboard. 'There's nothing to drink, I'm afraid, but I've tea and coffee.'

'Coffee, please.'

She filled the kettle from the bathroom and lit the spirit stove. She said, 'Thank you for stopping me making a fool of myself, back there.'

'It's OK.' A quick grin. 'Any time.'

She spooned coffee into a jug. Her head pounded sharply. She considered whether to tell him and thought that she might as well, because it didn't seem to matter any more. After all, what had she to lose?

'I found out what happened to my father,' she said. She brushed back her hair from her forehead with her hand. Her voice still shook a little. 'It was what you thought. He left my mother for another woman.'

'Ah.' He frowned. 'I'm sorry, Ruby.'

'He'd gone by the time I got there — he'd left years ago. But he *married* her, Theo! While he was still married to my mother!'

'Jesus. Any idea where he went?'

'No. Neither has Claire.'

'Claire?'

'My father's other wife,' she said drily. She gave a short laugh. 'It's not hard to work out what happened, is it? He couldn't cope with the expense — and the deceit — of having two families, so he cut and run. He did a lot of cutting and running, my father.'

'Have you told your mother?'

'Of course not. She thinks he's a hero.'

He came to stand beside her. 'He was. Nothing changes that.'

'Oh, *Theo*. Such nonsense.' She felt suddenly very tired. 'My father was a liar and a cheat. And hardly a stayer — he left *two* families.' She squeezed his hand. 'So there's the mad parent and the bigamist parent. You're not so badly off.'

'Were there children?'

'Two, Archie and Anne. I only met Anne; Archie was at school.' She stirred the coffee, letting it brew. 'I expect he preferred them to us. I would have, if I were him.'

He said gently, 'Perhaps he loved you both in different ways.'

'Perhaps. The place they lived — I could see it was the sort of house where people *do* things. I expect,' she said slowly, 'that when my father met Claire, he felt alive again. I expect that after all those years of having to be quiet for the sake of my mother's nerves, it was glorious to be with Claire.'

There had been a question she had never before wanted to voice. She knew that she had always wanted to keep them all together, the Finboroughs, all in the same place, so that they could be what they had always been to her, a refuge, enviable and glittering and always slightly unobtainable. But now they were scattering; what had happened tonight would divide them permanently, she thought.

'Will you always live in Paris, Theo?'

'Probably not. It depends what happens. For one thing, it depends whether there's another war, and if so, whether it touches Paris.'

'Do you think it will?'

He did not speak for several moments, and then he said, 'Sometimes I'm afraid that everything is falling apart. Europe feels old and tired and fraying at the seams. It's as if we're leaving something behind but we haven't found anything to replace it. There's a loss of belief in all the old institutions, and the new ones frighten me. Germany frightens me, Ruby. What Aaron was saying the other night isn't the half of it. But communism frightens me too — I haven't travelled in the Soviet Union, but Aleksandra and her people know something of what's going on. So there's Stalin murdering people in Russia, and Germany and Italy have fallen to fascism, and Spain's on the verge of civil war. France is chaotic and lacking in conviction and America stands aside, keeping out of it all, of course. As for us, our timidity, our hypocrisy, appals me.'

After they had drunk the coffee, he kissed her cheek, said a quick farewell and left the room. Ruby listened to his footsteps, running down the stairs, and then she curled up on the bed, and, rather to her surprise, drifted off to sleep.

Part Three

Until Tomorrow

1936–1940

10

Scotland, where Sara and Gil went on their honeymoon, was glorious, and almost made up for Sara's disappointment with sex. In their hotel in Fort William, Gil divested her of her nightdress and embraced her in a thorough, conscientious way, and then made love to her. The act itself was efficient rather than transformatory. As Sara caught sight of the antlered stag staring down at them mournfully from above the fireplace, she let out a peal of laughter. Gil seemed offended, so she explained that she was laughing because of the stag, because it looked so *shocked*, but she didn't think he saw the joke.

Her marriage went on like that. They — and she understood quite quickly that Gil and Caroline would always be a very united *they* — didn't seem to find the same things funny as she did. It did not amuse them to discover Mrs Regan, the cook, wearing a sou'wester as she made pastry because the kitchen roof was leaking, and nor did they roar with laughter, as Sara did, when the cat they kept for mousing found the salmon trout that Jimmy Coulter had left for them in the porch and carried it off to a cupboard and devoured it, and the bones and skin made such a terrible smell and it took them days to work out what had happened.

Each morning, Caroline rose early and took the dogs for a walk. Quite often, Sara went with her. Then the three of them had breakfast, where they discussed their arrangements for the day. Caroline always had a boiled egg, Gil eggs and bacon. After breakfast, Gil worked in his study while Caroline gave Mrs Regan her orders; then Caroline spent the rest of the morning in the garden. After lunch at half-past one, Caroline wrote letters or visited neighbours while Gil drove to beaches and sand dunes to continue his study of the flora and fauna of the coastal areas. In the evening, they dined at half-past seven — Caroline explained to Sara that Mrs Regan disapproved of late dining. After dinner, they read or listened to a gramophone record or played whist. They dined out only occasionally.

There was little variation in their daily routine. Sara's suggestions of a picnic or a day out in the motor car were met with little enthusiasm. Both Gil and Caroline disliked change, Caroline because she had an innate sense of the rightness of her daily round and her status in the neighbourhood, and Gil because he found it unsettling. Perhaps Gil and Caroline's need for order was also in reaction to the chaos that surrounded them — the mouldy plaster and leaking roofs of the house, the weeds in the garden, even the struggle and violence of Ireland's history.

Sara quickly realised that she was expected to slot into the life of Vernon Court, not to try to alter it. Vernon Court's handful of servants — Mrs Regan in the kitchen, Jimmy Coulter the odd-job man, the maid and the gardener, had a greater influence on day-to-day affairs than she. At first, she tried to carry out her intention of helping Gil in his scientific research, of becoming his helpmeet. Yet she recognised after a while that he was merely tolerating her, keeping her amused, that he did not need her. The mechanisms that fascinated Gil — DNA and genes and chromosomes — Sara knew nothing of. She lacked even the most basic scientific vocabulary to enable her to understand them, and Gil hadn't the knack of explaining difficult concepts to someone so ignorant. There were, Sara realised, great areas of knowledge that were closed off to her. She found herself remembering the time she had visited Anton in the East End, of her discovery that she had not known the city of her birth.

Offering to help Caroline in the garden, she felt on safer ground. She had often helped her mother in both Hampstead and Cornwall — surely gardening would be much the same anywhere? Yet Vernon Court's garden was on a different scale to Isabel's. There were acres of it, surrounded by yet more acres of woodland. Though much of the garden was pleasingly natural in style, that appearance was, Sara came to learn, achieved at the expense of a great deal of work and planning. The walled garden for which Vernon Court was famous had been constructed, Caroline explained, to shelter tender plants from the prevailing winds. The rockery, with its azaleas, alpines and conifers, had been the best solution for a patch of land pitted with large boulders. Even the woodland had to be tamed and managed and coppiced, so that vigorous species did not overpower the rest.

Caroline managed the garden herself with the aid of Dickie, a strong, mute man who lived in a shack on the perimeter of the estate. 'His parents were cousins,' Gil said dismissively of Dickie. 'Too much interbreeding, I'm afraid.' Dickie did the heavy work that Caroline could not manage, hauling stones out of the soil and hacking out tree roots. Caroline did everything else. Vernon Court's garden was Caroline's passion. She showed the same depth of feeling for it that she did for her son. The garden showed Caroline at her truest and best, content and in her element, informed and expert and patient. Recognising that Sara needed something to do, Caroline gave her little tasks and explained to her how to pot on seedlings and prune shrubs. But Sara saw that Caroline, like Gil, distrusted her, and kept a careful eye on her as she worked.

Caroline sewed on Gil's buttons, darned the elbows of his sweaters, reminded him to have his hair cut and to take his indigestion powders. One evening, when they were invited out to dinner, Caroline retied Gil's bow tie, which Sara had earlier tied, and, with a tut, took out the flower Sara had put in his lapel and replaced it with one of her own choice. In the same way, Caroline made adjustments to any table that Sara had laid and returned to its original arrangement any alteration to the positioning of furniture or ornaments. None of these things was done with spite or with any intention of diminishing Sara, it was just that Caroline meant Vernon Court to be run the way it always had been run — and it was Sara who must adapt, not Caroline or Gil. The addition of a daughter-in-law to the household meant only that there was an extra place to lay at the table and that Sara now accompanied Caroline on visits to her neighbours, where they drank tea or sherry and ate boiled fruitcake. And the substantial dowry that Sara had brought to the marriage meant that the work on Vernon Court's roof had begun at last. The old slates had been stripped off and carpenters had begun to replace the rotten timbers.

Pregnancy relieved Sara of the need to find an occupation for herself. The earliest symptom of her condition was a disabling nausea that seized her as soon as she opened her eyes in the morning and excused her from sharing breakfast with Caroline and Gil. The news that she was pregnant lifted the slight but measurable air of disapproval that Sara had begun to sense. Pregnancy put an end to both riding and sex. Sara was aware that it was the riding she missed most.

Lying on a sofa in front of the drawing-room fire, with the dogs her companions, trying not to be sick again, Sara heard the news of the abdication of Edward VIII. On the covers of Gil's newspaper were photographs of a veiled, tight-lipped Wallis Simpson. Caroline's friends were starchier than Alice Finborough's; in drawing rooms and dining rooms, Sara caught snippets of conversation — an American . . . a divorce . . . *shocking*.

After a scare in the third month of her pregnancy, the

doctor told Sara to rest, which, as she felt very unwell, was not so much of an imposition as she might once have thought. Sometimes she sat in the drawing room with the dogs, sometimes she retreated to the conservatory, which was warmed by its high glass roof. The fecundity of the room, with its smothering vines and pendulous figs, seemed to Sara suited to her condition, and she loved to hear the rain batter against the glass. She thought of Edward, who had given up his kingdom for the woman he loved. She wondered whether he had thought about it for a long time, whether he had hummed and hawed, unable to make up his mind. Or whether, given the choice, the decision had been simple, as easy as choosing between lemon meringue pie and semolina, or between a ride along the beach and a cocktail party. When she tried to talk to Caroline about the Abdication, her mother-in-law said disapprovingly, 'He should have done his duty,' and made it clear that she did not wish to discuss the subject any further. But which had been the King's greatest duty, wondered Sara — to his country or to his love? To which one had he owed his deepest loyalty? Could love be so important that it made all other loyalties insignificant?

With the coming of spring, as her belly grew fatter and when the weather was fine, Sara lay wrapped up in a fur coat and blankets on a wicker chaise-longue in the little games room beside the conservatory, where she could look out through the open front to the lawn and the woodland. Now and then Caroline would bring her a cup of tea and sit and chat to her about the garden or the neighbours, and sometimes Gil would stop by and tell her what he was doing that day. Though, more and more, Sara thought he had a rather startled expression, as if he was surprised to discover that he had a wife resting in the games room.

She would have said that it was because of her

pregnancy that she and Gil had drifted apart — but had they ever really been together? Or had she been mistaken again, had she persuaded herself he was something that he was not? Had she married Gil Vernon because he had been the opposite of Anton, solid and dark and grown from the same Anglo-Irish stock as herself? Had she married him because he had not been tall, fair, foreign, different?

There were advantages to loneliness, though: for one thing, she was able to think. Her thoughts drifted, as they always did, to Anton, and what he had meant to her, and how he had seemed to be the answer to the problem of what to do with her life. It had been easier for the boys, for Philip and Theo, because they had always known that they would work for Finboroughs — the fact that neither of them did so now was beside the point — they had had a purpose, and Sara had come to the conclusion that it was that initial discovery of a purpose, that starting off, that was so difficult. The assumption had always been that she would marry. Yet she had known little of what marriage would involve, had been kept intentionally ignorant of important parts of it, and marriage, as she had found out, could leave one's day-to-day life as aimless as it had been before.

So thank goodness for the baby. Once the baby was born, everything would be all right. Gil and Caroline would be pleased with her, and she would have someone to love. Enfolded in furs, Sara watched as the spring rains gave way to sunshine. Her palms rested on her belly, feeling the baby moving inside her. In the last few days of her pregnancy, she took to wandering through the garden, tracing the loops and crisscrosses of the paths in the walled garden. Caroline begged her to rest, to sit in the shade, but Sara kept walking until she felt the first labour pains stabbing into her back.

Her son was born two days later, after a long and difficult labour. The infant was whisked away to the nursery; Sara's life hung in the balance and, on the doctor's advice, Caroline sent for Isabel. Out of concern for her daughter-in-law and the baby, Caroline had halted the roofers' work, but in her fever Sara still seemed to hear the hammering and banging. When her temperature eventually dropped, she felt weak and exhausted. To her immense joy and relief, her mother was sitting beside her bed — had been sitting there some time, she suspected.

★ ★ ★

While Sara had been ill, Caroline and Nanny Duggan, who lived in a cottage in the village, and who had been Gil and Marcus's nanny, looked after the baby. Caroline and Gil chose the infant's name. He was to be called David Marcus, after Gil's dead father and brother.

When she held her son for the first time, Sara's strongest feeling was one of dismay. David was large and red-cheeked and dark like his father, not at all the baby she had imagined she would have. In fact, she didn't feel as though he was anything to do with her. Sometimes she found herself wondering whether a mistake had somehow been made, whether her baby had accidentally been exchanged for someone else's, which was ridiculous, she knew.

Sara made sure that no one, not even her mother, guessed what she was thinking. Affection would come, she assumed. She felt like this because she was so tired and because she had been ill for such a long time. Every mother loved her baby, didn't she?

After six weeks, Isabel returned to England. David was a wakeful, restless baby. He cried a lot, day and night, and Sara did not seem able to soothe him. When she bathed him, she felt clumsy and incompetent. Nanny Duggan or Caroline always seemed to be in the nursery, watching her as the soapy infant threatened to slither out of her grasp. Feeding him was a nightmare of coaxing him to take the bottle while he recoiled, screaming, red-faced and windy.

Mostly, she felt relieved to hand him back to Nanny or Caroline. Once, on Nanny Duggan's half-day, while Caroline was working in the garden, David woke, howling bitterly. Sara put him against her shoulder and patted his back, but he became rigid and crimson-faced, his yells piercing. And Sara was aware of a feeling of terror, that sprang, she knew, from a great lack in herself, a lack of love for her own son, a lack of expertise and of instinct. She went outside and found Caroline, who peeled off her gardening gloves and cradled her grandson. The crying stopped within minutes and Sara went to the games room, where she cried as bitterly as the baby had, for hours.

She became convinced that there must be something wrong with David, he cried so much. Dr Kennedy looked him over and David went red and screamed when the stethoscope was placed on his chest.

'He's a fine little chap,' said Dr Kennedy, when he had finished examining the child, 'fit and healthy, though he seems to have a touch of colic. You must be very proud of him, Mrs Vernon.' Then, looking at her closely, he said, 'You must make time to have a little outing now and then, Mrs Vernon. Don't spend all your days in the nursery. Ask your husband to take you shopping, perhaps.'

If there was nothing wrong with David, Sara reasoned, then there must be something wrong with her. Though she didn't mention the doctor's suggestion of a shopping trip to Gil, Dr Kennedy must have spoken to him because Gil offered to drive her to Downpatrick the following week. The expedition was not a success. Sara had never much enjoyed shopping. Over tea and buns in a café, Gil spoke to her of the paper he was working on, something to do with eradicating the weaker strains in a type of grass. She understood little of what he was telling her — she didn't try to understand because she felt too tired to bother. It was a relief when Gil, who also seemed to have found the afternoon a strain, suggested they go home.

As the months passed, Sara spent less and less time with her son. Dutifully, she pushed him round the estate in his pram each morning and gave him his bottle at night because Caroline seemed to expect her to. Yet David was Caroline and Nanny Duggan's, and Sara had begun to suspect he always would be. She had no belief in herself; she knew that she had failed.

Throughout her pregnancy and since David's birth, her grandmother had been a regular visitor. For Alice Finborough, whom she loved, Sara always found a smile and a funny remark. But one day, after she had wept for much of the night, she could not raise a smile. After tea with Caroline and Gil, Alice suggested that she and Sara go out for a ride. As they left the Vernon estate in the dogcart, Sara was aware of a feeling of relief, as if a black cloud had lifted. Vernon Court, that had seemed enchanted to Sara when she had first seen it, had become a cage.

They drove into the village, where Alice bought eggs and apples from a cottage. As she climbed back on to the dogcart and took the reins, she asked, 'What's wrong, Sara?'

'Nothing's wrong,' said Sara. 'I'm fine.'

'Nonsense. You are deeply unhappy. How is the child?'

'Just the same.'

'David is a colicky baby and they can be unrewarding. But he'll grow out of it, they always do.' Alice flicked the reins and the horse began to walk. 'What about Gil? Is he unkind to you?'

'Not at all. Most of the time he doesn't seem to notice I'm here.'

'Ah.' Alice Finborough looked troubled. 'That can be worse, in some ways, than cruelty. Your grandfather was a little like that. He had his passions, which he didn't share with me.'

Sara looked up at her. 'How did you bear it?'

'I had my horses, of course, and my child. And then, when Richard was a little older and needed me less, I had my friends.'

'Friends?' repeated Sara.

'Lovers, dear girl. I mean, I took lovers.'

For what seemed the first time in months, Sara could not keep back a smile. 'Granny, I had no idea.'

'One had to find a way of surviving living in the middle of nowhere with a man who, though sometimes perfectly sweet, could at other times be a tyrant,' said Alice crisply. 'And that was my way. The horses weren't quite enough for me, you see.' She patted Sara's hand. 'You remind me of myself at your age, my darling. We are alike. We both need someone to love. We do not feel whole unless we love, even if loving doesn't always make us happy.'

Sara felt miserable again. 'I ought to love David.'

'Plenty of women adore babies, but I found Richard far more interesting when he was older. As a very small child, he was given to tantrums, which was quite exhausting. I'm sure you'll come to love David when he's grown.'

'Did you have a lot of lovers, Granny?'

'Half a dozen, I believe,' said Alice. 'I can't remember the exact number now. It's a rather sad reflection, my dear, that these things that seem so important, so compelling, at the time, become rather a blur as one becomes older.'

'Was there one you loved more than the others?'

Alice gave a secret smile. 'I have always believed that my dear Tom was the love of my life. Everything was an adventure with Tom. He made even the most mundane event wonderful. He was my last lover. I've managed on my own since he died.'

'What happened to him, Granny?'

'He was killed in the war, God rest him.' A shadow crossed Alice Finborough's face. Then, urging the horses to a trot, she said pointedly, 'I was always very discreet, Sara. It's so important to avoid scandal.'

Christmas was a turning-point for Sara. By then, David was almost six months old. He had begun to sleep better and he cried less. Richard and Isabel stayed at Raheen for Christmas as usual and visited Vernon Court, where David was played with and admired. In the company of her family, the fog of depression that had overtaken Sara lifted a little.

Her parents returned to England in the New Year, leaving her without any alternative but to face up to her difficult, troubling thoughts. She knew that there was no place for her at Vernon Court. Caroline and Gil tolerated her; they did not need her. Love for her child had not come naturally, as Sara had believed it would, and she suspected that for Caroline that absence marked her out as less than a woman. Both Caroline and Gil now treated her with a mixture of condescension and wariness, as if she was a little unhinged.

One rainy day, she found herself roaming round the house, peering into unused bedrooms and attics. In one corner of an attic, a steady drip of water was leaking through the new roof on to the floor. Automatically, Sara looked round for a bucket or tin to place beneath the leak, because that was what one did at Vernon Court. One stopped up the leaks, brushed away the worst of the dust and cobwebs. But they always came back.

If she left Gil — and she had begun to think that she must — then what would she do? She imagined her father's fury if she were to leave her husband; she imagined returning to Raheen, and remembered the emptiness of the months before her marriage.

And then there was David. Often now, he greeted her with a smile. At six months old, he no longer cried when she sat him on her lap, but examined, with a concentrated seriousness she found touching, her necklace or earrings or the buttons on her blouse. She had begun to see that her grandmother was right, that love might come as he grew up, that they might get to know each other, that they might have a second chance.

Yet her grandmother had also said, 'Tom was the love of my life,' and Sara knew now Anton had been the love of hers. That he had not loved her as much as she had loved him made no difference. She had been in love with the idea of Gil rather than the reality of him, and with the house a little, perhaps, and the escape into adulthood that marriage had seemed to offer. But living at Vernon Court had demonstrated to her the depth of her ignorance, as well as the depth of her feelings for Anton. It was time, she thought, to learn to live.

Caroline was in the nursery, kneeling on the floor, playing with David, when Sara went to see her. Seeing them together, Sara thought, that's what I was for: the boy. And the roof, of course.

After Sara had spoken, Caroline said, 'Must you do this?'

'Yes, I think I must.'

Caroline rose to her feet. She regarded Sara shrewdly. 'I understand that Gil may not, in some ways, be the ideal husband. If you are unhappy, then I wouldn't object to you spending more time pursuing your own interests. If you wished to travel, for instance.'

'I thought about that. But I know it wouldn't be enough.'

'Then I'm sorry.' Caroline looked troubled. 'And David?'

'Perhaps, if it was just me and him, I might be better at it.'

'You mean to take him with you? I beg you to think carefully, Sara. I beg you to think what's best for David.' Caroline picked up the baby, cradling him protectively against her. 'Of course I understand that you must want him with you. But, alone, what have you to offer him? How would you care for him?'

'I'll learn. I'll make myself learn.'

'I'm afraid I must speak bluntly. Have you considered what this will mean to you? What will your parents say? Will they take you back, if you leave your husband? As for Alice Finborough, I know she's always been an unconventional woman, but even she might balk at what you intend to do. The scandal . . . you will be the talk of the county, I'm afraid.'

Sara shook her head. 'I won't go home. And I won't go back to Raheen. It wouldn't do, I know it wouldn't.'

'Then where will you live? And what will you live on? The estate's income has been negligible for years. If you are expecting Gil to continue to maintain you — '

'I don't want any money from Gil.'

'Then, I say again, how will you live? And how will you support a child? The bringing up of a child costs a great deal of money. Food . . . clothing . . . school fees . . . There is another matter you must consider. I will not countenance a divorce in the family. If you leave Vernon Court, you must continue to live as Gil's estranged wife. And that will not be a *comfortable* position in which to be. Do you understand?'

'Yes,' she murmured. 'Yes, I see that.'

'And then there are all the intangible things that a family such as ours will be able to give to a child, and that you, on your own, will not. The introductions, the connections that will be so useful to David as he grows older. I don't mean to be cruel, but I must point out to you that a woman on her own by and large lives outside society.'

Sara cried, 'I don't care about my position in society! I hate all that!'

'But you care about your son, surely? If you insist on taking David with you, then you would deny him so much. He would share in your ostracism. He would inevitably be less favourably thought of than if he had remained part of the Vernon family.'

Sara stared at Caroline, horrified. 'Is that what you believe?'

'It's what I *know*. And if you care about David, you would not wish that for him, surely.'

'No,' she whispered. 'No, of course not.'

'Sara, I beg you not to take David away from what is familiar to him. Familiarity — security — is so important to a child. I have brought up two sons — you must trust my judgement in this.'

Sara went to the window. Through the glass and through the softly falling rain, she could see the walled outline of Caroline's garden. She imagined herself walking through the paths that twisted and turned through the trees and shrubs. Trying to find a direction, trying to see the way ahead.

David would share in your ostracism. She knew that Caroline had spoken the truth. There had been a girl at school whose parents had been divorced. She had never been wholly accepted by her classmates, had always stood a little apart from the rest. Some taint, some whiff of shame, had clung to her. Society disapproved of those who broke its bonds — little more than a year ago a king had been forced to give up crown and country because he had chosen to marry a divorcee.

Caroline added, 'Just think what Vernon Court can offer David. He'll be happy here, I'll make sure of that. It's such a magical place for a child. Marcus and Gil had such wonderful childhoods.'

The outline of the garden blurred. Was it the rain, or were there tears in her eyes? Sara whispered, 'But just to go away . . .'

'It need not be a permanent separation. You'll be able to visit him as often as you like. Neither Gil nor I will stand in your way.'

'May he visit me in England?'

'If that's what you wish. And when he goes to school in England, when he is seven, it will be easier for you, of course.'

David's life was mapped out already, thought Sara. It had been mapped out for him before he was born — before she and Gil had married — before, perhaps, they had met. And one thing was certain, she saw that with great clarity. She could not stay. Vernon Court had crushed her, reduced her: there would be nothing left of her if she remained. The price of leaving Gil would be separation from her child. The price of staying would be the knowledge that she was only half alive.

★ ★ ★

Telling Gil that she was leaving him was like saying goodbye to someone she had been acquainted with for some time, but had never really got to know properly.

'Leave?' He looked startled. 'You mean — for good?'

They were in his study; he had risen from his desk. 'Yes,' she said.

'Sara, this is preposterous.'

'Is it? Why do you say that?'

'I should have thought that was obvious.'

'I've no wish to hurt you, Gil, but then, I don't think I am. I think . . . I think that after a week or so, you'll hardly notice that I'm gone.'

Walking away from him, she felt a flicker of surprise that they had managed to produce a child. They should have been sterile, surely, like the hybrid plants Gil bred.

During the sea crossing, she sat on deck of the ferry, though it was bitterly cold. A young man who sold brushes and boot polish came and talked to her: he gave her a wave as she boarded the train at Heysham. It was seven o'clock when she reached London. She had been travelling all day and she was very tired. Ruby had promised to meet her at Euston Station. Sara searched through the crowds, but there was no sign of Ruby, so she stood on the concourse with her suitcases, waiting.

A voice said, 'I beg your pardon, are you Mrs Vernon?'

Sara turned to see a tall, thin man, with a long, mournful face that reminded her of a bloodhound's, standing at her side. 'Yes, I am,' she said.

'I'm Edward Carrington.' They shook hands. 'Ruby had to stay late at the office,' he explained. 'Her section has some frightful flap on so she asked me to meet you instead.'

'How kind of you.'

He smiled. 'Ruby told me to look for a beautiful redhead. I knew it must be you the moment I saw you. Shall I take your cases?'

★ ★ ★

Isabel met Philip at the Lyons at Piccadilly Circus. A trio played dance tunes and couples moved round the floor. Joining her, Philip kissed her cheek.

'I wouldn't have thought this was your sort of place, Mum. Too showy.'

'I like the music.' The waitress arrived and Philip ordered a glass of Médoc for himself and tea for Isabel.

Isabel said, 'Has Sara written to you?'

'Not recently, no.'

'She's left Gil. And the child.'

'Good Lord.' Philip sat back in his seat. 'For good?'

'I believe so.'

'Where is she now?'

'She's living with Ruby. She doesn't want to come home and even if she did, Richard wouldn't let her.' Isabel folded her gloves and put them in her handbag.

'Will Gil divorce her?'

Isabel shook her head. 'The family won't consider divorce. One can hardly blame them. There's never been a divorce in the Vernon family. Or in ours, for that matter.'

'I suppose Dad's furious.'

'He refuses to speak to her.' She pressed her lips together tightly. 'Though I dare say he'll forgive her eventually.'

Philip said nothing.

'Yes, I know,' said Isabel, rather heatedly. 'Really, it's too ridiculous, Philip. What has happened to my family? One of my children lives hundreds of miles away, and Richard seems to think he can pretend the other two don't exist! And we used to be so happy!'

Philip shrugged. 'It's up to Dad. He needs to make the first move.'

The waitress arrived with the tea. When they were alone again, Isabel said, her voice low, 'It's all very well saying that your father must make the first move but you were hardly without blame, Philip. That Sunday —'

'I didn't mean to tell you like that. It just happened. And anyway, however I'd told you, you would have hated it.' He shrugged. 'Dad has to understand that Elaine and I love each other.'

His tone, his gaze, was unyielding. 'There's no point going over old ground again,' she said stiffly. She turned away, watching the couples on the dance floor.

But she hated to quarrel with him, her firstborn, so it was she who broke the silence. 'You look well, Philip,' she said, and thought how awful it was that they were

325

reduced to pleasantries.

'I'm very well. Working hard, though.' Philip had set up a business importing furniture from the Far East. 'Elaine and I had a good look at the figures last night. We had a bit of a celebration. We've made quite a respectable profit over the last six months.'

We, Isabel thought, we. He isn't mine any more, he's hers.

Philip was looking down, fiddling with the tasselled edge of the tablecloth. 'That wasn't the only reason we were celebrating,' he said. 'Elaine's expecting a baby. September-ish, she thinks.'

Isabel struggled to absorb her shock. If she had, however unreasonably, wondered whether — sometimes hoped that — this unsuitable marriage would not last, that hope crumbled now.

But she made an enormous effort. 'Congratulations, Philip. You must be very excited. I hope she — I hope Elaine — keeps well.'

'Won't you meet her?'

She could see the hope in his eyes. She reached out and touched his hand. 'No, Philip. This is what you must understand. I can't.'

Isabel left shortly afterwards, hailing a taxi to take her to her dressmaker's in Bayswater. In the taxi, she opened her compact and powdered her nose. Never having worn cosmetics before, she had recently taken to applying a little lipstick and powder. Without it, she looked so grey. It was the change of life, she supposed. That, and all the dreadful upheavals of the past two years.

Elaine was having a baby. She had been very good, Isabel thought, she had said all the right things, but there was a part of her that could hardly bear it. And then there was Sara. How could she walk away from her baby, how could she? Isabel could see why she had left Gil — he had never been the right man for her, she saw that now, though goodness knows, plenty of women had to cope with husbands far more dreadful than Gil — but to leave her *baby*! And he had been such a dear little thing. Her first grandchild. What she couldn't understand was why such a decision hadn't torn Sara apart. She had believed that she and Sara were close, but now she often felt they can't have of been at all.

Yet above all the sadness and her sense of loss, her most powerful emotion recently had been rage. Though she might reasonably be considered to have been wounded the deepest, it had nevertheless been left to her to paper over the cracks. *She* was the one who had to talk to Sara and to Philip, to try to understand why they had acted as they had, when all she could see was that they had ruined their lives. *She* was required to be patient and tactful when what she really wanted to do was to give them both a good shake. She had had to endure Philip's description of his wedding — a rather hole-in-the-corner affair, she couldn't help thinking, in a drab little church in Hendon, and Ruby the only representative of the Finborough family to attend — she had had to do that while the fissures that Philip's marriage had opened up in the family remained, exposing, in the most horribly melodramatic way, rifts that had already existed. And all the time Richard sulked and cut off both Philip and Sara without a penny. She daren't even tell him she'd been seeing Philip because she knew he'd only fly off the handle. And when you thought that he was to blame for so much of what had happened . . .

The cab drew up in Bayswater. As she rang the doorbell, Isabel acknowledged that mixed with her resentment was a different emotion. Something in Richard — some jauntiness, some previously irrepressible confidence — had taken a knock. Sometimes she felt sorry for him.

Ruby's friends had discussed, with the seriousness they usually applied to knotty political problems, how Sara should earn her living. As cookery and riding were her only skills, it was decided that someone should have a word with Big Frank, who ran a café in Romilly Street. Sara now worked in the café every lunchtime as well as three evenings a week. Many of the café's customers were communists. They sat for hours, drinking their coffee very slowly and discussing great events while condensation trailed down the windows — condensation generated, Sara thought, by the heat of their conversation. She made them buttered toast and Welsh rarebit, and always gave anyone with holes in their shoes an extra piece of toast.

She enjoyed working in the café, she even enjoyed her journey to Romilly Street. 'Sara, you can't possibly,' said Ruby. 'You can't be a proper Londoner and not complain about the Tube.' But it was true, she didn't even mind rush hour, when she was squeezed between bowler-hatted men with briefcases and typists clutching bags containing novels and knitting. She liked the buses too, where the passengers talked to each other more than they did on the Tube, and she caught snatches of their conversation, slices of their lives. *Triplets, dear, and him in the navy . . . and I said to her, don't you even think about it, love, it'll be just the same as it was with Mavis . . .*

At the weekends, Sara and Ruby cleaned and tidied the flat, which was bigger than Ruby's old one, two rooms instead of one. When the housework was finished, they always had a treat — a bar of chocolate or a bowl of pears and tinned cream. At the café, Sara wiped the tables and washed dishes and mopped the floor. All these things were new to her, just as buses and the Tube were new to her. At Vernon Court and growing up in Hampstead, the maids had done the housework. Sara had not known how often a shelf needed dusting or how one applied wax polish or scrubbed a washbasin. Cleaning the floor in the café, she liked the way the mop made pale stripes through the muddy lino; rubbing lemon juice on to the taps, as Frank, who owned the café, had shown her, she saw the metal gleam through the limescale.

Edward Carrington often looked in on the café after work. One night, he arrived shedding flakes of snow from his shoulders. 'Brrr, it's freezing.' He unwound his scarf and took off his hat. His nose and the tips of his ears were pink.

'Shall I make you a coffee, Edward?' Sara asked. 'And some cheese on toast, perhaps?'

'Just coffee, thanks. I can't stay long. I'll be dining with my mother.' Edward sat down at a table.

The café was almost empty so Sara made two coffees and sat down with him. 'One of the girls brought the loveliest little poodle in today,' she told him. 'You wouldn't think communists would like poodles, would you?'

'They do seem a rather frivolous sort of dog.' He stirred sugar in his coffee. 'How are you, Sara?'

'I'm very well. And you?'

'Bit of a cold, but otherwise fine.'

She touched his hand. 'There's something I wanted to ask you about.'

'Fire away, I'm all ears.'

'This thing that's happened in Austria — '

'The Anschluss?'

'That, yes. Germany invading Austria.'

'There were big crowds out in the streets of Vienna, the papers said, to welcome the German troops. Funny sort of invasion.'

'So they — the Austrians — didn't mind?'

'It would depend which side you were on. If you were

a Nazi, for instance, you'd have welcomed the Germans with open arms.'

'What if you were a socialist?'

'I think you'd be pretty fed up. Frightened too, I should say.'

'Frightened?'

'The Nazis don't much care for socialists.' Edward glanced at her. 'I've never thought of you as interested in politics, Sara.'

'I can't get away from it, working in this place.' She thought how kind Edward Carrington had been to her and decided to confide in him. 'But it isn't that. I know — knew — someone who lives in Vienna.'

'Ah. Have you heard from her recently?'

'Him, Anton's a him. And no, we don't write. I haven't heard from him for a very long time.'

Edward sneezed. 'Poor Edward,' said Sara. 'I should of ~~have~~ made you a whisky toddy instead of coffee, shouldn't I?'

'I'm all right. I've rather a thick head, that's all.' He folded his handkerchief and put it back in his pocket. 'This chap — '

'Anton.'

'You knew him before you were married?'

'Anton and I were in love with each other.'

'*Oh.* But you married someone else.'

'Anton wasn't in love with me. I thought he was, but it turned out he wasn't really. I suppose that was why I married Gil, because I knew I couldn't have Anton. But it turned out to have been the most awful mistake.' She sighed. 'I do seem to have made a terrible muddle of everything. I've tried falling in love and I've tried getting married and having a baby, and nothing has worked out. I think I shall work here until I'm an old lady. It seems to be the only thing I can do properly.' She looked at him fondly. 'Have you ever thought of marrying, Edward?'

'It's difficult with my mother being so unwell. There was someone once but she didn't hit it off with Mother and it never really came to anything. Anyway, you were telling me about that chap.'

'Years ago, Anton was forced to leave Vienna. The last thing I heard, he'd gone back to Austria. I expect he was worried about his father. I wondered whether, after what's happened, he'd have to leave again. And — and whether he might come back to London.'

Edward cleared his throat. 'If he wanted to stay in Vienna he'd have to modify his views a little, let's say. And even if he did, he'd be on some list or other, by the sound of things.' He glanced at his watch, then he rose. 'I'd better go. Mother will worry. Thanks for the coffee, Sara.'

★   ★   ★

The Carringtons lived in a first-floor flat in Belgravia. Edward whistled to himself as he said good evening to the caretaker, then collected the late post and went upstairs to the flat. He hung his coat, scarf and hat on the stand before he entered the drawing room.

His mother was sitting in a chair by the fire. She shivered. 'You always seem to bring the cold in with you, Edward.'

'Sorry, Mother.' He kissed her cheek. 'How are you today?'

'Very poorly. My hip . . . Dr Steadman came round and he prescribed me some powders but they don't seem to have done any good. But at least he was company for a little while, though he always seems to rush off.'

'I'm here now.' Edward smiled at his mother. 'You have my undivided attention for as long as you like.'

'Yes, I dare say.' Mrs Carrington shivered again.

'Shall I fetch your rug, Mother?'

331

Mrs Carrington glanced at the clock. 'It's almost half-past seven. I'd have to put it on and take it off again and I'm far too tired for all that fuss. If I'd had it earlier, I might not feel so cold.'

'You could ~~have~~ OF asked Gladys to fetch it for you, Mother.'

'I didn't like to trouble her. The cooking . . . ' she added vaguely.

'It's what we pay her for. I'll have a word with her.'

'No, no. You mustn't upset her. We don't want to lose another girl.'

'I promise I'll choose my words carefully.'

Edward went into the kitchen, where Gladys, the cook-general, was clanging pots and pans. There was a great deal of steam and an aroma that reminded Edward of wet flannel, but he said: 'It smells delicious, Gladys.'

'The fish has broken up in the pan, Mr Carrington, but that's always the way with cod. And madam wanted blancmange. I told her it'd have to be packet, my egg custards always curdle.'

'I'm sure dinner will be lovely, as always.' Then, after few moments' silence in which Gladys, sighing, drained potatoes into a colander and spooned sauce into a boat, Edward ventured, 'I wonder if you could remember to tuck my mother's rug over her in the afternoons, Gladys, the quilted rug she keeps on the bed. She gets so frightfully cold, you see.'

Gladys looked offended. 'I offered madam the rug, sir, but she said it was too heavy and made her legs ache.'

'Ah. Perhaps her cashmere shawl, then.'

'If you say so, Mr Carrington. Now I must get on, I'm all behind.'

Edward took the hint. Muttering thanks, he left the kitchen.

Over dinner, he told his mother about his day at

work. Mrs Carrington's responses were limited to brief phrases and requests to pass the butter. Though she had been ill for many years, she had a good appetite. When Edward ran out of anecdotes he coaxed his mother into telling him the events of her day. Because of her rheumatism, she was able to walk only short distances, so Mrs Carrington spent a lot of time sitting by the front window, watching the comings and goings into the block of flats at the entrance way below. Visitors were noted, their destinations discovered by some means Edward had never been able to fathom. His mother knew the names of every other resident of the large building, as well as a great deal about their health and the state of their marriages.

Over pudding, she said to Edward, 'That Mrs Pritchard had a visitor today.'

Gladys's lumpy blancmange looked unpromising; warily, Edward scraped off a spoonful. 'Oh, yes?'

'Another man,' said Mrs Carrington meaningfully. 'He looked like a travelling salesman or some such type. He had one of those little suitcases.'

'Perhaps Mrs Pritchard had run out of polish.'

Mrs Carrington made a scornful sound. 'She's no housewife. No, I expect he was another of her *friends.*' She looked across the table to Edward. 'You're not going to take more jam, are you, Edward? You shouldn't take so many sweet things. You're looking bilious as it is.'

'I've a cold, that's all, Mother,' said Edward, and endured the blancmange without extra jam.

After dinner, over coffee, they sat by the fire, listening to the wireless. Edward could not remember his mother ever being well. He supposed she must have been well when he was little, but he had no recollection of it. His father had died not long after Edward had left boarding school at the age of nineteen, and his mother's health had deteriorated after that. Five years ago, they had sold their Surrey house and moved into London. Edward missed the Surrey house, where he had liked to fish in the streams, but the move to London had undeniable advantages — the flat was easier to run, his journey to work was short, and his mother was near the best doctors in Harley Street.

Though Edward had originally suggested a ground-floor flat, his mother had worried about noise and burglars, so they had settled for one on the first floor. If his mother wanted to go out, she used the lift, and then, with the aid of a stick, walked to the house of her friend, Mrs Collins, who lived on the other side of the square, or to Mrs Dixon, where she played bridge once a week. On Saturday afternoons, Edward drove his mother to the Odeon in Leicester Square. Mrs Carrington enjoyed both thrillers and romances; her favourite film was *The Prisoner of Zenda*, starring Ronald Colman, which Edward had taken her to see five times.

At ten o'clock, his mother put off the wireless and went to bed, with instructions to Edward not to make a noise when he retired later. Edward poured himself a whisky, taking care not to clink the decanter, and found his place in his Margery Allingham. Though his head ached because of his cold he treasured this hour to himself in the evenings too much to waste it in bed with cocoa and an aspirin.

He kept the hour after work free for himself as well. When they had moved from Surrey to London, he had told his mother that he finished work at six, rather than at five. The lie had made him a piece of time for himself, to pursue his own friends and interests. In the space between leaving work and going home, he joined colleagues for a drink or had coffee with friends, or, if no one was available, drank a beer in a pub while he did *The Times* crossword. He sucked peppermints on the way home so that his mother would not detect the smell of alcohol. More substantial outings — a party or dinner at a restaurant — needed careful preparation and planning. His mother had to be warned weeks ahead, Mrs Collins or Mrs Dixon had to be fetched to keep her company, treats had to be promised to compensate for his desertion.

Edward knew that he wasn't the sort of man girls fell in love with at first sight. He lacked something — or other men *had* something. What it was that they had always puzzled him. Girls seemed to fall in love with the most frightful asses. Though any glance in the mirror told him he wasn't handsome, that there was something skewwhiff about his face, that it had a malleable, rubbery quality, its separate parts nondescript — it was nevertheless a pleasant enough, inoffensive sort of face. Yet he had never had a wide circle of friends. If he did not repel, neither did he attract. Girls told him he was a sweetie, men considered him a decent chap. But he was never the person people sought first: he was always an addition, an understudy. 'And we must ask Edward,' he imagined them saying, those people who threw parties or scratched up weekend cricket teams, once their list was half a dozen strong.

He didn't mind, had never expected to be first. He had had few serious girlfriends. 'There was someone once,' he had said to Sara, but he had exaggerated. He had taken Barbara Cooper out a dozen times, had been permitted to kiss her and touch her breasts. Any attempt to go further had met with a downward tug of her skirt hem, and a 'Not here, Edward, for goodness' sake!' — understandable when he recalled the sorts of places they had been obliged to court. Mrs Carrington had taken a dislike to Barbara even though Barbara had made every effort to be agreeable, and eventually they had parted.

'It's not going anywhere, Ned,' Barbara had said on the day she had told him she had broken off with him. 'I'm twenty-five now. I want to get married and have children, not neck in pub car parks.'

The feelings he had for Sara Vernon went far deeper than any stirrings of lust he had felt for Barbara, far deeper than he had felt for any other woman. He remembered the first time he had set eyes on Sara at Euston Station. 'I'm in an awful mess, Edward,' Ruby had said to him earlier that day. 'I promised to meet a friend at Euston Station at seven o'clock and blasted Horniman has just told me that I have to stay late because of the audit.' Edward had good-naturedly offered to help. At Euston, he had caught sight of a woman wearing a fur coat and a little black hat, two suitcases beside her, standing alone in the centre of the concourse.

She had been, quite simply, the most beautiful woman he had ever seen. He had not gone to her straight away, but had stood beside the indicator board, watching her for a few moments. When they were among a crowd, he often found himself looking at her, his gaze drinking in the fall of her auburn hair and the grace of her movements.

Sara was married, of course, but the marriage must be dissolved eventually. He recalled the fellow she had told him about tonight, the Viennese. Edward hoped Anton Wolff stayed in Vienna. Or, if it became too hot for him there, that he headed for Paris, or New York.

★ ★ ★

At the beginning of June, Isabel went to stay at Porthglas. Richard was to join her in the middle of the month. On the day before he was due, Isabel took the bus to St Ives. Grey-roofed, whitewashed stone cottages clustered round the steep, narrow streets that led down to the harbour. In July and August, the boarding houses and beaches would be crowded with holidaymakers.

Isabel bought brill for supper the following evening from one of the fishermen at the harbour and had a sandwich lunch in a café. After lunch, she visited some of the artists' studios in the town. Artists had been coming to St Ives since the latter half of the previous century, attracted by the clear, bright light and the Mediterranean-blue sea. Over the years, Isabel had bought sketches and paintings to hang on the walls of Porthglas Cottage. Her treasures included a tiny Whistler, a dark, moody seascape executed on the wooden lid of a cigar box, that she had discovered hidden beneath clutter in an antique shop.

Passing the open entrance to a studio, Isabel heard a wolf whistle. Beside the door, a green parrot in a cage was looking pleased with himself. Isabel talked to the parrot for a few moments, and then, seeing that the studio was empty, ventured a little way inside, drawn by the paintings stacked against the walls.

She was studying a coastal scene when she heard footsteps on the steps outside. A tall, rangy man with wild salt-and-pepper hair appeared in the entrance way.

'Good afternoon,' said Isabel. 'I do apologise for coming in uninvited, but your parrot whistled to me and the door was open.'

'You're a harlot, aren't you, Charlie?' Opening the door to the parrot's cage, the man put in his hand and the bird stepped on his finger, then clambered up his arm to his shoulder. 'Invite in any passing stranger, wouldn't you?'

He turned to Isabel. 'Feel free to look around. Is there anything particular you're looking for? Because I've got the lot — seascapes, harbour scenes, fishing boats . . .'

'I was just browsing.'

'Ah.' He clenched a fist against his heart. 'Those words that strike such pain into the bosom of the poverty-stricken artist. I *was just browsing*.'

She couldn't help smiling. 'I'm sorry to be a disappointment.'

'Can't I tempt you? I accept commissions — landscapes, portraits. I'll even paint the pet dog, damn it.'

Isabel laughed. 'I'm afraid my husband and I are between dogs at the moment.'

'Now you do disappoint me.' He made a forlorn face. ' 'My husband', you said, didn't you?'

'He's driving down from London tomorrow.'

'Can't you put him off? Then I could make you supper and tell you the story of my life.'

'I'm sure that would be most entertaining,' Isabel said, suppressing a smile, 'but I'm afraid it's not possible.'

'Then at least buy a seascape to console me.' He offered her a sketch. 'How about this? I'll sell it to you for five bob. I should buy it, if I were you, or I might die of a broken heart and then you'd feel guilty for the rest of your days.'

She laughed again. 'It's very pretty, so yes, why not?'

He rolled up the sketch and wrapped it in brown paper as Isabel took five shillings from her purse. On the bus back to Porthglas, she found herself looking at the roll of paper every now and then and smiling. At home, she put the watercolour on the mantelpiece and admired its luminous light. She read the signature scrawled across the bottom right-hand corner: 'Blaze Penrose'.

Richard arrived late the following evening. Isabel was weeding between the lavender hedges when she heard the sound of the car coming down the lane. She went to meet him.

'How was your journey?'

'Fine.' He took his case out of the boot. Then he said, 'Isabel, I'm sorry, but I've bad news.'

A stab of fear. 'The children — '

'As far as I know, they're well. Not that they'd have

the goodness to let me know if they weren't.' His expression altered. 'Isabel, I'm afraid John Temple has died.'

Her hands flew to her mouth. 'Richard, no.'

They went into the house. As Isabel poured him a drink Richard told her that John Temple had died in his sleep on Thursday night. His wife, Margot, had woken in the morning to find him lying cold beside her. His heart had given out, the doctor said.

'I've done what I can,' Richard said. 'I went to the house and made sure Margot had everything she needed. I've instructed Dunning to collect their children and grandchildren from the railway station — the daughters all live some distance away, remember. We'll have to drive back to London tomorrow, because of the funeral.'

'Of course.'

He sat down by the fireplace; he looked pale and strained. He said, 'Isabel, this was my fault. John wanted to retire two years ago, remember, when he turned sixty-five. But I asked him to stay until we'd seen through the takeover.'

Isabel came to sit beside him. 'John was an adult. It was his decision.'

Richard looked grim. 'He knew that I needed him. He was too loyal an employee to leave me fighting for air. I asked him to put off his retirement. I made it very difficult for him refuse.'

She put her hand over his. 'Richard, please don't torment yourself.'

'I don't blame only myself. I blame Philip too. He didn't think twice about walking away from Finboroughs at the worst possible time.'

'You don't know that. He may have found it a difficult decision as well.'

Richard shook his head. 'He knew when to put in the knife.'

Isabel suppressed a sigh, and said quietly, 'Richard, it was you who made it impossible for Philip to remain at Finboroughs.'

'*He* made it impossible for me to do otherwise!'

She could hear the rising anger in his voice. 'You are tired and upset,' she said gently. 'We shouldn't talk about this now. Why don't you change and then we'll go out for a walk?'

Later, walking along the beach, Richard strode ahead, stooping every now and then to pick up a pebble and hurl it into the sea.

'I wonder if he'll have the nerve to show himself at the funeral,' he said.

'Who?'

'Philip, of course. Who else?'

'Philip has known John since he was a baby. Of course he must come to the funeral. Richard, you can't blame Philip for John's death. That would be unfair and wrong. John died of heart failure. It's terrible, but I expect it could have happened at any time.'

He roared, 'Why do you make excuses for him? And when he has hurt you, too?'

Because he's my son, she thought, but said calmly, 'We can't change what has happened. We might like to, but we can't. Philip is married. He's been married for more than eighteen months. Nothing's going to change that.' She thought for a moment, took a decision. 'There's something you should know. Elaine is pregnant.'

His expression became blacker, but he said, 'That's no concern of ours.'

'Oh, Richard, of course it is! The baby will be our grandchild.'

'Philip is no longer a Finborough,' said Richard coldly. 'Whatever progeny he manages to — ' He broke off, his eyes narrowed. 'How do you know?'

'He told me.'

'You've seen him?'

'Yes.'

'When?'

'A few weeks ago.'

'And you didn't see fit to let me know?'

She met his gaze. 'Don't browbeat me, Richard.'

'*Browbeat*! As if I ever could!'

'Philip and I meet up from time to time,' she said tiredly. 'I didn't tell you because I thought you'd be angry. And I was right, wasn't I?'

He had picked up another pebble and was passing it from hand to hand. 'Do I take it this meeting wasn't the first one? That this has been going on for some time?'

'Yes.'

'I see. And the deceit didn't trouble you at all?'

She said furiously, '*You* dare to lecture *me* on deceit?'

'I thought I made it clear that we should have nothing more to do with him.'

'That was your decision, Richard, not mine.'

'You were of the same mind. You felt as I did.'

'I was very angry with Philip, yes. But I was angrier with you.'

He snarled, flung the stone into the sea, and strode ahead. She hurried to catch up with him. She said, 'It was hard at first, seeing Philip, but not as hard, I found, as not seeing him.'

'I suppose you've been to his home . . . I suppose all is forgiven . . .'

'No,' she said sharply. 'I have not been able to bear that.'

'You surprise me.' His voice was laced with sarcasm.

She studied him dispassionately. 'You're angry with Philip because he humiliated you in front of our friends. You're angry with him because he walked away from the business you've spent a lifetime building up. But you're also angry with him because he took something you wanted, and you can't bear that. You can't bear to be

341

beaten, Richard, you never could, and nor can you bear to admit that you were in the wrong. You translate hurt and grief into anger and you don't allow the people who love you to come close to you. I grieve for John Temple too, you know. He was a good man.' Shaking her head, Isabel turned on her heel. 'I find it impossible to talk to you when you are like this. I'm going back to the house.'

She walked away. The only time she looked back, Richard was a stroke of grey against the sand. On the cliff-top, sea pinks quivered in the grass as she headed towards the house.

In the kitchen, she checked the stew in the oven and washed and dried the dishes. She was wiping the sink dry with a cloth when she heard Richard come into the house. She put down the cloth and went into the sitting room.

She said, 'I thought you might drive away.'

'I considered it.' Sitting down on the sofa, he pressed the heels of his hand against his eyes. 'But I was too tired, I'm afraid.' He gave a wry smile. 'Perhaps after dinner.'

'It's almost ready.'

'I'll light a fire.'

Richard crumpled newspaper and stacked kindling. He lit the fire, then sat down on the bench in the inglenook. 'I can't imagine how I'll manage without John,' he said. He looked exhausted, the lines around his mouth and eyes scored more deeply than before. 'He's always been there, from the earliest days. He was such a tower of strength, the one person I knew I could rely on absolutely. I remember how kind he was to me when you were so ill after having Theo, when I was almost out of my mind with worry and fear. And it makes me so sad that he hasn't had his years in the sun. John and Margot were planning to leave London, you know, to move to Bournemouth to be near their daughters. He ought to ~~have~~ *of* had those years — he deserved it.'

Isabel kneeled in front of him, taking his clenched hands in her own, pressing them against her face. 'I know, Richard, I know. I'm so sorry.'

He said, 'Philip may come to the funeral if he wishes to. I shall not speak to him but he may come.'

She knew how much the offer had cost him. 'And Sara?'

'Yes, of course. John was very fond of her. And I was wondering . . . she must be short of money. I thought I might give you something to give to her. You could say you've saved it from the housekeeping.'

After Sara had left Vernon Court, Richard had written to Gil, telling him that he was putting a sum in trust to be used in the future for David's school fees, and to grow into a lump sum that he would receive when he reached his majority. He had refused, however, to support Sara — hoping, Isabel suspected, that Sara would return to Gil.

At last, thank God, he seemed to have softened a little. But she said exasperatedly, 'Why don't you give it to Sara yourself? You know how much you miss her.'

'No.' Richard glowered. 'She's behaved abominably. She needn't think I'll just forgive and forget. But I don't want her to go hungry. I don't want her to suffer.'

'If you won't change your mind, of course I'll give Sara the money.' Isabel stifled a sigh.

★   ★   ★

A fortnight later, Isabel was back in London, walking home from a visit to the library, when she caught sight of the man waiting outside the entrance to her house. He was smoking a cigarette, glancing every now and then up and down the pavement. There was a small suitcase beside him. A travelling salesman, she thought, or one of the army of unemployed men from the mill towns of northern England or the coalfields of South Wales who had come to London in search of work.

His gaze fixed on her as she neared the gates. His clothes were cheap yet flashy. He was wearing a tan jacket of which the cuffs had frayed, and the sole of one of his patent-leather shoes gaped away from the upper. As she approached him, he snuffed out his cigarette between thumb and forefinger, put the stub in a tin and slid the tin into his pocket. Then he raised his hat.

'Mrs Finborough?'

His voice had an American twang, which surprised her. 'Yes?' she said briskly. 'Can I help you? I'm afraid we've no work at present, but if you ask at the kitchen, Mrs Finch will give you some bread and tea.'

He said, 'Don't you remember me?'

She searched his face, wondering whether he had once been in service with the family or was an ex-employee of Richard's, perhaps. Apart from that unexpected American accent, he appeared much the same as any one of the thousands of men who had fallen on hard times. He was fiftyish, weather-beaten with purplish broken veins in his cheeks and on his nose. His only striking feature were his eyes, which were a very dark brown, set between puffy red lids.

Then he said, 'I remember *you*, Isabel.'

'I think you must be mistaken,' she said coldly. 'If you will excuse me . . . '

He said, 'Broadstairs beach,' and Isabel froze, her hand on the gate.

She heard him say, 'You *do* remember.'

'I've no idea what you're talking about.' Yet she found her gaze drawn back to him, and she was aware of a flicker of recognition, mixed at first with disbelief and then with a rising horror, as she looked once more into his eyes.

A brown so dark it was almost black. The colour of treacle toffee.

'I don't know you,' she whispered. 'I've never met you before.'

He smiled. 'I know the years haven't done me many favours, but you can't have forgotten me. You can't have forgotten your old friend Alfie Broughton, can you, Isabel?'

11

In September, the country found itself teetering on the brink of war with Germany. All other concerns shrank away, made small by comparison. Hitler had laid claim to the Sudetenland, a part of Czechoslovakia with a significant German-speaking population. Eduard Beneš, the Czech president, had used his country's alliance with France to stave off Hitler's demands. But now Hitler had raised the stakes, threatening to invade Czechoslovakia unless France and Britain conceded the Sudetenland.

There was the fear that any local European war would turn into a wider, global conflict, as it had in 1914. In memory of the slaughter of the Somme and Passchendaele, war memorials stood in every town and village. There was also the realisation that Britain was not ready for war. And, Ruby thought, there was no heart for war.

Preparations for civil defence, put off for years, went into action. Ruby attended a lecture on the dangers of poison gas. Vans fitted with loudspeakers toured the streets, reminding everyone that they must receive gas masks. In an infants' school in West Brompton, Ruby joined the queue of men, women and children waiting to be fitted for gas masks. Her gaze wandered over the pictures on the walls, the wax-crayoned stick figures and the prints of beach and farmyard, idyllic, sunlit, untroubled. The gas mask had a rubbery smell when she pulled it on over her head, and the babies screamed when they were fitted into the bags designed to protect them from poison gas. Their mothers' voices rose, outraged and alarmed, when they discovered that there were not enough baby-bags to go round. Walking home,

Ruby slung the gas mask, in its ugly cardboard container, over one shoulder and felt a sense of disbelief.

Something different, something frightening, was being slowly but relentlessly conjured into life. The apparatus of war — sandbags stacked against the public buildings, an anti-aircraft gun on Westminster Bridge, machine-gun emplacements prickling against the skyline on the roofs of the power stations — emphasised the vulnerability of the city. The familiar took on a threatening aspect. An aeroplane soaring high in the sky brought with it memories of newspaper photographs of the bombed cities of Madrid and Guernica. The Royal Parks, their lawns now scarred by trenches, foretold an uncertain future. She went to work, she shopped, she went out with her friends, yet at the back of her mind Ruby saw London, *her* London, breaking up, falling apart, consumed by fire.

At the end of the month, Neville Chamberlain flew to Munich in a last, dramatic bid for peace. Returning the next day, he brandished the scrap of paper that promised, he declared, peace in our time. The crisis was over, the price of peace the handing over of the Sudetenland to Germany, and the relief was at first almost palpable. They could go back to complaining about the weather or the lateness of the buses.

But after the first day or two relief seemed to dissipate, to be replaced by unease, and by shame, perhaps. And besides, the gas masks still hung in the hallways, the planes still left their vapour trails across the sky.

★ ★ ★

Nineveh farmhouse: the dogs barking and the geese hissing and wet sheets hanging dispiritedly from washing lines slung between the apple trees.

347

Ruby found Aunt Maude at the back of the house. A boy in his late teens was standing in front of her. Behind the scullery window, Hannah's face was a frightened white blur.

'A dozen eggs!' Maude was screaming at the boy. There was a smear of broken shells and egg yolk on the paving stones and an upturned basket had rolled beneath the old wicker chair to one side of the scullery door. 'Do you know how much money you've lost me, you careless fool?' The stick flailed, cracking the boy on the side of his head. 'I'll dock every penny from your wages!'

The stick swung up once more, but this time, the boy grabbed it, wrenching it out of Maude's hands and throwing it aside.

Maude's eyes narrowed. 'Pick it up,' she said softly.

'I won't.'

'Pick it up, George Drake, or I'll have you and your family out of that cottage by nightfall.'

There was a long silence. Then the boy picked up the stick and handed it back to Maude.

'Now clear up that mess you've made. Scrub it hard. I don't want to see a speck of eggshell left on those stones.' Catching sight of Ruby, Maude snapped, 'You're late. Midday, I told you. Dinner will be getting cold.'

They went into the house. Maude leaned her mountainous frame heavily on the stick. Folds of flesh fell round her neck, ankles and wrists. Her dark hair had greyed and excess weight had reduced her eyes to little black pebbles.

And like Maude Quinn herself, Nineveh farmhouse seemed to be slipping into age and decay. A felting of dust greyed the small window-panes and the rooms were cold and damp. It always struck Ruby, visiting Nineveh at half-yearly intervals, how little the house changed. Other families replaced worn furniture or

348

hung new curtains or put another coat of paint on a dingy room — not the Quinns. Other families threw out or passed on unwanted items, but at Nineveh nothing was too worn or too old to be kept. Ruby found herself wondering whether those were the same coats on the pegs as the last time she had visited, whether that was the same stub of candle on a saucer. Whether, in fact, those coats and that candle had been there the first time she had come to Nineveh as a small girl.

Ruby ate lunch with Maude and Hannah, and then helped Hannah with the washing-up. When it was time to leave, Ruby asked Hannah to walk down the track to the drove with her.

Her cousin was now nearly as tall as Ruby herself. Her frame was slight and her long, light brown hair was tightly plaited. If she had a decent haircut, thought Ruby, if she had a new dress instead of that old-fashioned, faded thing, covered with an even more worn and faded apron; if she stood up straighter and met your eye when she was speaking to you, then she might not look too bad.

Ruby imagined introducing Hannah, in her plaits and faded cottons, to her fashionable friends. Then, making a huge effort, she shoved the ignoble thought to the back of her mind.

'Why don't you come and visit me in London, Hannah?'

Hannah's eyes widened. 'London?'

'Yes, why not? It isn't the other side of the world, you know.'

'Oh, I couldn't . . . '

'Of course you could. You just buy a ticket and get on a train.'

'I haven't any money.'

'What, none?'

Hannah shook her head.

'Doesn't Aunt Maude give you any money?'

Another shake of the head. Of course Aunt Maude didn't pay her daughter a wage, thought Ruby — why would she, when she could get her services free?

'I'll lend you some, then.'

'Thank you, Cousin Ruby, but no. Neither a borrower nor a lender be, Mother says.'

'You don't always have to do what your mother tells you.'

Hannah glanced nervously over her shoulder, back to the farm-house. Ruby said, 'I'll post you a train ticket. It could be your Christmas present.'

'I couldn't. You don't understand, I just couldn't.'

A thought struck Ruby. 'You have been on a train before, haven't you, Hannah?'

'No.'

'*Never?* Good grief. A bus, then?'

'Once, when I went to March for Mother, and the wheel of the trap had broken.'

'But don't you go shopping? Or out on Sundays?'

'Sometimes I walk to Manea, but we don't need to buy much food, we make our own. Mother and I go to church on Sundays, in the pony and trap.' Hannah was twisting her apron. 'I have to go. Mother'll want her tea.' Pausing only long enough for Ruby to kiss her goodbye, she rushed back to the farm.

As she walked along the track to Manea Ruby caught sight of the plough horses nearing the bottom of the field. She waved to George Drake. He came to the hedgerow. He was a skinny lad with bright blue eyes and a scattering of freckles over his nose. A red weal ran down one side of his face, the legacy of Maude Quinn's stick.

'Are you all right?' Ruby asked him.

'A few bruises, that's all.' He grinned. 'My ma always says I've got a skull an inch thick.' The grin faded; he muttered, 'She's an evil old bitch, though. Sorry, miss. Shouldn't say that — she's your aunt, isn't she?'

'For my sins, yes. Why do you stay here? How can you bear to work for her? Why don't you just go?'

'Can't. You heard her — my family lives in one of her tied cottages. My dad's always worked for the Quinns. He was scaring birds from Nineveh's fields when he was eight years old. I've worked for Mrs Quinn since I left school at twelve. Had to, no choice, else we'd have lost the house, see.'

'Aren't there other farms? Nicer farms?'

'There's no work round here, miss. Times are hard.'

The land that surrounded them bore an air of neglect. Reeds grew in the ditches and the hedgerows were overgrown, spikes of hawthorn and blackthorn shooting high into the air. Earlier, walking from Manea to Nineveh, Ruby had passed fields left fallow, and tumble-down cottages whose blackened and dishevelled thatch must give scant protection from the elements.

George wiped the sweat from his forehead with the back of his hand. 'It's been bad for years. Some of the smaller places are empty now — no one'll buy them. My Uncle Walter biked from farm to farm in the summer, looking for work, but they all told him they ain't got none. I've got four little brothers, miss. They'd all be out in the street if I told Mrs Quinn what I thought of her.' His expression became determined. 'I'll be away from here as soon as I find something better, though. You won't see me for dust. No need to feel sorry for me. It's poor Hannah has the worst of it.'

On the way to Cambridge, the train crossed the flood plain that lay between the Hundred Foot Washes and the Old Bedford River. The water had already begun to gather in the hollows, rippling like grey silk in the late afternoon sunlight. At Cambridge, Ruby changed trains. The London train was crowded, so she walked along the corridor, threading between other standing passengers, peering into compartments, searching for an empty seat. Reaching the engine, she turned back. As she passed the first-class compartments she looked inside and saw the plentiful empty seats.

She ached with tiredness and tension, as she always did after visiting Nineveh. Catching sight of the ticket inspector, she stood in the corridor, staring out of the window at the passing countryside, waiting until he had gone into the next carriage. Then she ducked inside a compartment. There was only one other passenger, reading *The Times*. The open paper hid his face.

Ruby unbuttoned her coat and sank thankfully into a seat. As she took a book out of her bag, the other passenger drawled, 'Don't worry, I won't tell.'

'Tell what?'

'Travelling in a first-class compartment on a third-class ticket.'

'I've paid for a seat,' she said belligerently. 'I don't see why I should have to stand up all the way to London.'

'Oh, quite. Perfectly reasonable.'

Her fellow passenger flicked the newspaper in half and she saw him properly. He had dark hair, dark eyes, chiselled cheekbones and a strong jawline. There was a glint in his eyes, as if he found a great many things amusing. He was elegantly and expensively dressed in a light grey jacket, trousers and waistcoat and a dark red silk tie, and there was a navy-blue overcoat and a black hat in the luggage rack overhead.

His gaze drifted over Ruby and came to rest on the bag at her feet. His smile widened. 'Do you always take Wellington boots with you when you're visiting Cambridge?'

'I haven't been visiting Cambridge. I've been to the Fens.'

'Good Lord. What on earth for?'

'I've been to see my mad relations.'

His smile, she noticed, was lopsided, one side of his face bright and amused, the other faintly sardonic.

'Do you have mad relations?' he asked.

'Doesn't everyone?'

'Probably,' he conceded. 'Why do you visit them? Out of a sense of duty?'

'No, guilt, I think. I go to Nineveh every six months. That's about the length of time it takes for the guilt to get so bad I can't ignore it any longer.'

'You're not a Catholic, are you?'

'No, I'm not anything. Why?'

'Oh, the guilt. Catholics are rather good at guilt. Although confession is a handy way of expurgating guilt. I wonder how non-Catholics manage without it.'

'Do you believe in all that?'

'Since you ask, not any more.'

'I'm sorry, that was rather rude of me. You're not even supposed to talk about religion at dinner, are you?'

He laughed. 'I don't believe so.'

'Or politics.'

'Politics are my bread and butter, so I'm afraid they do creep into my dinner engagements sometimes.'

'Are you an MP?'

He shook his head. 'I work at the Foreign Office. It's quite fun, I get to travel around a fair bit. And you?'

Ruby told him where she worked. He looked interested, and said, 'You must know Leonard Speers, then. We were at Trinity Hall together.'

'Hardly. I glimpse him very occasionally in a corridor. It's a bit like seeing God.'

'Leonard has a rather godlike manner, it's true. He was always aloof, even when we were undergrads.'

'I take it you haven't been visiting mad relations?'

'No, I called on my old tutor. First afternoon off in months, after all the fuss.'

'Munich, you mean?'

'Mmm. I thought I'd better take the opportunity while I could, before it all starts up all over again.'

'Do you think it will?'

'Of course. Don't you?'

Ruby glanced out of the window. Everything, even the ugliest redbrick house and the dreariest little village, seemed so precious now. 'Yes,' she said.

'No point burying our heads in the sand, is there?' he said cheerfully. 'We've been doing that for a remarkably long time as it is. We've managed to buy ourselves some time at Czechoslovakia's expense so we'd better make use of it.'

'Do you think we should have *of* stood by Czechoslova-kia?'

'Morally, yes. What we did was craven and reprehensible. It was a betrayal. Hitler's a tyrant, and one should stand up to tyrants.'

Ruby found herself remembering the ugly little scene at Nineveh: Aunt Maude striking her labourer with her stick. A flicker of dislike, mostly directed at herself. She had not intervened on George Drake's behalf, she had not stood up to Maude Quinn, tyrant though she undoubtedly was.

She said slowly, 'I suppose its partly that we can't believe people can really do such terrible things. It paralyses us — we stand there stupidly, too shocked to do anything. Too polite, almost.'

'Quite. Chamberlain and his ilk seem to think that beneath it all, Hitler must be a gentleman and must eventually play fair. They can't seem to comprehend his true nature. And besides, practically, we had little alternative.' He threw Ruby a glance. 'You're not a pacifist, are you?'

'No.'

'Pacifism's all very fine in theory — perfectly noble sentiments and all that — but it's left us terribly behindhand.' He gave his lopsided smile again. 'These past few years, the dear old British public has seemed convinced that to make a few aeroplanes is to *invite* war.'

'Don't you think that's true?'

'Well, the *idea* is that rattling the sabre deters. Though you may have a point. Make a lot of shiny new weapons and all the military types will want to play with them.' He flicked an invisible speck of dust from the knife-crease down the front of his trousers. 'Our efforts to rearm ourselves haven't come soon enough for poor old Czechoslovakia. And by selling them down the river, we've made our task in the future much harder for ourselves.'

'Because Czechoslovakia is weaker now Hitler has some of it, you mean?'

'Weaker? It's utterly indefensible. We've given away the very part of the country that has a strong frontier. Hitler can just march into what's left.' His smile faded. 'Which he will do.'

'When?'

'Oh, quite soon, I should imagine. It's only a matter of time. He'll want Czechoslovakia's arms factories. I say, don't look so glum. You were right — we shouldn't discuss religion or politics over dinner.'

'But we're not having dinner.'

'Aren't we? You do disappoint me. I'd hoped we might.' Leaning forward, he offered her his hand. 'My name's Gascoigne, Lewis Gascoigne.'

'Ruby Chance,' she said.

'Well, Miss Chance? Won't you have dinner with me? Please say that you will.' His eyes pleaded: even if she had wanted to, how could she resist?

★ ★ ★

'I was hoping you'd help out an old friend who's fallen on hard times,' Alfie had said, that first time he had come to the Finboroughs' house. Isabel had scrabbled in her purse for pound notes and half-crowns.

Later, she had wondered whether that had been a

355

mistake. Whether, if she had pretended to have no recollection of him, he would have gone away, left her alone.

It was six weeks before she saw him again. She had begun to hope that he would not return. Her dreams, those old dreams of Broadstairs and a man walking out of the sea, became less frequent. Then, one Sunday afternoon, glancing out of an upstairs window, she saw him at the gate.

She hurried down the path. 'Why have you come here? What do you want?'

'To see you. To talk to you.'

'My husband is at home. You mustn't come here.'

'There's a bench down the road beneath some tall trees,' he said. 'I'll wait for you there.'

'But my husband . . . '

He smiled. 'You'll think of something.' Then he walked away.

She wondered whether there had been a threat in his words, or whether she had imagined it. Richard was in his study, working; she called to him that she was going out for a walk and he grunted, but did not look up from his desk.

She put on her hat and coat and put the new puppy, Tuppence, on a lead. Alfie Broughton was sitting on a bench beneath a row of tall horse chestnuts. He rose and tipped his hat as she approached him.

'Hello, Isabel.'

'I wish you wouldn't call me that.'

'But we're old friends.'

'No, we're not.' She studied him coldly, noting the bloodshot eyes, the sulky turn of his mouth. All his beauty had crumbled away. How could she have ever loved him? What poor taste she had had.

She said, 'What do you want?'

'I thought we should have a little talk.'

'There's nothing to talk about.' But there was

something she wanted to know, she realised. 'How did you find me?'

'Do you remember Jim Cottle? My old friend Jim?'

'No.'

'Surely you do, Isabel. We went out on his boat one day.'

She frowned, racking her brain. 'He was a fisherman,' she said.

'See, you do remember. I looked up Jim when I came back to England. He's still living in Ramsgate. He's married, though. His wife, Liddy, was a friend of yours.'

The puppy was frisky; she spoke to it sharply. 'Liddy . . . ' she said. 'You mean the parlourmaid at the Clarewoods' house? Liddy married Jim Cottle?'

'Yeah. She showed me pictures of their kids and grandkids. And other pictures too, of you.'

'Of me?'

'She collects them. She's made a scrapbook. She likes to read about all the film stars and rich toffs. She saw your photo in the paper, years ago, and cut it out and pasted it in her book. You and your old man at some charity ball. She recognised you. She was mighty proud to have known someone like you. Proper fairy-tale romance, she thought it was. Touching, isn't it?' His eyes ran her up and down. 'You've done well for yourself, haven't you, Isabel? That's a swell house — must have cost a bob or two. And wasn't that a Roller I saw in your front yard?'

'My house — my life — is nothing to do with you. You made that perfectly clear when you left me.'

'Yes. Naughty of me, wasn't it, running off like that?'

His smile was practised, a charming crinkling of the skin around his eyes. A young girl, that smile had melted her heart. Now she found it loathsome.

'I wasn't ready to settle down,' he said. 'I went to America.'

'You should have stayed there.'

357

'Don't be like that. I did pretty well at first, but it's been hard since the Crash of '29. I did this and that, but things got a bit hot for me recently so I thought I'd come back to the old country, see how it's getting on.'

'You made your choice years ago,' she said coldly. 'You made it clear that you wanted nothing more to do with me. And now we've talked, as you wished, and I must go.'

She stood up. Alfie took a packet of Lucky Strikes out of his pocket and struck a match. 'To tell the truth,' he said 'I was hoping you could help me out.'

'Help you out?' She felt frightened.

'I'm a bit short of cash. You're a rich lady, now — I guess I thought you could lend me a few bob.'

'No,' she said coldly. If she was strong this time, surely he would give up, go away. 'No, I can't do that.'

She began to walk away, the dog skittering beside her. Then he called out, 'What happened to the baby, Isabel?' and her heart missed a beat.

'Baby?' she repeated.

'Yes.' Alfie had risen to his feet. 'Our baby.'

She forced herself to meet his eyes. 'There was no baby. I made a mistake.'

'That wasn't what Liddy thought. She always wondered why you rushed off, left a good place.'

Isabel's mouth was dry. She repeated, 'There was no baby.'

'I don't believe you.' He took a few steps towards her. 'What did you do with the baby, Isabel? Did you get rid of it?'

She was aware of the rumble of traffic and the sound of the wind in the trees, and this man, who had once been her lover, standing in the shadows, watching her.

'She died,' she said. 'My baby died.'

'Ah.' He frowned, studying her. 'I wonder whether you're telling me the truth?' He inhaled his cigarette, then blew out a stream of smoke. 'Does hubby know about us?' he asked. 'And about the kiddie?'

'Go away!' Her voice was a scream. 'Go away and leave me alone!'

'Hush,' he said softly. 'People are staring at us.'

She pressed her fingers against her mouth. She was shaking.

'There's no need to take on like that, sweetie,' he said. 'I'll go as soon as you've helped me out. I'm a bit short of cash — I need something to get myself started up again. Fifty quid should do it.'

'Fifty pounds?' She stared at him, appalled. 'I don't have that sort of money.'

'Rot,' he said. 'Tommy rot.'

'I only have my housekeeping.'

'Then use that.'

'And how would I pay the tradesmen?' There was an hysterical edge to her voice.

'Oh, you'll find a way.' He glanced at his watch. 'I'll be waiting here, same place, let me see, on Tuesday. That'll give you two days. Should be long enough. Six o'clock, Tuesday. Make sure you're not late.'

He turned and walked away. Isabel watched as his shadow was swallowed up in the darker shadows of the trees.

★   ★   ★

Big Frank, who owned the café in Romilly Street, asked Sara to deliver a package to an address in Liverpool Street one afternoon. She had carried out the errand and was waiting at the Circle Line station when she saw him.

Anton. Standing on the opposite platform, reading a book.

A flash of golden hair, hidden for a moment as people walked in front of him. A feeling of heart-stopping disbelief. The crowds parted; she saw him again.

Then, as a train came into the opposite platform, Sara began to run, darting round bags and briefcases and carrycots, rushing up the steps and along the bridge. As she dashed down the second flight of stairs, she called out his name, but her voice was drowned by the sound of the engine as the carriage doors closed and the train pulled away.

When she looked round, she saw that the platform was deserted but for a cleaner pushing round a brush, gathering up cigarette boxes and sweet wrappers. Still, she searched for him. Then she returned to the other platform and took the next train, alighting at Sloane Square and then walking to Ruby's flat in Fulham Road.

The flat was empty. Sara washed her face and brushed her hair. There was a knock at the door. Anton, she thought, with a rush of joy, and went to open it.

Edward Carrington was standing in the hallway. 'Oh,' she said.

'Are you expecting someone?'

'No, no. How nice to see you, Edward. Come in.'

He came into the room. He said, 'I wondered if you'd like to come to the pictures. *Jezebel*'s on at the Odeon.'

'That would be lovely — ' she began, and then broke off, saying, 'I *saw* him, Edward!'

'Who?'

'Anton. I saw him only an hour ago!'

'That foreign chap you told me about? The one you were keen on?'

'Yes. He's *here*! He's in London!'

'Is he visiting, or what?'

'I don't know.' She felt restless, bubbling over with energy, as if someone had flicked a switch and she had come alive again. 'I was waiting on the Circle Line platform at Liverpool Street and I looked up and there he was, on the other side of the rails.'

'Did he see you?'

'No, I don't think so. I ran across, but a train came in and by the time I'd got there he'd gone.'

He rubbed his chin. 'Sara, are you absolutely sure it was him? Couldn't you have made a mistake?'

She shook her head vigorously. 'No, no, I'm sure.' Yet even as she spoke, doubts began to form. She had seen him so fleetingly. He had been looking down at his book. The light had been poor, casting shadows . . .

'If you *wanted* to see him — are you sure it wasn't just someone who looked a bit like him?'

'No, I'm certain. Almost certain.'

'And even if it was him . . .'

'What?'

'I thought you'd said he wasn't keen. I mean, wouldn't you only be raking up a lot of unhappiness for yourself if you met up with him again? Why stir things up?'

Some of her elation ebbed away. 'Perhaps you're right,' she said slowly. 'Perhaps he wouldn't want to see me. Perhaps he's forgotten me.'

Yet she remembered a taxi ride through London in winter, and Anton's voice, from a long time ago, saying, 'I wouldn't have thought anyone could forget you, Fräulein Finborough.'

Edward reached across the table and squeezed her hand. 'So how about the pictures? It might take your mind off all this. And anyway, my mother's given me a late pass, and you wouldn't want me to waste that, would you?'

* * *

The following morning, Sara went to Peter Curthoys' office in Golden Square. A girl with brown hair coiled into earphones was sitting in the reception room, typing.

She looked up as Sara came into the room. 'Can I help you, madam?'

'I wondered whether I might speak to Mr Curthoys.'

'He's rather busy at the moment, I'm afraid.'

'It'll only take a moment or two.'

'I'll see, then. What name shall I give, please?'

'Mrs Vernon.'

The girl rose, knocked on the opaque glass door of an office, put her head round the door and went inside. A few moments later, she came back, saying, 'Mr Curthoys will see you now, Mrs Vernon.'

'Thank you.'

Sara introduced herself to Peter Curthoys, who was tall and balding with quick, intelligent eyes. She said, 'I'm sorry to disturb you, Mr Curthoys, but I believe you know a friend of mine, Mr Wolff.'

'Anton?' He beamed. 'I certainly do. Would you like a word with him?'

Sara's heart began to batter against her ribs. 'Do you know where he is?'

'He's right here, in the next room.' Opening an inner door, Peter put his head round the jamb, and called, 'Anton! A lady to see you, a Mrs Vernon.'

And then he was there, standing in the doorway. She was about to run to him, but as he caught sight of her, his expression of enquiry altered, and he frowned, saying, 'Sara . . . good morning.'

His formal politeness made her pause. She found herself responding in kind, holding out her hand, murmuring a greeting.

Peter Curthoys muttered something about coffee and left the room. Sara said, 'You look well, Anton.' Though he didn't, particularly: he looked thin and strained. 'How are you?'

'I'm fine, thank you. And you, you look well also.'

'When did you come back to London?'

'Two months ago.'

'Oh,' she said, dismayed.

'Is there something I can help you with?'

'I thought . . . Where are you staying?'

'Peter has been kind enough to let me have a room in his house.'

'And your father, is he with you?'

'I'm afraid my father died six months ago.' Cutting off her words of condolence, he said abruptly, 'And now, it has been pleasant to renew our acquaintance, but you must excuse me, I have work to do.'

'Yes, of course.'

He held open the door for her. On her way out Sara said, 'I'm living with Ruby now. You must come and see us.'

'Thank you. Perhaps one day.' He bowed.

Sara left the room. Walking downstairs, her sight blurred and her eyes filled with tears. Outside, in the street, the autumn sunshine glittered on the roofs of the cars and on the panes of glass in the shop windows. She realised that she had never quite given up hope, that she had nursed a grain of it inside her, a small kernel that just now Anton had taken in his hand and crushed.

★ ★ ★

On their first date, Lewis Gascoigne took Ruby to Simpson's in the Strand, where they dined on lobster soup and steak and kidney pudding. On their second evening together, they went to a cabaret at the Trocadero. Then Lewis went away for several weeks to Europe. After he came back he and Ruby dined at a quiet restaurant in Knightsbridge. At the end of the meal, he suggested she come back to his flat for coffee. They took a taxi to an address in Mayfair: inside his flat, they sat on leather sofas to either side of the fire while a manservant produced coffee and then melted discreetly away into the background.

Lewis said, 'You are a very beautiful and intelligent woman, and I've enjoyed our evenings enormously, Ruby.'

She felt a pang of regret; she had come to like him. '*But* . . . ?' she said. 'I sense that you're about to say something beginning with 'but', Lewis.'

'But there's something I must tell you.'

'You don't have to be tactful, if you're dropping me. You can be quick and brutal, if you like. Gets it over with.'

'I'm not dropping you, you silly girl. Though you may decide to drop me. I'm married, Ruby.'

She glanced round the flat, which was masculine in taste and furnishings. 'But your wife — '

'Theresa lives in our other house, in the Lake District. We have lived separately for some years. We're not divorced, though, and we never will divorce. Theresa is a devout Roman Catholic. She believes that marriage is truly until death do us part.'

Ruby considered what he had told her. 'Have you any children?'

'No. There was a stillborn boy — there have been no others.'

'I'm sorry.'

'Ours has been a marriage in name only for some years. It has to be. The doctors have told Theresa that she mustn't risk another pregnancy. Her religion doesn't allow contraception, so . . . ' He spread out his hands.

'*Oh*. I see.'

'Quite. I suppose that if I was a better man, I'd put up with it and live with my wife as if we were brother and sister. But I'm not able to do that, so now we live apart.'

'Do you still see her?'

'Yes, every now and then. Theresa prefers to keep up some semblance of a marriage. And there are inevitably financial matters to discuss.' He steepled his hands, looking thoughtful. 'I don't think she minds too much. She has her garden and she's very involved with the Church.' He gave his little lopsided smile. 'What I'm trying to say, Ruby, is that if you're the sort of girl who'd like marriage and babies, then now's the time to beat a hasty retreat.'

'And if I'm not?'

'Then I would very much like to continue seeing you.'

'And I you.'

'Good. I hoped you'd say that.'

'Do you still love Theresa?'

'You're very forthright.' He held up a hand, staving off her response. 'With complete justification. I did love her — I loved her very much to begin with. She has an intensity that I found very attractive. I'm not sure what it was that destroyed my feelings for her. The knowledge that her convictions were of greater significance to her than love, perhaps. Or the discovery that something that was hugely important to me meant little to her — and vice versa, of course. Or perhaps I didn't like to find out that I'd always taken second place.' His voice was dry, self-mocking. 'What you said to me on the train, about being driven by guilt, struck a chord. I visit Theresa and we are civilised to each other, even though both of us, I suspect, feel suffocated by each other's company. I leave her, light-headed with relief and consumed by guilt.'

She rose from her seat and came to sit beside him. 'Dear Lewis,' she said, and kissed his cheek. 'I'm glad you've told me. Are you worried about my reputation? How gallant of you.'

'More,' he said 'that I may be a disappointment to you.'

'I doubt if I'll be disappointed. My mother might, I suppose.' She stirred her coffee. 'I'm afraid she assumes I'm still a virgin and hopes that sooner or later I'll marry a nice young man who works in the office.'

'Will you?'

'Good Lord, no.'

'No hankerings for wedding bells and orange blossom . . . ?'

'Not at all. I suppose my mother might mind that I never bring the nice young man home to meet her, but she's had to live with a great deal of disappointment in her life and I dare say she's used to it.'

He took her cup and saucer out of her hands and put it on the table. Then he scooped her on to his lap. 'My lovely little Ruby,' he murmured. He kissed her shoulder blades as he undid the buttons at the back of her gown. She felt a shiver of anticipation. Then he threaded his hands beneath her dress to stroke her breasts. Her eyes closed and she lay back against him and gave a sigh of contentment.

★   ★   ★

A foggy night and the café crowded with customers.

The door opened, letting in a curl of fog and Anton. Sara moved between tables and kitchen, her pencil slippery in her hand, a trail of plates balanced on her arm.

His table: a plate shivered. He said, 'You told me you were living with Ruby. You did say that, didn't you?'

'Since February. Since I left my husband.'

She walked away, unloaded the plates, gathered up dirty ones. His coat was slung over the back of his chair. Her arm brushed against it, picking up beads of moisture.

'I have to speak to you,' he said. 'When do you finish work?'

She told him, then she took the crockery back into the kitchen. She heard the hiss of the kettle, watched the cups slide into the water with a plop. She noticed the way her hand shook as she turned on the tap.

Don't hope too much. He's probably just being polite. He might have a girlfriend, he might be married, he might have a child. He might, quite reasonably, not love you any more.

When her shift finished, she put on her hat and coat and they went outside. The fog made hazy yellow circles around the streetlights. Walking beside him, she felt as if she was slipping back into something beloved and familiar.

He asked her if she would like a drink, but she shook her head. 'I'd rather walk.'

'Where shall we go?'

'To the river. I like the river in the fog.'

They crossed Shaftesbury Avenue. The cars and lorries, heading along the road, were visible as twin circles of dull, dissipated light. Passers-by loomed towards them and then were gone again.

He said, 'When I heard that you were married . . . ' The sentence trailed off, unfinished. Then, 'But you've left your husband?'

'Gil and I separated at the beginning of the year. I have a son, David.'

'A son?'

'Yes. He's eighteen months old. He lives with his father and grandmother in Ireland.'

She saw him frown, taking it in. Taking in that she had a child, but had deserted that child. What would he make of that? Would he understand the reasons for her choice, or would he despise her?

Hazards obstructed their path, separating them: a woman pushing a pram, someone cycling on the pavement, a letterbox. 'I was so sorry to hear about your father,' she said. 'You must miss him very much. Was he ill for a long time?'

'He suffered from bronchitis. That was why I went back to Vienna, because a friend wrote to me that he was unwell. But it wasn't the bronchitis that killed him. My father was beaten to death in an alleyway.'

She stared at him, appalled. 'Oh, Anton, no.'

'Half a dozen young thugs beating an old man to death — so brave, don't you think?'

'How horrible. I'm so sorry.'

He had paused beneath a streetlamp. The collar of his coat was turned up and the mist curled his hair into tendrils. She took a step towards him, but then he began to walk again and they set off down Charing Cross Road side by side, not touching.

'Nothing happened to his murderers,' he said. 'I never even knew their names. They were our Nazis or they were German Nazis or they were sadists looking for some sport — I'll never know.'

'And you, Anton? What happened to you?'

'I was in prison when my father died.'

'Why? What happened?'

He shrugged. 'Why did they imprison me? Because I no longer fit in with the times, perhaps. Because I no longer fit in with a country that allows old men to be beaten to death in the street. Because Vienna is not my Vienna any more.' His voice was savage.

They crossed Trafalgar Square. There were sandbags round the plinth of Nelson's column; Nelson himself was lost in the fog. Anton told Sara how Kurt von Schuschnigg, the Austrian Chancellor, had at first tried to resist Hitler, while attempting to lessen the influence of the Nazi party within Austria's own borders.

'But in the end we were alone,' he said. 'Schuschnigg had no choice but to permit the German army to enter Vienna. He offered no resistance because he knew that to do so would have invited a bloodbath. I have no country now, Sara. The country in which I was born and brought up has been humiliated and obliterated. Schuschnigg is in prison. Austria is now a state of the German Reich. Our army is under Hitler's command.

My country has gone.'

They walked in silence to the river. Through the smoke and petrol fumes that seemed to settle in the fog, Sara sensed the tang of that indefinable watery smell, that always transported her back to childhood visits to her father's warehouse on Butler's Wharf. The ships and bridges were masked by the fog, but she could hear the low moan of a foghorn and the soft plash of water against the piers. Every now and then the mist cleared, showing a gleam of black.

He touched her wrist. 'Are you sure you don't want to stop somewhere? You must be cold.'

She shook her head. 'My coat keeps me warm.'

'You must be the only waitress in London who comes to work in a fur coat.'

She looked up at him, drinking him in, recalling what was familiar, searching for what had altered. Searching through night and fog to check that his eyes were the exact grey of her memory, reminding herself of the way he smiled, the way he put up a hand to rub his forehead when he was puzzled or abashed or distressed.

'So you came to England.'

'Yes.'

'Alone?'

'Of course.'

'I thought you might have found someone in Vienna, you see.'

'No, never. I came back to England to find you, Sara.'

Her heart leaped. 'Truly?'

'You were all I thought about while I was in prison. You were all that kept me alive, that kept me fighting. And I hoped — '

'What, darling?'

'That you'd waited for me. I knew you'd come of age. When I found out you'd married, that was when I despaired.'

Her feet ached: waitress's feet, she thought. There

369

was a bench nearby. She ran her hand over it, wiping the drops of rain from the slats before she sat down. She thought of Ireland and Vernon Court, that now seemed so oddly distant, as if they had been part of someone else's life.

'I suppose I must seem fickle. I tell you I'm in love with you but then I marry someone else.' She turned the collar of her coat up around her face. 'Things have happened to you, Anton, dreadful things, I can see that, but nothing at all was happening to me. I wonder if you can imagine that. I wonder if you can understand how *dead* that made me feel. So I made things happen. I thought you didn't love me. I thought I'd never see you again. And I didn't know how to bear it.'

He sat down beside her. 'How could you think I didn't love you?' There was anger in his voice. 'Why didn't you trust me?'

'That letter you wrote to me — '

'You must know I had no choice. Your father gave me no choice.'

'My father? I don't understand.'

'He made it clear to me that he would never allow me to marry you. Never, ever.'

She leaned forward to him, seized by a sudden terror. 'You saw my father? You spoke to him? When?'

'You didn't know?'

'Of course not. I had no idea.' Now, she felt cold. 'What did he say to you?'

'That I must keep away from you, of course.'

'But, still — the letter — ' And then, a dreadful intuition. 'Did my father *make* you write that letter? Anton, did he?'

'He was most insistent, yes.'

'But why didn't you refuse?'

'I was in no position to refuse. As I said, he gave me no choice.'

'I still don't understand. Did he threaten you?'

'Sara, it was a long time ago.' He scowled. 'What do you say? Water beneath the bridge.'

The fog had thinned and, for the first time, she caught sight of the far bank of the river, with its warehouses and cranes and factories. 'I want to know,' she said harshly. 'What did my father do? What did he say to you?'

A sigh. 'That I did not have enough money to support you, which was true. And that I would make you unhappy.'

'I don't care about money! And you'd never make me unhappy!'

'Only saints don't care about money,' said Anton gently. 'The rest of us do, a little, I think. I didn't want you to suffer — I didn't want you to be cold or hungry. I didn't want to take you out of your own world and put you into the one I know. Why should I want that for you?'

'There's something else, isn't there?' And when he did not answer: 'Anton, tell me.'

On the river, every now and then, part of a boat — a hull, a funnel, a mast — was revealed by the thinning mist. She heard him say, 'Your father told me that if I didn't do as he asked I would be forced to leave the country.'

No, she almost said, *he wouldn't do that.* Yet she had learned to take a step back, to see her father from the outside, as a stranger, a strong, forceful man, convinced of his own rightness. A man capable of ruthlessness, even cruelty. Her father, whom she loved and trusted, had deceived her and betrayed her, and had manipulated her into abandoning the man she loved.

'I didn't know,' she whispered. 'I hate him for that.'

'He thought he was protecting you. He thought he was doing his best for you.'

Sara shook her head slowly. 'My father was doing what he thought was best for *himself*. For the

371

Finboroughs. Well, I'm not a Finborough any more. I never thought I'd be proud of being a Vernon, but I am now.' She had not been quick enough to escape her parents' influence, she thought. Philip confronted, Theo had got away, but she had tried to please. In forcing her to give up Anton, her father had almost broken her.

He took her hand; they sat in silence for a while. Eventually he said, 'Your husband, what was he like, Sara? Why did he let you leave him? I'm very glad he did, but he must be a fool.'

'No, Gil isn't a fool. He's very clever, very learned. Though he doesn't understand people at all.' She sighed. 'But we both made rather a lot of mistakes.'

'And your child — your son?'

'David never felt as though he was mine. Caroline and the nanny cared for him, not me. I couldn't seem to make him happy.' She pressed her hands together. 'I always assumed I'd be a good mother. To have left my child — that's monstrous, isn't it? What sort of woman does it make me?'

'Someone who tried her best, perhaps?' he said gently.

'Someone who failed,' she said bitterly. 'Someone who couldn't manage what the poorest, least educated, least privileged woman does so easily. I couldn't love him, Anton.' She looked out to the river again. 'Though perhaps I'd begun to love him by the time I left Vernon Court. Only by then it was too late. I write to him every month — I draw him pictures, babies like pictures, don't they? — and I go back to Ireland as often as I can. In the summer, Caroline brought him over to London to stay with my parents. My mother adores him.' She frowned. 'Now that I no longer live with him, I can see what a dear little boy he is. So sweet and funny. He has an endearingly serious streak. That must come from Gil; I think it was what attracted me to him. We Finboroughs don't like to be serious, you see. We're frivolous, we're flippant, we mock and tease and quarrel — anything to avoid being serious. I wonder why that is?' She smiled sadly. 'When I lived at Vernon Court, it was as if I was some rather extraordinary ornament that someone's bought on the spur of the moment, and when they get it home no one knows quite what to do with it.'

'You are very ornamental, it's true.' When he kissed her, she closed her eyes, dizzy with the nearness of him. 'I can't believe I'm with you, Sara,' he murmured. 'I can't believe we're here. I think I'm dreaming. I have never stopped loving you. You must believe that. Never, ever. And all will be well, I know it will.' And then he said, 'Peter Curthoys has let me have a room in his house. He and Melissa are away for the weekend. Won't you come home with me?'

★　★　★

Whether sex was dull, unpleasant or ecstatic entirely depended, Sara discovered that night, on who you were doing it with.

After the first time, lying in his arms, she said, startled, 'That was really rather lovely.'

'Didn't you expect it to be?'

'With Gil, while I was doing that, I used to think of the book I was reading or whether the horses needed shoeing.'

He gave a crack of laughter. 'Sara, you are quite ridiculous.' Then he made love to her again.

In the early hours of the morning, he told her what had happened to him. After the Anschluss, the Nazis, both German and Austrian, had set out to destroy those they hated — the Jews, the socialists, the Catholics. The physical deprivations — the lack of food and the beatings — had been hard to bear, but Sara understood, listening to Anton, that it had been his confinement in the cramped, dark prison cell that had almost destroyed him.

One night, the authorities had been moving Anton and a dozen other prisoners when the van in which they were being transported had been halted by a disturbance in the street. In the mêlée, some of the prisoners had managed to escape. Anton had made for the house of a friend. Weeks had passed, weeks of hiding in cellars and attics, of being moved from one safe house to another, always under cover of darkness. Eventually, using a route over the Alps, he had been smuggled into Switzerland. From there he had travelled first to Paris, and then, after Peter Curthoys had agreed to sponsor him, he had come to London.

They had both changed, she thought. There was a sadness inside him and, as for her, the years of their separation had altered her, leaving her with a layer of regret. Sara wrapped herself in a blanket, climbed out of bed and went to the window. Pressing her face against the pane, she tried to make out the garden below, the slick black branches of the trees, the crisscrossed lines of fence and wall, and beyond, the houses and squares and bridges of the city. And it seemed to her that the sky had lightened a little, that the night was not so dark.

12

The next time Alfie Broughton came to the house, it was a weekday evening. Isabel was in the music room, playing the piano, when the maid tapped on the door and announced they had a visitor.

Richard, who was sitting in an armchair, gave the newspaper an irritable flick. 'Who is it?'

'He didn't give his name. He said he wanted to speak to madame.'

A premonition of danger and Isabel rose from the piano stool, saying, 'It's probably nothing important. I'll go, darling.'

Through the window beside the front door, she made out Alfie Broughton's blurred form, his bulky shape distorted and made monstrous by the porch light and the coloured glass in the panel.

She went outside to him, saying softly, angrily, 'You shouldn't have come here! I told you not to come here!'

'Hello, Isabel.' His wink, with its assumption of complicity, repelled her.

Hurrying him along the drive, she drew him into the shelter of the garage.

'Why are you here?'

'I wanted a little chat, that's all. Haven't got many friends left in the Old Country.'

'I'm not your friend. I thought I'd made that perfectly clear.' Worse even than her anger and fear was her sense of being trapped. 'If you've come here to ask for more money, then you're wasting your time because I'm not going to give you any.'

His face altered, the wheedling replaced by resentment. 'Better think carefully before you say things like that, Isabel.'

375

'I won't be blackmailed.' There, she had said the word, and in the familiar, oily interior of the garage it sounded so improbable, so melodramatic.

He put his hands in his coat pockets and studied her, frowning. 'Got used to calling the tune, haven't you? It wasn't like that in the old days. Time was when you were a sweet, biddable little thing. Time was when you'd do anything I asked. Though, come to think of it, you always had a temper, didn't you? I remember you were jealous as hell if I so much as looked at another woman.'

She hated to think of him touching her, kissing her. He revolted her. 'I have to go,' she said icily. 'Don't come here again.'

'Or what? What will you do? Will you call the police, *Mrs Finborough*?' His tone mocked her.

'If I have to.'

'I don't believe you.' He moved closer to her. His eyes were hard. 'Be careful, Isabel. A woman in your position can't afford to have this sort of thing get out. What would your fancy friends think if they were to find out the truth about you? What would your husband do if he were to find out you'd had another man's baby? And I'm sure I could find a gossip columnist who'd be interested in such a nice, juicy story.'

'You wouldn't — you mustn't — '

'I will if you make me.' Then his mood changed again, conciliatory now. 'I need the money, you see — a man's got to make a living somehow and it's damned hard these days. Another fifty quid should do it.'

'And if I give you more money, what then? Will you come back again in a few weeks or months, asking for more?'

Alfie took out his cigarette case and regarded her through narrowed eyes. 'You'll have to hope I don't, won't you, Isabel?' Tapping the cigarette against the case, he said, 'Two days' time, at the bench by the Heath. Six o'clock. Make sure you're not late.'

★ ★ ★

Praying that she would see no one she knew, Isabel went to a shop in Hatton Garden, where she sold two old, unfashionable brooches. Another secret meeting, as with a lover. An ice-cold evening, when the frozen air stung her skin. As she handed Alfie the money, his fingers brushed against hers. His touch made her shudder. She knew that he would never go away, that he would bleed her dry.

She went with a friend to hear Myra Hess play Schumann at the Wigmore Hall. Closing her eyes, letting the music sink into her, Isabel thought of all that her marriage had given her — the cultural and intellectual satisfaction she had craved as a young woman, freedom from want, the opportunity to make for herself a beautiful home, a home that reflected her own tastes and interests, and, of course, most important of all, family life. All this Alfie Broughton could destroy; all this, she might lose.

She considered her alternatives. She could go on paying him, always afraid that he might give her away, her heart lurching at every knock at the door, every step on the garden path, resorting to ever more degrading ruses to raise the money he demanded. And his demands would increase, she had no doubt about that.

Or, she could refuse to pay him and call his bluff. Alfie might tell Richard — but he might not have the nerve. She remembered her horror when he had threatened to tell her secret to a gossip columnist. He would do that, she thought. She could imagine him doing that. And then, the public disgrace and, so much worse, Richard finding out about her past in such a way.

Or she could tell Richard the truth. What would he

do, what would he say? Alfie Broughton and the baby had been more than thirty years ago, old history, finished with. Yet, of course, these things never completely went away. They left shadows, and besides, their embodiments lingered on — one of them, in the unwelcome form of Alfie Broughton, haunted her. And there was another, that she had not allowed herself to think about for years.

Might Richard understand? She thought that best part of him, the part she loved most, might do. He had, after all, on that long-ago day she had agreed to marry him, told her that her past did not concern him. *If you marry me, you can start again. You'll have a new name, a new home in a new city. You can put all the hardships you've suffered behind you.*

Yet he had changed, they both had changed. Their relationship had never fully recovered from Philip's marriage to Elaine Davenport. They evaded the subject because to confront it would be to pick at too many unhealed wounds — at her own hurt and resentment that Richard had felt an attachment for another woman, and at Richard's discovery that for first time in his life he had been bested. And by his own son. His crown had been jolted, toppled. These days, Richard was preoccupied and angry — and stubborn. So wretchedly, self-defeatingly stubborn. The news that Sara was now living with Anton Wolff had done nothing to improve his mood. His behaviour punished them both, thought Isabel; she seemed to live her life in compartments these days, a section for each of the children, another for Richard, all to be kept apart.

The concerto came to an end and there was a burst of applause. Parting from her friend outside the concert hall, Isabel caught the bus home. Handing her fare to the conductor, she wondered how much the compromises she had made so long ago had shaped the path of her life. What different roads she might have taken, what other person she might have been. How much she had really altered, and whether the earlier Isabel still existed beneath the changes that age and wealth and experience had made. Whether the person she had become would survive what she must do.

Yet what choice had she? She was living on a knife-edge and she did not know how long she could bear it. And it would be better, far better, for Richard to learn the truth from her instead of from Alfie Broughton. Or — and she gave an involuntary shudder, causing the woman sitting beside her to stare at her — from the pages of a newspaper.

★ ★ ★

The last year had been difficult. There had been John Temple's death, and then, the previous week, one of the clerks had been caught fiddling the books. No large sums of money had been lost but it had been a messy business, the police involved and a bad taste left in Richard's mouth. Time was when he would have known every one of his clerks by name, would have known what sort of man they were. He missed John Temple, missed the presence of the one other person who had been with him since the beginning. He missed the clean, fresh smell of tea and the excitement of a new cargo unloaded at the wharf. These days, too much of his time was spent in his office or speaking to lawyers, accountants or government ministers. Business was booming: with the rush to rearmament that had followed the Munich crisis the demand for machine parts had become acute, and he was working long hours, weekends too, sometimes. He should have been revelling in it, yet he felt out of tune, distant from the business that had always absorbed him, no longer fired by it.

He took a stack of papers home with him to go

through that evening. Isabel greeted him when he arrived at the house, then went to check the dinner.

'Where's Mrs Finch?' he asked her as she came back.

'I gave her the evening off.'

Unstoppering the whisky decanter, he asked, 'Drink?' and she shook her head.

'Not for me.' She hesitated; she looked nervous. 'Richard, we have to talk.'

He thought of the papers — he had meant to start work before dinner, over a drink. 'Can't it wait till dinnertime?'

'No, I'm afraid not.'

He sat down. 'Fire away, then.'

She was twisting her hands together. 'I'm being blackmailed,' she said.

He gave a short, incredulous laugh. 'Blackmailed?'

'Yes.'

He wondered whether she was exaggerating, or fooling about. Though she was in the habit of doing neither.

'Blackmailed . . . by whom? Why? For how long?'

'His name's Alfie Broughton. He's been asking me for money. He came here first towards the end of June.'

June, he thought. It was November. 'You haven't given this scoundrel any money, have you, Isabel?'

'I'm afraid I have.'

'How much?'

'More than a hundred pounds.'

'Good God. Why?'

'Because he knows something about me. Something bad.'

'What?' He tried to lighten the heavy atmosphere in the room by making a joke. 'Have you been defrauding the Art Club's subscriptions?'

'Something bad,' she repeated steadily, 'that happened to me before you and I met. Alfie Broughton was my lover.'

'Your lover?' he repeated mechanically.

'Yes. A long time ago.'

'How long?'

'More than thirty years.'

'In Lynton?'

'No, Alfie lived in Broadstairs. I worked in Broadstairs, remember, before I went to Devon.'

He had assumed that when they had married she had been a virgin. Why? Because he had wanted to, he supposed.

He said, 'And you didn't think to mention this?'

She looked away. 'I did try, but I couldn't. It was all over long before I met you. I hadn't seen Alfie for years. I never thought I'd see him again. I had no reason to believe — I thought . . . ' She pressed her lips together. 'I suppose I thought you'd never find out. And after so long . . . but then, in June, he came here.'

'So this fellow — Broughton — I assume he's threatening to tell me? I assume that's why you've been paying him off?'

'Yes. No.' She looked panicked. 'If it had been just that — '

'It's bad enough, surely?' He found that he was afraid of what she was going to say next. But he forced himself to ask, 'There's more?'

'Yes, I'm afraid so.' She met his eyes. 'I had a child, Richard. Alfie's child.'

At first, his mind was blank. It had been a long, demanding day and he could not seem to seize on to these preposterous, unreal snippets of information. What he wanted was to leave the house and get in his car and drive far away, somewhere, anywhere.

But he stayed where he was, forcing himself to focus. He wanted to think that he hadn't understood her correctly. He repeated, 'You had a child before you met me?'

'Yes. A daughter.'

'When, exactly?'

'The summer of 1907. Long before we met.'

'And what became of this child?'

'I gave her away.'

'Gave her away . . . ?' he repeated: he felt stupefied, caught up in a nightmare.

'Yes. I put an advertisement in the newspaper. A couple who had no children of their own adopted her. There was nothing else I could do. I couldn't care for her myself. Alfie left me, you see, as soon as he knew I was expecting a baby.'

Richard was aware of the sensation one has on learning of a death, of disbelief, horror, of being unable to absorb the bad news. He wanted to know that it was not true, that she had invented it all, made it up, that they could go back to being what they had been before.

'I'm sorry, Richard,' she said. 'I'm so sorry,' and something inside him snapped.

He said slowly, 'Our entire marriage has been founded upon a lie and you tell me that you're *sorry*?'

There was a tightness in his chest. He went to the decanter to refill his glass. His hand shook as he poured out the whisky. He wasn't sure whether he would be able to drink it, or whether he would be sick — or whether, God forbid, he might weep.

'I know I should have told you before, but I couldn't.' She faltered, then seemed to gather herself together. 'Richard, please try to understand. Please try to forgive me.'

'What do you want me to say?' He gave a raw laugh. ' 'It doesn't matter, let's forget about it'?'

'No, of course not.'

'Perhaps you just forgot — '

'Richard, don't — '

'Perhaps it slipped your mind, this child.'

'My past — my history — was one of the reasons I wanted nothing to do with you when we first met.

Because I felt so ashamed!'

He drank the whisky, letting it scorch his throat. He heard her say, 'I know it was wrong of me, but it makes no difference to how I feel about you. It need make no difference to us — '

'Of course it makes a difference.' His voice cut through hers. 'It means I can't trust you.'

'Richard, please — '

'Rather an important thing to neglect to tell me, Isabel, that you had a child by another man. It makes me wonder what else you haven't told me about.'

'There's nothing else!'

'Any other love affairs? Any other children?'

'This is why I didn't tell you — because I was afraid you'd take it like this!'

His fragile hold on himself dissolved; he slammed the glass down hard on top of the sideboard. Whisky pooled on the polished wood. 'How else do you expect me to take it?' he shouted.

There was the tick of a clock, and, somewhere in the distance, an ambulance bell rang out. Isabel said quietly, 'You have every right to be angry. I deserve it. But, Richard, please try to understand. I was desperate. I was very young — only seventeen — younger than Sara is now. I had no one to turn to, no one to take care of me.'

He searched for the worst thing he could think of to say: found it. 'No wonder Sara's turned out the way she has with you for a mother.'

Isabel took a step back, as if he had struck her. She whispered, 'That's a terrible thing to say!'

He couldn't stop himself saying, 'Broughton . . . did you love him?'

'Richard — '

'I want to know. Did you?'

It was several moments before she answered. 'Yes, I did.'

He had to turn away, to hide his pain. He said softly, 'How you must have laughed at me, for the fool I was!'

Her face contorted. 'No, Richard, never! How can you say that, when we've known each other so long, when we've been through so much together?'

He remembered the first time he had seen her, standing on the harbour arm at Lynton. The banner-flare of her skirts, the dashing scarlet of her jacket. He shook his head slowly. 'Ah, but I didn't know you, did I? I thought I did, but I was wrong.'

'Richard, for God's sake! I made a mistake! It was foolish and wrong of me, but it was a mistake!'

'A mistake . . . is that what you call it?'

'We all make mistakes,' she said harshly. 'Even you.'

'Mine are not of quite the same magnitude.' Thinking it through, his anger intensified. 'Dear God, for you to have accused *me* of deceit — the fuss you made over a few kisses!'

'It's not the same!' she cried. '*I* wasn't married!'

'And that makes it *better*?'

She flushed. 'No, of course not. I didn't mean . . . '

'Such hypocrisy, when all the time you've been hiding *this* from me!'

'If I doubted you it was *because* of what Alfie had done to me! Can't you see that? I'd been betrayed once already and I was always afraid it might happen again! Richard, please, try to see how it was! When Alfie left me I wanted to die!'

'Feel free to change your mind even at this late stage, Isabel,' he said sarcastically. 'Go to him — to *Alfie* — if that's what you want.'

'I don't.' Her face was drained of colour. 'I hate him.' Then she said, 'The day I agreed to marry you, you promised me that my past would make no difference to you.'

'Did I?' He stared at her, his eyes wild. Then he shook his head slowly. 'But *this* . . . I never imagined *this*. To

keep something like this from me for so long ... '
Inside him a fire raged. He turned away, gathering up
his papers, his pen, and went to the door.

'Where are you going?' Her voice was small and
frightened.

'To my club.'

'But dinner — '

'I'm not hungry.'

'Don't do this, Richard!'

In the hall, he took his hat and coat from the stand.
As he opened the front door, she ran to him, grasping
his sleeve.

'Richard — don't go — not like this — forgive
me — ' She was weeping openly now.

Shaking her off, he went outside and started up the
car. As he drove away, he glimpsed her in his rearview
mirror, standing outside the house. He pressed his foot
down on the accelerator and she was lost in the curve of
the drive.

★ ★ ★

He remained at his club for a week. He thought how,
through all the time he had known Isabel, it had mad-
dened and frustrated him that she had always seemed
out of his reach, that he had never felt he knew her
completely, that she kept a part of herself back from him.
Well, now he knew what that part was. A lover, a child.

Memories bobbed up, monsters from some deep,
dark pool. That she had not loved him when she had
married him. That she had married him to escape a
difficult situation — penniless, workless, soon to be
homeless, the object of suspicion and jealousy in the
town. That she had married him for his money and
for position. That she had been everything the
townspeople had believed her to be — promiscuous,
calculating, avaricious.

Sometimes, in brief moments of sobriety, he remembered all they had shared — the hopes and the fears, the children, the passion. But his doubts remained, unmoving and poisonous. That he had been a stopgap, second best.

Waking in the morning, his eyes felt gritty and there was a sour taste in his mouth. Driving into work one day, he misjudged a junction and by a fraction of an inch avoided a collision with a tram. The incident shook him: afterwards, he forced himself to eat, to sleep, to attend to practical matters. He caught up at work, and found a private detective, a rat-faced man with nicotine-stained fingers, in a dingy office behind King's Cross Station.

There were questions he needed answers to: he went home. He spoke to Isabel in the bedroom, so that the servants would not over-hear.

'This fellow, Broughton, do you know where he may be found?'

She shook her head. 'I'm sorry, no.'

'Is he in employment?'

'I don't think so.'

'Describe him to me.'

When she had finished, he said, 'This mess will be sorted out discreetly. He'll have to be paid off, no doubt, and the consequences of trying to extort more money from me will be made clear to him. I shall make sure there's no scandal.'

'Thank you, Richard.'

He said coldly, 'I'm doing this for the family, not for you, Isabel. For the Finboroughs. I've no wish to see my name publicly disgraced.'

'Yes, of course.'

He glanced round the room which, after his week's absence, seemed oddly unfamiliar. 'I shall return home on one condition.'

'Anything, Richard.'

'You are never to mention Broughton again. Do you understand?'

'Yes, Richard.'

'And the child. The same goes for the child.'

This time, she did not reply. He prompted her. 'Isabel. You are to promise me.'

A silence, then, 'I have no wish to speak of Alfie. If I could forget him, I would. But my daughter — that's different.'

'I insist.'

She twisted her hands together. She was frowning. 'I don't think I can do as you ask, Richard.'

'I ask this one thing of you — '

She interrupted him: 'I think what you're asking me to do is to pretend the child never existed. To pretend none of it ever happened. But I don't believe that will mend things between us. Not now.'

'So you refuse?'

'I have denied the existence of my child for most of my life,' she said tiredly. 'There is a certain — a certain relief in you knowing at last.'

'*Relief!*' he repeated angrily.

'For me. Not for you, of course. If I could take the hurt away from you I would, but I can't.' She took a deep breath. 'Richard, I have always tried to be a good wife to you. I've endured social occasions I loathe and I've lived in a city I dislike because I've always known how much I owed you and how much I love you. But I can't let you control my thoughts. There would be nothing left of me if I did. If I were able to choose, I would choose that you forgive me. As, in the past, I have forgiven you. Can you do that?'

He said softly, 'No.'

Momentarily, she closed her eyes. 'Then I'll leave for Cornwall tomorrow.'

'Do as you wish. What you do is no longer any

concern of mine. Go to Cornwall — go to hell, for all I care.'

The next day, after leaving certain instructions with his solicitor, he left London for an extended business trip to Europe.

★ ★ ★

At Porthglas, Isabel remembered her baby. Her first baby, her first daughter. She had left the Clarewoods' house when she was six months pregnant, when she had known she would be unable to disguise her condition any longer. She had gone to London because where else would a girl like her, a girl in trouble, go? Travelling into the city, she had looked out of the window of the railway carriage and seen how the houses and factories and public buildings went on for ever.

She had worn her mother's old wedding ring and told the few who cared to ask that she was a widow. She searched for the cheapest room in the cheapest lodging house and found it in Stepney in the East End. She was fortunate to find piecework embroidering collars and cuffs for blouses. She placed an advertisement in *Exchange & Mart* and received in reply a letter from a Mrs Wellbeloved, a doctor's wife who lived in Lancaster, in the north of England. The surname, with its suggestion of affection and popularity, seemed a good omen.

Her baby was born towards the beginning of May, a little earlier than Isabel had expected. A neighbour went for the midwife and her tiny, perfect daughter came into the world at dawn — at cock's crow, the midwife said, had there been any cocks to crow in Stepney. The baby was healthy and pretty, with dark hair and blue eyes. Isabel called her Martha, after her own mother. A few days later, she wrote to Mrs Wellbeloved, to tell her of the safe arrival of the child. Another letter arrived, asking that Isabel take the baby, when she was six weeks old, to Euston Station, where the Wellbeloveds would meet her.

Those six weeks had passed quickly. Then Isabel tied up a bundle containing her baby's clothing, wrapped Martha in a shawl, and made her way to Euston. There, she had handed her daughter to her adoptive parents. On her way home, she bought a newspaper and studied the 'Situations Vacant' columns. She chose to apply for the post of housekeeper to a Mr Charles Hawkins, of Lynton, Devon, because she longed to see the sea again.

On her first evening in Lynton, after she had cooked Mr Hawkins his tea, she made her way down the steep hill to Lynmouth harbour. There, she walked out along the harbour arm and stood beneath the Rhenish Tower. Surrounded by sea, the emptiness that had overcome her since she had given her baby to the Wellbeloveds failed her, and she wept bitterly, a long howl of grief. Then, spent and exhausted, she walked back to Orchard House. There were flowers in the garden and rows of books in the house, and it occurred to her that perhaps, at last, she had found a refuge. She put on her pinafore and cooked Mr Hawkins his supper and he had the kindness to pretend not to notice that she had been crying and to talk to her instead about other things.

Now, walking along Porthglas beach, she remembered those precious six weeks she and her daughter had spent together. She remembered sitting in her room in Stepney, feeding her baby, screened from the outside world by a scrap of yellowing newspaper pasted over the lower part of the window. She remembered the joy of feeling the baby tug at her breast and the pearl of milk at the corner of her daughter's mouth and the fine dark hair on her head. She remembered that she had thought of taking her child and running with her, as far as she could, away from all that she knew and all who knew her, so that they could be together.

'This is what I did,' she wrote to Richard. 'Condemn me if you must, but this is what I did.' In her letter, she told him everything — the Clarewoods, Alfie, London, the birth of the child and the giving away of the child. She laid her heart bare for him.

She received in return a letter from Richard's solicitor. It told her, in cold legal language, that her husband had instructed him to set up a bank account in her name and that a sum of money to cover her living expenses would be paid into it each month.

Isabel threw the letter into the fire. Then she wrote back to him. ''Your past is no concern of mine.' That was what you said to me on the day I agreed to marry you. Have you forgotten, Richard? Don't you keep your promises?'

It was not until some weeks later that she received a reply. This time, the envelope was addressed in Richard's hand. Inside, one sentence was scrawled on the single piece of paper.

'But that was when I loved you.'

★ ★ ★

The world was shuffling itself about, jostling people up, displacing them and spitting them out in unexpected places. After the violence of Kristallnacht — the Night of Broken Glass — in the November of 1938, when shops owned by German Jews were looted and smashed, synagogues destroyed and hundreds of Jews murdered, there was a mass exodus of refugees from Germany, adding to the numbers who had already fled the regimes of Hitler and Mussolini and the Civil War in Spain. Ruby saw them in pubs and cafés and libraries, the Italian musicians and the students from Berlin, huddled in threadbare coats. The newspapers told stories of boatloads of refugees forced to wander the seas, turned away from port after port in their search for

390

places of safety. The popular press wrote of the flood of foreigners who would take jobs from a population who had been starved of work for a decade.

A few of Ruby's friends had already left London to fight with the Republicans in Spain. Others were joining the RAF. Jewish friends, scientists and writers who, during the upheavals of the thirties had found themselves washed up in London, glanced over the Channel with trepidation and bought themselves tickets for New York, kissing her goodbye and promising to write.

Sara and Anton lived in a room in a house in the maze of streets behind Euston Station. In the mornings, Sara was woken by the clip-clop of the milkman's horse in the street and the hurrying footsteps of passengers dashing for their trains. Her gaze drifted to Anton, sleeping beside her. Propping herself up on one elbow, she tried to see whether she could wake him just by looking at him, and gave a delighted crow of laughter when his eyelids opened and he drew her to him, kissing her.

Anton showed her his London, a different London from the one Sara had known all her life. His friends, many of them drawn from the refugee community that had gathered in the poorer parts of London, became her friends. They were journalists and playwrights and trades-unionists, economists and musicians and scientists. Most of them now lived hand-to-mouth existences. Many of the women worked as domestic servants. Their stories, of parents dumped without any possessions on to rusty ships that faltered down the Danube, of brothers in concentration camps or little sisters thrust into the arms of a stranger on a train transporting Jews from Vienna to Amsterdam, shocked her. She made them coffee and admired the photographs they showed her, photographs so much looked at their corners had begun to crinkle and roughen.

One fine morning, Sara and Anton took the train to Bexhill-on-Sea, to see the De La Warr Pavilion, a glittering palace of concrete, glass and steel that looked out over the sea. 'One day,' said Anton, 'I'll build you a house like that, Sara. A house that's full of space and light. It will be in the middle of a forest and it will look out over a lake and we'll be together for always and no one will ever trouble us again.'

★ ★ ★

Anton Wolff's turning up out of the blue had shaken Edward. Sara had introduced Wolff to him one evening in the café. *Edward, come and meet Anton. Anton, this is my dear friend Edward.* He had managed to murmur greetings.

Sara had taken it for granted that he and Anton Wolff would become friends. And on the surface, that was what they were. Wolff asked Edward's advice on matters connected with the rental of rooms or the filling in of forms, that sort of thing; sometimes, when Sara was working, the two men went out for a drink. He played the part of the helpful friend because, really, what else could he do? He knew the alternative would have meant not seeing Sara any more and that would have been unbearable.

Yet he felt a deep, visceral dislike of Wolff. It hurt to see Wolff with his arm round Sara's shoulders or pulling her to him for a kiss. Wolff was handsome, Edward supposed, with the matinée-star looks that girls often went for, and he had the natural, easy manner that Edward himself tried to cultivate but never quite succeeded. But he was not good enough for Sara. Edward noted his threadbare clothing, his lack of a decent occupation or income. Even his accent and the occasional stumble in his English, grated. He was too *different*.

Edward longed to turn back time. If only Wolff had stayed in Austria, then he might have had a chance. If Wolff had not turned up, perhaps she would have loved him.

★ ★ ★

In coming to live at Porthglas Cottage, Isabel sometimes felt that she had returned to the solitariness she had known as a young woman. She was aware of a degree of social ostracism, caused, she assumed, by the fact that she was living apart from her husband. She didn't mind, had no wish to become a part of any clique or set. She had been the subject of gossip years ago, in Lynton, and, throughout her marriage, her background in service had often left her feeling an outsider in the company of Richard's friends and colleagues. She minded her difference, and her solitariness, far less at forty-nine than she had at twenty.

More and more, she felt relieved at no longer having to pretend she was something she was not. There was a certain relief in the quietness of her life, its absence of storms and tempests. Living on her own was easier, less troublesome. She had put passion behind her, and she felt, at last, on an even keel. There was even relief in having escaped the tension of her marriage — she had always, she recognised, been afraid that she might lose Richard. Well then, she had lost him, so what else had she to fear? During her marriage she had known such extremes of emotion. Love had sometimes elated, but often excoriated.

She left Cornwall as little as possible. Something else that she need hide no longer: her dislike of London. She enjoyed the neatness and quietness of her home, took pleasure in the fact that her belongings remained exactly where she had put them — no more lost scissors or paper gum, no used cups or glasses left abandoned in

393

the sitting room or the garden. Her fine clothes hung forlornly in the wardrobe, denied any outings, and she rarely opened her jewellery box. And oh, the relief of not having servants, of no longer having to live her life exposed to a servant's watchful, critical eye, her day-to-day business gossiped about in lowered tones in the kitchen. She did not think of Mrs Spry as a servant; they addressed each other by their Christian names and had become friends who worked and talked together.

And she was free, after so long, to try to find out what had become of the child she had given away. She wrote to the Wellbeloveds, in Lancaster, pleading for news of her daughter. She still remembered their address: it had been printed on her heart all those years ago.

A few days later, the letter was returned to her unopened, with the words 'No longer at this address' scrawled on the envelope. The following week, Isabel travelled to Lancaster. On reaching the city, she walked to the Wellbeloveds' house. Enquiries confirmed that the family had moved away long ago, during the Great War. No, a neighbour told Isabel, she did not know where the family had gone. Yes, she remembered the Wellbeloveds' daughter, a pretty, dark-haired little thing.

Questions asked of other neighbours and local shopkeepers told her nothing more. Isabel caught the train back to the south; sitting in the carriage, she acknowledged the hopelessness of her quest. She had no idea where the Wellbeloveds had gone. They might have left the country, they might even have died. As for her child, how could she possibly find her when she did not even know her name? The Wellbeloveds would have given their adopted child a new Christian name; her daughter, who would be in her early thirties now, would most likely have married and changed her surname. In bed that night, she found herself reaching out for Richard, missing him with a raw grief that she managed to cover over during the day, angry with him for not being there when she most needed the comfort of his strength, his certainty.

But it helped her make up her mind about something. There were papers to be signed that would make actual her new status as Richard Finborough's estranged wife. Isabel made an appointment to call at the solicitor's office in Throckmorton Street and caught the train to London. Arriving at Paddington Station the day before her appointment, she took the Tube to Sloane Square and from there went by foot to Cheyne Walk.

After the weeks on her own in Cornwall, London seemed garish, noisy, crowded. Passing the Royal Hospital, Chelsea, she paused for a while, putting down her overnight bag. She found that she was not afraid. Her only regret was that she had not done this long before. 'Jennifer . . . ' Isabel whispered the name aloud. 'Jennifer Finborough.' A lovely name, she thought. A Cornish name, of course, a variant of the English Guinevere. The baby had been born in September, but she, too stiff and proud, had refused to see her, and because of that she had missed those precious first months with her granddaughter.

She had endured too many separations in her life to allow this one to drift on. Perhaps the addition to her life of a granddaughter — and, she reminded herself with a stiffening of the spirits, a daughter-in-law — might lighten her heart. And if she did not at least try to learn to love Elaine, then she would lose Philip, she saw that now.

In Cheyne Walk, Isabel stopped outside Philip and Elaine's house. Then she knocked on the door.

★ ★ ★

In the March of 1939 German troops took over the remaining, and indefensible, rump of Czechoslovakia.

395

In the days immediately after the invasion, five thousand Czechs were arrested. Two weeks later, the British government formally guaranteed the independence of Poland. In April, the Military Training Bill was introduced to Parliament in London, making men liable for call-up during their twentieth year. A scattering of Ruby's friends and Ruby's friends' younger brothers made their way to army camps. At Nineveh, the army freed George Drake from the tyranny of Maude Quinn.

Every evening, Ruby bought a paper on her way home from work, and scanned it for alliances, pacts, guarantees, threats. She saw Lewis only for odd half-hours, snatched in a bar or in the privacy of his flat, meetings that were, because of his work, unpredictable and infrequent. Barrage balloons glittered in the sky and public information leaflets fell through letter boxes: 'Fire Precautions in Wartime', 'Your Gas Mask', 'Masking Your Windows'. Sandbags were stacked outside Air-Raid Precautions Control Centres, shelters appeared in streets and parks, and in back gardens Anderson shelters hunched beneath lawns and flower-beds. A Civil Defence exercise took place in Chelsea; sirens wailed and passers-by were herded into roped enclosures.

A hot, dry August. On the twenty-third, to the shock of the world and the horror of Ruby's communist friends, Germany and the USSR signed a treaty of friendship. Telegrams were sent out, recalling reservists, and holidaymakers abandoned guest-houses and hotels, and fled home. Parliament was recalled, the fleet was mobilised and evacuation plans set in motion. One and a half million children and their teachers, along with mothers and infants, were entrained, bused or shipped round the south coast to seaside towns and country villages, away from the threat of bombardment. As she made her way to work that Friday, Ruby saw them, the small faces pressed up against the windows of the buses, the long crocodiles of children heading into the London railway termini. Their names were printed on luggage labels attached to school blazers or jerseys and they carried their gas masks and their belongings packed into small suitcases, rucksacks or pillowcases. Inside the station, loudspeakered voices exhorted the children to take their seats quickly and not to play with the train doors. Though a few cried, most seemed excited. But the mothers, as they waved their sons and daughters goodbye, were pale and drawn, and when they turned to walk away from the station their eyes glittered with tears.

That same day, the German army crossed the frontier into Poland and the Luftwaffe bombed Warsaw. Two days later, on the morning of 3 September, the British people were told to listen for a radio broadcast by the Prime Minister. Silence in the flat as Ruby washed and ironed and tidied. The only sounds the distant conversation of radios from the other rooms in the building, the faint rise and fall of their chatter like the whining of wasps. Outside, a thundery, dusty heat. Indoors, a bunch of chrysanthemums in a vase, the slosh of stockings in water, the typewriter, untouched because she couldn't write today, the iron sweeping over cotton and linen, and the radio, of course, and Neville Chamberlain's strained, gentlemanly tones telling them that they were now at war with Germany.

★　★　★

Standing in the drawing room as the radio played the national anthem, Richard remembered what the last war had done to his generation. He thought of the schoolfriends who had never returned from Flanders, and of Major Woods, and Nicholas Chance, of course, and his mad dash to the British trenches, and of Lieutenant Buxton, whom he had known for only a week, and now remained in his memory as nothing more than a head of blond hair streaked with mud and blood. He thought of Freddie McCrory, with the arm of his jacket pinned emptily back. He thought of the men one still saw sometimes begging on the streets, madmen and crippled men and men who had never really got the hang of things again after the war was over. Then he looked down at his hand and saw the scar on his palm where the bullet had passed through it.

The air-raid siren wailed but Richard remained where he was. He thought of Philip and Theo and of what this war might do to his sons, and he pressed his fingers against the bones of his skull, and closed his eyes.

★   ★   ★

Towards the end of September, a letter from the police arrived for Anton. He was required to present himself at a tribunal, which would assess his status as an enemy alien. In October, he went before the tribunal, which was held in a local school, empty now because the children had been evacuated. Anton was not permitted to take a lawyer but Peter Curthoys went with him to provide a character reference.

Sara was at work. Whenever the café door opened her gaze jerked towards it. All enemy aliens going before the tribunals that were being held throughout the country were to be assigned a category of either A, B or C. Category A aliens, considered a threat to the state, would be immediately interned. Category B represented medium risk, C low risk. Peter Curthoys had reassured Sara that there was no possible reason for putting Anton into category A. 'This is just a formality, Sara,' he had said cheerfully before they had left that morning. 'A couple of hours and you'll have him back with you in no time, have no fear.' Yet the hours dragged on — two, three, four — and, inside her, something buzzed and agitated, reminding her that they had not always been lucky, she and Anton.

Two o'clock: the door opened and she saw them. She ran to him and he caught her in his arms.

'A lot of waiting around,' Anton said, kissing her. 'Here, you see — I'm still a free man.'

'The fool of a chairman classed him as category B,' said Peter. He put down his briefcase with a thump. 'He was an idiot. An utter, complete idiot.'

There were no other customers in the café. Sara made coffee and they sat at a window table. The chairman had been a barrister, Peter told her. All had seemed to go well at first. Peter had given Anton a glowing character reference; other similar letters and references had been read out, all attesting to Anton's loathing of the Nazi regime, his imprisonment by that regime, and his father's death at the hands of Nazi thugs.

Then Anton had been asked about his politics. He had received information, the chairman said, about Anton's involvement with left-wing groups — with socialism.

'Dyed-in-the-wool conservative,' Peter said with a sigh. 'When push comes to shove, the old buffer probably still distrusts the Reds as much as he does the Nazis.'

Anton had admitted to belonging to socialist organisations in Austria. But he had reiterated his commitment to the use of peaceful methods for political change as well as his admiration of the country that had provided him a refuge.

Then the chairman had dropped his bombshell. 'Is it true,' he had asked Anton, 'that during your stay in this country, you have had an immoral relationship with a young, married Englishwoman of good family, and that you have been living off her earnings?'

Anton had, for a moment, been too shocked to speak.

The chairman had explained, with looks of distaste in Anton's direction, that he had been provided with evidence of such an illicit liaison, a liaison made all the more sordid by the fact that the young woman in question was the mother of a little boy.

'He knew all about you, Sara,' said Peter furiously. 'God knows how.'

'What did you say?'

Anton shrugged. 'I told him the truth, what else could I do? That it was true that you were married and had a child, but your marriage had broken down irretrievably. And that I have always done my best to provide for you. Thought I ~~have~~ *or* not done well — I know I have not done well.'

'Anton,' said Peter, putting his hand on his friend's shoulder.

'Darling,' said Sara, kissing him, 'no one could have done better. No one could ~~have~~ made me happier.'

The chairman had been unimpressed, though, and Anton had been assigned to category B. 'There are no hard-and-fast rules of categorisation,' Peter explained to Sara. 'Some chairmen make judgements on character, on reputation. Others on their political prejudices.'

Anton kissed Sara's hand. 'B or C — who cares? I am free and we are together. Though no more days at the seaside, I'm afraid. I'm not allowed to travel more than five miles from my home. And I'm not allowed to own a car or a camera, but then I can't afford either, so no matter. Oh, and no maps, of course — dangerous characters like myself must not own a map.'

'We could appeal,' said Peter, but Anton shook his head.

'No. Better to accept it. Better not to draw attention to myself.'

On the bus, going home, Sara looked out of the window. But there was nothing much to see — night had already begun to fall and, in the blackout, the street lights and the headlamps of the cars remained unlit, so that the houses, traffic and people all melded together in darkness.

'The chairman knew all about you,' Peter had said. 'God knows how.'

But she knew. Who else, other than the one person who had so ruthlessly separated them before, would have volunteered such information to the tribunal? Her father had done this. Mixed with her anger was a deep hurt. How nearly she might have lost Anton again today, Sara thought. She threaded her fingers through his, making them linked, inextricable.

★ ★ ★

The old dog had died in the night. Hannah found her curled up in a weedy thicket beside the barn, as if she had sought out the most comfortable place and had then lain down to die.

Her mother wept when Hannah told her about Bonny. Hannah had only ever seen her mother cry for the dogs, never for anyone or anything else. Hannah wasn't strong enough to carry Bonny to the place where she was to be buried, and her mother leaned too much on her stick these days, so they rolled the dog up in a blanket and dragged her to the back of the house, then through the orchard and down the track.

The pets' graveyard stood a distance back from the house, at the edge of a field. Over the years, Maude Quinn had planted shrubs and flowers among the stumpy black headstones. Now, Maude walked among the headstones, choosing a spot for Bonny. 'Here', she said, pointing to a dank piece of land beneath a laurel.

Hannah began to dig. Her mother watched, leaning on her stick. As Hannah dug, she tasted something bitter at the back of her throat. Beads of sweat gathered on her forehead. A glancing blow from her mother's stick, which took her off guard while she was staring down into the hole, made her dig with renewed vigour. With every down-ward plunge of the spade, she was afraid she might unearth . . . something. A bone, perhaps. A skull with empty eyes.

But there was nothing. When the hole was deep enough, Hannah dragged Bonny into it. The corpse fell into the pit with a dull thud. Hannah was about to spade earth back into the grave when her mother said sharply, 'The blanket, you've forgotten the blanket. You mustn't waste a good blanket, you stupid girl.'

Kneeling down beside the open grave, Hannah heaved the blanket out from underneath the body of the dog. Then she scattered spadefuls of soil, levelling it out until the patch of earth was smooth again.

Part Four

The River and the Sea

1940–1942

13

April in Paris, early evening. Sunlight glittering on the new leaves of the plane trees and Aleksandra buttoning up her blouse and telling him that she planned to leave for North Africa.

'Casablanca, perhaps. I've never been to Casablanca.'

She stood up, gathering up clothes she had cast off an hour before. Theo liked the way she never troubled to dress in the right order, but would happily wander round a room wearing only her blouse and her little pearl necklace.

He said, because someone had to, 'But what about us?'

'Us, Theo darling?' She slid two gold bangles on to her wrist.

'Yes, us.' A thought struck him. 'Or were you assuming . . .'

'I never assume, you know that, *chérie*. But you will make your own plans, as you always do.'

He felt discomforted. As she pulled on knickers and a skirt, she laughed and said, 'Don't look so worried. I love you so much, you know.'

'Come here.' She sat on his lap; he kissed her. 'And I adore you.'

She gave him a thoughtful look. 'But not *love*. You never say 'love'.'

'But I do,' he protested.

'Yes, but you never say it.' She flapped her hands, silencing him. 'We are the same, you and me, we like to be on the move, busy little bees, we don't like to be trapped.'

'I would never think of you as a trap.'

'I know, darling. But if you took me home with you to

405

England then you might think you had to marry me.'

He kissed her ear. 'Who said I was going back to England?'

'Aren't you?' Her dark eyes regarded him seriously.

'I don't know. I hadn't thought.' Which was a lie, of course.

She stood up, bending to unroll a stocking on to her leg. 'When the Germans come, you will be interned. You are English, Theo — that's what they'll do to you. You must go home.'

'The Germans won't reach Paris.'

'Do you believe that?'

He stood up and went to the window. His room was a good size, though it was rather dark and adjacent to the bathroom, so that he heard the hissing of the geyser, the running of taps. The two years he had rented the room had been the longest time he had lived in the same place since leaving London. And already there was a warmth in the air, the promise of summer to come. He liked to fling open the window and look out and see the steep, cobbled streets, the lines of washing slung between the houses, the men spilling out of the bar opposite. He liked to hear the clack of women's high heels on the cobbles, the hoots of the Citroëns and Renaults, the shrieks of the children playing.

Though, these days, the radio was always on, cutting through the street sounds. It was on now. Making love to Aleksandra, he had reached out a hand and turned off the dial. But afterwards, as they lay tangled together, she had switched it back on.

That was what they did now, he thought. In bars, offices and bedrooms throughout France, they listened to the radio.

A week ago, Germany had invaded Denmark. Shortly afterwards, German armies had marched into Norway. The battle for Norway continued. British troops had been landed near Narvik and units of the French

Foreign Legion had been sent to stiffen the resistance.

He said, 'When are you leaving?'

'Tomorrow.'

'Sasha — '

'Vassily is driving to Marseilles tomorrow. He's offered me a lift in his car. I must leave Paris, *chérie*, you do see that, don't you?'

'Don't go.'

She touched her aquiline nose. 'I'm a little bit Jewish, remember. Only a little bit, but it makes me afraid.'

He was surprised how much he minded. He watched her pull a comb through her thick, black hair. 'The thing is,' she said, looking at him, hands on hips, 'that all of us will have to do something. Even you, darling, will have to choose. I mean, we shall have to fight or be obedient. Resist or do as we're told.' She flicked open a powder compact, swivelled her lipstick. 'You won't be able to stand back, Theo. They won't let you just watch.'

He thought how much he would miss her, his tall, dark, beautiful Sasha. How he would miss the way she uncurled herself like a cat in his bed in the mornings, stretching out, throwing off the sheets. How, when she was gone, he would think of the way she dug her fingers into his hair when he kissed her, pressing him to her as if she wanted to consume him.

'I could come with you,' he said.

'No.' She kissed him on the mouth. 'If we had wanted that then we would have planned it together, wouldn't we? But we didn't.'

★ ★ ★

Theo had been editing a cinema magazine — and writing most of the articles that went inside it — but the magazine had folded when its proprietor, a wealthy Belgian, had decided to head south. 'Seen it all before, in 1914,' he had said, patting Theo on the shoulder.

'Don't particularly care to see it again.'

Theo had never previously minded being between jobs; had taken the opportunity to travel, or to take a different, more interesting, turning. Though Paris was the place he kept returning to, he did not really think of it as his home. Things came up, taking him away — a friend of a friend who had decided to produce a series of gazetteers, which required someone to travel the length and breadth of Europe by train; a baroness with botanical leanings, who had employed him to draw the plants in her garden on the Côte d'Azur. A yearning to see cold lands or hot lands, to be on his own, away from streets, houses, cities. He had always survived. Sometimes, he had prospered. Busy little bee, he thought.

But now, without work, and without Aleksandra, he wasn't busy any more, wasn't quite sure what to do with himself, and it bothered him. Everyone else seemed to be making plans — *If this happens we will do this, if that happens we will do otherwise* — even if their only plan was to stay in Paris, to do what they had always done, whatever happened. He knew he ought to do the same. If Hitler didn't stop at Poland, Denmark and Norway . . . if his armies marched south, through the Netherlands and Belgium . . . and it wasn't really an if any more, more *a when*, because why stop now, when all those other countries had toppled so easily?

Even you, darling, will have to choose. Aleksandra's voice echoed. He knew that he had a dislike of alignment, reservations about putting his name to something, anything.

★ ★ ★

Fouquet on the Champs-Élysées: a drink with a friend from the British Embassy. They were talking about the battle for Norway.

'Absolute fucking shambles,' said the friend, and drank down his *marc*. 'Strictly between you and me, that is.'

They were sitting at a corner table. Across from them, a wealthy financier wooed his prospective mistress with a bottle of pink champagne.

The friend said, 'Not enough air support and the French chaps haven't even the right *clothes*, for Christ's sake. If Norway falls, Chamberlain won't survive, you know.' A snort, while he gestured to the waiter to bring more drinks. 'Only a couple weeks before the Jerries bombed our ships at Scapa Flow, we were still dropping fucking *leaflets* on Hamburg.'

The drinks arrived; his friend offered cigarettes. A flick of a lighter. Beside them, the prospective mistress, in her furs and silk, let out a shrill peal of laughter.

Theo said, 'How long, d'you think?'

'Till we start burning the files?' A sour twist of the mouth. 'Weeks, months . . . who knows?' The embassy man, usually genial, leaned across the table, his eyes a hard, flat yellowy brown. 'How old are you, Theo?'

'Twenty-eight.'

'They're up to twenty-six now, back in Blighty. They'll be conscripting your age group next. If I were you, I'd hitch a ride back. Get more of a choice if you join up before you have to, if you see what I mean. Don't want to end up in some blasted trench, do you? And there might not be many tickets home if you leave it much longer.'

★ ★ ★

A farewell walk round Paris. Not the tourist places, but *his* places — the bars and studios and cafés, the places where he met his friends.

He supposed that, whatever happened, some things would go on — the businessmen making love to their *cinq-à-septs* in bedrooms heavy with velvet and tassels, the rich old men courting pretty mistresses with pink champagne at Fouquet. They would still talk, his friends, they would still have those long, philosophical conversations that had so entranced him when he had first come to Paris at nineteen years old, with his schoolboy French and his fantasies of being an artist, his only experiences a cold English boarding school and six months working for his father at Finboroughs. That old dream was long dead, but he still loved Parisian talk, the civility of it, the depth and extravagance of it, the way the conversation rambled, blurred with Gitanes and wine, taking you along byways, down blind alleys, to different horizons. That first evening, he remembered, he had talked so much that, waking in the morning, his throat had been sore.

★　★　★

He was lucky. His embassy friend was flying back to England at the end of the week, there was a spare on the plane. Bobbing over the English Channel, trying not to look down, settled one thing: he wouldn't join the RAF. 'First time in a plane, is it?' his friend said cheerily. 'If you're going to puke, mind my shoes.'

At twenty-eight, he was too old for the RAF anyway, the pilot told him. They wanted boys straight out of school. 'Quicker reactions, you see,' the pilot yelled over his shoulder, as Theo's knuckles whitened. 'Kids like that, they don't know the meaning of fear.'

They landed at an airfield in Kent. A gleaming black Humber was waiting to whisk the embassy man with his boxes and briefcase to some unspecified destination; parting from Theo with a handshake, the flat yellow-brown eyes ran over him as he said, 'Your French is pretty fluent, isn't it? Could pass for a native. Could be handy.' A card was passed to him.

'Keep in touch, old chap.'

The London train was crowded with soldiers in khaki. Theo wedged himself and his rucksack into a gap in the corridor and closed his eyes.

★ ★ ★

Ruby was putting on her lipstick when the bell rang. She ran downstairs and opened the front door. 'Theo!' she shrieked and flung her arms round him.

In her rooms, he unhoisted his rucksack and she inspected him closely. Tall and lean, his straight black hair a little too long, but elegant, like all the Finboroughs always were, even in his travel-crumpled clothes. *Years* since she had seen him, she thought; it was hard to put her finger on how he had changed, but she saw that he had.

'Sherry?' she offered.

'I'd rather have tea.'

'You do look a bit green. Was it a rough crossing?'

'I've just flown over the Channel.'

'You've been in an *aeroplane*? You lucky thing.'

She made tea, offered biscuits. 'Pearls or garnets?' She held both pairs of earrings up, beside her face.

'Garnets. Who's the lucky fellow?'

'He's called Lewis Gascoigne and he's absolutely divine. He works for the Foreign Office. He's married, but they don't live together any more. It makes me feel very old and sophisticated, having a married lover.'

She put on her glasses to check her reflection in the mirror, was satisfied with it, turned to show herself to him. 'What do you think?'

He had been wandering round the room, inspecting her records and books. Now he blinked, gave her a proper look. 'You look wonderful.'

She felt a flicker of pleasure: she had impressed a Finborough. 'How's Sasha?'

'We've split up.'

A dash of powder; she said coolly, 'She was never the right woman for you.'

'I can't see why not.'

'No, not right at all. Too — too *tall*. Are you brokenhearted, Theo?'

'A little. Actually, I'm madly in love with you, Ruby — the other women are just a blind.'

She threw a cushion at him. He said, 'And your chap — Lewis — is he the right man for you?'

'Probably not,' she conceded. 'But he's terribly good fun.'

'Have you seen much of the others?'

She put her compact and lipstick into her bag. 'I see Sara quite often. And Anton, of course. Though it's rather sickening to be with them — they're always touching each other and they have pet names.'

'I suppose they're in love.'

'Oh, *hugely*. I must pop round to see Philip and Elaine but I've been so busy. The baby's gorgeous, though — so sweet. Have you been home yet, Theo?'

He shook his head. 'That's my next stop.'

'You can sleep on my sofa, if you like.'

'That's very kind of you, Ruby, but I'd better go and see Dad.'

'How is he?'

'Don't know. Haven't seen him since Christmas, and he doesn't write. Christmas was bloody awful. There was just him and me. He's quarrelled with everyone else, of course. I tried to sound him out about making things up with Philip and Sara, but he just blew up. So far as he's concerned, Sara's a scarlet woman because she's left her husband and child and is living in sin, and I can't see him ever forgiving Philip. Apart from everything else — Elaine, I mean — Philip sold his Finborough shares, and my father sees that as an act of betrayal.' Theo changed the subject, touching the stack of typed paper on the table. 'What's this?'

'It's my first novel,' she said proudly. 'It's called *Death in a Minor Key*. Set in a symphony orchestra, you see. Just a few more chapters to go.'

'Not a romance then?'

'No, I thought I'd try a whodunnit. I've no idea if it'll ever be published — I haven't much time to write these days, and none of the publishers has any paper.' She put on a little grey jacket, edged in crimson. 'Have Richard and Isabel ever fallen out for so long before?'

'I don't think so. Actually, I feel sorry for the poor old devil. Beneath it all, I think he's as lonely as hell.'

'Poor Richard. Now, darling, I'm afraid I must dash.'

Theo picked up his rucksack and they left the flat. Out on the street, parting from him, she said, 'We must have dinner sometime.'

'Better be quick. I might not be around too long.'

She gave him a sharp glance.

'I thought I'd join the navy,' he said.

Ruby was startled. Then she said, 'I'm sure you'll look very fetching in navy blue, Theo,' blew him a kiss, and walked smartly away down the street.

★　★　★

May 10 1940: the day everything changed. German forces advanced into Belgium and Holland, appeals from the Dutch and Belgian governments for assistance were received in London early that morning. In the Houses of Parliament, equally cataclysmic events. Only a few days before, during a debate on the Norway campaign, a Conservative Member of Parliament, L. S. Amery, had quoted Cromwell's words to the Rump Parliament while addressing Neville Chamberlain: 'Depart, I say, and let us have done with you! In the name of God, go!' Demands for Chamberlain's resignation swelled, gathering like a tidal wave,

413

unstoppable. Chamberlain was succeeded by Winston Churchill at the head of a coalition government.

Europe was tearing itself apart. Though the defence of the Netherlands and Belgium was resolute, German force was overwhelming. For the second time in twenty-five years, people fled the invading army, carrying their belongings in cars, on carts, in prams, on their backs, heading south. Troops swarmed through Belgium, funnelled through the forests of the Ardennes, crossing the Meuse and the Dyle, tanks cracking trees like matchsticks while overhead the Luftwaffe machine-gunned the long columns of refugees. Prevented by German bombardment from joining her forces in Zeeland, Queen Wilhelmina sailed for Britain to plead for more air support. She landed at Harwich, and took the train to London, where King George VI met her at Liverpool Street Station.

★ ★ ★

May 12: German and Austrian nationals living in the coastal counties were interned.

Sara and Anton lay in bed. 'I couldn't bear to lose you,' she said, laying the palm of her hand against his face. 'It won't happen, will it, darling?'

'It might,' he said. The popular newspapers screamed of fifth columnists, the enemy within.

'I couldn't bear it. Not again.' She pressed herself against him, her back against his chest, as he folded his arms round her. His hand traced the curves of her body, breast and belly and thigh. She felt him harden against her; with a sigh, she closed her eyes as he entered her.

Later, when the contented aftermath of sex had faded, he thought of prisons, guards, beatings, and something inside him tightened in terror. No, he thought. Not again.

They made plans. They told only their closest friends,

Ruby, Edward Carrington and Peter Curthoys, people who would keep an eye out for Anton, who might be able to tell which way the wind was blowing.

Walking round London they kept their eyes open for empty premises, for derelict buildings, somewhere off the beaten track. Somewhere he could hide, somewhere he could stick it out until things got better again. Somewhere, he thought, where he could see the sky. He'd be all right if only he could see a piece of sky.

★ ★ ★

May 14: the Luftwaffe bombed Rotterdam. More than eight hundred people died as bombs intended to destroy the bridges exploded in the city centre.

In an attempt to boost resistance, British soldiers landed in the Dutch port of IJmuiden. At the same time, two hundred Jews reached the port by bus, where they embarked on board ship to sail across the North Sea to Britain as, behind them, the oil refineries burned. Shortly afterwards, overwhelmed, the Dutch capitulated.

German troops continued to sweep south through Belgium and Northern France, prompting the fear that their forces would thrust towards the Channel ports, encirling the Allied armies. Soon, Rommel's army had pushed fifty miles into France. The French Prime Minister, Paul Reynaud, telephoning Winston Churchill, told him that the road to Paris now lay open.

★ ★ ★

Supper at Ruby's flat. By the time the evening ended, it was dark. To spare themselves the difficulty of travelling home through the blackout, Sara and Anton slept the night on Ruby's sofa.

Coming home the next morning, they saw, from the upper deck of the double-decker bus, the police car parked outside the lodging house. Sara gripped Anton's hand tightly. They stayed on the bus until the next stop, then made for Regent's Park. They talked little, there was nothing more to say. When Sara had to leave for the café they kissed and parted, Anton heading for the disused warehouse basement they had found earlier in the week.

The warehouse was in a narrow lane off Charrington Street in Somers Town. They had chosen it for its seclusion, its spaciousness and its enclosed square of courtyard. The single large room had once housed a small weaving shed that had fallen into disuse during the Depression. High windows, the panes cracked and dirty or absent, looked down on to rows of rusting machinery. A scuttle of tiny paws told Anton, as he entered the basement, that it was infested by vermin.

It wasn't so bad, he thought. A greyish sunlight, shadowed by the tall buildings opposite, cast itself in oblongs on the dusty floor. He could hear the rumble of traffic and the song of a blackbird. When he stood beneath the windows and looked up, he could see through those high panes a patch of blue sky.

Visiting that evening, Sara brought a haversack containing his clothes, books, paper, washing things and food. They sat on upturned packing cases and spread out their supper on an old cutting table.

He said, 'Did the police come back?'

'Yes, not long after I came home from work. I told them I didn't know where you were. I said we'd quarrelled and you'd gone away.'

'Good girl.'

'I think they believed me. I cried a lot and they got embarrassed and stopped asking questions. They're rounding up all category B aliens, they told me.'

'Have you spoken to Peter?'

'I telephoned him. He said — ' she frowned, getting it right — 'men were being detained under Regulation

18b of the Defence of the Realm Act.'

Anton shrugged. 'It means that Habeas Corpus has been suspended because of the war.'

'Max and Rudi have been taken away, Anton! When you think what Max went through in that concentration camp! And Ruby's friend, Aaron — he's gone too!'

'Britain is afraid of invasion. They're afraid of people like me. They fear that their enemy is living among them. They don't think they have time to sort out the good from the bad. Here — ' he patted his thigh — 'come here.'

She sat on his knee. She smelled of cherries and vanilla, he thought.

She took something from her pocket. 'Look what I've got. Chocolate! Ruby got it for you.' She broke off a piece and put it in his mouth.

The night had seeped into the room. Sara's face was a mixture of light and shadows.

'I wish I could have married you,' he said. 'I would have liked that.'

★ ★ ★

'The French are asking us to send more fighter squadrons,' Lewis Gascoigne said to Ruby. He smiled his sardonic smile. 'The thing is, even if we kept every single plane we'd got, we still wouldn't have enough left to defend ourselves.'

They were in his Mayfair flat. Lewis, who had worked without stopping for the last forty-eight hours, had bathed and shaved and changed while Ruby made omelettes and salad and took from a tin a home-made cake.

His words added to the shock she had felt on first seeing him. He, who was always so immaculately groomed, had looked slightly dishevelled, his shirt crumpled, dark shadows around his eyes.

'What will we do?' she asked.

He refilled their wine glasses. 'No choice, really — we'll send more planes. Partly because, obviously, it's imperative that France holds out. And partly because it would look damned bad if we turned them away and France were ruined. What a choice, eh?'

Beneath the smile, he looked exhausted. She changed the subject. 'You always have such lovely food, Lewis.'

'Theresa sends me hampers. I think she still feels herself responsible for my material welfare. She gave up on my spiritual welfare, of course, a long time ago.' He put his napkin on the table and rose. 'I have to get back to the office, I'm afraid. But stay, won't you?' He kissed her. 'Make yourself some coffee — finish the wine.'

After he had gone, Ruby went into the kitchen. There was a jar of coffee beans; opening it, she closed her eyes, breathing in the aroma. Then she put the lid back on the jar. Lewis, she felt, needed it more than she did just now.

Instead, she cleared up, wiping surfaces, washing dishes. Lewis's manservant, a Territorial, was in France with the BEF. Ruby rubbed a cloth over the taps and sink, squeezed the cork back into the wine bottle and put it in the fridge, then put the cutlery back in the drawer. We haven't enough planes left to defend ourselves, she thought, and had a vision, both terrifying and amusing, of her, Ruby Chance, fending off German paratroopers from the streets of London with a breadknife.

★   ★   ★

May 17: Brussels fell. The next day, Antwerp surrendered. German troops pushed through Amiens and Abbeville, border towns fought over for centuries, familiar to occupations, invasions, defeat. On 21 May, the first German troops reached the Channel coast.

418

Soon, most of the British Expeditionary Force, along with a great many French soldiers, were trapped, surrounded by German forces in an area inland from Dunkirk.

Then, at last, a miracle. After a fierce British counterattack at Arras had mauled Rommel's Panzer division, the German army halted, with Hitler's agreement, for three days. On 24 May, the British evacuation from France, from the port of Boulogne, began. Two days later, ships began evacuating troops from Dunkirk as, all around them, Belgian and British soldiers fought to close the gap that had opened and prevent German troops reaching the port. On 28 May, Belgium surrendered.

Over the next nine days ships rescued British and French soldiers stranded on the beaches, beaches that were under almost continuous enemy bombardment. The naval vessels were augmented by a patchwork flotilla of hundreds of little ships: paddle-steamers and shrimpers and tugs, trawlers and pleasure yachts and river cruisers, all crossing the Channel to take men back to Britain, all running the gauntlet of the Stukas. By 3 June, almost 340,000 men had been transported, exhausted, bloodied and traumatised, back to England.

★   ★   ★

Leaving the lodging house, Sara always glanced up and down the street, checking for policemen. Once, catching sight of a parked car with two men sitting inside it, she changed her mind and walked to the shops instead of to Somers Town.

Many of Anton's friends, those friends who had argued politics in cafés and bars, or who had come for supper, their clothes often shabby and too thin for the cold weather, their smiles and greetings sitting ill at ease with their bitten fingernails and their constantly tapping feet, had been taken away to internment camps. A few, realising they were likely to be imprisoned, had, like Anton, disappeared into the night; one, a silent, sad-looking boy whose face Sara found hard properly to recall, slit his wrists.

On 10 June, while the battle for France still raged, Mussolini declared war on Britain and France. *Collar the lot*, said Churchill, the next day, and so Italians, some of whom had lived in Britain for more than a decade — waiters from smart London hotels, the proprietors of ice-cream parlours, the cheerful owners of Soho delicatessens — were interned. Those brown-eyed boys with the faces of Renaissance princes who had flirted with Sara as she had served them coffee, those dark, thickset men who had sat at a corner table in the café, cigarette smoke gathering over their heads as their short, stubby fingers stabbed the air to make a point: all had gone.

Lured out by the lingering sunshine, Anton and Sara picnicked in the courtyard by the basement, surrounded by red-brick walls and rusted trailers and rotting tea-chests and the wheelless skeleton of a bicycle. Spreading a blanket on the flagstones, Sara saw the weeds pushing through the gaps between the paving stones and the buff-coloured wings of moths that took to the sky as dusk fell.

'Tell me how your day was,' she always said. As if, she thought with a smile, he'd talk about the office, the commute.

'Oh,' he said, 'I read a book and took some exercise — a hundred press-ups and running on the spot. You won't love me if I turn into a flabby old man.'

She kissed him. 'I'll always love you.'

'And,' he said, 'I've almost finished our house.'

In the dusty quiet of the basement he was drawing out the plans of the house he meant one day to build for them. 'Let me see it,' she said.

'Not yet.'

'*Anton.*'

'Patience.' He touched the tip of her nose. 'When I've finished. When it's perfect.'

'Look,' she said, brandishing a paper bag, 'fairy cakes. Elaine made them. And some books from Edward.'

Anton lay on his back on the blanket, his threaded hands cushioning his head, looking up at the sky. 'Come here.'

'Aren't you hungry?'

'Yes, but not for bread and cakes.' He drew her to him; she pressed tiny kisses over his face. Then he unbuttoned her dress, rolled down her stockings and made love to her. Afterwards, they lay together on the blanket. She thought how neatly her head fitted into the hollow of his collarbone. Beneath his ribs, she could feel his heart beating.

'Tell me what you're thinking,' he said.

'I was thinking about David. I'm glad he's in Ireland. I'm glad he's safe.'

He stroked her hair. 'When all this is over, I'd like to meet him.'

'I'd like that too. Though I don't know what Caroline would think of you, darling. She might find you rather disconcerting.' She stroked the fine golden hair on his chest. 'And you, darling — what are you thinking?'

'That I love you.'

'I know that. What else?'

He sighed. 'That I feel so useless, hiding here, doing nothing, *waiting*. Why won't they let me fight? I would prefer to fight.'

'I'm glad you're not fighting. I'd be frightened for you.' She sat up, buttoning the front of her dress. 'Anton, we don't have to just sit and wait. We should make plans. When it's safe, we should go to the countryside. Cornwall, perhaps. Somewhere far away.

The war might go on for years. You can't stay here for ever.'

'I'm safe here. If we're careful — '

'But I worry about you. I'm afraid you're lonely, and in winter it'll be cold.'

Anton rose, stretching out his limbs, running a hand through his tousled fair hair, straightening his clothing. 'Sara, how could I travel? If I were to take a train or a bus, what if someone were to ask to see my papers?'

'I've worked it out. We could cycle. It would take days, I know, but we could. If we went to Cornwall my mother would help, I know she would. And I could get work nearby.'

'We have no bicycles.'

'Philip's old push-bike is in the garage at home. You could ride that. And I'm sure I could find another bicycle somewhere. I used to have one at Porthglas — it's probably still there. Mummy could send it up on the train for me.'

He walked up and down the courtyard, frowning. 'It's too risky.'

'I looked at maps in the library. We'd use byroads, not the main roads. If anyone asks, we'll say we're on holiday.'

'But, Sara, what about food? What if more foods are rationed? They will be, you know — U-boats are picking off the Atlantic convoys. And I can't use my ration card.'

'There's mine. And — ' she interrupted him — 'if we were in the country, we could grow vegetables, couldn't we? And we could catch fish.'

'Fish?' In the dusk, she saw the flash of his white teeth as he smiled.

'We used to go fishing when we were children, in Cornwall. I was rather good at it.'

He rested his hands on her shoulders. 'Dear Sara, you would do this for me? You would cycle hundreds of miles — you would sail in a little fishing boat . . . ?'

'Of course I would,' she said calmly. 'I'd do anything for you. Tell me we'll do it, darling — tell me we'll go to Cornwall.'

A slow exhalation of breath. 'Yes. But not yet. When all this fuss has died down — when the authorities are worrying about something else.' He glanced at his watch. 'You'd better go. I don't like you walking home alone in the dark.'

She kissed him. 'Until tomorrow,' she said, and walked away.

★　★　★

He tried to imagine the two of them, fleeing London, hurtling down hills and through valleys to the narrow limb of the West Country, to a land of rock and sky and sea.

Sometimes, he almost convinced himself. Often, he longed for it. But most of the time he felt frightened. He tried to hide his fear from Sara but he was afraid she must scent it, sour and pervasive. 'When all this fuss dies down,' he had said to her, as if he expected it to end sometime soon. He knew that it might never end. What if imprisonment were not enough? What if there were killings, as there had been in Germany, Austria, Italy and Spain? What if Britain, too, learned to kill people for their nationality, their political beliefs, their religion? And what if the fears of invasion were to prove correct, and the Nazis were to sweep on, unstoppable, crossing the Channel, marching to London? What, then, would happen to people like him?

He traced the path of how he had come to this, to living in a cellar with the rats and the spiders. A happy childhood in Vienna, in spite of the war and privation, followed by the heady optimism of the early twenties, and Red Vienna. Carefree days at university, chasing girls and studying till the early hours of the morning. It had all come to an end when the American stockmarket Crash of 1929 had spread its ripple effect around the world, bringing instability to the European financial markets. Instability had fostered the rise of fascism. Fascism had reduced him and his father to outcasts. More than two years ago, at the time of the Anschluss, he had stood among the cheering crowds, listening to the peals of bells as Hitler, standing in an open car, had followed the tanks into Vienna. When Hitler had appeared on the balcony of the Hotel Imperial, the people surrounding Anton had raised their arms in the Nazi salute. Fearful that his non-compliance would be noted, Anton made his way out of the throng, but the sound of the cheers had resonated behind him. From that day, the foundations of his life — family, home, country — had been stripped away, until Sara was all he had left.

As the days passed, he began to find it intolerable to be immured in the warehouse, shut away from the events of the world, no longer a part of it. The first time he ventured outside he circled once round the block before, with a quick glance up and down the road, ducking back into the narrow side street. As if, he thought, he were a rabbit, running into its burrow. But, later, in the cobwebbed darkness, he found himself remembering the touch of the sun, that hardly reached inside this derelict place, and the comforting hum of noise and activity.

The next time, he went a little further. The confined space of the warehouse had become airless as the heat of summer intensified. He didn't tell Sara, he didn't want to worry her. Sometimes, he went out at night. Yet it seemed to him that daylight was safer — more people on the streets, more crowds in which to hide himself. Surrounded by people, cars, shops, he began to feel part of the human race again. He belonged nowhere, was on the run in two countries. Now, he felt as if he was still *there*, if only at the edges.

Yet his apprehension remained and, turning into Charrington Street, every passer-by seemed a threat. Was that soldier, leaning against a lamppost to light a cigarette, watching him? Was that motor cycle, which crawled so slowly along the street, following him? Sometimes he caught sight of himself reflected in the window of a shop and saw in his eyes the expression of the hunted. His clothing had a bedraggled appearance, even though Sara took his things away to wash and iron. But it was hard to keep up appearances when you shaved looking in a hand-mirror and rinsed your razor in a tin filled with rainwater.

One morning, he walked to Regent's Park. The cloudless sky was a vivid Mediterranean blue. Sitting down on a bench, taking out a paperback, he thought of Alpine meadows, holidays with his father. The flowers that sparkled in the long grass, the butterflies dancing in the warm summer sun. The heat not so solid, so compacted, as in London.

'Phew, it's going to be a hot one!'

He turned, startled. A young woman had sat down beside him. She wore a red and white summer dress and her brown hair was pinned in rolls over her forehead. She was fanning her face with a newspaper.

'Yes,' he agreed 'it's very warm.'

She offered him a cigarette. Anton shook his head. She lit one for herself. 'Bloke on the wireless said it was going to be in the eighties. Me, I like it hot. Do you?'

'Very much.'

He thought he sounded stilted. He had forgotten how to converse, he realised, during his weeks in the warehouse basement.

She peered over his shoulder. 'Wotcha reading?'

'Lawrence,' he said, showing her the cover of the book. And then, making an effort, 'It's very interesting.'

She laughed. 'He was a dirty bugger, wasn't he?'

Then, frowning, looking at him closely, she said, 'You're not English, are you?'

His heart pounded; he couldn't speak. She blew out a stream of smoke. She was looking at him curiously — suspiciously, he thought. 'Where're you from?'

'France,' he said. 'I am a French *poilu*. I came here after Dunkirk.'

'You don't look French. My sister lives in Dover, she said they was all dark.'

Rising, stumbling, he said, 'I must go. Goodbye, *mademoiselle*.' He felt her watching him as he walked away across the grass.

Leaving the park, sweat prickled at his collar and his mouth was dry. He needed a drink but didn't dare go into any of the cafés and bars he passed. He wanted to run, but knew he must not let himself. All he longed for was to be back in the darkness of the basement. He walked, waiting for the hand on his shoulder, the uniformed figure stepping into his path.

Nothing happened. He began to relax a little. She had been just a pretty girl looking for company, he told himself. Nothing to be frightened of.

A wave of relief as he turned into Charrington Street, and then, glancing quickly around to make sure no one was about, he headed down the narrow lane that led to the warehouse. As he ran down the steps and opened the door he felt elated, proud that he had reached safety. Inside, he let out a breath and felt the tension go from his muscles.

Footsteps in the darkness. Anton looked up. Two men coming towards him. 'Anton Wolff?' one of them said.

* * *

There was a note from Sara on Edward's desk in his office, delivered there by Ruby, presumably. He opened it and read it.

After work, he went to the house where Sara and Anton lived. Sara let him into the room. She looked pale and agitated.

'I'm sorry to drag you out here, Edward,' she said as soon as she saw him, 'but I need your help.'

'What's happened?'

'It's Anton. They found him — he's been interned.'

'Good Lord,' he said. And then, quickly, 'How awful. When did it happen?'

She was walking round the room, twisting her hands together. 'Last night I went to the basement and he wasn't there. His rucksack was gone. I waited for ages but he didn't come back. So I went to the police this morning. And they told me they'd arrested him last night.'

'Where is he now?'

'They've handed him over to the army.' She rubbed her hand over the windowpane and looked out. 'No one will tell me where he is. He's been taken away somewhere but I don't know where. I keep thinking of him, all alone in some horrible prison. I've phoned everyone I can think of. Lewis Gascoigne's trying to find out for me, and there's a girl I know whose husband works for the Ministry of Home Security, so I've spoken to her. I'm going to keep telephoning and writing to everyone until I find out.'

He said, 'If there's anything I can do, you only have to say, Sara, you know that.'

She turned to him, gave him a brilliant smile. Her eyes shone with tears. 'Dear Edward. Everyone's been so kind. If you could just ask around. It all seems such a muddle, you see. Apparently the poor foreigners have been put in all sorts of places — prisons and factories, and even a circus, someone said, and no one seems to know where anyone is. So if you could talk to anyone you can think of who might know, anyone at all, that's what I wanted to ask you.'

'Of course.'

She glanced back out of the window. 'If I just knew where they'd taken him it wouldn't be so bad. I keep thinking I'll just look out there and see him. That they'll realise they've made an awful mistake and will let him go, and he'll come home.'

'I say, old thing, cheer up.' He gave her a clumsy hug. 'How about a drink? Anton wouldn't want you moping at home by yourself, would he?'

She smiled. 'I suppose not, darling.'

They had a drink and then Sara remembered a friend from her débutante days whose brother had some hush-hush job and might be able to help, and she headed off in a taxi to Mayfair.

Edward went home. As he let himself into the flat, his mother limped slowly down the corridor towards him.

'Where have you been?'

'I had to stay late at work, Mother.'

'It's too bad! Left here all on my own and the invasion expected any moment!' Mrs Carrington sniffed the air suspiciously. 'What's that? Are you wearing cologne, Edward?'

'No, certainly not.'

'I can smell scent. Have you been with a girl?'

'No, Mother. Where's Gladys?'

But his mother would not be distracted. 'I'm sure I can smell scent.'

Edward opened his briefcase. 'I managed to get you some biscuits.'

Mrs Carrington glanced at the tin. 'Shortbread. You know I've never liked shortbread.'

'Fortnum's didn't have your favourites.'

Edward helped his mother back down the corridor and settled her in her chair. Then he washed his hands and ran a brush through his hair, humming to himself as he did so.

'I hope you're not going to make that dreadful noise

all evening,' said his mother, as he returned to the drawing room. 'You never could hold a tune, could you, Edward?'

'Where's Gladys?' he asked. 'Where is the divine Gladys, queen of the kitchen, empress of the cooking-stove?'

'She's gone out.' Mrs Carrington sniffed. 'Some nonsense about her cousin being unwell. She's left something cold in the larder. Too bad of her. I could have been shot.'

'Shot? I don't think so, Mother. I doubt if Belgravia will be the Germans' first port of call if the invasion comes. And if you're worried about being in London, then why not go back to Andover?'

At the outbreak of war, Mrs Carrington had gone to live with her friend, Mrs Collins, in a small hotel in Andover. It had not been a success; Mrs Carrington had returned to London six weeks later. Edward suspected some falling-out over the bridge table.

His mother looked evasive. 'It worries me, not being near Dr Steadman.'

As Edward settled his mother in her chair, he managed not to point out that, if the Germans did invade Britain, Dr Steadman might well be otherwise occupied.

'I'd better put up the blackout,' he said.

'*Must* you? So gloomy.'

'Don't want to find ourselves in court, do we?' he said cheerfully.

Edward attached squares of black rep with press studs. Then he laid the dining table and took from the larder a plate of sliced tongue and a potato salad. After he and his mother had dined, they listened to the wireless. Then his mother went to bed.

There was nothing he wanted to listen to on the wireless so he fetched his Graham Greene. But he could not concentrate. By now, his elation had faded, replaced

429

by a mixture of guilt and depression.

It was always the same. There was the delight of being with Sara, like listening to exquisite music, and then, after he parted from her, delight was gradually replaced by torment, an awareness of his own inadequacies and failings as he raked over their encounter in his head and saw where he had fallen short — his clumsiness, or things he had said that he could have phrased better. He remembered that she had smiled at him, that she had called him darling, both of which, in the earliest days of their acquaintance, would have given him hope. But he knew her better now, knew that she smiled at everyone, that she would call a dog darling. Because his family had never used endearments he was unused to them and placed too much importance on them. And though, this evening, Sara had seemed to need him, he knew, deep down, that she did not. He wondered whether she thought about him at all when she was not there. He wondered whether she would like him even the little bit she did if she could see into his heart.

★　★　★

First they took Anton to Ascot racecourse, where he had to sleep in the totaliser building. The long, narrow structure was lit by tiny windows, each covered with a steel grid. The internees slept in rows to either side, closely packed, with barely enough room to walk between them.

That was the worst night. The single door was at the far end of the building, a long way away. In the night, some of the men panicked — the lack of air, the lack of light, the dread of tomorrow. Anton hardly slept. When he did doze off, he woke what seemed like minutes later, bathed in sweat, convinced for a moment that he was in the prison in Vienna. He tried to breathe regularly but something seemed to weigh on his chest.

There was the fear that they'd keep him in here for ever, till he went mad or died, and there was the fear of what was to come. Images of deportation, or of the firing squad, flickered into his mind. And the terrible, irrational fear of the walls and ceiling closing in on him, crushing him. He tried to keep his fears at bay by thinking of the house he would build for Sara, with the great, wide windows that looked out over a lake, tried to see in his imagination the open sky, the cool water.

In the morning, he and several dozen other men were driven under armed guard to another racecourse, this time at Lingfield in Surrey. He slept on a straw palliasse in the stables. The stables had been cleaned out but they still smelled of horse. He felt a bit better at Lingfield, and he didn't mind the cold showers or the bucket toilets or the army food because by day he could see trees and sky. His fellow internees were merchant seamen who had been captured by the Royal Navy, and other sailors, socialists and communists who had sailed under neutral flags after escaping the Nazi regime in Germany and Austria. An internee from Edinburgh had brought with him a haversack full of Penguin paperbacks; Anton borrowed one and read it, sitting on the raked seats of the grandstand. He longed to receive word from Sara but there was nothing.

A week later they were made to assemble in the Collecting Ring, where a list of names was read out. Anton's name was on the list He gave *The Good Soldier Schweik* back to its owner and climbed into the truck. He saw his own fear written on the faces of the other men in the truck. Where were they going? What was to be done with them? Only the soldiers who escorted them, their bayonets fixed, looked untroubled, bored.

They were driven to the railway station and put on a train. One of the guards on the train told Anton that they were being taken to Huyton, in Liverpool. It was raining when they reached the Huyton camp, which had been hastily formed out of barely completed rows of newly built council houses. There was a strange look to the place, Anton thought, as if the ordinary had shifted out of joint — the rows of identical houses, with their unfinished gardens and fencing, the people who huddled in groups in the streets, all men, not a woman or child among them. The coils of barbed wire that divided them from the other houses, only a short distance away.

Once again, he was given a straw palliasse. Because the houses were already crowded he had to sleep in a tent in a field. Some of the other men complained about the mud that the rain had churned up, but Anton didn't mind. He regretted, though, that they hadn't gone to Cornwall as soon as Sara had suggested it. He shouldn't have waited.

Many of the thousands of prisoners at Huyton were Jewish. Some were elderly men, over sixty years old, their poor health exacerbated by years of privation and fear and imprisonment in concentration camps. They were amusing and erudite, these doctors and professors and rabbis, but Anton sensed the unease that lay beneath their conversation.

Still no letters. As the days went on, other fears grew. Had Sara given up on him? Had she forgotten him? Had something happened to her? He saw his own fear reflected in the eyes of the other men in the camp, fear for their families and friends, left behind in a world that was breaking up, falling apart. There was no radio at the camp and they were not allowed newspapers. No books, no distraction from their own thoughts. Many of the men had been through too much in the past to bear easily this latest dislocation. Fear filled the vacuum, fear sparked by rumours — London had been bombed to smithereens, German naval vessels were bombarding the south coast of England, paratroopers were floating like deadly thistledown into the arable pastures of England, as they had in Holland . . .

One morning, at roll call, a list of names was read out. The men who were called for collected their belongings and climbed into army trucks. Some of those who remained gathered near the entrance to the camp to watch as they were driven away.

'They're shipping them to Australia,' someone said. 'The British always send their prisoners to Australia.'

'Madagascar, I heard,' said someone else.

A gaunt-looking man said, 'They're sending us back to Germany, that's what they're doing.' He had smoked his cigarette down to the last quarter-inch; stubbing it between thumb and forefinger he put the unsmoked fragment into his jacket pocket. 'The Nazis have agreed to exchange us for English internees. I overheard someone say so.' They all turned to look up the road to where the barrier had been raised, allowing the trucks to drive through the barbed wire, away from the camp.

After roll call the next day, another list of names was read out. Anton's name was among them. He packed his belongings into his rucksack and managed to get a seat towards the open end of the truck, from where he could see the shops and housing estates they were driving through. Few of the people they passed troubled to glance up at the truck — why should they: after all, it was only another army truck transporting men somewhere.

But *where*? The houses became smaller and meaner, the parks replaced by light engineering workshops and warehouses. When the truck slowed for a junction, he wondered whether he should make a run for it and mentally measured the distance between the end of the truck and the road. But the soldiers sitting on guard at the back of the truck were nervous, jumpy little fellows. One of them caught his eye and Anton settled back in his seat, remembering rumours of internees shot dead after altercations with their guards.

Gulls wheeled in the bright blue sky. A ship sounded its foghorn. Anton made out on the skyline cranes and the superstructures of ships. Liverpool docks, he thought. His stomach churned uneasily.

They're shipping them to Australia. They're sending us back to Germany.

★ ★ ★

Early morning. Barrage balloons bobbing in blue skies, a flight of Hurricanes and Spitfires overhead; men, their sleeves rolled up, filling sandbags and stacking them against the public buildings. As she left the house, Sara's eyes flicked, as everyone else's did, to the headlines chalked on the news-vendors' billboards.

'Ship Sunk: Internees' Panic Lost Many Lives . . . Aliens Fight Each Other In Wild Panic.'

She scrabbled in her purse for coins to buy a paper. Ducking into a shop doorway, she scanned the columns to read the story of the *Arandora Star*.

In peacetime, the *Arandora Star* had been a luxury liner, carrying only first-class passengers on Mediterranean cruises or in search of the winter sun. At the beginning of the war, all British merchant vessels had been commandeered by the Admiralty, the *Arandora Star* among them. On 1 July the ship had left Liverpool, her cabins and staterooms filled with enemy aliens bound for an internment camp in Canada. The following day, shortly after seven o'clock in the morning, the *Arandora Star* been torpedoed by a German U-boat off the north coast of Ireland, and had sunk.

Phrases jumped from the page. 'Hundreds of men believed drowned . . . ', 'Ship's captain thought lost ... ', 'Italian, German and Austrian men on board ... '

Italian, German and Austrian men on board ...

★ ★ ★

Late that evening, a knock on the door. Ruby and Lewis came into the room. There was something ominous, Sara thought, about Lewis being there as well.

Sara said, 'Shall I make us some tea?' and Lewis shook his head and said, 'Not for me, thanks. Ruby?', and Ruby shook her head too.

Sara said, 'You've news, haven't you?'

'Some. Not all of it's definite, but some.'

She sat down on the bed. 'Do you know where he is?'

'He was at Huyton.'

'Huyton?'

'It's an internment camp in Liverpool. Rather a large one.'

'*Was*,' said Sara. 'You said he *was* at Huyton, Lewis.'

'Yes. He was shipped out a few days ago.'

She didn't like the word 'shipped'. It had a menacing, frightening sound. '*Tell me*,' she whispered.

'I don't know for certain. No one knows for certain.'

'Was he on the *Arandora Star*?'

'It's possible, yes.'

Ruby, sitting beside her, squeezed her hand. Sara said harshly, 'How possible?'

'I don't know. That's the honest truth, Sara. There were no proper records of who was on the ship and there's no clear list yet of — ' Lewis seemed to change his mind about the word he was going to use — 'of survivors. It's a mess,' he said angrily. 'No one seems to know what they're doing. I can't find a single person who seems able to get their hands on any reliable information. All I've been able to do is to speak to friends of friends, colleagues who might know

435

something. Anton was at Huyton, there seems no doubt about that. And he doesn't appear to be there any more. Some internees from Huyton appear to have been on the *Arandora Star*, but, if they were, I haven't been able to find out whether he was among them. I'm sorry, Sara. I wasn't sure whether to tell you. It's very possible that I've frightened you unnecessarily.'

'No, no, you were right to tell me.' She marvelled at the steadiness of her voice. 'And I was frightened anyway. At least now I know *something*.'

'I have to go, I'm afraid,' Lewis said. 'Ruby will stay with you.'

'He isn't dead,' she said, looking up at him. 'I know he isn't. I would feel it, I would *know*, if something had happened to him.'

She could see by the expression in his eyes that he didn't believe her, but he said, 'That's the spirit.' At the door, he paused. 'Policy made on the hoof is always the worst kind. Good God, we seem to have sent a boatload of Italian waiters and chefs to their deaths. Hardly our finest moment.'

'You'll let me know if you hear anything else, won't you, Lewis?'

A smile. 'The very minute, I promise.'

After he had gone, Ruby said, 'I'm sure Anton'll be all right, Sara,' and then, 'I'll make some tea, shall I?'

Ruby left the room. Alone, Sara remembered the mornings she had tried to wake Anton by thinking about him. If he had drowned, then she would know, she would have sensed that extinguishing of something so precious. Just as Anton had, on those lazy mornings, sensed her thoughts.

Ruby came back into the room with the tea. Sara said, 'I didn't know before how you must have felt about your father. Always waiting.'

Ruby said, 'I'm still waiting.'

Days when the hours, minutes, seconds dragged themselves out, aching. Days when every telephone call screwed her stomach up into a tight little ball and every letter, glimpsed on the hall table as she returned home from work, made her heart miss a beat. At night, she lay awake, her muscles sore from the tension of the day, listening to the tapping of a fly on the window, trapped between the glass and the blackout.

The story of the *Arandora Star* became clearer. After the torpedo had struck, the ship had taken only twenty minutes to sink. It became clear that the early newspaper reports had been inaccurate: there had been no panic, no fighting for places on the lifeboats. The ship's crew and the internees had helped each other. Many of those drowned had been older internees, who had been unable to reach the open decks in time.

She was afraid to go out in case word arrived while she was out; it was unbearable, though, to stay in. Quick visits to friends and relatives, in a hopeless attempt to distract herself. At Philip's house, Elaine was packing. Philip had been transferred to Portsmouth, Elaine told her. He had rented a cottage in Hampshire for Elaine and Jenny.

'We'll be nearby, you see. And he wants us to leave London, in case.' In case the bombs fall, in case of invasion. Elaine blushed. 'And with a baby coming . . .'

Sara hugged, congratulated, reassured. 'When's it due?'

'December, the doctor thinks.' Elaine was folding little pink cardigans. 'Why don't you come with us, Sara? Why don't you come and stay with us in the cottage? It's a bit primitive, but quite sweet, really. There's a spare bedroom, and Jenny would love you to

437

come. And I would too. Company, you see. I'm a city girl; I don't know how I shall manage in the countryside.'

'I can't,' said Sara. 'I have to stay in London for Anton. He has to know where to find me.'

'Of course.' Elaine folded terry squares. 'I understand. But you'll come and see us, won't you?' Sara promised.

At home, no letters, no telegrams. She couldn't face cooking, ate a piece of bread and Marmite, drank some tea. Too much tea, she thought: she must have drank, these past few days, gallons of tea.

She ironed a couple of blouses, polished her shoes, made the bed. All these ordinary tasks seemed to have taken on great import, to be made the most of, because they filled in the time. Then she put up the blackout, reread Caroline's latest letter telling her of David's progress, and wrote in reply. And then there was nothing left to do. Every button had been sewn on, every fallen hem mended. She couldn't read, forgot each sentence as soon as she came to the end of it. There was no one else to write to, pleading for help in finding Anton. There was only the room, which she and he had shared, and which was now filled with memories.

For the first time, she found herself thinking, what if he never comes back? What if all she had left was her memories? Would it have been worth it — the abandonment of her marriage and her child, the rift from her father, whom she missed so much, in spite of what he had done. Would it have been worth the loneliness, the pain? Would it have been better if she and Anton had never met? Would she have remained the old, blithe Sara Finborough? Might that have given her more happiness, less pain? She thought of the house Anton had promised to build her. Would they ever live in it? Or would it remain a house built only in the clouds, existing on scraps of paper and in her imagination?

But there were no answers to her questions. Only a sense of affinity, perhaps, with all the other women who watched and waited. With Ruby, of course, and with Elaine, waiting with Jenny and her cases for Philip to return to take her away from London. With all the other women whose husbands, sons, brothers were in the Forces.

Edward had given her a half-bottle of brandy. Sara drank a large glassful and curled up in Anton's side of the bed. Unexpectedly, she slept well, and the next morning, a Saturday, was woken by the clatter of mail falling through the letterbox.

She ran down the stairs to the hall. Among the buff envelopes and government pamphlets there was a postcard, addressed to her. Turning it over, she saw that it was from Anton. He was safe and well, he told her, and he was living in an internment camp on the Isle of Man.

14

At much the same time as France fell, a trainload of schoolchildren from the East End of London arrived in St Ives. They were shepherded from the railway station to Stennack School, where local people who had offered to take in evacuees chose those they wished to take home with them.

Isabel selected three brothers, all square-faced, snub-nosed and grubby, with hair the colour of sacking. Their shirts were threadbare, their shorts too big for them and tied up with lengths of string, their socks ruckled round their ankles above scuffed plimsolls. They came from Canning Town, they told her as they left the school together. On the bus back to Porthglas, the two elder boys, Robert and Ted, bobbed up and down in their seats, rushing every now and then to the back of the vehicle to peer out of the window and make rude remarks about the countryside and the other passengers. Alighting from the bus at the village, Robert and Ted ran ahead along the coastal path to the cottage, hitting each other with their gas masks and the brown paper parcels in which they carried their belongings, leaving Isabel to walk after them, six-year-old Stanley's hand in hers. There was rather a whiff to Stanley: Isabel suspected that somewhere in the course of his lengthy journey he had wet himself.

At the cottage, Robert and Ted fired off a barrage of questions while Isabel ran a bath.

'Why'd you live here?'

'Because I like it.'

'What are those stones for?' — with a swipe at a circle of pebbles arranged on the windowsill.

'Because I like them.'

'What d'you want them old stones for?'

'I think they're pretty.'

'Why've they got holes in 'em?'

'To keep away witches.'

A brief, shocked silence, then Robert recovered himself.

'Where's your old man?'

'In London.'

'Why's 'e there?'

'Because that's where he works.'

'Ain't you got no kids?'

'I have three children, but they're all grown up. There,' said Isabel, turning off the tap. 'In you get.'

All three brothers stared at the bath. Stanley's snuffles turned to wails. 'Not getting in *that*,' said Robert, very definitely. 'I'd get poorly. It'd go to my chest. I've got a bad chest.' He coughed loudly.

Isabel began to strip off Stanley's clothes. Beneath his outer garments, Stanley appeared to have been sewn into a wrapping of brown paper, in place of underclothes.

Isabel fetched scissors to snip off the brown paper. 'After you've had a bath, you can have tea. Boiled eggs and cake.'

'Eggs! Eurgh!' Ted made vomiting noises.

Robert said slyly, 'They come out of hens' bottoms. Mrs Wright told me.' Ted looked appalled.

Somehow, they were all persuaded to undress and climb into the bath, where Stanley howled and the elder boys amused themselves by sloshing water over the floor. When they were dry and dressed again, Isabel cooked tea. She helped Stanley eat his boiled egg, which he did with an expression of bewildered resignation, while his two brothers, who refused egg, insisting they always ate bread and jam for tea, hurtled round the room. After tea, Isabel sent Robert and Ted outside to play while she sat Stanley on her knee and read him a story. Her voice was low and hypnotic and he fell asleep before the end of the first page. She carried him upstairs and tucked him up in bed, then went outside to find his brothers.

No sign of Robert and Ted. Isabel circled the house, walked to the edge of the cliff, looked down over the tumbled rocks to the cove. An empty beach, no footprints in the sand. She walked a short way along the cliff, trying not to think of all the dangers Porthglas held for children who had never seen the sea before.

She went back indoors to clear up the tea things. She was cleaning the bath and had begun to put up the blackout when she heard voices from outside. Glancing out of the window, she saw Robert and Ted coming back along the path. Both boys were covered in mud and twigs and Robert had by the scruff of its neck a large piebald rabbit.

★　★　★

The next morning, after she had given the three brothers over to the care of their teacher, Miss Wright, in St Ives, Isabel went shopping.

She was coming out of the International Stores when a voice said, 'Good morning. Beautiful day, isn't it?'

'Glorious,' she said automatically. Looking up, she saw a tall, gangling man dressed in scruffy navy-blue trousers and a striped shirt. There was a parrot on his shoulder.

'Mr Penrose . . . I bought a painting from you, didn't I? And, of course, I remember Charlie.'

The parrot preened itself. 'Charlie likes an outing, don't you, Charlie?' Mr Penrose glanced at Isabel's bag. 'That looks heavy. Let me carry it for you.'

'There's no need.'

'I'm not offering because I *need* to. I'm offering because if I carry your bag then you'll be obliged to talk

442

to me. Where are you headed?'

'The bus station. Mr Penrose — '

'Blaze, you must call me Blaze.'

'I have to catch my bus.' She sounded ungracious, she thought: she made an effort, saying, 'Actually, I'd be very grateful if you carried my bag. I am rather exhausted.'

He cocked an eyebrow at her. She explained, 'First thing this morning I had to take one of my neighbours back his pet rabbit. Don't ask — it's too tiring even to think about it. Oh, and I gave three small boys their breakfast, when two of them will only eat bread and jam and don't seem to know what a chair is for, and the third one won't say a word, the poor little soul. I've been buying carbolic and a comb because they all have lice, I'm afraid, and I've just bought them more clothes because they've hardly a decent set between them.'

'I have an evacuee, you know.'

'Really?'

'Don't look so surprised. Didn't you think I was the fatherly type? Angus is the son of an old girlfriend of mine. She says she's worried about bombs and gas, but I think she's having far too much fun with the Free French soldiers to be bothered with him.'

'How old is he?'

'Ten. Too delicate for school, apparently. Seems as tough as old boots to me.'

They had reached the bus station. 'His education . . . ' said Isabel.

'He can read and write and add up. I'm trying to teach the little blighter to paint and to sail. What else does he need to know? There's your bus.' He laughed at her expression as he handed her the shopping bag. 'Porthglas Cottage, isn't it? I've seen you around. Perhaps I'll bring Angus over some day — he could do with someone to play with.'

Blaze Penrose's evacuee — Isabel was unclear whether
Angus Mackintyre was also Blaze Penrose's son — had
the face of a Botticelli cherub, flaxen curls, an olive skin
and hazel eyes. Meeting him for the first time a few days
after her encounter with Blaze Penrose in St Ives, Isabel
feared for him at the hands of Robert and Ted.

She soon discovered that her fears were groundless.
Angus was a survivor. His boundless self-confidence
meant that unkind remarks slid off him like water off a
duck's back. Any physical aggression he dealt with by
hair-pulling or biting, tactics that even Robert and Ted
considered underhand.

'Of course, Laura, his mother, is just the same,' said
Blaze, who had cycled over to Porthglas with Angus.
'Looks like an angel but winds you round her little
finger.'

They were in the kitchen. All four boys were upstairs:
Stanley's howls told Isabel that she might have to rescue
him soon.

Isabel said, 'Does she visit often?'

'Not once, the miserable bitch.'

'Doesn't Angus miss her?'

'Doesn't seem to. That boy was born with a heart of
steel.' Blaze leaned forward, elbows on the table, his
eyes, which were a washed-out blue, settling on her. 'A
bit like you, Isabel.'

She said, 'Do you want some gooseberries? I've rather
a lot and the boys refuse to eat them.'

Blaze groaned. 'I talk of love and she talks of
gooseberries.'

'I'm only being practical.'

'So am I. It must get lonely out here on your own.'

'I'm not on my own.' Isabel took a tray of biscuits out
of the oven. 'I have the boys.'

'I meant — ' he gave a stage leer — 'at night.'

'*Blaze*. I'm a married woman.'

'So? I may be a married man.'

'May be?'

'Marita may have divorced me, I'm not sure.' He lounged against the sink, tall and rangy and scruffy, with long, thin, spidery hands.

'Marita?'

'Italian . . . met her in Marseilles . . . ' he said vaguely. 'And anyway, you say you're married, but where's your husband?' He glanced round the room, as if expecting to see Richard hiding behind a sofa.

'In London,' she said briefly. And then, 'So, the gooseberries?'

'No, thanks,' he said. 'I don't like them either.' Then, whistling, he went to stand at the bottom of the stairs to bawl for Angus.

★ ★ ★

The river and the sea.

The sea, which the invasion force must cross to reach Britain. The river, which, on moonlit nights, guided the bombers into the heart of London.

Sometimes, in the taut, nervous months before the outbreak of war, Richard had felt bewildered. How had he come to be living alone, his entire family having deserted or betrayed him, when all he had ever wanted to do had been to keep them safe, to protect them?

Of course, he tried to distract himself from his loneliness. A dimpled, green-eyed little creature, encountered one night in a Mayfair bar. An old friend, now separated from her husband, with whom he had had a brief fling when in his prime, in the twenties.

But the dimpled creature made it clear to him that she expected trinkets and silk négligés and, when her demands rose to diamond earrings and sable stoles he ended the affair. And besides, her eyes were not so pleasant a green as Isabel's, but were a sourer, sharper shade. And the old friend proved to suit him more as just that, a friend, and one evening they found themselves drinking brandy and listing what they missed about their lost loves, until she was sobbing and he was murmuring comfort and sneaking glances at the clock because he had to be up at dawn for work these days.

He wondered why, when Isabel had been living with him, London had seemed to be full of pretty women, and why, now that she was gone, none of them seemed to suit.

Then, after the fall of France, the war picked up with a vengeance. Richard's experience in industry had led to him becoming closely involved with the work of the Ministry of Aircraft Production. Travelling south from London on business, he witnessed the battles that were being fought in the sky overhead. He saw the vapour trails drawing arcs and circles, heard the rattle of machine-guns and the scream of engines. Sometimes the dogfights ended with a plane spiralling into the sea. The news-vendors chalked on their billboards the outcome of battle, like cricket scores.

Philip and Theo were in the navy and Sara and Ruby were in London. And then there was Isabel, proud in her citadel in Cornwall. None of them was safe any more. Richard thought of ships torpedoed in the Atlantic and bombs falling on the cities. He thought of the unimaginable horror of occupation and all the everyday betrayals and humiliations and compromises that must come with it. His fears came to him in the early hours of the morning, when he struggled to wake up from a nightmare in which he was back in the shell-hole in no man's land, waiting for Nicholas Chance to rescue him — or he had picked up the soldier's corpse and the head had come off in his hands and was talking to him, the rotting mouth forming words, the sunken eyes blinking open.

He wrote to Isabel. She mustn't stay in Cornwall — the entire south of England was now at risk of invasion. She must go to Raheen, he said, and take Sara with her. Isabel wrote back a brief little note telling him that she had no intention of leaving Cornwall, and that he could ask Sara to go to Raheen if he chose, but she would not do so.

Richard cursed, ground his teeth, ripped up her note. The following week, he visited the aircraft works at Filton, near Bristol, to discuss an order for engine parts that were to be manufactured by Finboroughs. He made sure his business was completed quickly, checked out of his hotel, and caught the train to Exeter. At Exeter, he changed for the St Ives line, a miserably slow journey, stopping and starting between stations, so that by the time he reached his destination, it was early evening. In St Ives, he went to the garage that he had used before the war, and managed, through a mixture of coercion and bribery, to rent a car with sufficient petrol to take him to Porthglas. The car, an ancient Austin 7, refused to drive above twenty miles an hour and had long ago lost what little suspension it had ever had, and rattled bone-shakingly along the unsurfaced track from the village to the house. To one side of him were the fields, to the other, only a few yards away, was the steep cliff that fell to the sea. There was the feeling, familiar to him from previous journeys, of having entered a different domain, a land of clouds and sea and sky, at the end of the world.

Parking the car beside the low, white fence, Richard climbed out. He walked a short way down the slope that led to the beach, trying to ease his joints, which were stiff after his long journey. He saw the coils of barbed wire and the concrete blocks that had been placed across the access to the beach to impede the invasion forces.

He looked back at the house. It seemed unchanged since the last time he had visited — whitewashed walls bright against the blue sky, a line of washing flapping in the breeze. There was the scent he always associated with Porthglas — salt and grass and the honey fragrance of the clover that grew on the cliffs. And he heard the distant rush and hiss of the waves on the sand and, some way away, the sound of children playing — a shriek, a burst of laughter. And he had the curious sensation of having shifted back in time, so that the years fell away and he was a young man again, and Isabel was inside the house, waiting for him to come home, while the children played in the garden.

The door opened and Isabel came out. Richard's heart seemed to miss a beat, to take a breath, as if it had been starved of oxygen for too long. He stood motionless, watching her go to the washing-line, take down the dry clothes and put them in a wicker basket.

He stepped forward. 'Hello, Isabel.'

'Richard.' Her hand went to her mouth. Then, 'Has something happened? The children — '

'No, no, nothing like that. They're all fine, as far as I know. I came here to see you.'

'*Oh.*' She was still clutching the peg bag; she glanced up to the track. 'The car . . . ?'

'No petrol — blasted rationing. I took the train, then I borrowed an old boneshaker from Fred Gribbin.'

'You received my letter?'

'Yes, that's what I came about.'

He saw her mouth purse. She frowned. 'You're not still trying to insist I go to Raheen, are you, Richard?'

'Of course you must! It's only sensible!'

She gave him a cool look. 'As we no longer live as man and wife, why should you be concerned about my safety?'

'You are still the mother of my children. Whatever

happened — whatever you have done — *that* is unchanged.'

'Whatever I have done . . . ' she repeated slowly. 'Go back to London, please, Richard. You're wasting your time here.' Turning away, she bent to lift the washing basket.

He tried to control his rising temper. 'Isabel, for God's sake. Think of what's happened on the Continent. I've seen war, I've seen what it can do. Don't be fooled into thinking life will go on much as before, because it won't.'

'I'm sure you're right,' she said calmly. 'But I won't leave Porthglas.'

'Isabel — ' he began again, and then the door of the house was flung open and a man stuck his head round it, and said, 'It's all fixed, my darling Isabel. May I have a reward?'

'*Blaze*,' said Isabel sharply.

Richard said, 'Who the hell are you?'

'Richard,' Isabel said quickly, 'this is a friend of mine, Blaze Penrose. Blaze, this is my husband, Richard.'

Blaze Penrose — scruffy, no jacket, overlong hair, and his cuffs and the top button of his shirt undone — sauntered out of the house, and said, 'Good afternoon, Mr Finborough.'

He held out his hand. Richard ignored it. Isabel said, '*Richard*,' and Richard said, 'I didn't realise I was interrupting something,' and Isabel said furiously, 'Oh, Richard, don't be so ridiculous!'

'Ridiculous?' His gaze flicked between the two of them, forming the worst possible conclusion. 'Yes, you're right. I suppose I must seem ridiculous to you.'

'*Richard*!' she cried. 'For once in your life, listen to me! It's not what you think. Blaze was fixing the blackout over the landing window, that's all!'

The man — Blaze — said, 'That's right, just fixing the blackout,' and Richard, infuriated by his tone and his smile, hit him. Blaze Penrose gave a little surprised grunt, collapsed on to the grass, struggled to his feet again, and hit Richard back, a badly aimed blow that struck his chest, winding him. Then a few more messy, furious punches until they were both sprawled on the lawn, knuckles bloody and gasping for breath.

'*Bugger*,' said Blaze, sitting up, inspecting his fist. 'I think I've dislocated a finger.'

Richard dabbed at his mouth with his handkerchief, which came away scarlet. Isabel and the laundry basket were no longer there. Blaze said, 'She's damn well left us to it. Gone back into the house,' and then fell back on the grass, eyes closed, breathing heavily.

Richard's gaze came to rest on the four small boys who were standing at the fence, watching them wide-eyed. Then he wiped the blood from his mouth, gathered up what remained of his dignity and walked back to the car.

★ ★ ★

Unable to bear the transformation of her sedate seaside town into a battleground, Etta Chance fled to London to stay with her daughter. The city, with its noise and traffic and busy, unfamiliar people, frightened Etta. London on Black Saturday, the first night of the London Blitz proper, terrified her.

The first warning siren sounded in the late afternoon. They all trooped down to the boiler room in the basement below the flats and sat in the hot, clanking darkness listening to the crump-crump-crump of the bombs obliterating the decaying Victorian terraces and Dickensian warehouses of the East End. At six o'clock, the all clear sounded and they emerged, blinking and dazed, into the light. To the east, an enormous mushroom cloud of smoke hung in the sky.

Two hours later the raiders returned, guided now by

the crimson glow of the burning houses and factories, a beacon for bombers. High-explosive bombs rained down not only on the East End but on other wealthier, more exclusive, parts of the city. Fire-fighters battled to direct hoses on buildings where flames leaped thirty feet into the sky. Fire barges jostled on the Thames, and rats, like a muddy brown wave, escaped a burning grain warehouse.

Ruby dragged down a mattress, blankets, pillows to the boiler room, made tea, tried to comfort and distract. The bombardment continued throughout the night. Etta recoiled at every shiver of the building, every thunderous crash and whirr and screech. Her hands shook too much to hold the mug of tea.

In the morning, they emerged to a changed city. Fires still burned to the east, flecks of soot hung in the air, speckling the forgotten washing on the line. A sooty taste on the tongue and an acrid scent; an unpleasant mixture of burned paint, tar, sugar, rubber, drifting from the east. In nearby Earls Court, a house had been swallowed up in a bomb crater, a chaotic jumble of brick, planks and tile, scattered with someone's furnishings, someone's keepsakes.

The raiders returned the next night and the night after that and the night after that. Relentless, crowing, circling over the rubble and the homes peeled open like oranges to reveal the soft, vulnerable parts — that cheap wallpaper that should have been replaced years ago, that worn armchair with horsehair bulging out like fungus — before dropping their payload of bombs.

Ruby met Lewis for a quick drink in the Berkeley.

'I have to find somewhere for my mother,' she told him. 'It's making her ill. And all the guesthouses are full.'

He frowned. 'Theresa has taken in several distressed Catholic gentlewomen. I could ask her if she has room for another.'

451

A vision of her mother serene among the lakes and the daffodils: Ruby shook her head. 'The Lake District's too far away. I wouldn't be able to visit. And though my mother's very mild about most things, I'm afraid she's rather disapproving where Roman Catholics are concerned. And anyway, Lewis, your mistress's mother staying with your wife? It wouldn't do, would it?'

He smiled his lopsided smile. 'When you put it like that . . .'

'Thank you for thinking of it, though.' She touched his hand.

'I'm hoping to get a free hour later on. Could you come to the flat?'

His brown eyes talked wordlessly of sex; there was a curl of desire inside her.

'Darling Lewis, I'm sorry, but I can't. I have to get back to Mum.' She finished her drink, gave him a lingering kiss, left the bar.

Edward knew of a little hotel in Andover. More expensive than Ruby had budgeted for, but all the guesthouses were packed with refugees from the Blitz, so it would have to do. There was something in Etta's eyes that frightened Ruby, that made her feel twelve years old again, struggling to cope in the months that had followed her father's disappearance, when her mother had seemed to disintegrate, the fragile strands that held her together unravelling like knitting wool.

The next day they left for Andover. A taxi took them to Waterloo, but the station was closed due to bomb damage, so they headed on for Clapham Junction. Some of the area had been sealed off because of a time bomb and, as they made their way to the station, the warning siren sounded. They pressed on, catching a train that carried them into a raid. Anti-aircraft guns clattered, and the passengers crouched on the floor among the cigarette butts and chewing gum and sweet wrappers. In Ruby's arms, her mother's ribs and shoulder blades felt like the bones of birds. The rat-tat-tat of the guns, the drone of the bombers, and her mother's lips moving in prayer. 'O God, who knowest us to be in the midst of so many and great dangers . . . ' Eventually, the train moved on.

Changing trains at Surbiton, a Polish airman offered Etta his seat on a bench. Etta sat down. Her face was grey, her lips blueish and she was trembling. 'We'll be there soon, Mum,' said Ruby. Such feeble consolation. Her mother was sinking into herself, losing herself.

Come on, Ruby, you're supposed to be good at words. Something different, something distracting.

'I wonder how Maude and Hannah are getting on.'

A small flicker of interest.

Ruby smiled. 'I can't imagine Aunt Maude letting a few Germans bother her.'

A whispered, 'No.'

'She'll be out there, blazing away with her shotgun.'

'Yes.'

'What do you think Hannah will do?'

Etta blinked. 'Do?'

'She could leave the farm. She could join one of the women's services.'

A shake of the head. 'Hannah will never leave the farm. Not while Maude is alive.' An unexpected strength in her mother's voice.

In the distance, a cotton-wool tuft of smoke as the engine came into sight. 'Everyone's moving,' said Ruby. 'Everyone's going somewhere different. Hannah might.'

Something altered in Etta's gaze. 'Maude was always a hoarder. Once she got hold of something she'd never let it out of her grasp. She'd never give you one of her sweets or let you play with her skipping-rope. She always had a tight fist, did Maude.'

A billow of smoke and a screech of steam as the train pulled into the platform. Ruby's elbows pushing, fighting, to get her mother a seat. Reaching Andover,

453

they walked to the hotel.

The Lees was smarter than Etta's old guesthouse in Eastbourne. Its proprietor, a Mrs Weston, was brisk and efficient in tweeds and twinset and pearls, and lacked, Ruby felt instinctively, Mrs Sykes's kindness.

They had tea, and then Ruby kissed her mother goodbye and headed back to London. The train was busy, every seat taken. She stood in the corridor, facing the window, feeling a heady relief at being alone again, as well as guilt at her relief. Her mother was safe now, she told herself, and that was the most important thing. There was nothing to be ashamed of in being pleased to have her flat back to herself, in wanting her life back, in returning to the Ruby she had made herself into, the Ruby they depended on at work, the Ruby with her married lover, the Ruby who, alone in the evenings, plotted sticky little thrillers, spider's webs of greed and love and desire in which to catch her characters.

But there was an ache behind her eyes at the memory of her mother, lost in the unfamiliar room. What would Etta be doing now? Still sitting in her room, Ruby feared, afraid to go down to the lounge in case the other women stared at her. Or torn between the horror of entering the dining room alone and the ordeal of requesting a tray. It hurt to think of her mother: Ruby wished the raiders would come back, take her mind off things.

★   ★   ★

At night, Ruby slept in the boiler room with the other residents of the house. There was Kit and Daisy Mae, and Linda, knitting something fluffy and orange, and Stephen, who had one leg shorter than the other and was a pacifist and a vegetarian and who snored, and Jorge, a Spanish exile, who smoked little black cigars, and Jorge's girlfriend, Panda, who always came down to the boiler room wearing a royal-blue silk robe, whatever the time of day. The nights were a symphony of clicking knitting needles, Jorge cursing in Spanish, and Stephen's snores. And the bombs and the ack-ack guns, the shrieks and whines and whirrs and thumps and crumps that they became intimate with, as if they had known them for years, so that soon they could tell the swoosh of a high-explosive bomb from a parachute mine.

One evening, an odd experience. The siren had sounded and Ruby was gathering together book, Thermos, notepad and blanket, when the house filled with an eerie light, and something — some force — whipped through the air. As if the air itself had been seized and shaken. Then the tension relaxed and she made her way downstairs, sickened, frightened, as if she had seen something from another world.

And then, going to work.

Different each day, now, and no more complaints about crowded carriages on the Tube because that was the least of it. Sometimes there was a train; when there wasn't, she caught a bus, hitched a lift. The buses were a challenge — unmarked, because telling you where they were going might help invaders trying to find their way to Whitehall or wherever, and then teetering round the edges of craters, squeezing between heaps of rubble or areas fenced off because of unexploded bombs. A lorry driver who gave her a lift from Brompton Road to Westminster Bridge told her that Buckingham Palace had been bombed the previous day, and she saw in her mind's eye a lone German plane, shooting up the Mall, aiming for all that gilt and mahogany and damask curtaining.

When there weren't any trains or lifts, she walked. Great swathes of them walked, all over London, migrations of typists and clerks and bank managers and postmen and shopgirls. The girls in their smart work coats and hats, the men armed with umbrellas and briefcases, stepping round the bomb craters, picking their way over the rubble, wading through the dead leaves that lay in the gutters, that this autumn were mixed with broken glass, their route dictated by fires, UXBs, fallen girders and railings.

The things she saw as she walked: a burned-out house, doors and windows gone, charcoaled window-frames like empty eyes circled with black kohl. A shelter that had received a direct hit — in the street outside, a child's pink, buttoned shoe. A fireman, face blackened, drifting off to sleep as he stood beside his engine: she gave him the sandwich she had meant to have for lunch. John Lewis's, in Oxford Street, a few days after the store had been hit by a bomb, the window dresser's mannequins strewn stiff-limbed and naked over what was left of the pavement, the arches and columns and empty interior reminding her of photographs of the ruins of the Colosseum in Rome.

It was the nights that did it, though. The nights that made the daytime seem not quite solid any more, the nights that stopped you being able to fix your mind properly on to anything. For endless nights without interruption, London was bombed. Sometimes, when she couldn't face Stephen's snoring and Panda in her blue robe, Ruby slept in her own bed in her own room. She pulled the blankets over her head, as if that could keep her safe from the bombs, and slept through the crashes and booms and thumps, and woke in the morning, blurred with sleep, fumbling for face flannel, toothbrush, clothes. The windowpanes in her flat had cracked and little pyramids of plaster dust had formed beneath the fissures that now showed in the ceiling. A few doors down, a crater had opened up in the back garden.

Ruby swept up the dust, taped up the windows. One evening, she was caught in a raid walking home and spent the night in a public shelter. Puddles glistened on the floor because it had rained that day. Women sat on the benches, babies on their knees. That night, the babies wailed and the mothers soothed — next time, Ruby thought, she'd take her chance with the bombs. The following day, a Friday, she caught the train to Andover after work to visit her mother and slept for twelve hours.

You got used to it. That was the funny thing. The wail of the siren, the daily challenge of making your way to work, became routine, almost mundane. You thought more about your laddered stockings than the possibility of sudden death.

And then, one day, Ruby arrived at the office to find that the roof was holed and rain was pouring through the yawning gaps, stewing the dust and rubble to a beige porridge. The rooms were littered with broken glass and upturned chairs and desks. Blinds and curtains, torn from their fastenings, flopped like dirty dishcloths. Filing cabinets, emptied by the blast, had strewn their contents over the floor. A janitor wandered through the heaps, looking dazed. A woman righted a pot plant, blew plaster-dust from files.

Ruby began to gather up scattered pieces of paper. The ledger cards, hundreds of them, had to be arranged in alphabetical order. The requisition notes and the flimsy carbon copies of letters and notes of telephone calls had to be sorted by date and by subject. Splinters of broken glass sparkled inside every file. She opened them up, took out their contents, tapped them over a wastepaper basket.

Cold and rain oozed through the empty window-panes. They worked in their coats and scarves, Ruby wore sheepskin ankle boots. There was no electricity and no water, so no tea trolley, no canteen, and the lavatories didn't flush. At two in the afternoon, she escaped with some colleagues to a café for lunch.

Except for requests to pass the salt or cadge an aspirin, they were all too tired to speak. By four o'clock, the furniture had been set right, wiped and dusted, and the files put back in the cabinets. Ruby noticed the hundreds of tiny cuts and scratches on her hands, the legacy of the glass splinters.

Arriving home that evening, she lay on her bed, too tired to eat, too tired to move. Too tired to phone Lewis, too tired to boil a kettle to fill a hot-water bottle to warm herself up. Ruby Chance, she thought, who had once believed herself *chic*, lying on a bed in wet, dirty coat and boots, with laddered stockings and plaster dust in her hair.

There was a knock on the door. Jorge, wanting to borrow matches again, Ruby thought, and ignored it.

Another knock, a hard rat-tat-tat-tat. An insistent, official tone.

Ruby slid off the bed, opened the door. Two policemen were standing outside.

'Miss Chance? Miss Ruby Chance?' said the older one. 'I'm afraid I've some bad news for you.'

★ ★ ★

Her mother had died suddenly of a heart attack. Ruby got to know the horror of unexpected death, the way you kept forgetting it for a second or two and then remembered and had to get used to it all over again.

Yet her mother's death should not have been unexpected. Etta Chance had had a weak heart for years, and the shocks and displacements of the past months must have strained it to breaking point. *Breaking point*, thought Ruby, as, in the hotel in Andover, she sorted through her mother's belongings. Her mother's heart had been broken years ago, when Nicholas Chance had walked away from her.

All the dreadful things one had to do after the death

458

of a close relative: the only compensation was that it kept you busy. She packed up her mother's clothing to give to the WVS, the hand-knitted sweaters and cardigans, the darned stockings and gloves, the shoes that had been resoled so many times. All her mother's belongings — all Etta Chance had possessed in the world — fitted into one wardrobe and one chest of drawers. A postcard, sent by Ruby herself, years ago, from Cornwall. A handful of photographs, a pair of baby shoes. Letters from her father, tied with a pink ribbon. Inside the bottom drawer, a stack of magazines, carefully preserved, each one containing a short story written by Ruby herself.

They had come to appreciate each other, she and her mother. If their relationship had never been easy — they had been two such different people — they had learned to enjoy each other's company and had respected each other's good qualities. Yet, oh, the smallness of her mother's treats, the unremitting hardness of her life!

Ruby paid Mrs Weston's bill, visited the doctor to obtain the death certificate, arranged the funeral. Swallowed down her rage that her mother, who had asked so little of life, had spent her last months in a strange room in an unfamiliar town. Swallowed down her anger that the funeral could not take place in the church her mother had attended for years. *Don't you know there's a war on?* she reminded herself sourly.

Mrs Weston, with a tight little smile, offered to attend the funeral. 'Thank you, but that won't be necessary,' said Ruby, with an equally small smile. On the day, having gone far too early to the church, she wondered whether she should have accepted Mrs Weston's offer. Perhaps no one would come. Perhaps she would be the only mourner.

But then they began to arrive, in dribs and drabs, from the railway station, in their best blacks and funeral hats. Mrs Sykes from the boarding house and the vicar from Eastbourne and a sprinkling of old friends from the Eastbourne congregation.

But no Aunt Maude, no Hannah. Nor the person for whom, against all reason, she kept looking, hoping to see him striding into the churchyard, wearing his army greatcoat, the brass buttons glinting in the autumn sunlight. No *family*.

And then she glimpsed them, Sara and Isabel, dashing up the road from the station. A flurry of hugs and kisses and elegant hats and veils, and voices saying the right things, the things she needed to hear. And then, to her astonishment, at the last minute, when they were all in the church and the service was about to begin, Richard Finborough arrived.

Her foster family. The comfort of friends, she thought, and began to cry as the organist played the opening chords of the hymn.

★　★　★

Richard tried to think about poor Etta Chance, but his gaze kept drifting to Isabel, standing in the front pew, next to Ruby. Then to Sara, and then back to Isabel again.

He had to drive back to London as soon as the service was over. He kissed Ruby and offered her his condolences and then, because she looked so small and lost, gave her a big hug and said that if there was anything she needed . . .

Then he found himself face to face with his estranged wife and daughter. He told Sara that she was looking well, and Sara said, 'You, too, Dad,' and then she walked away to Ruby and together they looked at the floral tributes.

It hurt him that she had walked away.

He found himself alone with Isabel, standing a little apart from the others, in the dark shade of a yew.

He said, 'That day I came to see you — '

'You were wrong, Richard. You were wrong about me and Blaze. There was never anything between us, and there never will be.'

'Yes. I'm sorry. Made a fool of myself.'

He hung his head a little, then she touched his arm and said, more kindly, 'It was good of you to come today, Richard. You must be very busy. It means a lot to Ruby.'

He said, 'I've been thinking about poor old Nick,' and, during the silence, he found himself very aware of her — the curl of her hair beneath her black hat, the glitter of an opal eye beneath the mesh of her veil.

He said, 'I have to go,' kissed her cheek, put his hat back on and walked to the car.

★ ★ ★

Shortly after the beginning of the Blitz, Mrs Carrington had gone to stay with a friend in Harrogate. Gladys, the maid, had also left, to live with her sister in Wales, so now Edward had the flat to himself.

He and Sara met up for a drink every now and then. One evening, Edward met her outside the British Restaurant in St Pancras in which she had been working since Big Frank had closed up the café to rejoin the Merchant Navy. Tonight, she was wearing a dress of a soft blue-green colour, the same shade as her eyes, and a grey, square-shouldered jacket. She wore no hat and her hair fell loose to her shoulders in red-gold curls.

She kissed his cheek. He said, as they walked along the road, 'You look beautiful, Sara.'

She glanced down at herself and laughed. 'That's very sweet of you, darling, but I don't, at all. I'm a fright, I know. I've hardly had time to comb my hair today. There's a UXB in Euston Road — a big one, someone said — and hundreds of people have been

461

evacuated and they all came to us for lunch. And I'm so sorry, but I can't go for a drink tonight. One of the girls has a birthday, and I promised her I'd have supper with her. Do you mind awfully?'

'No, no, it's fine,' he said quickly. And then, to hide his disappointment, 'I brought you a present.' He took a small package out of his pocket and gave it to her.

'Hairgrips!' she cried. 'Oh Edward, you are wonderful. Where did you find them?'

'That little chemist in Pimlico Road. I was passing and there was a notice up saying they had hairgrips and I remembered you said you were short.'

'Down to my last three. Thank you so much.' Peering into a shop window, she began, with deft movements of her hands, to pin up her hair.

They walked on. 'I had a letter from Anton,' she said. 'How is he?'

'He seems well. He says the boarding house is quite cold but the Irish Sea is even colder.'

'He's been sea-bathing?' said Edward, surprised.

'On their bit of beach.' She beamed. 'He's like me — he loves to swim. He says you can see the horizon through the barbed wire. And he went to a concert — some of the other internees have made up a string quartet. And he's giving a series of lectures on architecture.'

Edward said, 'Sounds more like a holiday camp than a prison,' and she went very quiet and walked more quickly, looking ahead of her.

He felt himself redden. 'I didn't mean — I'm sorry, Sara, that came out all wrong.'

She said softly, 'He hates it. He doesn't say so but I can tell he does. Can you imagine what it's like, always having to think before you speak, having limits set on where you can go, what you can do? Anton's lived like that for years and years. Once, he told me that it made him feel less than a person.'

462

'I'm sorry,' he said again. 'Stupid of me. I only meant — well, at least he's safe. At least they're not mistreating him.'

'Yes.' She bit her lip, then she sighed. 'I shouldn't be so touchy — I know you didn't mean to be unkind. I'm just a little tired, that's why I'm so snappy. It's so good to talk to someone who knows him, who cares about him.' She gave a rueful smile. '*He* worries about *me*, you know.'

As if on cue, the air-raid siren started up, its ululating wail cutting through the noise of the street. Soon, they heard the deep, vibrating rumble of the bombers. The air filled with the bells of the fire engines and the staccato bursts of anti-aircraft fire.

A louder, more concentrated rumbling. The sky was lit up by fires and, looking up, Edward saw the black, heavy shapes of the aircraft. He took her hand and they began to run. Then a strange sensation — an absence of sound that he seemed to *feel* — and, without forethought, he swept Sara into a doorway, sheltering her with his body. There was a deafening crash, and then shards of glass fell around them like frozen rain. He could smell brick dust and something foul — a sewer had been struck, he thought.

Sara was trembling. 'There, you're safe,' he murmured, and stroked her hair. His voice sounded muffled, his ears were ringing.

He heard her whisper, 'Are you all right, Edward?'

'Yes, I think so. You?'

'Yes.'

They drew apart. She was white-faced. A fog of dust greyed the air. They walked through a sea of rubble to the entrance to the Tube station, where they parted, and he watched her disappear into safety. It was only then that he put up his hand to the back of his head and discovered that it came away streaked with red. He must have been gashed

463

by the broken glass in the blast: until now, he had not felt the pain.

★ ★ ★

December 29, an ice-cold winter's night. After a lull over Christmas, the Luftwaffe returned, this time to bomb the City. The low growl of the bombers overhead, then an eerie white light and balls of greenish-white flame as incendiaries fell on houses, offices, factories, churches. Whipped up by the wind, the fires soon burned out of control. Sheets of flame soared from warehouses storing paint and polish, and then swept through the narrow alleyways and cramped courtyards. The heat became so intense buildings burst into flames spontaneously.

At St Paul's Cathedral, incendiaries lodged in the roofs and parapets. Teams of fire-fighters — members of the Royal Institute of British Architects, who understood the construction of the cathedral — put out the fires with buckets of sand and stirrup pumps. Then, from the dome above, a glow of light. An incendiary had lodged in the dome's outer shell. Burning lead dripped from the roof: the entire great structure of the dome, the symbol of London's survival in the Blitz, was threatened. Then a miracle: as a firewatcher prepared to crawl precariously along the timbers of the dome with a stirrup pump, the incendiary burned through the wood and fell harmlessly outwards to the Stone Gallery.

The next day, the air was still made of ice, but, as you neared the City, you felt the heat. Philip, who had stayed in London overnight, had to go, felt drawn by it. Fires still burned, much smaller now. Ropes cordoned areas off and the remains of walls, like blackened teeth, jutted from the rubble.

The tea-packing factory was in Moorgate. Or, *had been* in Moorgate. Moorgate was now a wasteland of blackened timbers and scorched bricks, and civil defence workers and firemen, searching through the wreckage for whatever remained of the dead. Philip passed the remains of a bombed-out shelter that had entombed the people who had sought refuge inside it. When you breathed in the air it felt gritty. Philip wondered what he was breathing in — ashes, ashes of what?

Among the workers and onlookers who drifted, dazed, through the wreckage, he caught sight of a familiar figure. His father, bulky and square-shouldered in his heavy overcoat. Philip wondered whether to walk away.

He crossed the road. 'Bit of a blinder, Dad.'

Seeing him, Richard glowered.

'How bad is it?'

Richard spread out his hands. 'The factory's gone. They wouldn't let me near enough to see, but they told me nothing's left.' His gaze jerked, settling fleetingly on a heap of rubble, then a fire engine. He looked shocked, tired, old. 'It was only a building. No one was inside, thank God.'

'Makes your throat dry, doesn't it? How about a drink, Dad?'

'Haven't time.'

Philip felt a familiar flicker of anger. *Unforgiving old bastard.*

Then Richard said, 'Too much to do. Paperwork, you know.'

Which was the nearest, Philip realised, his father was going to come to an olive branch. He asked, 'Where are you heading?'

'My club.'

'I'm meeting someone in the American Bar at twelve. We may as well walk together.'

Walking to the Savoy, Philip steered the conversation, kept it safe, factual, unprovoking. Business and the

465

navy, filling in the distance between them in a civilised way until they reached the Strand.

Outside the hotel, Philip was about to take his leave when his father said suddenly, 'It was the beginning, that factory.'

'You can start up again, once all this is over.'

Richard shook his head. 'No point. You were right, I should have sold it years ago. It was an anachronism. But I was fond of it. Sentimental, I suppose — sentiment should have no place in business. But John Temple and I set it up. That was before I bought the button workshop. And to disappear, just like that, overnight . . . ' He seemed to give himself a shake. 'You'd better go. You'll be late for your appointment.'

Philip said quickly, before he could have second thoughts, 'You should come and see us. We're living in Hampshire now, but Elaine and I come up to London quite often.'

'I don't think — ' Richard began haughtily.

Philip made for the entrance of the Savoy. Looking back at his father, he said, 'I have a son now, Dad. Rufus was born three weeks ago. Wouldn't you like to see your grandson?' He caught a glimpse of something — pride? longing? — in his father's eyes. He added, 'Rufus is a Finborough, no doubt about it. Red-haired and bad-tempered, just like us.'

★ ★ ★

Robert, Ted and Stanley stayed with Blaze and Angus for a week in the New Year, allowing Isabel to visit Philip and Elaine in Hampshire, to help with Jennifer and the new baby.

She had three grandchildren now. David, the eldest, she was able to see least often; it saddened her that contact had been made more difficult by the war. She did her best to maintain a relationship through correspondence with Caroline Vernon, and hoped that Caroline would agree to bring David to England in the summer, to stay at Porthglas.

Isabel's granddaughter, Jenny, was a bright, uncomplicated little thing, fair, like Elaine, and sweet-tempered. As for Rufus, the newest addition to the family, he seemed strong and healthy. His howls, when he woke to be fed at night, threatened to raise the rafters of the damp, old cottage Philip had rented for his family to escape the Blitz.

Isabel's relationship with Elaine had not, at first, been easy. Too much past conflict, too many jealousies simmering just beneath the surface. When, once, Elaine had begun to speak of the past, Isabel had cut her off. 'I don't wish to talk about it,' she had said crisply, and Elaine had not raised the subject again. It was easier to talk about the children. They could talk for hours about the children, were both endlessly amused and absorbed and engaged by them. Isabel recognised that Elaine was a good mother, attentive but not fussy, sensitive but not over-anxious. More reluctantly, she acknowledged to herself that Elaine was also a good wife to Philip, teasing him out of his moodiness yet giving him the affection he needed.

It had at first required a huge effort on Isabel's part simply to tolerate being in the same room as Elaine. She had persisted because she had known that she must, that if she did not come to terms with her daughter-in-law she would lose both her son and her grandchildren. And, over time, dislike had been tempered by respect for Elaine's good qualities. And even, sometimes, by the beginnings of affection.

Returning from a visit to London, Philip had told them about the destruction of the factory. Isabel remembered the afternoon, not long after they had married, when Richard had showed her round Finborough's Quality Teas. The clean, fresh smell of the tea, the rows of women and girls in their long, high-collared dresses and aprons, pasting labels on to packets.

After taking her leave of Philip and Elaine and the grandchildren, Isabel endured a slow, uncomfortable train journey to London. London shocked her. You could read about the Blitz, you could see the photographs in the newspapers, hear the news on the wireless, but the reality of it, as the train clanked and stopped and started through suburbs and into the heart of the city, was devastating. She had always been a tidy person, she hated to see everything so utterly in the wrong place.

It was six o'clock, so she went straight to Hampstead. Richard wasn't home yet, but Isabel bore the stares of the housemaid with cool equanimity and waited in the drawing room with a tray of tea. Odd to be once more in the house that had been her home for more than a quarter of a century. She noticed the things that were not quite right: dust in corners, a lack of care in the arrangement of furniture and ornaments, the place no longer graceful or at its best.

Hearing Richard come into the house, Isabel rose from the chair and went to the window. As he entered the room, she said quickly, 'It's all right, I'm not staying. I only wanted to tell you how sorry I was about the factory. Philip told me and I thought of writing, but that seemed cowardly.'

A heartbeat's pause, then he said, 'Good of you.'

'Can anything be salvaged?'

'Nothing, nothing at all. It's hard enough even to tell where it was.'

'I'm so sorry, Richard.'

He shrugged. 'Financially, it wasn't important. It's only . . . '

'Yes,' she said gently. 'Yes, I know.'

He went to the sideboard. 'Drink?'

'Thank you.'

He poured her a sherry. She said, 'How are you, Richard?'

'I'm fine.'

'You look tired.'

He ran his hand over his face. 'We were working twenty-four hours a day during the Battle of Britain, making oil-filter casings for Hurricanes. And then, since the bombing started, it's been difficult, of course. Keeping up production in the air raids, especially since we lost some of our best men into the Territorials right at the beginning.' He splashed whisky into a glass, frowning. 'The funny thing is, I don't mind. Not really. To be honest, I've been enjoying my work more than I have for years. There's a point to it all again, something worth making an effort for.'

She murmured, 'You always have liked to be in the thick of things.'

'Yes. I like a challenge. I'm better when my back's up against the wall. I'm better when I've something to pit myself against, when there's something worth fighting for.'

She felt his eyes on her; she looked away. 'And I've always preferred tranquillity. We never were well-suited, were we, Richard?'

'Rot,' he said calmly. 'You're a fighter, like me. The only difference between us is you don't make so much noise about it.'

A pause, in which neither of them spoke, and then Richard said, 'Cornwall must suit you. You look well, Isabel.'

'I am, thank you. I've had a lovely week with Philip and Elaine and the babies.'

'I saw Philip. He told me he had a son.'

'Yes, Rufus, such a dear. He looks just like Philip did when he was a baby. It was rather unsettling — and very touching.' She put down her empty glass. 'My train . . .'

469

'Have dinner with me, Isabel, for God's sake.' His voice was quick and rough. 'You can't believe how pleasant it is to talk to someone *familiar*. Someone I don't have to explain things to.'

'Yes, of course,' she said. 'If you like.'

'Good.' He gave a short laugh. 'You may regret your decision. Mrs Rogers isn't a patch on Mrs Finch.'

'What happened to Mrs Finch?'

'Retired. Gone to live with her sister in Suffolk. I think she missed you. Damned agency can't get the staff these days — none of these girls they send me lasts more than a month or two. More fun in the WAAF, better pay in the factories.'

Isabel gave her coat and hat to the maid, washed her hands and checked her face in the bathroom and then went to the kitchen. It seemed cavernous, untidy — again, so many things in the wrong place, she had to bite her lip to stop herself pointing them out. Saucepan lids rattled, there was a lot of steam and a cookbook opened on the table.

Mrs Rogers was a gaunt, high-coloured woman in her mid-twenties. Her husband was in the army, she explained to Isabel, but a private's pay was barely enough to live on, so she did for Mr Finborough in the evenings while her mother kept an eye on the twins.

'There won't be enough potatoes,' Mrs Rogers said, harassed. 'I only peeled for one. I make stews and meat loafs at home, but Mrs Wilson at the agency said stews won't do for Mr Finborough. I've never followed a recipe before, I always cooked the same things my mother cooked.'

'Mr Finborough will be delighted with whatever you put in front of him,' said Isabel firmly. 'He's not fussy about food. And I don't want any potatoes, thank you. I have to think of my figure.'

When she went back to the drawing room, Richard had fallen asleep in the armchair. Isabel took the glass out of his hand and put it on the side table.

At the sound of the dinner gong, he stirred. 'Do you mind if I don't dress for dinner?' he asked. 'I've rather let things slip, since . . .'

'Do you imagine I put on an evening gown and my jewels whenever I sit down for supper with my evacuees?'

'No.' He grinned. 'Though I rather like to think of you doing so.'

Over the soup, he said, 'I keep thinking about the first fire. Do you remember? It was at the time we met. John Temple telegraphed me in Lynton. I knew I should go back to London straight away, but I went to see you instead.'

'We quarrelled, didn't we?'

'I'm afraid so. I almost drove away, left for good.'

'Do you wish that you had?'

A pause; he put down his spoon. 'Sometimes, after you left, yes. Sometimes I wished I'd never met you. When you told me about that man, Broughton, I thought that was why you'd married me. Because you'd had no option.'

'No, Richard.'

'There's some truth in it, though, isn't there?'

She thought hard. It had never been so important, she sensed, to tease out the truth. 'I didn't love you the day I agreed to marry you.' She saw his expression freeze, but she persevered. 'Or I didn't think I did. Though I was attracted to you. But I began to love you very soon after that. It's hard to say exactly when — these things aren't always obvious, are they, like a light bulb switched on.'

'I loved you the first time I saw you.'

She sighed. 'I was *bruised*, Richard. I didn't *want* to love anyone else, I didn't *intend* to love anyone else. To begin with, I resented you pushing your way into my life. I'd become used to being on my own. I married you

471

because I began to see that I might have a future again. And it was a long time since I'd thought that.'

'Why didn't you tell me about Broughton and the child before, Isabel? Why didn't you tell me back then, in Lynton?'

'If I had, what would you have done?'

'I don't know. I honestly don't know.'

'Would it have made you think differently of me?'

'Perhaps,' he acknowledged.

The maid cleared the first course, served the second. Richard said, 'You can go home, Doreen. And tell Mrs Rogers she may go home as well.'

When they were alone again, he said, his voice low, 'I wanted you above all reason, Isabel. It wasn't *rational*, what happened back then. So it might not have made any difference at all.'

'At first, I wasn't sure whether I could trust you. I hadn't told anyone about Alfie or the baby, no one at all. And I suppose I'd become used to secrecy, to keeping things to myself. I was ashamed, of course, so ashamed. And then, once we were married, I couldn't tell you what had happened because I knew I should have told you before. And then, as time went on, it became impossible.'

Outside, the wail of the siren. Richard glanced at the blacked-out windows. 'All this gives one a different perspective, don't you think?'

War and babies, she thought. Beginnings and endings. 'That's why I came here. I didn't like to think of you on your own, after you'd lost the factory. I don't suppose there are many people left who'd realise what it meant to you.'

'No,' he said. 'No one but you.'

In the distance, the thunder of the bombardment. She looked up at Richard. 'What do you do when . . . ?'

'Nothing, usually. If they're overhead, I might go under the stairs. If you'd prefer to — '

'No.'

He smiled. 'I remember, when I first brought you to London, you wondered whether my real motive was to persuade you to become my mistress.'

She too smiled, remembering. 'I imagined myself in scarlet satin and lace, in a love nest.'

'A love nest — good God.' A roar of laughter.

She said, 'We quarrelled about that too, didn't we?'

'We were in a restaurant — '

'Freddie McCrory came in.'

'Yes. I'd ordered *crêpes au citron*. But we didn't eat it.'

'No,' she said. 'We didn't.' She paused. 'I tried to tell you that night about my daughter, Richard. But, in the end, I couldn't. I didn't want to lose you.'

A louder whine, then a crash. Isabel said, 'When I left you, I tried to find her.'

'The child?'

'Yes.'

'And did you?'

She shook her head. 'The family had moved away — oh, decades ago.'

There was a loud explosion. The windows rattled and the cutlery jumped on the table. Richard put down his napkin. 'Perhaps,' he said, 'we should take shelter.'

Inside the cupboard under the stairs, mementoes of childhood — Sara's ice skates, Theo's fishing rod, a jumble of Wellington boots. To Isabel, sitting in the cramped darkness, it felt as if the German bombers were overhead, their missiles aimed deliberately at the Finboroughs' house in Hampstead.

'Is it always like this?' she asked Richard.

'Quite often, yes.'

'How do you bear it?'

'I've been through worse. Sometimes, when I'm tired and it starts up, I catch myself thinking I'm back in the trenches. Find myself looking round for the mud and rats.'

He put his hand on her shoulder, steadying her. She found herself pressing her lips together, trying to stop herself trembling — the bombs, his nearness.

'It'll be all right,' he said. 'They sound nearer than they are. They're probably ten miles away. And these stairs are very strong.'

A high-pitched, screeching noise made her turn in alarm and bury her head in his chest. He put his arms round her, murmuring comfort. His thumb stroked her neck. When she raised her head, she felt his lips brush against her forehead. Oh God, how I hate this, she thought. And, oh God, how I've missed this.

When, eventually, the intensity of the bombardment lessened and the all clear sounded, they drew apart. Richard opened the door and they stepped back into the hallway.

'I really should be getting on,' Isabel said, her voice a little unsteady. 'Daphne Mountjoy said I could stay with her.' She went to the coat-stand, fumbling for her things.

'*Stay*,' he said.

Her head jerked up. She was trembling again. 'Richard?'

'Please, Isabel, *stay*.'

'Yes,' she whispered. 'If you like.'

* * *

If the raiders returned that night, she did not hear them. She slept more deeply than she had done in a long time, curled up against Richard in bed, exhausted by the passion of their lovemaking. Sex had been quick, desperate, fumbling, almost painful in its intensity.

In the morning, waking, she felt a deep pleasure and relief in the nearness of him, in the touch of skin against skin after so long on her own. She lay still, not wishing to break the spell. She had forgotten the sheer delight of physical love, the pleasure of deep intimacy with the man she loved. She had believed she had put passion behind her — what a fool she had been. She had become too used to solitude, had almost deceived herself into thinking she preferred it.

But eventually, glancing at the clock, she rose, went to the bathroom, bathed and dressed. It was still dark and the house was very cold. When she returned to the bedroom, Richard was in his dressing room. She could hear him singing to himself as he shaved.

Emerging, he kissed her. 'You're up early. I thought you'd have a lie-in.'

'I ought to get to the station. You know what the trains are like these days.'

He was tying his tie. He frowned. 'The station?'

'I'd rather go early and queue. I don't want to find myself stuck in the middle of nowhere overnight.'

'I assumed you'd stay here. After last night.'

'Darling, I'd love to.' She kissed him. 'But I must get back home. I'm a day late as it is.'

'Home . . . ' he repeated.

She said quickly, 'Porthglas, I meant.'

'There's no need to go back to Porthglas. If you're worried about the blasted air raids, I'll have a shelter put in.'

'It's not that,' she said, as she began to fold clothes and put them in her case. 'It's the boys.'

'Philip and Theo?'

'No, no, my evacuees. It's been hard enough finding someone to take care of them for only a week. I can't leave them for any longer.'

She pressed down the clasps of the case; when she looked up at him, his expression had become colder.

'Someone else could look after them, surely?'

'No, I don't think so.' She looked round for the

jewellery she had taken off the previous night. 'I took them in because no one else wanted them. Not many people will take in three brothers.'

'I want you to stay, Isabel. I want you to come back to me.'

She could see that he was growing angry. She had forgotten his anger, what a force it was. She said, her voice level, 'They're children, Richard — not, perhaps, particularly attractive or appealing children, but they are children and not machines. I can't just shunt them off to someone else, even if that someone else could be found, which I seriously doubt. And I can't bring them here because they wouldn't be safe. It was weeks before Stanley would say a word and I'm afraid he might become permanently mute if he were to be uprooted all over again.' Richard began to speak: she interrupted him, 'Children are being sent from pillar to post all over the country. Everyone seems to think it's fine because they're just children, and children are adaptable, aren't they, but actually I don't think it's fine at all.'

He said furiously, 'I can't believe that you are refusing to come home because of *evacuees*.'

'No,' she said. 'I don't suppose you can.' She could feel her drowsy happiness chilling, drying up, replaced by disappointment and weariness.

Almost, knowing his inability, often, to listen, it did not seem worth the effort of explaining, but she tried. 'They are — children are — what I'm good at. When we brought up our own children I made certain compromises. Sending Philip and Theo to boarding school — that would not have been my choice. Sara's coming out, when I knew it would never suit her, when I knew she felt as I did about that sort of thing — I would not have chosen that either. When I see Sara now, I know that I was right. I should have followed my instincts. I need to follow them now.'

He said coldly, 'I'm sorry you felt you had to keep

your true feelings from me. Still, you seem to have done a great deal of that during the time we were together.'

'Richard, please . . . ' She said tiredly, 'I've made a life for myself. What did you expect me to do when we separated? Shut myself away, sit and mope, do nothing, see no one? And then come back to you as soon as it suited you? I can't just drop my obligations, even if I wanted to. There are the boys, as I've explained, and there's the garden and the WVS — I can't just walk away from them.'

'I hardly think,' he said sarcastically 'that the war effort will grind to a halt without you. And I don't doubt that the WVS would be able find you something to do in London.'

'But that's my point!' she cried, with exasperation. 'I don't *want* someone else to find me something to do! This is what I have *chosen* to do — this is what I have made for myself. My contribution may not seem much to you, but I'm proud of it. *That's* what I'm trying to tell you!'

'So you prefer to live as you do now?'

'Sometimes,' she said levelly. 'Not all the time.'

'And you insist on returning to Cornwall?'

'Yes, I must go. But you need not infer — '

'I'll call you a taxi.'

'Richard,' she said, but he had already gone downstairs.

★   ★   ★

Reaching Paddington Station, she wondered whether she had done the right thing. Too many partings, she thought. They were not like those Golden Wedding couples one sometimes saw in the local papers, who boasted of never having been apart for a single night. They had been parted so often, she and Richard — by his work, by wars, by their differences.

477

As the train pulled away from the platform, she wanted to run out of the carriage, to find him and plead with him, to tell him that she had made a mistake. But she remained where she was, staring out of the window as the engine gathered speed and the fragments of the shattered city passed her, remembering the events of the night, wondering what it had meant, whether it had meant anything at all.

Yet something unexpected: when, eventually, after a dreadful journey that she had to break overnight in Exeter, she reached the cottage, a letter from Richard was waiting for her.

I was too hasty this morning, perhaps. I understand that you prefer to stay in Cornwall — you will be safer there, Isabel. Because of my work and the Home Guard, I am rarely at home anyway, so there would be little point in your returning to London at present.

He had signed the letter, 'With love, Richard'.

15

Ruby's section was evacuated to a house in the countryside. Greenhayes Hall was in chilly Cambridgeshire. Not all that far away were the East Anglian airbases. Often, hearing the drone of engines, the workers looked up and saw formations of planes fanning out across the sky.

If Ruby had been asked to find the one word that would sum up her war, that word would have been 'cold'. She was always cold. There seemed only to be a brief couple of months in the middle of the year in which she was not cold. Greenhayes Hall was built on a shallow rise across which an east wind always seemed to be blowing. Ruby and two other girls from the office shared a bedroom in the attic. On the coldest mornings, their breath clouded the air, and their stockings, washed out the previous night, froze to brownish pennants on the bath rail. To save fuel, there was only one small fire lit at the far end of the room in which Ruby and a dozen other women worked. They built barriers of files round their desks to keep off the draughts. If she could have worn gloves while she typed, Ruby would have. As it was, she kept them on most of the time, only whipping them off for a brief, icy tussle with the keyboard. The food served at meal-times was awful: bread and margarine and sausagemeat and carrots, so many carrots she began to hate them, cooked by a disgruntled woman who had once catered for the family who owned the house.

And oh, the lack of privacy. The ever-present other girls, chattering and bitching and borrowing — or swiping — your last stub of lipstick, your hairpins, your Tampax, your headache tablets, your comb. The shriek of conversation at the breakfast table and the smell of cheap perfume got from some shady dealer in a pub. The hot, animal smell of woollens drying on the fireguard and the stockings and knickers always looped over pieces of string run up in the bathroom — and the bathroom was the one place in the house where you could be alone, and that only until someone hammered on the door, telling you it was freezing outside and to get a move on. And then, some song that some girl had fallen in love to, blasting out over and over again on the gramophone.

In the coldest months, they drew up a rota to get up at night to turn on the taps and flush the lavatories, because otherwise the pipes burst. Dressed in pyjamas, jersey, dressing gown and coat, clutching a candle, Ruby roamed the darkened house from one bathroom to another. Some of the other girls disliked their turn on the rota because, in the big, old house, they were afraid of ghosts. In the bleak months after her mother died, when she couldn't seem to write any more, Ruby would have welcomed the distraction of a ghost. Once, plodding silently through the old, wood-panelled rooms and having forgotten her glasses, Ruby saw a greyish shape form in the distance — but it was only Mr Spencer from accounts, and, once they had both got over their fright, they shared the biscuits his wife had sent him.

When, eventually, she became able to write again, she set to work on a different sort of book. The mainstream publishers had cut their lists drastically because of the shortage of paper, and dozens of small publishers had sprung up to take advantage of a gap in the market that had not been there before — the thousands of bored young men spirited away from factories, farms and building sites to moulder in army camps or on convoy ships or in submarines, men who, denied the company of women — and sometimes also the solace of alcohol

— needed distraction. The stories these publishers demanded were short, fast-moving and salacious, with a tang of the war, the times. The novels were printed on flimsy yellow paper and covered with lurid pictures of fast cars and faster women, and had titles like *Death in Convoy* or *The Deadly Redhead*. Not, Ruby wrote to Theo, the sort of fiction she could ~~have~~ of shown to her mother.

But still, the ghosts, the girls, the food, the cold . . . She had to escape.

She escaped to Nineveh for the food, had to, even though she hated Aunt Maude and Hannah for not having come to the funeral. But there were her mother's bequests to deliver, a brooch for Hannah and a prayer-book for Maude, and besides, she found herself fantasising about the large hams studded with cloves on Nineveh's kitchen table, the smell of freshly baked bread and apple pies, and the boxes of Turkish delight.

At Nineveh, an explosion of noise from behind the farmyard. The dogs were yelping and the geese were honking and the hens fussing; from the group of people arguing in the distance, Ruby made out Hannah and two men, perspiring in their suits.

And Aunt Maude — but, Ruby noticed with a shock, a different, diminished Aunt Maude, who had lost weight and leaned heavily on her stick as she waved her fist at the two men.

'They're from the War Agricultural Committee,' Hannah whispered to Ruby. 'They want Mother to plough up the graveyard. Mother won't let them.'

'Graveyard?' asked Ruby.

Hannah pointed to the field behind the orchard. 'Where Mother buries the dogs — ' A yell from one of the committee men as a goose charged him, neck outstretched.

As the War Ag men left and Hannah helped Aunt Maude back into the house, Ruby followed the path

Hannah had indicated behind the farmyard, through the orchard, down the shallow slope of the island on which Nineveh was built. Halfway along the field boundary she found a garden of about twenty foot square, an odd little oasis among a sea of green wheatfields. All these years of visiting Nineveh, thought Ruby, and she had never known such a place existed. Narrow cinder paths wound between shrubs and geraniums. Dotted among the plants were stubby headstones, some marked with a name. Bonny . . . Malachi . . . Dido . . . The dank patch of ground had the rotting smell of drying river-beds, and even in the spring sunshine the conifers and laurels cast it into shade. Ruby shivered.

Yet the alchemy of war had altered even unchangeable Nineveh. The farm was tidier, licked into shape, hedges trimmed and ditches cleared and almost every inch of earth cultivated. A landgirl was emptying swill into the pig trough. Yet the greatest change was in Aunt Maude. She couldn't walk more than a short distance, her sight was failing and on her foot there were sores that refused to heal. Her mother had fallen out with the doctor, Hannah confided, and he no longer visited. She hadn't been to church for months, but sometimes the vicar called and they prayed together.

The fire had gone out of Maude Quinn. Exhausted by her confrontation with the War Ag men, she sat in the parlour, her bandaged foot raised on a stool, and accepted the prayer-book her sister had bequeathed to her with a nod and a grunt. Reduced, lame, felled at last, Maude was trapped in the parlour among the layers of Nineveh's past, the teacups and the sweet wrappings and the jars of buttons and pieces of string.

Whenever she could, Ruby escaped to London, prised herself into a crowded, unheated railway carriage, squeezed into the corridor between soldiers and their kitbags, crammed up against the stiff, scratchy khaki of their uniforms. Slogans — 'Is your journey really necessary?' — admonished her from the advertising hoardings. Well, yes, or I shall go mad. The train stopped in a siding, the soldiers cursed under their breath, rolled cigarettes, offered her a piece of gum. Reaching the city, she caught the Tube — and, oh, that familiar warm, dusty darkness! — or walked while searchlights sliced through the black, star-speckled sky, catching every now and then on the gleaming silver bubbles of the barrage balloons.

In the summer, she had a phone call from Theo to say that he had a few days' leave. They met up in London, her friends and Theo's friends, picking up the threads of conversation as if there had not been the months of her cold exile or his thousands of miles across the Atlantic. There was always some girl who attached herself to Theo — a small blonde cockney Waaf who operated barrage balloons, or an ex-deb who worked in a draughty country mansion like Ruby's. They piled into a show or a dance hall or squeezed into the Marquess of Granby in Fitzrovia, with the black-marketeers and the queers and the deserters.

They were always the last to leave, she and Theo. They'd find themselves still talking when everyone else had gone, even the Waaf and the deb, marooned among the empty glasses and the cigarette stubs while the landlord called closing time or the band packed up their instruments. She wanted to know what it was like, serving on a corvette, escorting the ships that brought the provisions, raw materials and oil that kept Britain from starving and enabled her to keep fighting the war. She wanted to know the names of the parts of his ship, what his duties were and what it felt like, out there, hiding in the vast empty darkness from the U-boats; whether it was for Theo as it was for her, people all the time, only a few feet of space you could call your own, hard to think.

'I try not to think about home, when I'm out there,' he said. 'I don't think about my family or my friends. Not even of you, Ruby, because if I did, I'd feel so bloody lonely.'

She liked the way he said, 'Not even of you, Ruby.' That 'even'. As though she was important to him.

★ ★ ★

In the February of 1941, Anton's status as an internee had been reduced from B to C. The following month, to Sara's immense joy, he was released from the internment camp on the Isle of Man on condition that he join the Pioneer Corps.

They had a week together before he was required to report to an army camp in Devon. Philip and Elaine lent them their Hampshire cottage. They walked, talked, made love, got to know each other again. Sara saw how his seven months in the camp had changed Anton — he was quieter, there was a little more sadness in his eyes.

When the week was over, they took the train to Ilfracombe. He would not let her see him to the base; instead, they said their farewells in the guesthouse. Then Anton left for the camp in which he would spend the next six weeks and Sara went on to Cornwall, to spend a week with her mother.

Then Sara returned to London and went back to work at the British Restaurant, peeling potatoes and making pastry. After he had completed his training, Anton was posted to Newbury. Refused permission, because he was an enemy alien, to join a fighting regiment, his work was mostly labouring, loading and unloading lorries, felling trees, clearing rubble from bombsites and repairing bomb-damaged ports and railways.

In the summer, in late June, when Anton had leave, they spent a long weekend in Hungerford, ten miles from Newbury. They stayed in a boarding house in a street off the High Street, where they slept in a room wallpapered with tiny pink and blue flowers. They spent a day walking on the downs. Lying in Anton's arms in a meadow with the wide blue sky above them, Sara felt at peace. They talked about the events of the previous months and about the past. When she tried to talk about the future, Anton changed the subject. He no longer believed in the future. Sara was afraid that he had lost faith in it.

In the afternoon, they went back to the guesthouse. Sara lay on the bed, an open book in front of her, dozing off every now and then; beside her, Anton slept. After a while, she left the room and went downstairs in search of a cup of tea.

She was passing the sitting room when she heard someone say, 'With the Russkies on our side now . . . '

She put her head round the door. Two RAF officers were sitting in armchairs to either side of the fireplace. One of them smiled at her.

'Anything I can do for you, beautiful?'

'I couldn't help overhearing,' she said. 'What did you say about the Russians?'

'Didn't you know? The Nazis invaded the Soviet Union this morning.' He flicked open a gold case. 'Like a ciggie, darling?'

'No, thanks. So the Soviet Union's on the same side as us now?'

'Looks like it. We're best buddies with Uncle Joe.' He smoothed his moustache. 'Fancy the pictures?'

'I don't think so.'

'Or I know a nice little pub . . . '

She smiled. 'It sounds lovely, but my husband might not like it.'

Groans of disappointment followed her as she hurried upstairs to wake Anton and tell him the news. Anton dashed out to buy a newspaper. For the first time since the fall of France the previous year, Britain and her Dominions were no longer fighting the Nazis alone, and for the first time in a very long time, Sara saw hope in Anton's eyes.

★　★　★

In the autumn, to her immense relief, Ruby left Greenhayes Hall after being seconded to a new position at the Ministry of Supply. Since the last, devastating air raid on the night of 10 May, the German bombers had not returned to London. A semblance of normality had returned to the streets, so that, if you disregarded the absence of cars on the roads, you could almost imagine yourself back in the pre-war capital.

Yet a closer look showed the gaps between the houses where a bomb had struck, the churches without spires and the heaps of old tiles and bricks on the bombsites. They had taken down the railings round the parks and the private gardens in the squares, so that the iron could be melted down and reused; the secret gardens the railings had once enclosed had now been turned into allotments. The people in the streets were shabbier because there were few new clothes to buy, and they walked burdened with string bags and baskets because the shops did not wrap goods any more.

Ruby found a room to rent in Ladbroke Grove. It had high ceilings and tall sash windows and was rather frayed round the edges but then, weren't they all, nowadays? She collected her boxes and pieces of furniture from the various places she had left them during her exile in the countryside and arranged them in her room.

Her new job involved visiting factories on Ministry of Supply contracts and finding out whether the work was being carried out efficiently and whether there were any problems in labour supply. When she saw that a factory in Salisbury was on her list of visits, she immediately thought of Claire Chance.

She would not make the same mistake as last time, though: she would not turn up on the doorstep unannounced. She wrote to the Moberly Road address; a few days later she received a reply, inviting her to call.

As Claire showed her indoors and took her coat to hang it on the hall stand, she said, 'Funny you should write. I've often thought I'd like to talk to you. You were always the only other person who could possibly know what it felt like.' She gave Ruby a searching look. 'You haven't heard from Nicky, have you? You didn't say in your letter, but I wondered . . .'

'No. I'm sorry.'

'It's all right.' Claire showed Ruby into the sitting room. 'I don't know what I'd do if he turned up now.' She offered Ruby a cigarette.

'No, thanks.'

'You don't mind if I do?' Claire flicked her lighter. 'I've met someone else, you see. He's good fun — works at the airbase at Boscombe Down. Not husband material, but then, that's not what I'm looking for. Sit down, won't you? I'll get us some tea.'

She returned a few minutes later with a tray of tea and biscuits. She said, 'I suppose my marriage to Nicky — if one can call it that — was enough to put me off the institution for life.' She drew on her cigarette, studying Ruby. There were questions in her eyes.

'My mother died a year ago,' Ruby explained.

'I'm sorry. Rotten for you.'

'And in her things, there were some letters from my father. He wrote to her when he was away in the war.'

'Have you read them?'

'Bits of them. I couldn't bear to read all of them.' She took a biscuit. 'When I was little, I thought my father was the most wonderful person in the world.'

'You were a daddy's girl.'

'Yes, I suppose I was. And then, when I found out about you, I despised him. And now, I can't seem to put the pieces of him together. They don't seem to match. I'd like to know what he was really like. It would be a way of finding him. That's why I wanted to talk to you.' She gave Claire a quick smile. 'There's not many other people left who remember him, you see.'

Claire frowned. Ruby said quickly, 'You can be honest. I'd like you to be honest. If he was, well, not a good person, then I'd like to know.'

'A good person . . . ' Claire blew out a stream of smoke, her eyes narrowed. 'If you look at it one way, he was a complete bastard. He cheated me in the worst possible way — and of course he cheated you and your mother too. But I'll tell you what I remember most about Nicky. He was always so *alive*. You were never bored when he was around.' She stubbed out her cigarette in the ashtray. 'Wait there a mo.' She rose and went out of the door. Ruby heard her running upstairs.

While Claire was gone, Ruby looked round the room. Paintings — rather good ones — on the walls; photographs in silver frames on the sideboard. A young man in RAF uniform, and a girl, dark and striking like her mother. Archie and Anne, she supposed. Her half-brother and half-sister.

Claire came back holding a large envelope. 'I can't count the times I've nearly burned these,' she said. 'But they're snapshots of the children too, so I hung on to them.'

Ruby looked through the photographs Claire handed to her. A portrait of her father with a younger, dazzlingly pretty Claire. Her father wearing a short-sleeved shirt, standing in a garden, smiling in the sunlight, holding a surprised-looking baby in a romper-suit. Anne, with ribbons in her hair, sitting on her father's knee while he buttoned her shoe. A snapshot taken at the seaside — a sandcastle, the two

488

children, and Nicholas wielding a spade.

Claire said, 'Nicky was a good father, I'll tell you that. If I was tired, he'd give them a bottle, change a nappy — an awful lot of men wouldn't dream of doing that. When I was a bit down after I had Anne, he looked after them for a few days while I went to stay with a friend. He had all sorts of plans for when they were older. He was going to teach Archie to play cricket, Anne was going to have ballet lessons, he was going to take them to see the White Horse of Uffingham. He loved the children. You can tell, can't you, from the photos? He didn't seem the sort of man who'd just *go*.' She laughed. 'Listen to me, what a sentimental fool.'

'Have you told Archie and Anne about Dad?'

Claire shook her head. 'Not everything, not yet. They know he left me. I'd like to tell them, but only with your agreement, of course. Secrets didn't do me much good, you see, and I'd hate Archie and Anne to find out by accident, somehow.'

A moment's thought. Then: 'OK, if you think it's best.'

'Maybe you'd like to meet them someday. It's up to you.'

She hadn't enough relations, Ruby thought, to turn down the addition of two more. 'Yes, I'd like that.'

'Thank you.' Claire stubbed out her cigarette. 'What about you? Have you told anyone?'

'Only Theo.'

'Boyfriend?'

'No, no, Theo's not my boyfriend. I haven't told my boyfriend about my father.'

They talked about their jobs for a while — Claire had gone back to teaching art — and then Ruby left and walked back to her digs in Castle Street.

She couldn't sleep that night. The train journey, the series of interviews she had carried out at the factory, her conversation with Claire, seemed to go round and round in her head.

I haven't told my boyfriend about my father. She'd hardly told Lewis anything about her father or her mother, and he'd never really asked. After her mother's death, it had been Theo and Sara she had talked to, not Lewis. And Lewis had told her very little about his own family — the necessary information about Theresa, nothing more. Families weren't the sort of thing they talked about. They talked about the war, the latest songs and plays. Why, she wondered, was that?

And then, *He didn't seem the sort of man who'd just go . . .*

★ ★ ★

Sara's latest visit to Vernon Court, in the summer, had been to celebrate David's fourth birthday. He had grown into a bright, sturdy little boy, with dark hair and round blackcurrant eyes like Gil's.

In the autumn, she received a letter from Gil, who was engaged in war work at a research laboratory near Bristol. The letter told her that Caroline Vernon had died suddenly, following an operation to remove a gallstone. Sara wrote back, offering her sympathy; she and Gil arranged to meet up in London to discuss David's future a few weeks later.

Gil was staying at the Savoy. He was in the foyer when she arrived at the hotel. Sara kissed him. 'I was so sorry about Caroline. It's hard to believe she's gone. You must miss her so much. How are you, Gil?'

'Oh, bearing up.' He looked forlorn. 'When I think of home, I always imagine Mother there, in the garden.'

'How's David?'

'He misses her terribly. Thank goodness for Nanny Duggan.'

'Yes, of course,' she said. 'I'd like to help — David

could come and stay with me for a while, I thought. It would give Nanny a break.'

'Oh, no, no, that won't be necessary.' He gave a little cough. 'Actually, I wanted to ask you something, Sara.'

'Anything, darling.'

'I wondered whether you'd agree to a divorce.'

She stared at him, surprised. 'But I thought you'd never consider divorce?'

'Mother wouldn't,' he said. 'But times have changed, and now that she's gone . . . ' He stopped, had another stab. 'The thing is, for quite some time now . . . ' Then, looking properly at her, he said, 'I want to get married, Sara. To someone else, I mean.'

'*Oh.*' She smiled. 'How marvellous for you, Gil.'

'I could, of course, sue for divorce on grounds of desertion, but it would be better all round if you gave your consent.'

'Yes, I see that. Of course I will.' She kissed his cheek. 'What's your fiancée called? Where did you meet her?'

'Her name's Janet Radbourne and she works at the lab. We've been collaborating on a project concerned with the pollination of fruit trees.' Another cough. 'Actually, she's here. Would you like to meet her?'

'I'd be delighted to.'

Gil dashed off to a reception room, returning a few moments later accompanied by a big-boned, strong-featured young woman whose thick, dark hair was cut in a pageboy bob. She was wearing a plain navy skirt and jacket with a white blouse underneath.

'Sara, this is my fiancée, Janet Radbourne. Janet, this is Sara.'

They shook hands. Then there was a brief, awkward conversation, and then Miss Radbourne took control and decided they should all have tea together.

Miss Radbourne poured the tea. 'After we've married,' she said, wielding the milk jug, 'we'll close up the house and bring David and Nanny over to England.'

491

Sara was shocked. 'Close up Vernon Court?'

'Yes, it's the most sensible thing to do.'

'But what about the garden?'

'I'm afraid the garden will have to look after itself now,' Gil said. 'Dickie Lynch has joined up — I suppose armies can always use brute strength.' He reached out to the cake stand.

'Better not have another, Gil,' advised Miss Radbourne. 'It may be dried egg, and that's so indigestible.'

Gil's hand retreated. 'Perhaps the scones . . . '

'Currants, dear, I'm afraid.' Miss Radbourne addressed herself to Sara. 'We plan to let out the house to a school or some other suitable organisation.'

Sara thought of children trampling Vernon Court's borders, cricket balls smashing through the old glass of the conservatory, and ivies and bindweeds straggling over the plants that Caroline had loved. But she said, 'Well, you know best, Gil.'

Two days later, she met Edward for their usual after-work drink. She told him about her conversation with Gil.

'I can hardly believe it,' she said. 'It'll mean that Anton and I will be able to get married at last.'

'You can't.'

His tone of voice, and his words, startled her; she stared at him. 'Well, not *now*. But when my divorce comes through.'

Edward closed his eyes and pressed the palms of his hands against his face.

'Darling,' she said, concerned. 'Are you all right? What is it?'

'Nothing.' He rose, went to the bar to fetch more drinks. When he came back, he was smiling. 'I'm very pleased for you, Sara.'

She squeezed his hand. 'Are you sure you're all right, Edward? You do look awfully tired.'

'Yes.' A short burst of laughter. 'Aren't we all? Work, you know. And Mother isn't easy.'

'I know, darling, I know.'

★ ★ ★

Ruby worked long hours that winter, travelling round the country, inspecting factories for the Ministry of Supply. At Christmas, she received a card from Claire Chance. Inside the card, a note. 'I've told Archie and Anne about you and your mother,' Claire had written. 'It was a bit tricky at first, but we've talked and they would both like to meet you.' They were intending to visit London for a few days in the New Year, when Archie had leave, Claire added. Perhaps they could have a meal together?

Ruby met her half-sister and -brother for the first time in the dining room of a hotel in Marylebone. The conversation, awkward at first as Nicholas Chance's children assessed each other, improved as the evening went on. Anne was vivacious and outspoken, like her mother, and seemed to regard the fact of her illegitimacy as a great joke — 'Frightfully romantic, don't you think, to be a lovechild? I feel like a character in a historical novel.' Archie minded more, thought Ruby. He said little at first; every now and then, she found her gaze drifting to him, searching for her father's features in his.

The following month, she received a note from Theo, telling her that he was in London for a few days' leave. They met in a bar on Shaftesbury Avenue. Theo introduced her to his friends. There was a girl called Nancy, an American journalist, who seemed to cling to Theo rather. Nancy's face was a narrow golden-skinned oval with just a dusting of freckles across the bridge of her thin, patrician nose.

They went on to supper in an Italian restaurant. Ruby

ended up at one end of the table, Theo at the other. Every now and then, Nancy, who was sitting next to Theo, would flick back her smooth fall of dark blonde hair with her hand, or lean forward, chin on fingers, to talk to him. Poor Theo, thought Ruby, the woman was almost in his soup. The man sitting next to Ruby, a sub-lieutenant on Theo's ship, engaged her in pleasant conversation, but as the meal went on she began to feel prickly and dissatisfied, and she was relieved when the last person finished their coffee and they all headed off to a nightclub in Piccadilly.

Gold gauze curtains, a dusty chandelier swinging overhead, and an RAF band playing 'Jealousy'. The dance floor a blur of khaki and airforce and navy blue, and the bright colours of the girls' frocks. Ruby danced with the sub-lieutenant and a Czech airman and a man from the Canadian fire service. Nancy always seemed to be dancing with Theo. So impolite of her, thought Ruby, monopolising him like that, when the rest of them hadn't seen him for ages. The sublieutenant became a bit too friendly and she had to give him the brush-off, and he ended up at the bar, drinking for comfort. Ruby hid in a dark corner to avoid him. It irked her that she had been so looking forward to this evening and now she didn't seem to be in the mood. She went through the litter of empty glasses on the table but there was nothing left to drink. She had drunk too much anyway: that was probably what was wrong with her.

It was late, a few couples were still circling the dance floor and the music was soft, sleepy and seductive. Nancy slid into the seat beside her. 'So — ' voice lowered, sisterly, conspiratorial — 'Theo Finborough. Rather gorgeous. What I want to know is why no girl has had the sense to snap him up. Is there a wife I don't know about?'

'No, Theo's never married.'

'He isn't queer, is he?'

'Of course not,' said Ruby coldly.

'You never know, honey. These cool, aloof types . . . '

'I don't think,' said Ruby, icy now, 'that Theo wants to be *snapped up*.'

'Oh, they all do, darling, they just don't realise it.' Nancy's elbow was balanced on the table, her chin on her fist as her eyes followed Theo. Her mouth curled in a smile. 'I think he's quite a heartbreaker. A little *distant*, perhaps, but I bet I can bring him out.'

'Theo *is* distant. He's always been distant. It's what he is.'

'I always like to have a project. Theo Finborough shall be my next project.' A quick glance at Ruby. 'I wouldn't be treading on any toes, would I?'

'Theo and me? No, of course not. We're just old friends.'

'How old?'

'I've known Theo since I was twelve.'

'How fascinating.' Nancy leaned towards her. 'What was he like when he was a boy? You must tell me all about it.'

Ruby said, 'Actually, you must excuse me, but I have to go to the bathroom,' and picked up her bag and left the table.

Heading for the powder room, she thought furiously: loathsome, conceited woman . . . *I bet I can bring him out . . . Theo Finborough shall be my next project* . . . The nerve of it! Peering at her reflection, nose to mirror because she never wore her glasses when she went out, she checked her face and did her hair. Three girls giggled in one corner of the powder room, and, from one of the cubicles, she heard the sound of weeping. Ruby knocked tentatively on the door and said, 'Hello? Are you all right?' and a watery voice came back:

'Yes. Fine.' Then a lot of nose-blowing.

She wondered whether she should just leave — but her evening jacket was on the back of a chair so she headed back to the dance hall. Now, the band was playing 'A Nightingale Sang in Berkeley Square'. The lyrics, nostalgic and overly familiar, ran through her head. Pausing at the entrance to the room, she let her gaze wander round until she found Theo, standing at the bar. Short-sighted or not, she could always pick him out — something about his stance, the way he moved, familiar yet always interesting, always fascinating to her. *I bet I can bring him out* . . . How dare that awful woman try to change Theo when he was just perfect as he was?

And a moment of realisation, of understanding, and she stepped back into the shadow of a curtain, as if she was afraid her thoughts might be written on her face, afraid that anyone — that he — might read them.

She was in love with Theo Finborough. She had been in love with him for a long time but had been too blind to see it. She fumbled in her bag for her glasses, put them on, watched him properly. Just seeing him gave her pleasure. She knew the sweep of his heavy black hair, the way he curled his mouth as he smiled or raised his straight black brows in disapproval. She knew the pent-up energy in his stance, the way he always seemed to be watching, waiting. She knew everything about him and yet so little about herself.

Then he turned, looked across the room and, catching sight of her, raised a hand. Ruby stuffed her glasses into her bag and hurried over to the table.

Theo reached it at much the same time as she did. 'Dance with me, Ruby.'

'Where's Nancy?'

'She's gone. She has to be up early next morning. She took a taxi back to her hotel. Come on, you haven't danced with me all evening.'

'I'm tired. I was going to go home.'

'Just one. Please.' His eyes coaxed, he held out a hand to her.

Just one, she thought, and allowed him to lead her out on to the floor. Just this one dance and then she wouldn't dance with him ever again. She'd always be busy or she'd get herself posted to the north of Scotland.

But oh, the bittersweet delight as he held her closely and she shut her eyes and let her head rest against his shoulder. When the dance ended, he ruffled her hair and said, 'Hey, sleepy head,' and she straightened.

'It's late. I should go.'

'I'll see you home.'

He fetched their coats and they left the nightclub. As they walked to the Tube station, the silence seemed an almost physical barrier, veiling the space between them.

She broke it, saying, 'Have you been home?'

'Briefly, this afternoon.'

'How is everyone? Is Richard well?'

'As far as I know — he wasn't in.'

They headed down the escalator towards the platforms. As they reached the foot of the escalator they heard a train head into the station so they hurried down the last few steps. Squeezing into the carriage before the doors closed, they sat down next to each other.

He said, 'How's the new job?'

'Fine.'

He turned to look at her. '*Fine*? Nothing more? Decent people? A new office?'

If she had moved her fingers only half an inch she would have touched his hand. She jammed her hands into her coat pockets. 'It's fun. Better than being stuck in an office all day. I like going to all the different towns. And you? How's it been?'

'Fine,' he said. And then, 'The last one was a bit rough.'

'Ship still in one piece?'

497

'A little the worse for wear. She's into dock for refitting.'

They left the train at Oxford Circus and changed to the Central Line. He asked, 'What did you think of Nancy?'

'She's OK — rather full of herself.'

That raising of the brows. 'She's an impressive woman. She watched the Battle of Britain from the cliffs at Dover with all the other reporters and she's just come back from three months in Cairo. She had a hell of a journey through the Med.'

Ruby said, rather acidly, 'You sound quite taken with her, Theo.'

'I like her.'

'She won't last. They never do.'

He looked away, gaze roaming the carriage, avoiding, as one always did in the Tube, meeting the eyes of the other passengers. Her words seemed to echo: they sounded mean, she thought.

'I meant,' she said, 'she'll go back to America, won't she?'

'She hopes to stay here till the end of the war.'

A silence. Inside her, a raw and dejected feeling that she must at all costs hide. And how ridiculous, how humiliating, to fall in love first with one unobtainable Finborough brother and then the other!

He said, 'And anyway, you can talk.'

'What do you mean?'

'Lewis Gascoigne. Married, will never divorce, so not the smallest chance of risking anything lasting *there*.'

'Yes, it's bad luck, isn't it?'

'Bad luck?' He made a scathing sound. 'That's what you like about him, that he's permanently unavailable.'

'Rubbish. I'm very fond of Lewis.'

'Yes, but you don't love him, do you?'

'Of course I do,' she said stiffly.

'No, you don't. How often do you think of him when he's not there?'

'Often.'

'But not all the time. How do you feel when you get a letter from him?'

'I'm always pleased when Lewis writes to me.'

His eyes, that mixture of green and hazel, studied her and he said mockingly, '*Pleased*. That's not *passion*, Ruby.'

But she had known that for some time. She and Lewis had seen each other only infrequently over the past few months. Often, he was away on some mysterious errand that he could not talk about. And, looking back, she saw that her exile in Cambridgeshire had put an emotional as well as physical distance between them. Every now and then they went to a restaurant or a show and then they sometimes ended up in bed. *Sometimes*, but no longer always.

She liked to compartmentalise, she thought. One friend to talk politics with, another for going to the theatre. Another friend for sex, and yet another for long conversations that drifted on into the night. It was safer that way. There wasn't the risk that any one person would start to mean too much to you. She felt suddenly miserable and had to pretend to fiddle around in her bag to hide the tears that stung her eyes. Nothing worse than drunk, crying girls; Theo wouldn't want to see her again.

They left the train at Notting Hill Gate and walked to Ladbroke Grove. The sharp, crystalline coldness stung her face. When, in the blackout, she stumbled on the kerb, Theo took her hand.

'We're two of a kind, aren't we?' he said, more kindly. 'My problem is that I want everything to be perfect. Which is why, as you pointed out, no one ever lasts.'

'Nancy certainly isn't perfect.'

'Ruby, I don't think you've ever approved of any

499

girlfriend I've ever had.'

'That's because you have such bad taste.' She had meant it to be humorous, but it came out tart, stinging. 'And anyway,' she said quickly, to cover it up, 'you're mistaken: we're not two of a kind. I'm not like you at all.'

He said coolly, 'I suppose you're thinking of Philip. Do you still . . . ? Yes, I suppose you do.'

In the thick, inky darkness, she could not see his expression. They walked on, arm in arm but a vast distance between them, and did not speak again until they reached her house.

At the steps, she said, 'Will you have coffee?'

'No, I'd better head off.'

Something inside her was hurting very badly. 'Shall I see you?'

'I have to go back to my ship tomorrow.'

He kissed her cheek and was swallowed up in the darkness. Ruby let herself into the house and went upstairs to her room. She took off her coat, kicked off her high-heeled shoes. The room, *her* room — and she had always been so proud of having her own place — seemed small and shabby tonight. It had a transient look: she would not stay here for long. She filled the kettle, lit the gas burner. Took out one mug. Wondered if she would ever automatically take out two. Looked at the fold-down sofa and thought of all the unfolding and making it up and decided she wouldn't bother, but would sleep on it as it was, with some blankets to keep her warm. And felt adrift, horribly aware that she was one tiny, lonely atom in a city full of other atoms, buzzing around from place to place, sometimes colliding, but rarely coinciding.

★　★　★

Theo phoned Sara.
'How's Anton?'

'He's very well. We're going to get married as soon as my divorce comes through.'

'Congratulations. And about time too.'

'How are you, Theo?'

'Fighting fit. Actually, I'm a bit worried about Dad.'

'He's not ill, is he?'

'Not ill. But he doesn't look after himself. All the servants except Dunning have gone and the house is a mess and he hasn't a clue how to cook. Can't even make himself a piece of toast. I suppose he's never had to. He eats out at his club most evenings, of course, but the rest of the time he has to fend for himself. I found him eating sardines for breakfast this morning. Out of a tin.'

'Poor Dad.'

'And he has nightmares, you know.'

'Nightmares?'

'About his time in the trenches. I hear him almost every night. He cries out.'

'Oh, Theo, that's so awful!'

'I tried to talk to him about it and he told me to mind my own business.'

'Well, that's the trouble.'

'Yes, he always bloody does.'

A silence, while the phone line crackled and neither of them spoke. Then Theo said, 'I wonder if this war will be the same — whether we'll be haunted by it, like Dad's generation were. Or whether the last one was different. Maybe people didn't expect it to be how it was. Maybe they thought it would be glorious — cavalry charges, officers in red coats with swords.'

'Anton's trying to join the proper army,' said Sara. 'I mean, not the Pioneer Corps, but a fighting regiment. He's always wanted to but they wouldn't let him. But now they're talking about letting enemy nationals like Anton bear arms.' She wound the telephone line round her fingers. 'I know what'll happen,' she said quietly.

'We'll get married at last, and then he'll be sent away to North Africa or the Far East and I'll lose him all over again. I can't bear it. Sometimes I just can't bear it.'

'Oh, Sara. Have you talked to him about it?'

'Yes, we talk about everything. I won't try to persuade him not to go. That wouldn't be fair, would it? And, you see, it's one of the things I love about him — that he's so brave and courageous and he'll fight for what's right. And that he still wants to fight for this country even after everything that's happened to him.'

'Tough on you, though.'

'Oh, men must work and women must weep . . . or whatever it is.'

'At least the Americans will be in the war properly now.'

Two days earlier, on 7 December, the Japanese had bombed the American Fleet at Pearl Harbor. Now the war had swept round the entire globe and was being fought on many fronts at once.

Sara said, 'How are you, Theo? How are you *really*?'

'The last one was pretty bloody awful. We lost six of the ships in our convoy.' A pause. 'One of them was an oil tanker. It was torpedoed — it went up like an inferno. The men were swimming in burning oil . . . trying to swim in burning oil . . . ' His voice faded.

'Oh, Theo . . . You do sound a bit fed up.'

'I'm all right. But why is it that when you have leave at last, when you've been looking forward to it for months, it never works out how you think it will? You think of all the things you're going to say to people and then, somehow, you don't?'

'People . . . ?'

'Yes,' he said in the ending-this-particular-strand-of-conversation tone Sara knew so well. 'People.'

★ ★ ★

That evening, Sara went home.

It was years since she had last gone back to the house in which she had been born. The ending of a marriage, the rediscovery of love. Walking up the drive, she noticed the vegetables growing in the flowerbed, the ruts in the gravel, the peeling paintwork on the windows.

She rang the doorbell. Why had she come here? Because, she thought, it made her sad to think of her father eating sardines out of a tin.

A long wait, in which she had time to try to think of what to say, but then, when her father opened the door, she just put her arms round him and said, 'Oh, Dad,' and cried.

He looked so much older, his hair faded, no longer fiery, his eyes puffy. In spite of the cold, he was in his shirtsleeves — a rather crumpled shirt, without a collar.

He patted her back and said, 'There's no need for that,' and then, 'You're making my shirt wet and none of them is ironed.'

Sara sniffed, wiped her eyes, followed him into the house. Richard said, 'If you're looking for Theo, he's out.'

'I'm not looking for Theo. I came to see you, Dad.'

He looked surprised, but very pleased. 'Really?'

'I came to see if you were all right.'

'I'm fine, as you see.'

'Oh, *Dad*,' she said crossly, glancing around her. 'Look at it!'

The hallway was freezing. She could have drawn pictures in the dust on the table and the sideboard. Everything was left just anyhow — coats and hats on the window seat, newspapers and umbrellas and opened envelopes, their contents spewing out of them, discarded at random. She remembered that her mother and the servants had always tidied up after him.

He said, 'Are you cold?'

Sara shook her head. 'I've got my coat.'

'Would you like some cocoa? I'm rather nifty at making cocoa.'

'Yes, please, Dad.'

The kitchen was warmer and cleaner than the rest of the house. Theo had had a go at it, she suspected.

She said, 'Fetch me your shirts and I'll iron them.'

He went away, returning in a few minutes with an armful of shirts. Sara put up the ironing board while her father measured out dried milk and mixed it into the water and put the mixture on the hob to boil.

He asked, 'Are you still working in that canteen?'

'Actually, I've applied to join the Land Army.'

He threw her a glance. 'You'd like that, I'd have ~~have~~ of thought.'

'Especially the horses.' She lightly touched the hotplate of the iron to see whether it was warm enough. Then she said, 'Gil has asked me for a divorce.'

He looked back at her. 'Has he now?'

'Yes. He wants to get married again, you see.'

'Good God. I didn't think he had it in him.'

'When the divorce comes through, I'm going to marry Anton.' Her father started to speak, but she interrupted him. 'It's all right, I'm not asking for your blessing or anything. I know you don't like him.'

Richard had put on his glasses to read the instructions on the cocoa tin. He frowned. 'It wasn't a question of not liking him — well, a little, perhaps. I can't say that I was happy seeing you throw yourself away on some damned German — '

'Austrian, Dad.'

'Austrian, then.' Richard put down the spoon and turned to look at her. 'I didn't think he was good enough for you, Sara. All I've ever wanted was the best for you.'

'Anton is best for me,' she said firmly. 'I love him. I've loved him for years — I think I loved him from the first moment I saw him. I shouldn't think I'll ever love anyone else.' The iron swooped along a shirtsleeve. 'And as soon as I can, I'm going to marry him and you mustn't try to stop me again.'

His back was to her as he stood over the hob. He said, 'I've no intention of trying to stop you. You're a grown woman, Sara, and you must do what you think is best. That other time, you were just a child. Only twenty. I was trying to protect you.'

A wave of bitterness welled up inside her. 'And last year,' she said, 'when you gave Anton away to the authorities, were you trying to protect me then, too?'

He turned to look at her. 'Gave him away to the authorities? What are you talking about?'

'You know perfectly well what I'm talking about!'

'Sara, I don't.'

'I don't believe you, Dad,' she said angrily. 'You told the police where he was hiding. And they came and took him away.'

He shook his head. 'No,' he said, 'not me.'

Then the milk pan boiled over. 'Hell,' said Richard, and poured what was left into the cocoa mugs and then mopped ineffectually at the burned milk.

Sara said, 'Let me, Dad,' and took the dishcloth from him. As she wiped the hob and rinsed the cloth in the sink, she said, 'Someone told the Tribunal that Anton and I were living together. It must have been someone who knew us well.'

'Well, it wasn't me.'

'And when Anton went into hiding last summer, someone told the police where he was. I thought you must have had him followed, or something.'

Richard looked annoyed. 'How could you think I could do such a thing? Such a weaselly, underhand thing!'

'What about the time you threatened to have Anton thrown out of the country? Wasn't that underhand?'

505

'Not at all. That was completely different. As I said, you weren't much more than a child and I was trying to protect you. But sell a fellow to the police? No, I'd never do that.'

She looked at him closely. 'Honestly?'

'How many times do I have to tell you?'

'But if it wasn't you, then who was it?' But she knew, suddenly, and said very quietly, '*Oh.*'

Her father said, 'Drink up your cocoa or it'll get skin on it, and you know how you hate that.'

★   ★   ★

Tuesday evening: Sara waited for Edward at a pub in Westminster, wrapped in her fur coat in the dim, smoky bar, fending off offers of drinks, cigarettes and company. When Edward came into the pub she let him kiss her cheek — out of habit, she supposed.

'Your usual?' he said, but she shook her head.

'I won't be staying.'

'Oh.' He looked disappointed. 'I'll walk you to wherever you're going, if you like.'

'No, thanks.'

He looked at her sharply. 'What is it, Sara?'

'A couple of nights ago, I went to see my father. I always thought it was he who'd told the police where Anton was hiding, but it wasn't, was it?'

He had sat down next to her. She saw that he had paled. She said, 'The only other people who knew where he was were Ruby and Peter. And I don't think either of them would betray him.'

He started to speak, then he stopped himself. Then he said softly, 'I'm sorry. I'm so sorry. I knew it was wrong, but I couldn't stop myself.'

'So it was you?'

'Yes.'

Just then she hated him. She remembered the months

of separation and the anguish she had suffered, afraid that Anton had drowned in the sinking of the *Arandora Star*.

'How could you?' When he did not reply, she said, 'You knew what he'd been through in Vienna. You knew how afraid he was of going to prison again.'

'Yes.' A single, dull syllable as he stared down at the table-top.

'*Why* Edward?'

He turned to look at her. 'You don't know?'

'No.'

He gave a loud crack of laughter; some of the other people in the pub turned to look at him. Then he said, 'Because I love you, of course. You hadn't realised? No, of course you hadn't. Why should you ever consider the possibility? Why should you think that dull old Edward, everyone's friend but no one's *best* friend, could possibly be in love with you?'

It took her a moment to recover herself, but then she said, 'If what you say is true, that's no excuse.'

'No, I don't suppose it is.'

'And it isn't *love*,' she said fiercely, 'to hurt someone like that. Love is selfless — love puts the other person first.'

'Does it? I wouldn't know. I haven't a great deal of experience.' He rubbed his forehead with his fingertips. 'You were the best thing that ever happened to me, Sara. The first time I saw you at Euston Station, it changed my life. Oh, I know you've never thought of me in that way and it hasn't been all that often I've managed to convince myself that I had a chance with you. But since then, I've felt alive. There's been a reason for getting up in the morning, a reason for keeping going. Since I met you, I haven't been standing on the outside any more. I've been in the centre, the centre of my own story. *Our* story.'

She stood up, gathering up her handbag and gloves.

'We never had a story, you and I, Edward,' she said coldly. 'There never was *our* story.'

★ ★ ★

He went home.

His mother had returned to London six weeks after the Blitz had ended. As he hung up his coat and hat, she called out, 'Did you get any oranges?'

'No, Mother, there aren't any. But I managed to get bread and vegetables and a little bit of steak.'

'Mrs Dixon's son bought her oranges.'

'Lucky Mrs Dixon,' he said, rather sharply.

Edward went into the kitchen. While he had been living on his own, Edward had eaten out most of the time. Since his mother had returned to London after the Blitz had ended, he had done the cooking himself. There was a woman who came in two or three times a week to clean and peel the potatoes, but sometimes she didn't turn up and, when she did, her work was slapdash — not that he said anything, he didn't dare, knew he'd find himself scrubbing floors and bathtubs if he complained.

After dinner, Edward washed and dried the dishes and wiped the table. Then he helped his mother get ready for bed — turned down the covers for her, made her a cup of tea, helped her into the bathroom. She had become frailer recently, and he could see that the time would come when she would not be able to undress or bathe herself. And how would they manage then, if the war had not ended, if it was still so hard to find help? She would hate to have him help her into her nightdress or the bath. Sometimes he wondered whether that was the root of her dislike of him: that she resented her dependency on him.

Alone again, he switched off the light, pulled the blackout aside and looked out of the window. The streets were quiet, no siren going off tonight. He had caught another cold and his throat was sore and he was too tired to read — so tired, not the tiredness born of sleepless nights that he had experienced during the Blitz, but a deeper weariness, born of the long, hard days and an exhaustion of spirit. He was tired of everything, tired of getting up in the morning and going to work, tired of spending his lunchtimes queuing for food or at the chemist for his mother's prescriptions.

But most of all, he was tired of himself. When he had betrayed Anton Wolff, he had told himself that he was doing it for his country. Wolff was an enemy alien: as a loyal citizen, he had only been doing his duty in letting the police know where Wolff was hiding. But he had known, deep down, that he had informed on Anton Wolff because he had disliked him — and because Sara loved him, of course. And perhaps also because Anton Wolff had always reminded him of an uncomfortable truth: that they had something in common, they were both outsiders. Yet in betraying Wolff, he had also betrayed himself. He had never liked himself much, liked himself less now, had lost a little more self-respect.

He remembered the evening he and Sara had run through the Blitz. The colours of the sky, the sounds filling the air, the whole bright, transforming orchestra of it. The soft warmth of her, in his arms, as he sheltered her from breaking glass. And he knew that he would never feel so happy and so free again, running hand in hand with a girl through the burning streets of London.

16

Her mother wouldn't have the doctor. In the last months of her illness, when she had become too infirm to go downstairs to the parlour, Maude Quinn was confined to her bedroom. Her large frame had shrunk to a shadow of its former size, her eyesight had almost gone and the ulcers on her legs wept. The only part of her that persisted was her iron will. She would not allow Hannah to send for the doctor — some sort of quarrel earlier in her illness, some never-forgotten insult, and besides, Maude Quinn had never thought much of doctors — so Hannah did all the nursing herself.

When her mother needed anything, she beat with the ferrule of her walking stick on the floor. The drumroll of the stick followed Hannah through the house. She might be washing clothes in the sink or baking in the kitchen when she heard the thump of the stick, summoning her. Thump, thump, thump . . . the sound reverberated throughout the house and Hannah ran upstairs to adjust her mother's pillows or help her drink a glass of water. Her mother always seemed to be thirsty. Hannah held the glass to her mother's dry, cracked lips and she gulped the water as if she hadn't anything to drink for days. Beads of water dribbled down the furrows to the side of her chin and on to her nightgown. Then she sank back on the pillows, her eyes closed, and for a while the house was peaceful. Then the walking stick would start up again. Thump, thump, thump . . . all round the clock, throughout the days and nights, beating in time to Hannah's heart.

When Mother banged her stick on the floor, the land girls just raised their eyebrows to the ceiling and then went on doing whatever they were doing — sorting the

510

eggs or scouring the milk churns or wolfing down the breakfast Hannah cooked for them. Hannah was afraid of the land girls, who were called Diana and Marie. Diana was broad-shouldered and strong, and her fair hair was rolled up in fat curls around her face. Whenever it was raining or windy, she tied a green and white headscarf over her hair. She pronounced words differently to Hannah; sometimes Hannah couldn't understand her and had to ask Diana to repeat what she had said, and then Diana repeated it very slowly and deliberately, as if Hannah was stupid.

Marie was small and slight with short, dark curls, but her slightness didn't stop her heaving stooks of corn on to the cart or guiding the carthorse up and down the fields. At intervals during the day, Marie would light up a cigarette and smoke it, her head flung back, her pinched little face screwed up as she inhaled, her eyes dreamy. Once, after she had first come to the farm, Marie had offered Hannah a cigarette. Hannah had started, surprised, and then shaken her head. Marie had not offered her one since. Walking through the farmyard, Hannah was sometimes aware of Marie, perched on the edge of the cart or taking shelter in the barn doorway, smoking her cigarette. She couldn't tell whether Marie was watching her or not.

Diana and Marie were a tight little band of two. Their conversations faded as Hannah came into the room. When Hannah heard them laugh, she wondered whether they were laughing at her. Diana and Marie had become bolder since Mother had taken to her bed. They slept on the ground floor of the house in a room in which, a long time ago, Hannah's father, Josiah Quinn, had written up the farm's books. When the land girls had arrived, there had been stacks of ledger-books and boxes on the shelves containing receipts, and the scraps of paper on which Josiah Quinn had calculated Nineveh's finances. Mother had told the land girls not

511

to touch the boxes. But, in winter, after Mother became bedridden, Diana and Marie used Josiah Quinn's old papers to light the fire. They also took logs from the log pile and food from the larder without asking first. Mother would have been furious if she had known about the papers and the logs and the slices of bread and apples, but Mother didn't know, because she was confined to her bed, her communication with the world limited to thumping her stick on the floor, and Hannah was too scared to say anything.

It was during her mother's last months that Hannah began to feel unwell. Sometimes there was a pain in her stomach and she felt nauseous. Then it would go away and she would forget about it, only for it to return again a few weeks later. When the pain was really bad, she was afraid to move for fear of provoking it. If her mother didn't need her, she curled up on the bed, motionless, until it had gone away.

As Maude Quinn sunk towards death she became too weak to use the stick, so Hannah sat day and night at the bedside. It was too cold outside to open the window and Hannah had banked up the fire to keep Mother warm, so the air was thick and fuggy. There was the stale smell of dirty bedclothes — her mother was no longer able to roll on to her side to allow Hannah to change the bed-linen, and even now, in her weakened state, Maude was too heavy for Hannah to lift. And there was the rotten odour of the sores on her mother's legs, sores that refused to heal, no matter how often Hannah bathed them and changed the bandages. Her mother slept a lot of the time, groaning when she surfaced.

A stormy February night: the tops of the trees tossed by the wind and rainwater filling the dykes. The land girls had gone out to a dance in Ely so there was no one in the farmhouse but Hannah and her mother. Her mother's eyes were closed and her face was pale and sunken. Hannah listened to the wind and to her mother's breathing.

Then, looking up, she saw that her mother's eyes were open. 'Mother?' she said.

Her mother's lips moved, framing words. Hannah leaned forward, trying to make out what she was saying.

'The farm . . .'

'Yes, Mother?'

'You have to stay here. You know that. You must never leave Nineveh. Promise me.'

A claw of a hand reached out and grasped Hannah's. 'Yes, Mother,' Hannah whispered. 'I promise.'

Maude Quinn's eyes closed, her hand relaxed its grip. As the night wore on, her breathing became noisy and strained. Her face appeared to Hannah as if it was made of wax, its colour a yellowish-white, the skin opaque and bloodless. The sound of her breathing seemed to fill the room so that Hannah no longer noticed the screaming of the wind outside. There was only the tick of the clock and the sound of her mother's breaths, further and further apart. And then, one last final breath.

Hannah sat on the edge of the chair, waiting. Waiting for what? For her mother to breathe, move, speak, scold, hit her. Impossible to believe that such a dominating presence had gone from her life for ever. Her mother's eyes were slightly open, little dulling black slits. As, with a shudder, Hannah closed her mother's eyes, she expected the pupils to dart, the lids to twitch, her mother's hand to reach out and strike her. Her mother to say, in that voice of concentrated fury, 'Careless girl. We know what happens to careless girls, don't we?'

Then one of the windows burst open, whipped ajar by the gale, banging against the wall of the house. A gust of icy air swept into the room, making the faded curtains billow and move, ruffling the heaps of paper on the chest of drawers and the frill on the counterpane.

The light from the oil lamp guttered, and shadows flickered over Maude Quinn's dead face, so that it seemed to move, and Hannah stood motionless, terrified, her clenched fists pressed against her mouth, as afraid of her mother in death as she had been in life.

* * *

Her stomach had begun to hurt again. As she left her mother's bedroom, Hannah felt the first twinge.

She went to her room and lay down on the bed, her knees curled up to her chest. She wanted to sleep, the weeks of nursing her mother had left her exhausted, but there was the noise of the wind and the pain in her belly and the knowledge that her mother was lying only a few rooms away. *Thump, thump, thump* — she thought it was her mother's stick, banging on the floor to summon her, and she sat up, shaking, perspiring. She looked wildly around, half-expecting the door to open and her mother to walk in. *Thump, thump, thump* . . . and she realised it was only the branch of a tree, tapping the windowpane.

You must never leave Nineveh . . . But then, Hannah had always known that.

After several hours, the pain went away. Moving carefully, Hannah rose and went to the drawer where she kept the letters that George Drake had written to her. Back in bed, she lay down on her side and pulled the blanket over her and began to read the letters. She knew them by heart already, but it made her feel better to see the words on the page. Her eyelids became heavy; she drifted off to sleep.

* * *

In the morning, going down the corridor, she heard Diana and Marie talking in the kitchen. Hannah stood

514

outside the door, screwing up her courage, nerving herself to open it. As she went inside, the land girls turned and stared at her and Hannah looked at the floor. They said hello and Hannah muttered a hello in return. The room was cold because she had overslept. The stove was on — it was never allowed to burn down — but the fire in the grate was not yet lit. Diana and Marie, wearing their coats and scarves, were huddled round the stove. They were buttering bread and they had taken down the side of bacon from its hook and were cutting slices from it.

Hannah felt very disjointed from everything, as if she was not really there. She managed to say, 'Mother passed away in the night. I have to go to Manea to fetch the vicar.'

A short silence, then Diana spluttered through a mouthful of bread and butter, 'Christ Almighty, you don't mean she's lying dead upstairs, do you?'

Marie said, '*Di*,' and crossed herself. Then she said to Hannah, 'I'll go, if you like. I can cycle, it'd be quicker.'

'Thank you.'

Marie put on her gloves, which had been warming on the stove. Diana muttered, 'Isn't this place the absolute bloody limit — freezing cold and no decent bath and now a dead body upstairs.' Then she began to fry bacon.

'You look done in, you poor thing,' said Marie kindly. 'Here, you may as well have this.' She put her mug of cocoa on the table in front of Hannah. Then she said, 'I've milked the cows but I haven't fed the pigs yet, Di. I'll be back in a tick, so save me a bacon sandwich,' and left the house.

★ ★ ★

Gil had rented a house near Bristol. Visiting David from the Wiltshire farm on which Sara was working meant a complicated journey involving three buses and a longish

515

walk. Arriving at the house, Sara had lunch with Gil and Janet. After David had had his rest, Nanny Duggan brought him down to the drawing room and Sara played with him while Gil and Janet worked in the greenhouse. David had grown into an attractive little boy with a mop of heavy black hair and dark, intelligent eyes. He had recently started nursery school and had taken to using mildly slangy terms — 'super' and 'frightful' — words Sara guessed he had picked up from school. He told her about his teacher, Miss Harcourt, and his best friend, Butterworth, who had a dog called Pepper.

'Darling, would you like a dog?' Sara cried. 'The Labrador at the farm has just had the most adorable puppies — I could get you one, if you like.' And David thanked her politely and said, yes, please, that would be super.

Then it was time for David's tea. Sara cut the top off his boiled egg for him and showed him how to dip bread soldiers into the yolk. Nanny watched with a disapproving glare, muttering about messy table manners. Then David ate some stewed apple and custard and afterwards they went downstairs, hand in hand.

And then Gil and Janet came back into the drawing room and David's hand slipped from Sara's, and he dashed across the room, shouting, 'I made bread soldiers, Mummy! I put them in my egg!' And Janet smiled and said, 'Did you, dear? How lovely,' and gathered him on her lap.

Her choice, Sara reminded herself, sitting at the rear of the bus as she travelled back to the farm. If David had come to think of Gil's soon-to-be second wife as his mother then that could only be a good thing. And she had no regrets about the choice she had made, no regrets at all. So it was foolish of her, wasn't it, to cry? Yet she had to fumble in her bag for her

516

handkerchief, pressing it against her eyes while, through the mud-spattered window, the bare trees and ploughed fields blurred as the bus rattled across the chalk downland.

* * *

A cold wind and floodwater glazing the paths and fields. After the service in the parish church, Ruby wandered through the graveyard, her gaze drifting over the inscriptions on the headstones. So many stories to be found in graveyards. Tragedies, infants only a few months old, or sometimes a whole family of children, dying from a fever. Great romances, marriages of forty or fifty years, that had only come to an end when the husband and wife died within a few weeks of each other. Some of the old stones were unreadable, the old-fashioned script worn and covered with lichen.

She glanced back to the group of people outside the church. Mr Merriman, the Quinns' solicitor, was still talking to Hannah. The two land girls had ducked outside the churchyard and were standing on the pavement, sharing a cigarette. The handful of other mourners, former labourers and servants of the Quinns, huddled together in a group by the church wall, as if to protect themselves from the wind.

There was, Ruby discovered, no headstone to mark the grave of Josiah Quinn, Maude's husband and Hannah's father. Of course, Josiah Quinn had died in the war. In front of the church stood the grey marble memorial to those of the parish of Manea who had died in the Great War. Listed for 1918, Ruby read: 'Smart . . . Newell . . . Pope . . . Marshall . . . ' and a handful of others. She looked through the list twice, just to make sure, then scanned the lists of the dead of earlier years. No Quinn. Funny, that.

A handful of them trailed back to Nineveh,

Wellington boots sloshing through the puddles. Ruby talked to Hannah, and to Mrs Drake, who lived in one of Nineveh's cottages.

'Was your father a Methodist, Hannah?'

Hannah gave Ruby her scared rabbit look. 'No, no, the Quinns have always been Anglicans.'

Ruby explained about the war memorial. 'Uncle Josiah was killed in the war, wasn't he? I thought he might have been on some other memorial if he didn't attend the parish church.'

Hannah shook her head. 'Mother would never have married a Nonconformist.'

Huge puddles blistered the low-lying land at the foot of the shallow island on which Nineveh had been built. Someone had put down duckboards; they headed across them in single file before making their way up the path between the fields. Here, the wind was savage, and they clutched at their hats. As they entered the farmyard, Hannah hushed the dogs and shooed the geese away.

Ruby was about to follow Hannah into the house when she felt a tug at her sleeve.

'Miss Chance,' said Mrs Drake. 'I heard you ask Hannah about old Josiah Quinn,' she said. She had lowered her voice. 'I thought you should know.'

Ruby said, 'Know what?'

'Why he isn't on the war memorial. Josiah Quinn was a deserter, you see.'

A stiff gust of wind blew Ruby's hair in her face; she brushed it back with her fingers as she stared at Mrs Drake. 'A deserter? Are you sure, Mrs Drake?'

'Oh, I'm sure. The whole village knew. Maude Quinn told you that he died in battle, did he?' Mrs Drake shook her head. 'She lied to you.'

'What happened?'

'Josiah Quinn came home on leave, not long before the end of the war, and he never went back to the army. Military police was here, looking for him, but he never showed up. None of us ever saw hide nor hair of him. And if Maude Quinn ever heard from him she didn't tell anyone.' Mrs Drake gave a grim smile. 'He was no great loss. A nasty piece of work, Josiah Quinn was, grasping and avaricious. I shouldn't think Mrs Quinn mourned his leaving.'

'They didn't love each other, then?'

'Love?' Mrs Drake looked scornful. 'She hated him. And with cause, I must say. The only time I ever felt sorry for Mrs Quinn was when that man was around. Maude married him for his money, and I dare say she lived to regret it. He'd show her his fist if she answered him back — and worse. He beat her black and blue sometimes. He hadn't an ounce of pity in him. Neither had she, of course, only he was stronger than her.' Mrs Drake frowned as she glanced up at Nineveh. 'They were two of a kind, I always thought. They brought out the devil in each other.'

★ ★ ★

Back in London, Ruby telephoned Richard, who invited her to dinner at his club.

Richard's club was just how Ruby had imagined it to be, cracked leather Chesterfields and dark wood panelling and wing-collared old men asleep in armchairs. Over the consommé, she told Richard about Aunt Maude.

'What was she like?' Richard asked.

'Horrible,' said Ruby. 'I think she was the most horrible person I've ever met.'

Richard gave a bark of laughter. 'I've never believed in mincing my words either — best to be honest. And your cousin?'

'Hannah's not like Aunt Maude. She isn't cruel.' She stirred her soup, which had a yeasty taste, like Marmite mixed with water. 'I always feel guilty about her.'

'Guilty?' He gave her a look. 'Why?'

Best to be honest, Richard Finborough had said. Ruby drank the last spoonful while she tried to frame an honest reply.

'I should feel sorry for her — and I do — but she irritates me as well. I find myself thinking, why doesn't she get away, why doesn't she *do* something? And then I feel ashamed of myself, because I know why she doesn't. That it's because she's had all the spirit knocked out of her by Aunt Maude.'

'Still, with the old lady gone . . . '

'I asked Hannah whether she was planning to leave Nineveh,' said Ruby exasperatedly. 'I even offered to let her share my room while she looked for a place of her own, though she would drive me mad, moping about, in a day. But she told me she was going to stay at the farm.'

'It's her home,' said Richard gently.

'But *we* left our homes, didn't we? You left Ireland — and I've left so many homes.'

'But you and I, we're the same, aren't we? We're restless, we're greedy, we always want more. I've always thought you were a true Finborough, Ruby, by adoption, if not by birth.'

The waiter came to take away the soup bowls and ask them if they preferred mutton or boeuf bourguignon — a lot more bourguignon than beef, Richard told her, so they both ordered the mutton.

Ruby said, 'I wanted to ask you about my father. I want you to tell me what he was really like.' She looked him in the eye. 'I'm not a child any more. I need you to tell me the truth.'

Richard's gaze became less focused; Ruby thought he was looking back into the past. 'Nicholas was strong and honest and dependable,' he said. 'When you asked him to do something, you always knew it would be done properly. And he was one of the bravest men I've ever met. What he did for me — there aren't many who'd have that sort of courage.'

'But . . . ?' she prompted.

Richard looked troubled. 'War does things to men. Some men lose their nerve, they can't take it any more. Back then, such a man might have been called a coward — or, worse, he might have been shot as a deserter. We don't do that today, thank God. But Nick was different — the war made him fearless. There wasn't anything he wouldn't do. And it isn't right for a man to be fearless. It takes something away from you. It's only human to be afraid.' He paused. 'Nicholas became more volatile as the war went on. He found it harder to control his anger.'

She said, 'Did you think he was the sort of man who would walk away from his family?'

Richard said, 'Well, he didn't leave *me*, did he?'

★　★　★

Suddenly, everything felt unsafe. That same feeling as at the height of the Blitz, when you thought the house might topple down on top of you. When she thought of Theo, on his ship, she seemed to see the vast Atlantic closing in on him and feel the limitless depth of the ocean.

Two men, Nicholas Chance and Josiah Quinn. Both men had disappeared from the face of the earth, Josiah Quinn in 1918, Nicholas Chance ten years later. Josiah Quinn was assumed to have deserted the army, Nicholas Chance was assumed to have run away from a bigamous marriage.

Too many coincidences, Ruby thought. It didn't fit. Hard to imagine violent, avaricious Josiah Quinn abandoning his land and wealth to the wife he had brutalised. And her own father? 'He didn't leave *me*,' Richard Finborough had said. 'He didn't seem the sort of man who'd just go,' Claire Chance had told her.

Two men, Nicholas Chance and Josiah Quinn. What was the link between them? Nineveh, thought Ruby. Maude Quinn.

★ ★ ★

The pain returned in the middle of the night, waking Hannah up. She lay still, curled up on her side, as it came and went in nauseating waves. Then, after several hours, it faded, and she dozed off to sleep again.

When she woke, it was dawn. She had only just time to reach the washstand before vomiting into the bowl. She lay down on the bed again, shivering. When the shivering lessened, she began to feel unpleasantly hot, and, very carefully, so as not to disturb the pain, she moved the blankets aside. She wished she could open the window and let in some fresh air, but she was afraid to move.

Eventually, she saw that it was daylight. She could hear the land girls talking in the yard and the pain had settled into a fierce, burning place low down on the right hand side of her abdomen. When, gingerly, she pressed the spot with her fingers, she flinched. Perspiration ran down her face and she moved a little, trying to find a cool place on the sheets.

She tried to think of George. She remembered the time he had walked back from Manea with her and what he had said to her and how he had smiled at her. He had carried her shopping bag for her. Hannah wasn't frightened of George Drake; she had known him all her life and he had always been kind to her. But she couldn't envisage him now, could see in her mind's eye only the separate pieces of him — sandy hair, freckles, blue eyes — and when she tried to put them together they did not, somehow, make George.

Another tearing pain: Hannah gasped. She knew that

there was something badly wrong with her. She was afraid she was going to die, like Mother. She wondered whether she should tell Diana and Marie that she was ill. Perhaps one of them would fetch the doctor. But she shrank from the thought of what Diana would say in that loud, haughty voice of hers, if she, Hannah Quinn, were to ask her to go to Manea. And the thought of walking downstairs appalled her: she did not think she could do it.

She drifted in and out of sleep. She dreamed she was a little girl again and her mother had shut her in the outhouse because she had been naughty. She could feel the sticky drift of the cobwebs, smell the musty, mushroomy smell.

Another dream, from long ago. A loud noise in the night, and then the dogs, barking in the yard. And Mother's voice, singing. 'What a friend we have in Jesus All our sins and grief to bear.'

Waking again, she tried to pray, but the only verses that came to her mind were some of Mother's favourites: 'The earth shall tremble at the look of him: if he do but touch the hills they shall smoke.' And besides, why should God love her? Why should he love plain, stupid Hannah Quinn? She was not good, and God loved only the good. She was wicked: she knew that because Mother had told her.

★ ★ ★

At Cambridge, when the loudspeaker announced that her train was delayed, Ruby almost gave up, turned back, headed home to London. Why travel all the way to Nineveh when Hannah would only look at her with those frightened, bruised eyes of hers and shake her head? Why go to Nineveh, which contained everything that was irrational, everything she was ashamed of? Why follow a whim, a suspicion, a drift of smoke in the wind?

523

But there were conversations that she and Hannah had never had. There were questions that needed to be asked. Suspicions, too terrible to voice, that she needed to lay to rest.

In the waiting room, she took out her novel and her glasses and began to read. There was no fire, her hands were cold. In the opposite corner of the room, a young man in RAF uniform dozed, his cap pulled over his face.

The train arrived. Through the carriage window, Ruby watched the countryside to the north of Cambridge flatten itself out into black fields with a silvering of floodwater or sometimes a green haze of winter wheat. The train headed out of Ely, across the Fens, seeming to glide over the surface of the water as it traversed the floodland between the Old Bedford River and the Hundred Foot Drain. Water to either side of her as she stared out of the window, wildfowl swimming on its glassy surface.

The train pulled into Manea station. Ruby walked through the village and along the track to Nineveh. The sun had emerged from behind the clouds and the furrows in the fields were as black and shining as liquorice. Coming out of the copse, she looked up and saw Nineveh, perched like a fortress on its island.

No one in the farmyard, only the dogs and geese swarming round her, yelping and hooting. Ruby called out a hello: no answer. She walked round to the back of the building. The sunlight filtered between the trees in the orchard and over the cobbles in the yard. Aunt Maude's chair was still standing to one side of the back door, its wicker swollen and frayed.

She pushed open the door. 'Hannah?' she said. Her voice echoed.

There was the ghost of breakfast smells — bacon and sausages — in the kitchen, and dishes in the sink. But no fire in the grate and no Hannah washing clothes in the scullery or kneading dough on the kitchen table. Ruby peered into the adjacent rooms. Walking through the house, opening doors, she thought there was a stale, musty odour, as if the damp from the Fens had entered the fabric of the building. The blackout had not yet been taken down and the interior was in darkness.

Going upstairs, the heels of her shoes clattered on threadbare scraps of carpet. A long corridor, with doors opening off it. 'Hannah?' she called out, and heard a groan.

'Hannah?' That sound again: Ruby traced it to a door.

Inside the room, it took a second or two to accustom her eyes to the dim light. She saw that there was something — someone — folded up on the bed.

She kneeled down beside the bed. Hannah's face was white and she was doubled up in pain. 'Oh, dear God, *Hannah*,' said Ruby.

★   ★   ★

Someone had come into the yard, a very old, rather deaf man. Ruby yelled at him to sit with Hannah, then grabbed the bicycle that was propped against the wall and rode back to Manea as fast as she could, darting round puddles, slipping in the mud. In the village, a passerby directed her to the doctor's house. Dr Faulkner was eating his lunch when she arrived. After she had spoken to him, he collected his bag and they climbed into his car.

Then, a drive at speed back to Nineveh, where Dr Faulkner examined Hannah. He diagnosed acute appendicitis; they must get Hannah to the hospital straight away, he said, before the appendix ruptured. Dr Faulkner wrapped Hannah up in a blanket and carried her out to the car. Ruby sat in the back, Hannah's head cradled in her lap, and they set off for the hospital.

The surgeon operated on Hannah that afternoon. Ruby stayed at the hospital long enough to know she had come safely through the operation and then returned to Nineveh.

The land girls were in the kitchen, making a pot of tea. They looked up at Ruby and said hello, and Ruby said, 'Didn't you realise my cousin was ill?'

The blonde land girl stared at Ruby. 'I heard her throwing up this morning. Thought she had the collywobbles.'

'Actually,' said Ruby furiously, 'she has appendicitis.'

'Crikey,' said the blonde girl.

The dark one asked, 'Is she all right?'

'They think she will be. No thanks to you, though.'

Upstairs, in Hannah's room, Ruby lit an oil lamp and then went through the chest of drawers, searching for a spare nightgown. But she couldn't find one, and after a few moments she sat down on the bed. The room appalled her — the sparseness of the furniture, the old, threadbare items of clothing in the chest of drawers. Some Blitz victims, thought Ruby, had nicer clothes than Hannah Quinn.

There was a tap on the door. The dark land girl put her head round the jamb.

'Thought you might need this.' She held out a cup of tea to Ruby.

'Thanks.'

'Would you like a sandwich or anything?'

It was four o'clock in the afternoon; she hadn't eaten since breakfast. 'Yes, please.'

The girl went back to the door. 'Look,' she said, 'I know you must think we're awful, but I did try when I first came here. But she hardly said a word — she wouldn't even look at me. She was so shy, I suppose — and a bit strange, actually. And then, well, I know I shouldn't speak ill of the dead, but the old lady was such a bitch. She made our lives a misery. So Di and

526

me, we kept ourselves to ourselves.' She went back downstairs.

Ruby cradled the cup of tea in her hands. Her head ached. She took a sip of the tea but it was too hot. She put the cup and saucer on top of the chest of drawers and looked round the room again. The sister at the hospital had told her that Hannah would need a spare nightdress, dressing gown, slippers and washbag. There was a comb and flannel on the washstand, but the flannel was grey and the comb had a lot of broken teeth. Ruby dug her own comb out of her handbag and put it aside.

Nightgown, dressing gown, slippers . . . Hannah seemed to possess only one nightgown, the one in which she had gone to hospital. There might be another in the laundry, she must check that. Ruby glanced under the bed, searching for slippers, recoiling as she caught sight of the chamber pot.

Leaving Hannah's bedroom, she began to search through the house. Among all the useless detritus that filled Nineveh she must surely be able to find a dressing gown and slippers. There were bedrooms and boxrooms and rooms that seemed to have no particular purpose, in which strange collections of random objects — a grandfather clock, an old pram, a dozen pairs of shoes, soles gaping from their uppers, all in a heap — held the gaze. The light was failing and a greyish film veiled the furniture and all the things that Maude Quinn had collected. What had her mother said to her? *Maude was always a hoarder. Once she got hold of something she'd never let it out of her grasp.* Ruby saw a dog collar, its leather fractured, almost worn through. Empty tins, washed out, the lids cut away. Old envelopes and cotton reels and rusty pins. And pieces of string, too short to be of any use. What else had Maude Quinn kept? Her daughter, of course.

In Maude's bedroom there was a large iron bedstead

and wardrobes and chests of drawers and a bedside table. A heavy ruffled quilt in a dark purplish-pink on the bed. The glow from the oil lamp illuminated the patent medicine bottles on the side table and the jars of pennies and tablets of soap.

Ruby put one of the tablets of soap in her coat pocket. Then she opened the wardrobe. On the top shelf were a dozen hats, all black, adorned with a feather or a jet brooch. Beneath, rows of dresses and coats and skirts, so many they were squeezed tightly together. Maude Quinn had liked her clothes.

Ruby ran her eye along the rail. Among the sea of black, something khaki.

The land girl put her head round the door and said, 'There you are. I was looking for you. I say, what a nightmare this room is. What are you doing?'

'Trying to find a dressing gown for Hannah.'

'What's that?'

'It's an army greatcoat.' Ruby had taken it out of the wardrobe. 'My father used to have one like it.'

'Where shall I put this?' — holding out a plate of sandwiches.

'Oh, anywhere, thank you.'

Ruby laid the coat on the bed. One of the brass buttons was missing and there was a tear — no, a ragged hole — in the front of the coat. Around the hole, the material was stained darkly.

Then she read the name sewn into the collar.

'N. J. Chance.'

★   ★   ★

After eighteen months serving on a corvette, Theo knew the routine of the Atlantic convoys as well as he knew the rules of cricket or chess. The seven-day run out, sharing the guarding of the convoy of sixty or more merchant ships from German U-boats and aeroplanes with other corvettes and destroyers, and then — a triumph of navigation in the vast, empty ocean — the meeting in mid-Atlantic, when the convoy would be handed over to the Royal Canadian Navy or the American Navy, who would escort it to the New World, where the ships would be loaded up with oil, coal, machinery and food. Then, seven days escorting the laden ships, their speed dictated by their slowest member, back to Britain through the treacherous Western Approaches. And then, depending on timing, either a night in port or only a few hours to refuel before putting out to sea again and meeting up with the next convoy.

Of course, it was never routine. A ship might be damaged or break down and have to be towed. Or some puttering little merchantman might struggle to keep up with the remainder of the convoy and have to be rounded up like a straying sheep. And the weather was always a variable. There might be fog or sleet or snowstorms or furious Atlantic gales that tossed the corvette around like a cork in a bathtub. Bad weather meant nights without sleep because every lurch and lunge of the ship tossed you out of your bunk. And your food leaped from the plate and the liquid in your cup rose and flung itself to the floor — wherever the floor was. And everything was adrift in the cabins, furniture and clothing swilling about, and even the wireless hurled from its brackets. And you were soaked by the waves that crashed against the bridge — trousers, shirt, jersey, boots, gloves, duffel-coat, socks, all sodden, and no chance to dry out until, several days later, they got into port. The roar of the storm was deafening: in the lulls Theo heard it inside his head.

And then, there were the U-boats. The first sign they were in for a rough crossing was often the long-range reconnaissance planes circling overhead. Then, the next day, bombers, trying for a hit, getting a lucky one perhaps, on a straggler who had fallen behind the rest of the convoy. Then the attack. Ships sunk, the corvette on action stations throughout the night. Depth charges dropped in pursuit of the U-boat. The job of picking up survivors. When an oiltanker went up, it burned like a beacon and they searched through a sea of burning oil in the knowledge that they were silhouetted by the flames, an easy target for a U-boat. They rescued the survivors from life rafts and rowing boats, or plucked them from the sea, frozen, burned, wounded, choked with oil. Then they transported them back to the corvette and lifted them aboard, as gently as they could. All too often, if the men had swallowed oil or were badly burned, they watched them die before they reached port.

Perhaps the blessed respite of a day or two or lousy weather might hold off an attack. But eventually the clouds cleared and the aeroplanes peeped out their black noses from behind them and it all started all over again: the explosions at night, the burning ships, the debris on the water, the sweep round the seas, trying not to lose a single man left alive. The fear that they might miss a boat or a raft, because they all remembered the nightmarish experience of coming across a lifeboat or raft crewed by dead men, still wearing their life-jackets. It didn't take much imagination to picture the horror of it, what it must have been like for the last man alive, as his fellow sailors died around him.

This convoy was, to begin with, uneventful. The weather was blustery, but every now and then, when it was calmer, a fog swept in. In quiet moments, Theo thought about Ruby. He remembered returning from France, in the summer of 1940. It had been Ruby he had gone to see first that day, not his family, nor his other friends. She had been wearing a dark red dress and she had taken his breath away. He had intended to

530

ask her out to dinner that night, but he had been put in his place. Her diary had been far too full to fit in a stray Finborough.

He had waited for her for years. And all his waiting had been futile, pointless, because she was still in love with Philip. She did not need him, she did not want him. He would never be anything more to her than a friend, a substitute for the brother she had never had. And that was not enough for him.

Out there, in the cold grey wastes of the Atlantic, he recognised that it was time to put an end to it. He must take a step back; he must not see her any more. It was a decision he reached with a great deal of anger, pain and regret, but he knew that it was the right one. And at least the war, for once, played into his hands — it was unlikely he'd have another leave for months.

One morning, they caught sight of a reconnaissance aeroplane, which darted away as soon as they blasted their guns at it. That night, three of the ships in the convoy were sunk. The weather worsened, the clouds darkened, and rain spat, pocking the seas. In the morning, you could feel the wolves gathering. Catching sight of the periscope of a U-boat, the chase began. The U-boat submerged, the corvette dropped depths charges, but the lack of the tell-tale spread of oil and wreckage on the surface showed that they had failed to strike their mark. The ship was on action stations throughout the day. On the bridge, they kept their eyes peeled, raking the sea.

A steward brought them mugs of cocoa laced with rum, which they held on to firmly because of the rising sea. 'Damned needles in damned haystacks,' the captain remarked.

And then, shockingly close, the U-boat emerged. The corvette engaged — both ships must have fired at much the same time. Shells ripped across the bows of the corvette and there was a scream, the sound of breaking glass, and then sea-water crashed over the bridge, hurling them all to the floor.

The ship righted itself, they picked themselves up from the shattered glass and shrapnel sloshing about in the water on the floor of the bridge. Flames leaped from the gun-turret, then another wave swept over the bows of the ship, dowsing them. They could no longer see the U-boat. It had dived, and as the weather closed in they knew they had lost it.

There were three casualties of the engagement: a gunner, shot by the U-boat, the corvette's gun-turret, severely damaged in the exchange of fire, and Theo, who had broken his collarbone.

★ ★ ★

Almost the worst thing was having to wait. They wouldn't let her speak to Hannah at first. When Ruby visited the hospital with Hannah's things, the sister told her that her cousin's condition was satisfactory but she was not yet allowed visitors. Ruby returned briefly to London to ask for leave from work and to pick up some clothes and her ration card.

Then she went back to Nineveh. She had remembered the treasures Hannah had shown her, years before. She searched the barn and found the Oxo tin, hidden behind a loose brick. The brass button was still there, and when Ruby took it to the house she saw that it matched the other buttons on the coat: it fitted like the last piece of a jigsaw.

At visiting hour in the hospital, relatives sat by the rows of beds, their conversation muted, as if they were in church. Hannah looked pale, but, Ruby thought, a little more *normal*. She was wearing the new nightdress Ruby had bought for her and her hair was washed and brushed and clipped back with a slide.

Ruby kissed her cousin, gave her the bunch of

snowdrops she had picked, and asked how she was feeling. Then, there was no easy way of saying it — *I think your mother killed my father* — and it was possible, of course, that Hannah knew nothing, but she had to try.

She said, 'I found my father's coat in your mother's wardrobe,' and Hannah became very still.

'I think my father came back to Nineveh. I think Aunt Maude lied to me when she told me he'd only been there twice. I think he came back again, years later, just before he disappeared.'

A whisper: '*Please.*'

'I'm not cross with you, Hannah. I don't blame *you*. Your mother hurt you, didn't she? And you couldn't stop her because you were only a child. And if you couldn't stop her hurting you, then how could you possibly stop her hurting someone else?'

Hannah's eyes closed, her fingers gripped the blankets tightly.

Ruby made herself go on. 'This is what I think happened. My mother was ill and my father hadn't enough money to pay the doctor. Perhaps he thought Maude ought to help her sick sister. And when she refused him, I expect he lost his temper. He had a temper, my father, I remember that. Perhaps he shouted at Maude, perhaps he threatened her. Perhaps he reminded her of her own husband. Perhaps she thought he might steal something from the farmhouse. Perhaps she thought he was going to hurt her. And so she shot him. Do you think,' said Ruby, very gently, 'it could have happened like that, Hannah?'

Silence. But a trail of tears down Hannah's face.

'Aunt Maude owned a shotgun,' said Ruby. 'There's what looks like a gunshot hole in the front of the coat. It must have happened years ago, when you were a little girl, but I wondered whether you remembered seeing anything. Or hearing anything.'

533

Hannah stared mutely ahead, her face stained with tears. An orderly had begun to move along the ward with the tea trolley.

Hannah said, 'The next day, there was a new grave dug. And none of the dogs had died.'

★ ★ ★

They erected a screen round the dogs' graveyard and then they began to dig. Some time in the afternoon, a policewoman broke the news to Ruby that human remains had been discovered buried in the graveyard. Shortly afterwards, evidence of a second body was found. Ruby imagined them sorting through the bones: *this one's dog and that one's human.*

A mortuary van came to take the remains away. Ruby stood at the front door, watching it head back down the track. Then the detective interviewed her again. His demeanour had altered since the previous time she had spoken to him, after her visit to Hannah at the hospital. Then, his tone, the expression in his eyes, and the questions he had asked — 'You mentioned you wrote detective novels, Miss Chance. Don't you think your imagination might have run away with you?' — had been sceptical. But she had been insistent, and, in the end — to get rid of her as much as anything else, she guessed — he had agreed to send a couple of men to the farm.

But now he wanted to know everything. Everything shameful, everything concealed. Josiah Quinn's character — 'He was a brute, by all accounts,' the detective said, and, in response to Ruby's enquiry, explained that he had spoken to the locals.

He wanted to know her father's background, war record and financial situation. And about Claire Chance, the bigamous marriage, and the apparent desertion of both 'wives'. And Aunt Maude, her self-imposed isolation, and her death, in all probability, from untreated diabetes. 'Nutty as a fruit cake, wasn't she?' said the detective, then drew on his cigarette and went back to his notes.

It would probably never be a hundred per cent certain, he told Ruby, that the two bodies exhumed from the dogs' graveyard were those of Josiah Quinn and Nicholas Chance, but there was sufficient circumstantial evidence to assume that the remains belonged to the two men. Josiah Quinn must of died in 1918, when on leave from the army. Josiah and Maude had quarrelled, perhaps, the detective suggested, and Josiah had become violent, so Maude had shot him and buried his body in secret. And perhaps, after committing murder that first time, Maude hadn't found it too hard to kill again, when, ten years later, Nicholas Chance had turned up at the farm.

★ ★ ★

After the wounded corvette had made port, and after he had had medical treatment, Theo was given a month's leave.

He caught the train at Liverpool and headed south, to London. At first, he dozed, exhausted. When he woke, the woman sitting opposite him offered him a cup of tea from her flask; after he had drunk it, he felt better.

One-handedly, he opened the newspaper he had bought in Liverpool. The news of the war was bad, however hard they tried to dress it up. In the last few months, Hong Kong, Manila and Singapore had fallen. Great battleships — the *Prince of Wales* and the *Repulse* — had been sunk by the Japanese. Theo felt a rush of fury, along with pity for the sailors who had died. They could do with a few less noble defeats, he thought bitterly. A change from the 'In spite of a brave defence . . .'

He turned the page. His attention was caught by a headline: 'Bodies Found on Remote Fen Farm'. Theo began to read the article. 'Nineveh . . . Maude Quinn . . . the bodies are assumed to be those of local farmer Josiah Quinn and his brother-in-law Nicholas Chance . . . '

'Bloody hell,' he said out loud, and the woman across the carriage stared at him.

★ ★ ★

Nineveh wasn't quiet any more. More policemen arrived, trudging across the field to the farmhouse and gathering in little clusters round the graveyard. More questions from the detective while his colleague searched the house and the outbuildings. Then the journalists and photographers turned up. They parked their cars beside the copse, where they smoked cigarettes and called out to each other. Every now and then one of them would tramp up the rise and take a photograph or ask for an interview.

The next day it was colder and a mist had settled on the low ground. The reporters and photographers retreated to their vehicles. In the afternoon, Ruby made cocoa for the policemen and the land girls, who drank it in the kitchen, warming their frozen hands.

Ruby put on her coat and gloves and went outside. She walked to the graveyard. The site was deserted now, but the screens were still up. It was twilight, and the fields that surrounded Nineveh were washed with charcoal grey. The policemen had dug deep holes in the soil. The low, dying sun cast shadows of such intense blackness that the rifts in the earth seemed fathomless. She thought of her father swinging her up on to his shoulders so that she could see over the heads of the crowd. She thought of him turning to her and smiling, the last time he had walked away from her. Her eyes

536

were gritty with crying and it took an effort of will not to howl aloud her fierce grief and regret.

She walked back along the path by the field. She caught sight of a figure, walking through the farmyard, coming closer, blurred by the mist. 'Theo,' she said, and began to run.

★ ★ ★

She had been going to fling herself into his arms, but then, as she drew closer to him, she saw that one sleeve of his duffel coat was hanging emptily. There was a yellowing bruise on his forehead.

She said, frightened, 'Oh my God, Theo, what happened to you?' and he said, 'It's nothing, a broken collarbone, that's all.' They were standing a little way apart from each other, and her heart was pounding.

'Does it hurt?'

'Not much, since they gave me the sling. It was my own damned fault anyway. I should have held on better. I read about what happened in the paper. That's why I came. I'm so sorry, Ruby. How terrible for you.'

He had not kissed her, she thought, not even a peck on the cheek. A dull ache settled inside her, augmenting the pain of the last few days.

As they went into the farmhouse kitchen, he told her about the corvette's hunt for the U-boat and the ensuing exchange of fire. In the kitchen, she offered him a drink and something to eat. He asked, 'Where's Hannah?'

'In hospital, recovering from appendicitis.'

'Jesus. The poor kid. Does she know about all this?'

Ruby explained about her discovery of Josiah Quinn's disappearance, Hannah's illness, and finding her father's army greatcoat in Maude Quinn's wardrobe.

'Hannah told me she'd heard my father and Aunt

Maude shouting at each other. And she heard a gunshot.'

'But she didn't tell anyone?'

'No, of course not.'

When he glanced at her, she couldn't stop herself saying, 'You have no idea what it's like to feel like that, have you? But then, how could you? I don't suppose you've ever for a moment felt ashamed of what you are, of *who* you are!'

'Ruby,' he said, and her flare of rage died.

She ran a hand over her face and said tiredly: 'I'm sorry. It's not your fault. I shouldn't shout at you, especially when you're hurt.'

He rose from the table. Now, at last, he put his arm round her. 'Hush,' he murmured. 'You can say what you like to me, you know that.'

She pressed her face against the scratchy wool of his jersey and took in a shaking breath. '*Everyone* will know, Theo! Not only your family, but my friends, my colleagues at work — everyone! Even people I've never met! I hate it!'

'They'll be interested for a while, and then they'll forget it.'

'No.' Disentangling herself, she dried her eyes. 'Even the people in the shops in Manea — I can see the way they look at me.'

'We're in the middle of a war, Ruby. There's so much drama and terror in the world people will soon move on to something else.'

She folded her arms in front of her. 'And I *miss* him,' she whispered. 'I keep thinking about him, remembering what he was like. I hate Aunt Maude for what she did. I hate her for taking him away from me.'

'But he didn't leave you deliberately,' he said gently. 'You know that now. Isn't that some consolation?'

'Yes, it is, of course it is. I keep reminding myself of that. And — '

She broke off, alarmed to find herself on the verge of confessing her feelings for him. But then, she thought furiously, why hold back? She couldn't possibly feel any more humiliated and upset than she did already, could she?

'And what?' he prompted.

'If Richard hadn't taken me home with him that day, I might never have known about love. Not properly.'

His anger took her by surprise. 'For God's sake, Ruby, isn't it about time you put that behind you? Philip's a happily married man. He has a wife and two children he loves dearly. I'm sorry if what I say seems cruel, but I can't bear to see you wasting yourself like this any longer!'

'I wasn't talking about Philip.' Her voice trembled. 'I was talking about *you*.'

'Me? I don't understand.'

'Don't you, Theo?' She got control of herself, gave a little laugh. 'Is it so impossible that I might be in love with you? Is it so ridiculous?'

'Ruby . . . ' He looked blank, dazed, and there was an expression in his eyes that she found impossible to interpret — she thought it might be embarrassment. He said, 'But you're in love with *Philip*.'

She shook her head. 'No, I'm not. I haven't been for ages.'

'But you *said*, the last time I saw you — '

'Actually, I didn't. You *assumed*. But I'm sorry you feel it's so awkward.' Her voice was sharp.

She heard, from the depths of the house, someone call out to her, and she muttered an excuse and quickly left the room. There was a policeman in the corridor; he wanted to know where to find a ladder. Ruby directed him to a barn.

Alone, she stood still, her eyes closed and her fingertips pressed against her forehead, listening to the sounds of the men's footsteps as they searched the rooms above. And she thought, Of all the stupid things you have ever done, Ruby Chance, that was the stupidest.

A footstep. Her eyes opened, she saw Theo.

'It's all right,' she said quickly. 'Forget it.'

'No.' A quick shake of the head. 'Never.'

'Please, Theo.' She had to dig her fingernails into her palms to stop the tears falling.

'I don't want to forget it. That's the last thing I want.' Gently, he touched her face with his fingertips. 'You should never be ashamed of what you are. You should be proud of yourself. *I'm* proud of you. I admire you. And I love you. I love you for what you've made of yourself and for who you are, because you're unique and clever and so very beautiful. You are my best friend, Ruby, and you are the woman I've been in love with for years, and if it's true that you love me too then you've made me the happiest man alive.'

The rest of her speech — *not expecting anything from you, feeling over-wrought, didn't mean it* — died on her lips.

'Theo,' she whispered. 'No, Theo, you can't be in love with me.'

'I can. And I am.'

When his lips brushed against her forehead, she shivered. But, wanting to get things absolutely straight, she said, 'Nancy — the others — if you'd just *said* — '

'I did, actually, once, but you weren't listening. Ages ago, when I came back from France.'

'But, *Theo* — '

'What do I have to do to convince you? Have your name tattooed on my forearm like a proper sailor? I will if you like. Or this?'

Crushing her to him, he kissed her. And the knot of grief and regret inside her seemed to dissolve, thawed by the love and desire that flooded through her, an inner warmth and longing that melted the ice of winter, of Nineveh, of the past. And they clung to each other, eyes closed, together at last, and when the policeman came back into the house, ladder in hand, they did not even hear him.

17

'I couldn't find any collar-studs,' said Richard.

'Collar-studs?' she said.

'When you were at home, Isabel, I always had collar-studs.'

It was May: Anton and Sara's wedding day. The wedding had taken place at the register office in Salisbury because the farm on which Sara was working was near Broadchalke. At the wedding breakfast, Richard and Isabel had sat on the same table, though not next to each other. There had been the speeches and the cake (small and mean-looking, but at least not cardboard icing) and then some dancing. Then everyone had seen Sara and Anton off on their honeymoon and afterwards Elaine had taken the children, who were getting fractious, up to bed. And now it was evening and, in spite of all Isabel's attempts to avoid a tête-à-tête, they were here, on their own, in the garden, sitting on a bench overlooking the river.

And he was talking about collar-studs.

She said, 'It's a shame Alice couldn't come. How is she?'

'Fragile, I'm afraid. She would have loved to have come today. Sara was always her favourite grandchild, but she wasn't well enough. I must get over to Raheen but it's so hard to find the time. And she won't have a telephone. I've offered to put one in for her but she refuses. Says she finds the ringing too imperious. Imperious! My mother's the most imperious woman I've ever known.'

'I've always been so fond of Alice. She was so kind to me when we were first married.'

'Of course she was kind. Why should she have been

542

anything other than kind?'

'Oh, *Richard*. She must have been horrified at you suddenly turning up married to some ignorant little girl who hadn't long before been someone's housekeeper.'

'Nonsense, she wasn't horrified, not at all.'

'She was,' said Isabel firmly. 'She just hid it well.'

'I've been thinking,' he said.

A flicker of dread — the commotion, the arguments — to head them off she said quickly, 'Do you think they'll be happy?'

'Sara and that fellow?'

'Richard, you really must call him Anton. He's your son-in-law now.'

'Dear Lord, so he is. I should damn well hope they'll be happy after all the trouble they've caused.'

'They looked happy.'

'Yes.'

It was a pleasant garden, with roses straggling over trellises and a lawn going down to the river. Isabel thought she might plant roses over trellises in Porthglas.

She could feel him looking at her; her own gaze was directed resolutely out to the river, to the swans and the reeds and the sun setting over the water meadows. He said, 'It was you I was thinking about, Isabel.'

She sighed. 'Richard — '

'I remembered you telling me you'd tried to find your child.'

She glanced at him, startled. 'My daughter?'

'Yes, who else? And you told me you couldn't find her. That you'd come to a dead end — the family had moved away, the girl had probably married and changed her name.'

'Yes. It was impossible.'

'I'm sure she could be traced, if you'd like that. There are always ways.'

Such a very Richard thing to say, she thought. His utter confidence that everything could be managed or coerced had often infuriated her, sometimes amused her, and now touched her. She said, 'Why are you saying this?'

'Because I want you to come home. I'm tired of living on my own. I don't think I do it very well.'

'No, Richard,' she said, eyeing him. 'I don't suppose you do. How's Mrs Rogers?'

'She left. I haven't anyone now.'

She gave him a worried look. 'You do look very tired.'

'Oh,' he said vaguely, 'I eat at my club most nights, it's no trouble. So — ' he leaned forward to her — 'will you come home?'

'No, Richard,' she said quietly. 'I'm sorry.'

'If I found the child for you . . . '

'I don't understand.'

'I know I've not always been a good husband to you. I'm afraid that sometimes I was careless with what we had, that sometimes I wasted it. I know I hurt you.'

'We hurt each other.'

'Yes, it's true, we did.'

'And, you see, I don't want us to hurt each other any more.'

She was very weary. It had been a long day. She would have an early night, she decided, and head back to Cornwall tomorrow morning.

Suddenly he smiled. 'Do you remember that when I first asked you to marry me, I sent you presents? There was a puppy.'

'In a basket, with a blue ribbon round his neck.' Isabel, too, smiled. 'A boy brought him all the way from London. And what else? Flowers, a book of poetry, an umbrella, a black silk umbrella.'

'So, you see, I thought I could trace your daughter for you. That was the best present I could think of. It was what our disagreement was about, after all.'

Was it? she wondered, but said, 'It's very kind of you, Richard — and I'm truly touched — but, you see, she isn't my daughter now, that's what I've realised. She was only my daughter for six weeks. Other people loved her and brought her up. It would be wrong of me — of either of us — to meddle.'

'But, Isabel — '

'I've thought about this a great deal and I'm certain I'm right. It's very possible — quite likely, in fact — that her parents have never told her she was adopted. Just think of the shock if she were to find out. It would turn her world upside down.' She paused, then said, 'She would have to know she was born out of wedlock. Think of poor Ruby, all that dreadful business with her father, and her half-brother and -sister finding out they were illegitimate. I know times have changed, but there's still a slur. I wouldn't want her — my child — to have to endure that.' She touched his hand. 'But thank you for thinking of it.'

'You wouldn't necessarily have to tell her. You could find out where she was living, that she was well, that she had thrived, and leave it like that.'

Isabel felt an almost unbearable surge of longing. To know that Martha was safe and well and happy — what relief, what delight, that would give her!

Yet her longing changed to sorrow as she realised the impossibility of what he had suggested. She would never be able to 'leave it like that'. If she were to know where her daughter lived, she would want to see her. If she saw her, she would be unable to resist speaking to her. If she spoke to her once, how could she walk away from her and never speak to her again?

The scars in her heart seemed to reopen, tearing along old wounds. She said quietly, 'No, Richard, I don't want you to look for her. For my own peace of mind as well as hers.'

They sat in silence, looking out to the river. She had never told Philip, Theo or Sara about her daughter. No matter that they were adults, no matter that they sailed ships across oceans or drove tractors and ploughed fields, her instinct was nevertheless to protect her children from all that was painful and difficult. Mentally, she wrapped up her secret up again and hid it in her heart.

She heard Richard say hopefully, 'But will you come home?'

'I don't think I can.'

She thought he might storm off, but he remained where he was. After a while, he said, 'Nothing works out how you think it will. All my plans for the business — what was the point? All the work I put in, so that there would be something for Philip and Theo, and neither of them want it.'

'After the war — '

'That's years away. A decade, perhaps.'

'Is that what they're saying in London?'

'There's Europe to be liberated and the Far East as well. We've the Americans and the Russians on our side now, and, in the end, that'll make all the difference, but it's not going to be easy. And even after we're pulled through — and I believe that we will — Philip and Theo still won't want a part in the business. They are — they have become — too separate from me. Too used to finding their own way.'

'There's always Rufus.'

'Rufus?' He laughed. 'I'll be dead by the time he's old enough to work for the company. I'll be worn out with overwork.'

'Nonsense,' she said. 'You've a good few years left in you yet.'

'Sometimes I wonder what it was all *for*.'

'It's not *for* anything, my dear. It's a journey.'

A silence, then he said, 'The other day, I was thinking about our holidays in Cornwall. Our summers, when all our friends used to come to Porthglas.'

'Thirty of us, once. The house was full and so were

the rooms in the pub in Zennor. You took every table we owned outside and we put them in a row. I sat at one end, you sat at the other.'

'You looked like a queen. My red queen.' He laughed. 'Do you remember when the boys capsized the boat?'

'And you had to swim out to the Black Rock and rescue them? I couldn't imagine how you'd get both of them back.'

'Philip only needed a word in his ear. He'd just had a fright and lost his confidence. But he was always a strong swimmer. Theo clung on to me the whole way back, like a monkey.' Richard rose and went to the riverbank. He picked up a pebble and dropped it in the water. 'It seems a long time since we talked like this.'

'Sometimes,' she said, 'I think that, when we were younger, we should have talked a little more, made love a little less.'

He gave her his particular look: considered and hungry. And she found herself remembering that night in the Blitz. The touch of his skin, their two bodies moving as one. Lovemaking without thought or calculation, the reduction of existence to touch and sensation, of an intensity that had left them both breathless, exhausted, incapable of anything but sleep.

She went back to looking at the river. The swans had drifted towards the millpond. 'Perhaps that was why we quarrelled,' she said. 'Because we knew we'd end up in bed together.'

'Perhaps.'

It was becoming chilly; she shivered. English summer evenings were so rarely warm. Voices from behind them: Isabel turned and saw Philip, Theo, Ruby and Elaine step out on to the terrace. Then, with a glance towards the bench by the river, they hurried back into the hotel. Irritated, Isabel thought: even my children are conspiring against me.

At the hotel bar, Richard finished his whisky and ordered a second one. A woman, fortyish, nice-looking — his type, tall, dark and slender, in a green suit with a dead fox round her shoulders — came into the room. Richard watched the waiter cross to her table. After she had placed her order she took out a cigarette, looked round. Seeing Richard, she said, in a low, husky voice, 'I don't seem to have brought my lighter.'

He lit her cigarette for her. She murmured, 'Sweet of you,' and then, 'Won't you join me?'

A moment when he thought he might, and then he said, 'I'm afraid I have to be getting on. Have a good evening.'

He left the bar and went upstairs to his room. He was dog-tired and there was a niggling pain under his ribs. A few days ago, he had visited his doctor for a checkup, and the doctor had listened to his heart and frowned. Some irregularities, he had muttered, signs of weakness. Richard should cut down on his drinking, take some rest, lose a little weight . . .

Overcome by a mixture of outrage and shock at his own vulnerability, Richard had hardly listened to the details of what the fellow was telling him, and had immediately forgotten the name of the heart specialist he had been recommended. Instead, he had dressed, left the surgery and found the nearest pub. Rest, he had thought angrily as he ordered a Scotch — he, who had never in his life rested! Lose weight, when any glance in the mirror told him he was still a fine figure of a man!

And yet, his heart. Lying on the hotel bed, he placed his palm on his chest. He thought of poor John Temple, who had died in the prime of life, with everything to live for. He himself had so much to lose, so much still to gain. He wanted to watch his grandchildren grow up. He wanted to see his children survive the war. He wanted to wake up in the morning and find Isabel lying beside him.

He was not unassailable, as he had believed for so much of his life. A warning shot had been fired, and it frightened him. And oh, the pain of it — far worse than the tightening in his chest — the thought of leaving those you loved!

He drifted off to sleep. In his dream, he was in Lynton again. He was walking down the steep, snaking path from the town to the harbour. He had a stitch in his chest and he was hurrying, because he knew he was late.

At the bridge, he paused to take a breath. The tide was in and the sea was rushing up the channel. Where it met the river, the salt water and the fresh propelled into each other, fighting, dancing, cascading, casting up droplets as bright as diamonds. He looked up and saw her, standing beneath the Rhenish Tower. She was wearing her red jacket; it stood out clearly against the stormy grey of the sky. He began to walk to her, knowing he must reach her before the tide turned. But as he neared her his sense of urgency was augmented by longing and by joy. A golden light suffused the harbour. When they embraced, they melted together, inseparable, like the river and the sea.

Richard woke. He lay still, at peace, made tranquil by the lingering memory of the dream. The pain in his ribs had gone. He rose, went to the bathroom and splashed cold water over his face, cleaned his teeth and brushed his hair. Isabel, he thought, his first and best love. So often closed and unknowable to him, but that only added to her fascination. So, this evening, she had refused to come back to him. But he wasn't going to give up. Finboroughs never gave up. Finboroughs fought, they battled against the odds. And he had always been good at battling against the odds.

★ ★ ★

Isabel remembered the last thing Richard had said to her before she had gone into the hotel. 'Do you regret it?' he had asked her. She had known he had meant their marriage.

'No, not at all,' she had said. 'It's been an adventure. The biggest adventure of my life.'

Then, once more, he had asked her to come home with him. 'No,' she had said again. He had asked her why. 'Because it's too late,' she had told him. 'Because I'm too tired. Because we would quarrel and I don't have the energy any more. Because I'm settled, Richard, I'm happy as I am.'

Now, in her room, she began to pack her suitcase. As she folded garments and paired stockings she admitted to herself that she had lied. She wasn't *happy*. She hadn't been *happy* for years. Oh, she'd had flashes of happiness, one always did. But being settled wasn't the same as being happy.

For so much of her life she had felt apart from people. In Lynton, she had always been an outsider. Married to Richard, she had felt excluded from his circle of wealthy and privileged friends. But perhaps she had colluded with her exclusion, perhaps she had sometimes chosen to keep herself separate. There was no need to stay in Porthglas now that, with the ending of the Blitz, her evacuees had returned to London. She could have gone home, but she had not. Instead, she had remained locked away in her citadel.

She sat down on the bed. Why do you impose such isolation upon yourself? she asked herself. Are you so afraid of love? Are you so fearful of what it might to do you? Are you so afraid of losing it again that you'll cut yourself off from it for ever?

Such a terrible choice. To expose herself once more to all the risks that love and involvement brought, or to go on living a half-life. She twisted her hands together, trying to make up her mind. What should she do? She did not know.

Footsteps in the corridor, coming to a halt outside her room. She knew the sound of his footsteps, the beat of his heart: they were printed on her own heart.

A knock on the door. 'Isabel?' His voice.

I can't, she thought. I don't know how.

Another knock. 'Isabel, please.'

After a silence, he walked away. And then, quite suddenly, she had the answer. A voice in her head said, *All you have to do is to tell him you love him. That's not so hard, is it?*

And she opened the door and called out his name.

We do hope that you have enjoyed reading
this large print book.

Did you know that all of our titles
are available for purchase?

We publish a wide range of high quality
large print books including:
Romances, Mysteries, Classics
General Fiction
Non Fiction and Westerns

Special interest titles available in
large print are:
The Little Oxford Dictionary
Music Book
Song Book
Hymn Book
Service Book

Also available from us courtesy of Oxford
University Press:
Young Readers' Dictionary
(large print edition)
Young Readers' Thesaurus
(large print edition)

For further information or a free
brochure, please contact us at:
Ulverscroft Large Print Books Ltd.,
The Green, Bradgate Road, Anstey,
Leicester, LE7 7FU, England.
Tel: (00 44) 0116 236 4325
Fax: (00 44) 0116 234 0205